XXX

Leila stood an  **drew her by t... floor, and gave... when he presse... joking about dir...**

She could hardly bre... ...aybe that was too much excitement. Heat was rampaging through her as she came into contact with every alarming contour of his body.

'I thought you wanted to dance,' Raffa prompted when she remained quite still.

'*You* wanted to dance,' she reminded him, reluctant to end her sensory exploration of a man who was every bit as hard as he looked.

'Yes. With you,' he confirmed, tightening his grip.

Raffa didn't take no for an answer, Leila discovered as he swept her round the floor.

'I like your style, Leila Skavanga,' he murmured, his voice all husky and rough.

'Really?' She prepared herself for some glowing compliment from the master of charm. 'Why?'

'Stubborn. Tricky. Unpredictable.' Raffa shrugged. 'I never know what to expect from you.'

Then he wouldn't be surprised when her stiletto hit his foot.

'What's wrong now, Leila?'

She sniffed. 'I'm waiting for the right beat of the music.'

'Ah, a perfectionist.'

'No. A novice.'

'A novice?' Raffa's warm breath brushed her ear. 'I could soon change that.'

Susan Stephens was a professional singer before meeting her husband on the tiny Mediterranean island of Malta. In true Mills & Boon® Modern™ Romance style they met on Monday, became engaged on Friday, and were married three months after that. Almost thirty years and three children later, they are still in love. (Susan does not advise her children to return home one day with a similar story, as she may not take the news with the same fortitude as her own mother!)

Susan had written several non-fiction books when fate took a hand. At a charity costume ball there was an after-dinner auction. One of the lots, 'Spend a Day with an Author', had been donated by Mills & Boon author Penny Jordan. Susan's husband bought this lot, and Penny was to become not just a great friend but a wonderful mentor, who encouraged Susan to write romance.

Susan loves her family, her pets, her friends and her writing. She enjoys entertaining, travel, and going to the theatre. She reads, cooks, and plays the piano to relax, and can occasionally be found throwing herself off mountains on a pair of skis or galloping through the countryside. Visit Susan's website: www.susanstephens.net She loves to hear from her readers all around the world!

Recent titles by the same author:

DIAMOND IN THE DESERT*
TAMING THE LAST ACOSTA**
THE MAN FROM HER WAYWARD PAST**
A TASTE OF THE UNTAMED**

*linked to the Skavanga family. Visit their website at:
  http://www.susanstephens.com/skavanga/index.html

**all linked to the Acosta family.

**Did you know these are also available as eBooks?
Visit www.millsandboon.co.uk**

THE PUREST
OF DIAMONDS?

BY
SUSAN STEPHENS

MILLS & BOON

Published in Great Britain 2014
by Mills & Boon, an imprint of Harlequin (UK) Limited,
Eton House, 18-24 Paradise Road, Richmond, Surrey, TW9 1SR

© 2014 Susan Stephens

ISBN: 978 0 263 24569 1

Harlequin (UK) Limited's policy is to use papers that are natural,
renewable and recyclable products and made from wood grown in
sustainable forests. The logging and manufacturing processes conform
to the legal environmental regulations of the country of origin.

Printed and bound in Spain
by Blackprint CPI, Barcelona

THE PUREST
OF DIAMONDS?

For Fiona, blogger and Tweeter extraordinaire.
Your enthusiasm for romance makes writing sheer pleasure.

CHAPTER ONE

TENSION COILED IN Leila's stomach as she peered out of the cab window to weigh up the party guests pouring into the hotel. This time of year wasn't great for holding an event in the frozen north. Leila's home town of Ska-vanga was beyond the Arctic Circle in the land of the midnight sun, but when her sister Britt threw a party no one cared about the weather. Sky-high heels and body-con was the order of the day for the women, while the men rocked formal suits beneath their silk scarves and alpaca overcoats. The mantra for the packs of girls head-ing up the steps to the hotel appeared to be: if you're going to freeze, do it on the way to Britt's party.

Leila was the only one of three Skavanga sisters who didn't shine at parties. Small talk wasn't her strength. She was happiest in her office in the basement of the mining museum, gathering and recording fascinating information—

Relax, Leila instructed herself firmly. Britt had lent her a gorgeous dress with a pair of spindle-heeled san-dals to match, and she had a fleece-lined jacket sitting next to her in the cab. All she had to do was run up the steps of the hotel, breeze into the lobby and get lost in the crush.

'You have a good time now!' the cabbie insisted as she

paid the fare, adding a hefty tip because she felt sorry for him having to work such a filthy night.

'Sorry I couldn't get you any closer to the hotel,' he added, pulling a long face. 'I've never seen so many cabs here before—'

The Britt effect, Leila thought as she smiled. 'Don't worry. This is fine for me—'

'Careful you don't slip, love—'

Too late!

'You all right?' The cab driver leaned out of his open window to take a look at her.

'Fine, thank you.'

Liar. She had just performed a series of skating moves that would have done any ice star proud—if that ice star were a clown, that was.

The cabbie shook his head with concern. 'The roads are really icy tonight.'

She'd noticed. She was currently lodged in an inelegant squatting position at the side of his cab, her tights were ripped, and her dress was…thankfully not completely ruined after a close encounter with the side of a mud-streaked cab. Thank goodness her dress was blue-black. Navy was a great colour. It could be sponged.

Picking herself up, she stood waiting for a gap in the traffic. The cabbie was also waiting for the cars to clear. 'Aren't those the three men in the consortium that saved the town?' he said, pointing.

Leila's heart lurched. Sure enough, heading in arrow formation up the steps of the hotel were her elder sister Britt's husband, the Sheikh of Kareshi; her middle sister Eva's fiancé, the impossibly handsome Italian Count Roman Quisvada; and the third man in the consortium, who drew her gaze like a heat-seeking missile to its target. Powering up the steps ahead of the other men, Raffa Leon. Dangerously attractive. Currently single.

Turning away from more trouble than most women could handle, Leila shook her head with impatience for allowing herself to indulge in a moment of sheer fantasy. She was the shy, virginal sister in a family of out-there go-getters, and Raffa spelled danger in any language. Even the most experienced woman would think twice before falling into his lap, and she was more of a small-town mouse.

But the cabbie was right in saying the three men had saved the town. Leila and her two sisters, Britt and Eva, along with their long-lost brother, Tyr, had used to own the Skavanga mine outright, but when the minerals ran out and diamonds were discovered, they couldn't afford the specialized equipment required to mine the precious stones. The town of Skavanga had always depended on the mine for its existence, so the future of everyone who lived there had been at stake too. It had been such a relief when the powerful consortium had moved in, saving both the business and the town.

'There's one billionaire left, if you hurry,' the cabbie commented with a wink. 'The other two are married—or about to be, I heard.'

'Yes.' Leila smiled. 'To my sisters—'

'So you're one of the famous Skavanga Diamonds,' the cabbie exclaimed, clearly impressed.

'That's what they call us,' Leila admitted. She laughed. 'I'm the smallest stone with the most flaws—'

'Which makes you the most interesting in my book,' the cabbie cut in. 'And you're still in with a chance, seeing as there's one billionaire left for you.'

She loved his sense of humour and couldn't stop herself laughing. 'I've got more sense than that,' she as-

sured him. 'And I'm definitely not Raffa Leon's type.'
She gave a theatrical sigh. 'Thank goodness.'

'He has got a bit of a reputation,' the cabbie agreed.
'But you don't want to believe everything you read about
people in the press.'

Remembering how the glossies made out that all three
Skavanga sisters were currently monopolising the world
stage, at least as far as celebrity went, Leila was inclined
to believe him. The only stage she stood a chance of
monopolising was the bus shelter on her way to work.

'And remember this,' the cabbie added, giving Leila
an appraising look. 'Billionaires like to marry down.
They want a quiet life at home. They have enough excitement in the office. Don't take offence,' he said quickly.
'I mean that as a compliment. You look like a nice, quiet
girl, is all.'

By this point Leila was convulsed with laughter. 'And
no offence taken. Now *you* be careful of the icy roads.
I'm guessing you've got a long, cold night ahead of you.'

'Too right, I have. Goodnight, love. You have fun at
that party.'

'I will,' she promised. Just as soon as she had visited
the restroom to sort out her dress. Parties might not be
her thing, but she had no intention of letting down her
glamorous sisters by arriving at their celebration looking as if she'd been mud wrestling before she arrived.

Picking her way carefully across the icy road as soon
as there was a gap in the traffic, she launched herself
into the shadows. Raffa Leon was standing at the top of
the steps scanning the street, probably waiting for some
glamorous socialite to decant from a limo.

God, he was gorgeous!

But bang went her plan for an anonymous entrance—
Not necessarily... All she had to do was choose

her moment and scoot past him. He wouldn't even notice her—

Wrong.

Everything was going so well. Raffa was looking one way while she was running up the steps on his blind side. But then she hit a patch of ice, and while her heels went one way she went the other. With a shriek, she prepared to hit the stone hard.

Wrong again.

'Leila Skavanga!'

She was shocked into silence for a moment as the most impossibly handsome face in the world hovered inches from her own.

'Raffa Leon!' She faked surprise. 'Goodness! Please forgive me. I didn't see you standing there—'

Much.

Surprise? Make that *deeply* embarrassing. If there was one lap she didn't want to land in tonight, it was this lap. And Raffa was holding her so firmly she had no option but to remain exactly where she was, with him shooting heat through her veins, and quite a lot of other places too. Trying not to breathe in case the cheese sandwich she'd chomped down earlier overrode the smell of toothpaste, she remained immobile, while he…while he just smelled amazing. *And those eyes…*

'Thank you,' she said, recovering her senses as he lifted her and steadied her on her feet.

'I'm glad I caught you.'

His voice was deep and sexy, and faintly accented in a way that would have made the call of a corncrake sound melodious. 'I'm glad you did too.' He had just performed a save that would have earned him a standing ovation if she'd been a rugby ball.

'You didn't twist your ankle, did you?'

The man for whom the phrase tall, dark and handsome had been invented was looking at her legs. Deeply conscious of her ruined tights, she made a big play of brushing herself down. 'No. I'm fine.' She shook both feet in turn as if to prove the point and then felt stupid. He made her feel so gauche.

'We have met before,' he said, easing his big, sexy shoulders in a shrug.

'In the reception line at Britt's wedding,' she confirmed. 'It's good to see you again.'

Not only did he smell divine, and he was unreasonably compelling in a swarthy, piratical way, but those wicked eyes and that energy flying off him, both were off the scale. This encounter was so far out of her comfort zone, it was embarrassing, and she was longing to escape, but Raffa seemed in no hurry to get away. In fact he was studying her face as if she were one of the exhibits in the museum. Was her mascara smudged? She wasn't very good at applying make-up. Worse! Did she have sandwich stuck in her teeth?

Closing her mouth, she checked discreetly with her tongue.

'Not only did we meet before, we're almost family, Leila.'

'Sorry...' When Raffa's eyes smiled into hers, she couldn't think straight. 'Family?'

'*Sí,*' Raffa insisted in his addictive Spanish drawl. 'Now the second member of the consortium is marrying a Skavanga sister, there's only us two left. There's no need to look so shocked, Señorita Skavanga. I only meant that perhaps we can get to know each other a little better now.'

Did he really want to?

Why did he want to?

Instantly suspicious of why such a devastatingly successful, good-looking man would want to get to know her better, she blurted, 'I don't have many shares in the company.'

Raffa laughed then forced a gasp out of her as he bowed over her hand. 'I don't have any intention of stealing your shares, Leila.'

How could someone brushing his lips over the back of her hand cause so much sensation? She'd read about things like this. Before they were married or engaged her sisters had talked incessantly about romantic encounters, but this was a whole new world for Leila. Not that Raffa meant to be romantic. It was just his way of putting her at ease.

So why was it having the opposite effect?

People were still pouring up the steps to the party, pressing in on them from every side, making conversation impossible, let alone making it easy to move away from each other. And she was hopeless at small talk. The weather? It was always cold in Skavanga. That would keep them talking for all of ten seconds. But this was a Skavanga sisters' party, and Raffa was their guest, so it was up to her to make him feel welcome.

Bracing herself, she launched in. 'I hope you're enjoying your trip to Skavanga.'

He seemed amused by her opening sally. 'I am now.'

This was accompanied by a slanting smile that would bring Hollywood to its knees.

'It's been back-to-back business meetings for me before tonight,' he explained, his face turning serious, which was another great look for him. 'I just finished another meeting.'

'So you're staying here at the hotel?'

She blushed as Raffa held her gaze and frowned

slightly. He probably thought she was coming on to him, when that was a typical example of Leila Skavanga out of her depth and swimming frantically to reach the shore. Or, to put it another way: she had zero small talk.

Fortunately, Raffa had turned to assess the logistics of making it through the door without being trampled on. 'It seems to have quietened down a bit. Shall we go in?'

'Oh, I can make it from here,' she insisted, guessing he was longing to get away.

'Don't look so worried, Leila,' he said, smiling. 'You're going to love the party. Trust me…'

Trust Raffa Leon? When everyone knew his reputation? 'I'd better find my sisters, but thank you for your assurance—and for your great save,' she added as an afterthought, smiling.

'Don't mention it.'

His eyes were warm and luminous, and they plumbed deep, considering Raffa Leon was practically a stranger. This only made her more determined to stick to her original plan, which was to share a quick drink with her sisters, eat dinner—without spilling food down her, if possible—and then indulge in a little non-controversial chit-chat before shooting off as soon as she politely could.

'You're shivering, Leila—'

Oh… She was, she realised now.

'And you're laughing?'

She bit her lip, to stop thinking about the Raffa effect, and how her shivering had nothing to do with the freezing cold.

'Here—put my overcoat on…'

'Oh, no, I—'

Too late! She might have a perfectly good jacket, but Raffa's reflexes were too fast for her and now she had his coat draped round her shoulders. It was hard to pretend she wasn't distracted by his residual heat in the coat, or by the fact that it still carried the faint imprint of his cologne.

'How did you get all this mud on your dress, Leila?'

As he noticed everything she decided to make a joke of it. 'I…um…slipped away for a minute?'

He laughed. 'And I thought I saved you.'

'Almost.'

'Next time I'll have to do better.'

'Hopefully, there won't be a next time. It was my fault for chatting to the cabbie instead of looking where I was going.'

Raffa's mouth kicked up at one corner as his eyes lit in a conspiratorial smile. 'The landing wasn't too hard, I hope?'

It was hard not to laugh. 'Only my pride got bruised.'

'I think we'd better go inside before you have another accident, don't you, Leila?'

His smile was indefensibly sexy, she concluded, dragging her gaze away, but it was nice to have a man take care of her for once, especially when she was Ms Independence—not that she was going to make a habit of it, but for a few short minutes on this one special night, it couldn't hurt to lap up his aura, and she was quite sure Don Leon would find some excuse or other to part company as soon as they were inside the hotel.

So, he'd finally met the third Skavanga sister. And for longer than a ten-second handshake in a receiving line. She had turned out to be quite a surprise. Tense, but funny, Leila Skavanga was hugely lacking in self-confidence for some reason. He didn't blame her for not relishing the prospect of a party—false smiles and

meaningless chit-chat weren't his favourite form of rec-
reation either.

It was hard being the youngest in a family, as he knew
only too well, though he'd broken free of the constraints
imposed on him at a young age. When he'd been young,
with absentee parents, and three older brothers to kick
him around, not to mention two older sisters, who took
great pleasure finishing the job, it was no surprise he'd
turned out to be a handful. In his experience you went
one of two ways as the youngest child: determined and
driven, as he was, or retiring and apologetic, like Leila
Skavanga.

'Let's find the restroom first, to sort out your clothes,'
he suggested as soon as they were inside the hotel. He
was feeling unusually protective towards this woman,
he realised as Leila glanced at him.

'That was my plan,' she confirmed as if to let him
know that she was setting the ground rules—and she
could look after herself, thank you very much.

'Before I intercepted you?'

'Before I landed in your lap,' she corrected him.

He laughed into her eyes. He liked the defiance he
saw there. There was more to Leila Skavanga than met
the eye. But then her cheeks flushed red and she looked
away.

Why was she embarrassed? Too much physical contact? Too much physical contact with him?

Could Leila really be that innocent? His ingénue
radar—rusty from lack of use—said yes. Her sisters
weren't noted for being shy and retiring, which only
made Leila all the more intriguing. And when she turned
to look at him with eyes that, apart from being very
beautiful, were wide and candid, he registered a most
definite physical response.

'Come,' he said, forging a passage for her through the crowd. 'Let's get you sorted out so you can enjoy the party.'

Leila bit her lip to hide her smile. The thought of Raffa Leon 'sorting her out' was rather appealing. Thank goodness she had more sense.

There was one good thing about all this. Everyone was so busy staring at Raffa as they walked through the lobby that no one noticed Leila, or the mud on her clothes.

Shame on you, Leila Skavanga! Wasn't this supposed to be your breakout year?

Pegged as the dreamer of the family—the youngest, the quietest, the peacemaker—if she was ever going to break out of that safe, cosy mould, she had to change, and she had to change now. But not all those changes had to happen tonight. In fact, it would be safer if they didn't. When she had made that promise to herself that she would change, and that she could change, she hadn't factored the devil at her side into the equation. Don Rafael Leon, the Duke of Cantalabria, to give Raffa his full title, was not the sort of man to practise anything on. She had set her heart on finding the modern-day equivalent of a pipe and slippers man— someone undemanding and kind. Someone safe. And Raffa Leon was not safe.

So what about his chivalry towards her?

Innate politeness, she decided. Even great whites had the decency to circle you before they struck.

She exclaimed as Raffa grabbed her hands to draw her in front of him beneath the searching light of one of the hotel's glittering chandeliers.

'*Dios,* Leila! This is worse than I thought!'

Standing back, he stared long and hard at her ruined

clothes, while she was only capable of registering the unaccustomed heat flooding through her.

'Are you sure you didn't hurt yourself?' Raffa demanded.

'No, not at all...' She just wanted to stand there for a moment longer, enjoying the heat and strength in his hands. How cold and limp hers must seem by comparison, she thought, tightening her grip. She quickly released her grip, realising she had given Raffa entirely the wrong message.

'Well, I'm not going to let you out of my sight tonight,' he said with a hint of humour in his eyes as if he knew how awkward she felt having touched him. 'We can't risk any more accidents.'

'Agreed,' she murmured, still staring at him like a loon.

'The restroom, Leila?'

'Of course.' Mentally, she shook herself. 'And, really, I'm fine—I can handle it.'

'Can you?'

'Without you,' she confirmed pleasantly.

So ignore my wishes, she thought as Raffa drew her by the hand across the lobby, where the crowd parted for him like the Red Sea.

'I'm sure you've got places to be, people to meet, Raffa.'

'Yes,' he agreed. 'Right here with you, making sure the rest of your evening goes better than the start has. And you're not keeping me, Leila. Any excuse to avoid a night of small talk with people I don't know, don't want to know and will never see again.' At this point he gave a delicious Latin shrug that drew her gaze to the width of his shoulders. 'Getting away from the crowd is great for me, Leila.'

She'd felt exactly the same when she'd left the house, but only because she was so shy in a crowd of people she didn't know, which surely couldn't be Raffa's problem.

'I've been thinking back to Britt's wedding,' Raffa admitted as they waited their turn in the queue for the cloakroom. 'I remember you playing tag with those tiny flower girls. You did a great job of keeping them entertained.'

'I enjoyed it too,' she admitted. 'I'm afraid sophistication is not my middle name.'

'Some might call it charming, Leila.'

Her secret was out. She loved children. In fact, she loved children and animals more than most adults outside her family, because they were straightforward and she wasn't good at playing mind games.

'Our turn,' Raffa prompted with his hand in the small of her back as the queue to the cloakroom cleared.

His touch lit every part of her with awareness. Maybe because his hand was so strong, and his touch was so light...

'So, you like children?'

'Yes, I do.' Handing his borrowed jacket over, she turned to face the man she was sure would rather be a million miles away and hit back defensively. 'As a matter of fact, I can't wait to have children. I just don't want the man.'

Raffa's lips pressed down in the most attractive way. 'Could be awkward.'

She frowned. 'Why?'

'Biology?'

If there was some sort of danger/beware register, Raffa should be put on it, Leila decided as he flashed his wicked smile.

She had a lucky escape from more verbal jousting

when her gorgeous sister Britt chose that moment to enter the hotel on the arm of her handsome sheikh. Spotting them immediately, Britt gave Leila a what-the-heck-are-you-doing-with-*him?* look, swiftly followed by a jerk of her beautiful blonde head in the direction of the elevators—a signal that Leila should get herself out of trouble and up to the family suite pronto, before she got herself into deeper water with the most dangerous man in town.

She returned Britt's look with a slanting smile that said, do I have to?

Did she want to? That was the question.

Britt shrugged as if to say, on your head be it.

It was all right for Britt. Fantastic in company like Leila's other sister, Eva, Britt would be an asset to any gathering, while Leila would only get in the way if she went up to the suite Britt had taken for her pre-party gathering.

'Put your ticket away safely, Leila.'

'Sorry?'

'Your cloakroom ticket,' Raffa prompted, handing it over. 'Now get yourself into the restroom to sort out your dress. And, okay—' His gaze descended and lingered for quite some time. 'Your stockings are shot.'

'My tights,' she corrected him primly.

'Please don't disillusion me.'

That smile!

Her equilibrium having been taken and turned upside down, it was definitely time to take a short break from the hottest man around. 'Don't bother waiting up for me,' she called over her shoulder with a grin as she headed at speed for the restroom.

She'd given him an out. Hopefully, he'd take the hint. Leaning over the washbasin, she took a much-needed moment to catch her breath. Forget the dress. Forget the mud. Her mind was full of the man outside that door. Would he wait for her? Almost certainly not, thank goodness. No one had ever had this sort of effect on her before. Which had to mean she was certifiably crazy. Raffa Leon had a reputation that made Casanova look like a choirboy. He was single because he played the field. And she had no intention of applying to become a member of his team.

Pulling back from the basin, she tore off a strip of paper towel and, wetting it, cleaned the mud off her dress. The dress was soon okay-ish, but, as Raffa had clearly identified, her tights were ruined. Stripping them off, she dumped them in the bin.

Bare legs?

She pulled a face. Chalk legs weren't exactly the look she'd been aiming for, but who would notice?

Raffa.

Raffa noticed everything.

But he probably wouldn't even speak to her again that night. And if he did, wasn't this year supposed to be about chilling out and freeing herself to do some of the things she had longed to do—like travelling, like meeting new people, for instance? And if he was waiting outside the door for her, why shouldn't she allow him to escort her to the party? Britt and Eva wouldn't miss her up in their suite. They would be heavily into hosting cocktails and canapés by now. And Raffa was surely more entertaining than the mayor of Skavanga, whose unofficial job it was to make a wallflower feel valued. Or the elderly vicar, who could always be relied upon to give Leila a pep talk on finding a husband before it was too late.

Too late at twenty-two?

And who needed a husband, anyway? All she wanted was a child—children, preferably. She was perennially broody. And, in the unlikely event that Raffa was desperate enough to be outside that door, she would be well chaperoned at the party. Britt and Eva would be there with their partners, along with a hundred or so guests. And it wasn't every day she got to swap small talk with a billionaire.

So... Would he be there? Or would Raffa Leon have breathed a sigh of relief the moment she closed the restroom door and made his escape? Before her courage deserted her completely, she opened the door to find out.

'Leila.'

'Raffa...'

So far, so disastrous. One glance into those laughing dark eyes and she could hardly breathe. Raffa looked amazing—even more than amazing. In a dark, formal suit that moulded his powerful body to perfection, he was taller than most of the other men present, and exuded energy like a fighter jet amongst a fleet of biplanes.

'I apologise for keeping you waiting so long.'

'It was worth the wait, Leila. You look sensational.'

What? She stopped just short of rolling her eyes. Then, remembering this was another example of his practised charm, she filed his compliment away under Trivia.

'Well, at least I'm mud free,' she agreed, glancing down at her clothes. Unfortunately, under the lights they still looked a bit ropey. 'I had to take my tights off—'

Uh? What kind of message did that send?

There was laughter in Raffa's eyes, but now she couldn't stop herself and nerves were starting to make her babble. 'Bare legs... Well... White legs, actually—'

Good of you to point it out, she could imagine him thinking.

Great legs, he thought. And the rest was very nicely packaged too. Leila was wearing the same dress she'd worn at Britt's wedding when she had been playing with the children. He remembered it now.

'Britt's dress,' Leila said, seeing him look at it. 'I wore it at my sister's wedding.'

'I remember.' And Leila would win any Who-looks-best-in-this-dress? contest hands down.

'It's the prettiest dress I've ever seen,' she rattled on as if she had to excuse the fact that she was wearing something that suited her so well. 'I begged Britt not to go to the expense of buying some silly bridesmaid's dress I'd never wear again—and, look! Here I am, wearing it again! That's what I call getting your money's worth…'

As Leila's hectic explanation petered out, he hummed, wondering why she didn't have any pretty dresses of her own to wear.

And why should he care?

'It's a bit too tight,' she said, getting her second wind. 'Britt's so slim—'

The tighter the better, as far as he was concerned. He'd never gone for the half-starved look. The dress would always look better on Leila because she was voluptuous.

'I don't go to many parties. Don't feel sorry for me,' she insisted before he had chance to say a word. 'I usually hang out somewhere quieter than this—'

'My preference too,' he said, shielding Leila with his arm as more guests piled into the lobby. Quiet rooms and hot women would be his preference every time. 'Here's an idea—' He had stopped in front of the elevator. 'There's a quiet lounge just down this corridor. Why don't we take five? It would give you chance to recover your composure.' And calm down a bit, he thought.

'You mean, I look a mess?'

She looked adorable and so trusting as she turned her face up to his. Well, she was safe tonight. He had already reined in his thoughts from champagne and seduction to soft drinks and a few very necessary moments of calm for Leila. She needed to relax before facing the bright lights of the party, and, surprising even himself, he wanted to get to know her a little better. 'Come on—let's get out of this crush. The party isn't due to start for another half hour,' he reassured her when she looked doubtful. 'We won't be missed.'

'But my sisters are expecting me.'

'Your sisters will be so busy doing what they do well, they won't miss either of us.'

Opening the door on the tempting setting of a quiet lounge, he stood back. They wouldn't be alone. There were quite a few residents who weren't going to the party sitting around reading newspapers and chatting quietly, and there was a big, welcoming log fire burning lustily in the grate. There were still plenty of cosy armchairs where they could sit and chat without being overheard. It was the perfect spot for a girl who wasn't sure of herself yet, or of her companion.

'This is lovely,' Leila said with relief, gazing round.

'Orange juice?' he suggested.

'With a splash of lemonade, please. How did you know?'

He loved the way Leila's smile lit up her face. 'Lucky guess.' Not such a stretch. It was going to be a long night, and, though Leila was reputedly the shyest of the Skavanga sisters, there was a hint of steel about her that suggested she would face the party clear-headed or not at all.

Leila intrigued him, if only because she was so different from her sisters. The middle sister, Eva, whose eve-of-wedding party this was, could be a headstrong handful, while Britt was a hard-nosed businesswoman who only softened for her sheikh. Leila's sisters and her brother, Tyr, had clearly protected her when their parents died, as Leila had been so very young when the tragic plane crash happened, but the intuition that had never let him down so far said there was more to Leila Skavanga than simply a sheltered girl who worked in the archive department of the Skavanga mining museum, and he was keen to find out what that was.

CHAPTER TWO

WHAT EXACTLY WAS she doing with Raffa Leon? What could they possibly have to talk about?

Anybody?

She had never done anything so out of character in her life. Yes, Raffa was charming, but he was practically a stranger—and a dangerous one at that, according to her sisters and the rather more scandalous tone of the press. Leila had always been glad she worked in a separate building from the mining company, if only because it put some space between herself and these high-powered, fast-living types.

But didn't this unexpected encounter with a leading player in the consortium dovetail nicely with her determination to make this her breakout year?

Roar mouse?

Great idea, if she had the courage to summon up something more than a squeak. And what was Raffa up to? Why choose to spend time with her?

'Shall we sit here?' he suggested, indicating two comfortable armchairs facing each other across a sleek glass table.

'Thank you.'

Even this close to such a powerhouse of testosterone made her feel incredibly aware and wary. His deep, velvety voice with that intriguing accent played in her head, and she had to remind herself that sweeping a woman away with whatever means he chose to employ was Raffa Leon's stock in trade. Though he was hardly out to seduce her with so many other attractive women at the party.

Out of the archive department into the fire, she concluded with amusement as Raffa turned to give their order to the waiter. He looked so relaxed, while she was more like a schoolgirl on parade, sitting stiff and upright in her chair, waiting for the pronouncements of the headmaster.

Raffa knocked that idea on its head the moment he turned back to her. No headmaster on earth looked like this—such compelling dark eyes with that touch of humour, and a wickedly curving mouth.

'I'm looking forward to a refreshing drink, without having it knocked out of our hands,' he said, turning up the voltage on his smile.

It took her a moment to speak, she was so captivated, and then she experienced a moment of panic. What could she possibly say to him? How did you launch into a conversation with a notorious billionaire? How's your yacht? Would that do?

'What are you smiling at, Leila?' he enquired, raising one sweeping ebony brow in a way that made her heart stop.

'Am I smiling?' She stopped smiling immediately. 'I was just thinking, this is a great place, isn't it? Such a good idea of yours.' She made a point of staring round. Anything was safer than looking at Raffa.

'It's good to see you relax,' he said, his eyes dark like the night and just as full of danger.

Relaxed? Was that what he thought? She doubted

any woman could relax around Raffa Leon. He had this way of staring directly into your eyes that made it hard to look away. Impossible to look away, she amended.

So come out of your shell. Live boldly for once.

'Here's your juice,' he said. 'With a splash of lemonade as requested.'

As he handed it to her he was doing that eye thing— the curving smile, the crinkle at the corner of his eyes. It was all too easy to fool herself into thinking he was interested in her, when this was just his way. Raffa Leon was a charming and accomplished seducer, both in business and with women, and she had to get it into her head that this was just an innocent encounter and a refreshing drink. She had never been the type of girl men took up to their room. She was the kid sister they brought into the very public hotel lounge to share an orange juice with before the party.

And she should be pleased about that.

She *was* pleased. But she would be lying if she tried to pretend it wouldn't be thrilling to have Raffa look at her with something other than humour in his eyes.

When she leaned forward to pick up her glass, her senses filled with the faint scent of his cologne. It was one of those intoxicating scents, hard to identify, but undoubtedly exclusive. She sat back again, wondering. What now? Raffa seemed content to let the silence hang between them, so maybe it was up to her to break the silence. Live boldly, for once! Pointing through one of the tall arched windows, she drew his attention to the park, picked out in lights at this time of night. 'My mother used to take me over there to the park when I was a little girl so I could terrorise people on my three-wheeler.'

'I never saw you as a hoodlum, Leila.'

So how did he see her? Raffa laughed as he set down his drink. A soft drink too, she noted.

Raffa felt his heart stir as he thought about a little girl taking every day with her mother for granted, and a young mother enjoying special time with her youngest child. Those days must have felt as if they would go on for ever. Neither of them could have anticipated Leila's father's descent into drunken violence, or the tragic plane crash and loss of life.

'What are you thinking about now?' he prompted, though he guessed Leila had inadvertently uncovered memories she didn't normally share with strangers, and was probably regretting being so open with him. Insanely, he wanted to hug her and tell her it would be all right, but they didn't know each other well enough for that. They had a party to go to, where Leila would have to be bright and cheerful, or her sisters would want to know why. He didn't want to leave her shakier than when she'd fallen into his arms outside the hotel. What had begun as basic attraction and curiosity had gained an edge of care. Not that he felt responsible for Leila, and she wouldn't want that. She'd been doing pretty well on her own up to now.

'More juice?'

'Please. Sorry, Raffa, I was miles away.'

Thinking about her mother's letter, Leila realised as Raffa turned away to order more drinks. She'd been doing a lot of that recently, and she'd had plenty of time to memorise every word over the years.

My darling Leila,
I love you more than life itself, and want you to
promise me that you will live your life to the full.
You're only a little girl now, but one day you'll be

*a woman with choices to make and I want you to
make the right choices.*

*Don't be afraid of life, Leila, as I have been. Be
bold in all you do—*

It still haunted her to think her mother must have
known she was in danger—maybe even that Leila's father would go too far and kill them both. Leila had been
too young to understand what had happened at the time
of the crash, and it was only later when she was older
that her sisters had explained that their father was most
likely drunk at the controls of the plane. She'd done
some investigating of her own at the local newspaper
office and had got the picture of a violent alcoholic and
a woman who had been the helpless victim of his rages.

'Ice in your juice?' Raffa broke into her thoughts.

'No. It's delicious as it is, thank you.'

'Spanish oranges,' he said, his dark face brightening
with a smile. 'The best.'

'You're partial.'

'Yes, I am,' he agreed, holding her gaze a beat too
long.

It was long enough for her heart to pound out of control. Raffa was so worldly, and it was almost funny, the
two of them being here together, when Skavanga was
just one stop on Raffa's round-the-world tour of his in-
ternational business interests, and she had never been
outside the town except for university, and even then
she'd only gone a few miles down the road to the local
college. As soon as she had qualified, she'd scuttled
back to the place she knew best, the place she felt safest,
where she could hide away in the archive department of
a mining museum where it was quiet, and where there

was no chance of meeting a wife beater, or an alcoholic. Or anyone for that matter.

'So you've stayed in Skavanga all your life, Leila? Leila?' Raffa prompted, his voice shaking her round.

She'd been trapped in the past, sitting on the stairs, listening to her parents arguing and hearing the inevitable thump when her mother hit the floor. And now, judging by the concerned look on Raffa's face, he was joining her on this trip down memory lane too.

'Yes, I've been here all my life,' she confirmed brightly to make up for her lapse in concentration.

She was actually quite good at being jolly. She'd had plenty of practice over the years. Having been totally eclipsed by her beautiful sisters, she'd had the choice of being the mouse in the background, or the jolly sister. She'd perfected both. 'I've always been close to my brother and sisters.' At least, she had been, until her brother, Tyr, had gone missing.

'It's great to have siblings,' Raffa agreed, 'even if you don't always get along.'

'We get along. I just miss my brother, and I wish I knew where he was.' Her stare met Raffa's, but, if he knew where Tyr was, he wasn't telling. 'I know it must look to you as if my sisters run roughshod over me, but believe me, Raffa, I can hold my own.'

'I never doubted it,' he agreed, to her surprise.

But as Raffa's smile faded, and a shadow crossed his face, she wondered about his family. She also realised they had relaxed into the last thing she had imagined sharing with Raffa Leon, which was a meaningful conversation.

'What about you?' she prompted gently. 'What about your family, Raffa?'

The look he shot her made her regret asking. 'I'm sorry. I didn't mean to probe.'

'That's all right,' he said, sitting back. He shrugged. 'Apart from the three brothers and two sisters I do know about, I'm told I have countless half brothers and sisters across the globe, thanks to the untiring efforts of my father.'

'And your mother—?' That was one question she definitely shouldn't have asked, Leila realised, breaking off when she saw the expression on Raffa's face. 'I'm sorry. I—'

'Don't be,' he interrupted. 'I was lucky enough to spend most of my youth with my grandmother. As soon as my elder brothers and sisters went off to college, my father made it quite clear that he was done with children.'

'So there was no place at home for you?'

He didn't answer that. He didn't need to. What Raffa had told her explained so much about him. He was the lone wolf, dangerous, hidden and unknowable.

'I'd like to meet your grandmother,' she said, trying to bring him back to the present. 'She must be an amazing woman.'

'To take me on?' Raffa queried, relaxing into a laugh. 'She is. And maybe you will meet her one day, Leila.'

He was just being polite, but it was a relief to see him smiling again.

'And you grew up with your sisters and brother,' he prompted.

'Who always teased me unmercifully,' she confirmed.

'And you don't mind that?'

'I tease them back. Families,' she added with a smile and a shrug.

Raffa huffed softly and smiled back at her.

His eyes were so incredibly expressive they warmed

her right through. The fact that Raffa was as hot as hell should have been warning enough for her to back off, but he was like a magnet drawing her closer, against her will. 'My sisters tease me because they love me as much as I love them,' she said to break the sudden electric tension between them. 'I guess they're always trying to make up for—'

'Your mother dying when you were so very young,' Raffa cut in.

The concern on his face surprised her. 'I suppose… Anyway, they've been great.' Massive understatement. 'Tyr too—' She stopped as the familiar ache washed over her.

'Your brother will come home one day soon, Leila.'

'You say that with such certainty. Have you heard from Tyr?' There was excitement in her voice, but Raffa disappointed her by saying nothing. And why was she surprised? Leila and her sisters had always suspected that the three men in the consortium knew exactly where Tyr was, but none of them would reveal his whereabouts. The four men had been at school together, and then again in Special Forces, so their loyalties cut deep. But still, she had to try. 'All I care about is that he's safe, Raffa.'

Her heart lurched as she stared deep into eyes that held her gaze steadily.

'Please don't ask me questions about your brother, Leila, because I can't tell you the answers you want to hear.'

'You won't tell me,' she argued.

'That's right,' Raffa agreed levelly. 'I won't.'

'But perhaps you could tell me he's safe?'

There was a long pause, and then Raffa said, 'He's safe.'

'Thank you.' Relief flooded through her as she sat

back. Tyr was safe. That was all she needed to hear, and the thought that Raffa knew her brother so well made everything she'd heard about him pale into insignificance.

'Tell me about your job at the museum, Leila.'

She relaxed. There was nothing she loved more than talking about her job. She enjoyed working at the museum so much she could talk about it endlessly. 'It's my passion—' She didn't need to try now. The words just came pouring out. 'I'd love to show you round. It's amazing. I wish you could see all the things we've found. To think my ancestors used them. And every day there's a new discovery...' She stopped in case she was boring him, but Raffa encouraged her to go on. And so it all came pouring out—her plans for the museum, her hopes and dreams for the future of the work she loved, her classes, her workshops, her tours, the exhibitions she had planned.

'I am so sorry,' she said at last. 'I must have bored the socks off you. No one can stop me once I get talking about the museum.'

'On the contrary, I don't want to stop you,' he insisted, 'though it is a revelation to discover you're not the quiet sister after all.'

'I'm not quiet at all,' she assured him.

No. Leila just needed the chance to be heard, he thought.

'What are you doing?' she said when he took the glass from her hand.

'I think we should go to the party. Have you seen the time?'

'No. Goodness me!' she exclaimed, springing up. 'I have been boring you!'

'Not at all,' he insisted. 'Far from it. This evening has

turned out far better than I anticipated, and we haven't even reached the party yet.'

We?

She laughed as Raffa smiled back at her. Even if he was just being polite, she was having a great time. Raffa Leon was so much more than she had expected in every way. It was hard not to be attracted to him—impossible. Which was in itself crazy. Who invited trouble, unless they were completely mad?

She did, apparently.

'So, are you completely recovered after your tumble?' he said as he escorted her across the crowded lobby.

'Completely,' she confirmed. 'And thank you for the drink. I feel ready for anything now.'

When Raffa laughed at this, she realised he must think her quaint and old-fashioned; sheltered, certainly.

'If I were as honest as you, Leila, I would never have succeeded in business,' he confided to her obvious alarm. 'Meaning everything shows on your face,' he was quick to explain when she frowned. 'I'm not quite the big bad wolf I'm reported to be.'

'But close.' She laughed.

He laughed too. It was good to see Leila relaxed. And he wanted her to know he did have principles. He didn't want her fretting about some rogue buying into her family business. Leila had certainly brought out the best in him. And that was a first.

'And now to find your sisters,' he said, realising that with any other attractive woman, finding her sisters would be the last thing on his mind.

'Must we?'

Leila had spoken without thinking, he realised as her cheeks flushed red. She was enjoying being relaxed.

She'd never been keen to join the pre-party scrum in Britt's suite.

'We don't have to go up to Britt's suite,' he reassured her. 'We can meet your sisters in the ballroom at our table. I'm looking forward to seeing the three of you together. Life is never boring with a Skavanga sister, so they tell me.'

'They're right,' Leila admitted wryly. 'Just your bad luck you got landed with me.'

'Am I complaining?'

She flashed him a mischievous look, and as her mouth curved in a smile Leila's eyes lit in a way that made him want to know more about this youngest Skavanga sister. It hit him out of nowhere that his grandmother would love her. His *abuelita,* as cute little grannies were known in Spain, was never off his case, always insisting he must find himself a *good* woman. He would do a lot of things for Abuelita, but not that, though his grandmother would put the bunting out if he brought a girl like Leila home.

And hadn't Leila said she wanted to meet his grandmother?

He glanced at her, thinking the best thing about Leila was she had no idea how attractive she was, and in his world that was definitely a breath of fresh air.

They were halfway across the ballroom when she got a call on her phone. 'Britt,' she mouthed. As she pressed the receiver to her ear her cheeks turned scarlet. He gathered she wasn't having the easiest of conversations with her sister.

'She wanted to know where I was,' Leila explained when she ended the call.

'I hope you told her, living dangerously?'

'With the big bad wolf? Yes, I did, as it happens.'

'And your sister hit the roof?'

'Pretty much.'

They shared an amused look.

'Do you believe everything you've heard about me, Leila?'

For a moment she didn't speak, but then she said quite bluntly, 'I don't know you well enough to pass judgement yet.'

He laughed at that. 'When you do—you will let me know?'

'I'll make sure of it.'

She hadn't told Raffa the whole truth about her conversation with Britt, who was clearly worried about her, and who had yelled in alarm at the prospect of her baby sister spending even one minute alone in the company of the notorious Raffa Leon. Worse luck, Raffa had turned out to be the perfect gentleman, though it might be fun to tease her sisters. It wasn't often Leila caused comment.

'You did reassure Britt?' Raffa commented as they approached the table.

'Actually, no,' she admitted. 'For once in my life, I was enigmatic. I was only having a bit of fun, but I couldn't resist it. My sisters tease me constantly, so this was my chance to get them back.'

'Well, I'm happy to go along with however you want to play it,' Raffa assured her, his dark eyes glinting in a way that filled her mind with all sorts of outrageous possibilities.

'I might take you up on that.'

'Please do.'

His smile could travel to places she had forgotten about, in no time flat. 'Then I will,' she added with a smile and a shrug, thinking this evening was going to be fun.

'Tonight will see Leila Skavanga come to the fore,' Raffa promised as he held her chair.

'But I don't want to upset them,' Leila was quick to add. 'Britt has gone to a lot of trouble to arrange the party for Eva, and I don't want anything to spoil Eva's night.'

'I promise you, it won't,' Raffa agreed, 'not through anything I do, anyway, though there's nothing to prevent us having a bit of fun. I just hope with all the Skavanga Diamonds glittering at once you don't dazzle me into a stupor.'

'No chance of that,' Leila said, laughing at Raffa's expression as she sat down.

Warmth flooded her as Raffa sat down in the next chair, close but not too close, almost touching but not touching, in a way that made her thighs tingle.

'You can rely on me to back you up with enough smouldering looks and dirty dancing to shock your sisters out of their killer shoes.'

'Wonderful.' Did she mean to say that? Yes, she did. 'That should make my home life a whole lot easier,' she commented dryly.

'Any time I can be of service…'

And this was a really bad time to be holding Raffa's stare. His eyes were dancing with laughter, which told her nothing about his thoughts, but if this connection between them was only for tonight, it was the most fun she'd had in a long time. And now Britt and Eva had arrived in the ballroom on the arms of their handsome partners, bringing an end to their conversation as every head in the ballroom swivelled round.

'Don't look so worried, Leila,' Raffa murmured, leaning in close. 'I promise not to do anything that might upset them.'

Once she stared at Raffa it was hard to look away. 'Something tells me Eva and Britt aren't going to believe we've been sitting, chatting in the lounge all this time.'

And the truth was even more complicated than that, Leila realised. Both of them had touched on subjects she guessed neither of them would dream of discussing with a stranger, and the connection she'd sensed between them at first had grown stronger because of it.

'You'll just have to put up with your sisters' suspicions,' Raffa said pragmatically, leaning back as he prepared to stand to greet their dinner companions.

'Just so long as we don't take this too far,' Leila agreed, already wondering what she'd got herself into as Raffa turned to bestow a lingering look on her face.

'You and I know what went on.'

Precisely nothing, she thought as the most handsome man in the room went on to list their harmless pastimes. 'You drank juice. We talked. We relaxed. But there's no way on earth your sisters are going to believe that, so unless you'd rather pretend we haven't been together every second since you arrived at the hotel—'

'You make our innocent time together sound so bad.'

'What fun would it be otherwise?' he murmured.

She hummed as Raffa's black gaze bored deep into hers.

'Let the teasing begin,' he said.

Had it already? she wondered as Raffa leaned in close. And was she the main target? If Britt and Eva had been suspicious before, seeing the two of them like this, so close they were practically kissing, would turn her sisters into tireless seekers after the truth. But she hadn't done anything wrong. She was following the advice in her mother's letter and being bold.

And even when Raffa smiled his slow, sexy smile, she asked herself, was it likely Britt and Eva would imagine she'd had hot monkey sex with Raffa Leon?

Absolutely not!

So what did she have to worry about?

She could relax.

Britt and Eva stared first at Raffa, and then at their sister. 'Well,' Britt said, smiling as they greeted her. 'Here you are, Leila.' She exchanged an arch-browed look with Eva.

'I'm really sorry we missed the reception upstairs,' Leila began, slipping easily back into the role of peace-maker, 'but—'

'But we got talking,' Raffa intervened smoothly.

'I'm sure you did,' Eva agreed dryly.

'We were in the lounge,' Leila chipped in.

'Of course you were,' Britt agreed.

Raffa was right. They were never going to believe her. She glanced at him, only for Raffa to give her an amused and conspiratorial look. Let the teasing begin, he'd said. But let's not overdo it, her eyes begged him as her sisters sat down. This was Eva's special night, and she didn't want anything to spoil it.

Raffa returned her look with a reassuring expression. She'd never had a co-conspirator before. And it was quite incredible to think she belonged with such a party of swans, Leila mused as everyone started talking at once. Eva looked off-the-scale stunning, with her long, flame-red hair caught back on either side of her beautiful face with glittering diamond combs, her fabulous figure displayed in a floor-length, body-hugging gown of flesh-coloured lace, embellished with tiny crystals. And the heat flying between Eva and Count Roman Quisvada, the man she would marry tomorrow, was off the scale.

Would a man ever look at her that way? Leila wondered as she turned her attention to Britt, whose husband, Sheikh Sharif, was currently shooting intensely personal messages into his wife's eyes. With her icy

Nordic looks, imposing height and slender figure, Britt was the perfect foil for her Arabian prince, and there was such closeness between them, Leila couldn't help but feel wistful.

There was such an overload of glamour at their table they were the focus of the room. Three amazing-looking men, two fabulous-looking women…and Leila. Her sisters set a standard she couldn't hope to compete with, but for one night, with Raffa at her side, she was going to give it a shot.

'Would you like me to help you choose from the menu, Leila?' Raffa murmured, leaning in close.

Britt and Eva were instantly on alert, but she felt obliged to point out, 'It's a fixed menu.'

'So it is,' Raffa agreed, not losing eye contact with her for a moment.

It was going to be hard remembering this was just pretence, but a glance at her sisters reassured her they were convinced.

'Would you like me to read the menu out to you?' Raffa now suggested.

'Yes, please,' she said, sitting back with the air of a woman for whom men peeled grapes.

Britt and Eva had designed the menu between them and Leila soon realised that her sisters had chosen food which was impossible to eat without appearing provocative—a look Leila was keen to avoid tonight, even if her intention was to tease them, as she had to balance the game with not taking things too far with Raffa.

The appetiser was a small baked cheese drizzled with truffle oil on a bed of salad leaves…

'Don't you like cheese, Leila?'

As Raffa asked the question Britt and Eva stared at her. She loved cheese and they knew it. Britt had probably designed this first course with Leila's preferences in mind. But the thought of all that soft, warm cheese glistening on her lips—

'Shall we swap plates?' Raffa suggested.

She lifted the plate. He reached for it, and their fingers touched. Heat exploded inside her. Her gasp could probably be heard in the car park.

'I love a man with a healthy appetite,' Britt commented, flashing a look at Eva.

'What's the matter, baby sister?' Eva contributed, picking up the virtual ball Britt had just lobbed across the net. 'Not enough hot food for you around this table?'

'I've got an enormous appetite,' Raffa confessed with every appearance of innocence. 'If any of you don't want your food, please pass it my way.'

The other men registered small smiles at this, while Britt and Eva exchanged a knowing look.

Okay. She got it. Leila was Little Red Riding Hood paired with the big bad wolf for the night. She gave her sisters a warning look, but they just smiled and raised a brow. As long as she could handle it, they were okay with it. Now she just had to watch out that the joke didn't end up on her.

The next course was asparagus, which was possibly Leila's favourite food, but the way Eva was sucking the butter off the tip...

'I can't believe you're not eating this,' Raffa scolded when she again offered to exchange her plate with him, but his eyes were laughing, as if he knew exactly what she was thinking.

'I don't want to risk butter dripping down my dress.' She raised a brow at him, conscious that her sisters were watching them closely. 'This dress has been through enough adventures for one night, don't you agree, Raffa?'

As Britt and Eva exchanged a look, Leila appeared to change her mind, and, lifting a buttery spear to her lips, she sucked on it thoughtfully.

'Here—have another one if you're hungry,' he prompted in a way that made her breath catch.

Her sisters were transfixed by now, while the look in Raffa's eyes wasn't doing all that much for her own equilibrium. It was just an act, she told herself, until he captured some butter from her lips on his thumb and sucked it clean. She felt an answering pulse of pleasure with each lazy tug of his mouth. It was such a sexy, intimate thing for him to do.

And she should look away.

When it came to the entrée, a black pepper filet mignon with a blob of Gorgonzola on top, resting on a bed of wilted spinach, she was still watching Raffa eat.

'Hmm, delicious,' he murmured, savouring the delicious meat. 'Why aren't you eating, Leila?'

'It's chocolate fondue for pudding,' Britt remarked innocently.

Okay, there was no leaving this game half played. 'Chocolate fondue?' She gazed deep into Raffa's eyes. 'My favourite…'

As Raffa paused, fork suspended, she tucked in with relish. This was easy. Where had she been hiding all these years?

'Leila.'

Why was Raffa whispering?

She turned to look at him with confidence. 'Yes? What is it? What's wrong?'

She prickled with awareness as he leaned in close.

'You've got spinach between your teeth…'

CHAPTER THREE

IT WAS INEVITABLE the conversation around the table would eventually return to the hottest topic of the night: where had Leila and Raffa been for such a long time? Britt and Eva clearly weren't convinced by the hotel lounge story.

'So, what did you two find to talk about up in Raffa's suite?' Britt asked casually.

'We weren't in Raffa's suite,' Leila said patiently. 'We were chatting in the hotel lounge, surrounded by other guests—' She was just getting into her stride when her eyes widened with surprise as Raffa's warm, strong hand covered hers in a cautionary gesture.

'We were discussing the mining museum, as a matter of fact,' he commented casually. 'Leila's got some great ideas,' he went on without missing a beat. 'And I was saying that, as I have one of the finest gem collections in the world, perhaps Leila should visit my island with a view to displaying a selection of her choice in Skavanga.'

The silence was absolute. Everyone was stunned, including Leila. Raffa had just hit them with the conversation stopper of all time. Was that a serious invitation? Or was he still playing games?

'Just say yes,' he suggested, easing back on his chair as she looked at him.

For once, Britt had nothing to say, and it was Eva who filled the gap in her usual blunt manner. 'What are you suggesting?' she asked Raffa suspiciously, flying in defence of her sister.

'I'm suggesting Leila comes to Isla Montaña de Fuego to take a look at my jewels,' Raffa responded quietly.

'Why?' Eva was keen to dig deeper before she let him off the hook. 'Why does Leila need to visit your island? Can't you bring the gems here?'

'I wouldn't presume to make a selection for Leila,' Raffa explained smoothly, his black stare confirming this with Leila.

'That's right.' Leila's heart was going crazy as she played along. 'I can't wait to see Raffa's collection. Everyone loves a big diamond, don't they, Eva?'

Britt and Eva quickly hid their ring hands under the table as Raffa added, 'Leila sees a great future for the mining museum.'

'You two have been chatting, haven't you?' Eva commented, relaxing back, defeated for once.

As her sisters exchanged a look Leila wondered how long she could keep this up. Visiting Raffa's island? As if! 'Yes, Raffa and I have been talking,' she confirmed blithely. 'It's only natural when we've got so much in common— The diamonds,' she added when her sisters stared at her in disbelief.

'Indeed,' Eva murmured with amusement. 'The diamonds. I'd almost forgotten them.'

'Well, I can't think of any other reason I'd visit the island—' As she spoke Leila was conscious of digging an even bigger hole for herself, but somehow she couldn't stop. 'As soon as I slipped on the ice and Raffa caught me, I thought—what luck! This is my chance to put my business proposition to him—'

'Your what?' Britt interrupted.

Fair enough. She'd gone too far. When were Leila Skavanga and business ever mentioned in the same sentence? Try never.

'Leila made a very good pitch, actually,' Raffa said, filling the gap. 'Water, anyone? Sparkling…? Still…?'

'Leila *is* brilliant at her job,' Britt mused out loud as if she was actually convinced.

'And has always seen her work as an opportunity to give a whole new generation an insight into the business that put the town on the map,' Eva added, shooting a proud-sister look at Leila.

Oh, no! Why were her sisters getting involved? She felt really bad now. If only they would stop being so helpful! Didn't they realise this was all a joke? It so obviously was—

She looked at Raffa, who was giving nothing away. But why pretend to invite her to his island? That was going a bit far, wasn't it?

She almost jumped out of her skin when he reached across to give her hand a reassuring squeeze, and realised she had to say something quickly to Britt and Eva or they would be completely sucked in. 'He's only joking about the trip—even Raffa couldn't be such a glutton for punishment as to invite me to spend more time with him.' She shared an amused look with Britt and Eva and saw them relax.

'Well, the invitation's on the table, Leila.'

Her head shot round to Raffa. *What?* 'An hour chatting with me isn't punishment enough?' she pressed, laughing to try and get him out of his predicament.

No dice. And she got the distinct impression her sisters were holding their breath.

'Not nearly long enough,' Raffa said. 'And in case

you're in any doubt,' he added, saying this to everyone around the table, 'I never joke where business is concerned.'

Britt and Eva were transfixed, while Leila's heart was pumping like crazy. If this was a serious offer, and it certainly seemed to be, it would be her first proper trip out of Skavanga. And with Raffa!

As the spotlight swung away and the conversation returned to less controversial topics Raffa's attention remained fixed on her face, leaving her to wonder if she'd survived this game of teasing, or if she was heading for a fall.

'We're going to dance,' Britt announced. 'Leila?'

'Oh, no. I'm okay, thank you.'

'Will you excuse us if we leave you two alone?' Britt pressed, still obviously concerned for Leila.

'Yes, of course,' Leila reassured her. 'You go right ahead.'

Raffa stood politely as both her sisters left the table with their partners, and then he sat down again, while Leila clung to a life raft in the shape of a chair.

'Shall we?' he suggested, glancing at the packed dance floor.

'You want to dance with me?'

'I don't see anyone else sitting here.'

As a smile curved Raffa's lips she knew this was not remotely sensible. 'Dancing's really not my thing.'

'But I thought we had a pact?'

To tease her sisters, not to bring disaster in the shape of a hot, bad man crashing down on her head. 'Don't worry. I won't hold you to our pact.'

'What if I want you to?'

As a catalogue of potential pitfalls flashed through

her head she felt it was time to come clean. 'Really—there's no need to continue being polite to me.'

'Who said I'm being polite?' Raffa demanded, reaching for her hand.

She couldn't refuse—not with people staring at them and shooting admiring glances at Raffa. She stood and exhaled shakily as he drew her by the hand towards the dance floor, and gave another shaky exclamation when he pressed her close. He hadn't been joking about dirty dancing. She could hardly breathe. Or maybe that was too much excitement. Heat was rampaging through her as she came into contact with every alarming contour of his body.

'I thought you wanted to dance,' Raffa prompted when she remained quite still.

'*You* wanted to dance,' she reminded him, reluctant to end her sensory exploration of a man who was every bit as hard as he looked.

'Yes. With you,' he confirmed, tightening his grip.

Raffa didn't take no for an answer, Leila discovered as he swept her round the floor.

And her sisters were watching. Watching? They were agog. And now they were dancing round her to take a closer look. 'Bandits at twelve o'clock,' she warned, making the mistake of meeting the slumbering sexual heat in Raffa's eyes.

'I like your style, Leila Skavanga,' he murmured, his voice all husky and rough.

'Really?' She prepared herself for some glowing compliment from the master of charm. 'Why?'

'Stubborn. Tricky. Unpredictable.' Raffa shrugged. 'I never know what to expect from you.'

Then he wouldn't be surprised when her stiletto hit his foot.

'What's wrong now, Leila?'

She sniffed. 'I'm waiting for the right beat of the music.'

'Ah, a perfectionist.'

'No. A novice.'

'A novice?' Raffa's warm breath brushed her ear. 'I could soon change that.'

Her sharp intake of breath could probably be heard outside the hotel. 'Practice makes perfect.'

'Another topic on which we agree. Have you got the beat yet, Leila?'

She'd got something!

How could they move so well together when they were a complete mismatch? Fire and ice. Raffa's great size compared to her— Well, truthfully, she wasn't exactly small, but she was a lot smaller than he was. But as the music wove its spell and she began to relax she started to enjoy herself, so that by the time they danced past her sisters there was mischief in her blood. She had always been content to stay beneath the radar, allowing Britt and Eva to slug it out, but not tonight. Not with Raffa. So as they danced past her sisters, instead of shrinking into the woodwork, she threw back her hair and sighed, leaving Britt and Eva in no doubt that she wouldn't have dusty archives on her mind tonight.

'Do you know? I think we've done our duty—'

Leila gasped as Raffa took her hand to lead her off the dance floor.

'I'm ready to leave,' he explained as he forged a passage for them through the milling crowd.

Oh, he was? 'But the party's just getting started,' she pointed out, hanging back.

'Haven't you had enough? I know I have...'

She could see the cabs lined up outside the hotel

through one of the windows. Raffa wasn't talking about the party, she realised, cursing herself for being such a dope. He'd had enough of her. She'd get her coat from the cloakroom, he would put her in one of the cabs and she'd be drinking cocoa before you knew it.

'We'll grab our coats before we go up,' he said as they headed for the door.

'Go up where?'

'To my suite,' Raffa said, frowning as if that were obvious.

'Your suite?' She sounded like a parrot now, which was hardly surprising when his suggestion had turned her brain to mush.

'We need to talk,' he said, 'about the project for the museum? Your visit to the island to choose the gems, Leila?' he prompted. 'There are a lot of details we need to sort out before I leave Skavanga after the wedding tomorrow.'

'But I thought that was—' A joke, she had been about to add when Raffa turned away to speak to the cloakroom attendant.

'Ticket, Leila.' He held out his hand as she fumbled in her bag.

So Raffa was serious about her visiting his island. Her throat dried at the thought of working with the man at her side. She wasn't worried about the business side of things—she knew her stuff. But where anything else was concerned...

There wasn't going to be *anything else,* Leila reassured herself as Raffa handed over her jacket. And this opportunity to inspect his famous gem collection was too good to miss. If Raffa would allow her to display some of his world-famous pieces, it would really put Skavanga on the map.

'Ready, Leila?'

'Ready,' she confirmed.

This was her breakout year after all, she consoled herself as they walked towards the bank of elevators. And she was good at her job. What did she have to worry about? This was an amazing opportunity and she should seize it with both hands.

Let the mouse roar?

Yes. But couldn't she have started at a lower volume with a milder man?

It was too late to turn back now. Raffa was already swiping his card for the penthouse floor. 'After you,' he said as the doors slid open.

There couldn't be anything more to this invitation, could there?

Almost certainly not, but as she stared into the small steel cabin she got the sense that once she stepped inside her fate was sealed.

So go back home. Drink cocoa for the rest of your life. Resume mouse duties.

She chose to be bold.

CHAPTER FOUR

LEILA SPENT MOST of the journey up to his suite rattling off her credentials, perhaps because she needed to reassure herself that her degree in Gemology and Business Studies was the only thing that could possibly interest him. She kept this going until the elevator slowed and he pulled away from the wall where he'd been leaning.

'Very interesting,' he assured her. 'But the fact that you played hockey for the university team, and have Grade Eight piano with Distinction, isn't really relevant to me.'

'What is?'

For a moment there was something in his eyes that really, *really* made Leila wish she hadn't asked that question. But then the look was gone, leaving her wondering if she'd imagined it, as Raffa returned to being the soigné billionaire with the slanting smile that could conquer the world.

'Your enthusiasm, Leila,' he explained. 'Your enthusiasm when you talk about the mining museum. Your plans for it, and your dedication to the work you're doing there—with the children especially. You impressed me.'

'Are you saying you were giving me a job interview all the time we were sitting in the lounge?'

'You could put it that way.'

'I see.' Raffa's job offer was no joke, she realised as her heart began to pound.

'I'll square it with Britt,' he added as she frowned in thought. 'I'm sure your sister can get someone to cover for you while you're away.'

Leila smiled at that suggestion. 'I'll square it with Britt. She is my sister, Raffa.' And would have plenty to say about this plan, Leila was sure. 'I should get word to Britt now, in fact, to let her know where I am.'

'You don't have to tell her everything tonight. I recommend choosing another time. You don't want to spoil her party, do you, Leila?'

Raffa's eyes were dark and enigmatic as he held her gaze. 'You can't talk business tonight—or tomorrow at your sister's wedding, for that matter,' he pointed out.

'You're right.' But she also knew her sisters would be discussing her right now. Does Leila have any idea what she's getting herself into? she could imagine them saying as she left the ballroom. Should we rescue her or let her stew? For the first time in their lives, she guessed Britt and Eva wouldn't have a clue what to do for the best.

'Hey,' Raffa murmured when she frowned. 'Let your sisters sort themselves out for once.'

No one had ever seen her as the pivot of the family before. Leila Skavanga, hub of calm, around which the whirlwind that was Britt and Eva spun?

'What are you smiling at?'

'Your comment about my sisters needing me to sort them out.'

'Well, don't they?'

'Not all the time—'

'All the time, I would say.'

Raffa didn't give her chance to argue. She drew in a shocked breath as he dipped his head to brush her lips with his. It was such a gentle kiss it disarmed her completely. The thought of such a big, brutal-looking man being able to kiss like that was beguiling to the point where she had to tell him. 'You're not supposed to kiss like that.'

'How am I supposed to kiss?'

Heat flashed through her veins as Raffa demonstrated another, more insistent variation on a theme that sucked the breath from her lungs. It wasn't a case of when she roared now, but only how loud.

The elevator slowing to a halt broke them apart, giving her a moment to compose herself before the doors peeled back on a brightly lit Scandi-style corridor.

'We need to get into that detail fast,' Raffa said, throwing her with his change of gear. He stood back, allowing her to go ahead of him. 'I need all the loose ends tied up before I go.'

'Of course.' How stupid was she, thinking Raffa was bringing her upstairs for some sort of romantic tryst? Closing her eyes, she took a moment to reason that at least he was being honest with her. This was all about business. The kiss was just a kiss. Raffa probably handed kisses out like candy. They meant nothing to him. Sexy confidence was simply his default setting. But then he turned, and she hesitated as he held out his hand. It was a moment of decision. There was no mistaking the look in Raffa's eyes. He definitely wanted to sort out the business side of things, but, unless she was very much mistaken, he was offering to sort her out too.

She'd never had a one-night stand. She'd never had any sort of casual relationship. But she would like more of those kisses. And when Raffa smiled into her eyes, as if he were challenging her to go or stay, she was torn between retracing her steps and being bold. The elevator doors were still open. In a couple of steps she could be whisked down to the lobby, where normal service could be resumed: no excitement, no risk, lots of cocoa…

Slipping the lock, he backed Leila through the door of his suite. The bedroom was close, but the sofa was closer. Lowering her onto the cushions, he joined her. She was tiny beneath him, but responsive to the point where she was fierce. He hadn't expected Leila to show quite so much passion, or that she would use her sharp white teeth to nip his skin, and then pluck off her clothes with such abandon. Tugging impatiently at his shirt buttons, she was like a tigress set free from a self-imposed cage. She was innocent, yet deeply sensual, and when he dragged her close and kissed her again her mouth opened under his.

'Do you have any idea how beautiful you are?' he said as she whimpered, wanting more when his stubble raked her skin.

She pulled her head back to look at him. 'Do you have any idea how cheesy that sounds?'

He laughed. 'And you're the quiet sister?'

'Before you came along—'

He didn't let her finish and as his hands mapped the lush curve of her breasts and the smooth line of her thighs she writhed impatiently beneath him. 'Did you wear this underwear with the sole intention of driving me crazy?'

As Raffa was teasing her nipples through the fine fabric of her bra it took her a moment to answer him, and when she gazed down and saw the red filmy lace, she had to admit, 'I'd forgotten that I bought this to…' To build her confidence to face the party, she remembered.

Raffa, dropping kisses on her neck, drew a groaning

response from her throat, and, lacing her fingers through his hair, she kept him close. 'Oh…that's so good.'

'How good?' Raffa demanded, pulling back to look at her.

'Good enough for you not to stop.' Arching her back, she thrust her breasts towards him, wondering what else he could do for other parts of her body. She'd never had such erotic thoughts before and a deep throb of pleasure followed each wicked thought. 'I need you,' she gasped out at one point, hardly knowing what that meant.

'I think I've got that,' Raffa whispered, and when he shifted position she felt how much he wanted her… and when he slipped his fingers beneath the edge of her thong…

'It's almost a shame to take this off.'

'Please don't let that deter you,' she whispered against his mouth.

'That's very forward of you, Leila Skavanga.'

As Raffa was stroking her to a leisurely rhythm, she had no intention of distracting him with any sort of conversation.

'You don't have to do anything,' he promised as he removed what few remaining clothes she had on.

Sounds good to me, she mused, lost in an erotic haze.

'You can safely leave everything to me.'

Safely? And Raffa? Her brain examined this notion sketchily and then drifted away. Leaving everything to him was so good, as was leaving reality behind to pick up another day. Theirs was such a crazy pairing she knew it could never happen again. By the time she visited his island it would be all about business. They'd forget this had ever happened.

Hopefully.

She sighed with pleasure as Raffa feathered kisses

down her neck, to her nipples and on to the area marked danger at the apex of her thighs. She had never been so aware, or so aroused before. And when Raffa teased her lips apart with his tongue…and when he tumbled her beneath him… 'You're impossible,' she exclaimed softly when he did something amazing with his hands.

'So I've been told,' he agreed, sounding not one bit concerned about it.

'I don't want to hear what anyone else said.'

'There is no one else, Leila.'

'For now.'

'There is no one else,' Raffa repeated, staring her straight in the eyes.

'And I'm in control.'

'Absolutely,' Raffa confirmed as she did battle with his belt.

The leather was like butter and she freed the tine in seconds. Whipping the belt from its loops, she was left with a classy horn button and a zipper to tangle with…

'Giving up so easily?' Raffa mocked when she pulled back.

'Just taking a moment.'

In control? Her shaking voice gave her away. She was losing courage with every second that passed. Raffa was so experienced. And she wasn't even a bit experienced where this was concerned.

'Take as long as you want,' he suggested. 'It all adds to the suspense.'

It might take rather longer for the pay-off than he imagined.

'Or would you rather be seduced than be the seducer?'

Thankfully, Raffa didn't wait for her answer. Swinging her into his arms, he carried her into his bedroom, where he laid her down on his enormous bed, his laughing eyes smiling into hers as he kissed her neck…

It was even better when he pinned her wrists above her head. Leave it all to him? She was more than happy to do so.

It wasn't so much a case of seducing Leila, but more of holding her back. His lightest touch sent her over the edge. She was so aroused he had to curb his intentions and go as slowly as he could, which wasn't as easy when Leila Skavanga was the most desirable woman he'd ever known. Her hunger added to her seductive lure and fired his appetite, so that what had begun as an intriguing encounter was transformed into a challenging exercise in restraint for him. His only regret was that there wasn't enough time for them to enjoy each other for as long as he would like.

'Don't stop! Don't you dare stop,' Leila warned him when he drew back. Guiding his hand, she was quite open about what she wanted. He could feel the heat of her need without exploring, and he had to tell her to slow down as he felt around for his jacket.

'I said, don't stop,' she complained, grabbing on to him impatiently.

'And I say we need to take a minute.'

He kissed her into compliance, but he was lost too. He wanted this woman—and not just for easy sex. His hunger defied reason. Wanting Leila had hit him like a freight train. He had never felt this with any woman. And he wanted Leila to want him as he wanted her. He wanted to ride her into Hades and back as he watched pleasure unfold on her face and felt her body bloom beneath him. He wanted to burn his brand into her mind, so there could never be anyone else—

'And I'm bad?' he murmured, when, finally losing patience with him taking so much time to protect them both, Leila grabbed hold of his hand to urge him on.

'You make me bad.'

'Weak argument,' he countered, feeling dangerous heat rush through him as Leila laced her hands around his neck, trusting him with that one small gesture.

'We make each other bad,' she amended, smiling as he drew her into his arms.

Now that he wouldn't argue with. There was something between them he couldn't explain, a fire like nothing he'd ever experienced before. He'd barely touched her before she flew screaming over the edge again, forcing him to hold her firmly in place as, lost to pleasure, she bucked mindlessly beneath him. When she'd calmed down, he smiled. 'This could be a long night, Señorita Skavanga.'

'I certainly hope so,' she said groggily, but then, slowly coming round, she pulled back to look at him and her cheeks flushed red.

'There's no need to apologise for enthusiasm where sex is concerned,' he assured her, kissing her to reassure her as he stroked her hair to soothe her down. 'But if you'd like me to stop—'

'No,' she said fiercely. 'Don't you dare stop.'

Laughing, he dropped kisses on her mouth. This was turning from intriguing to extraordinary. Leila was unique in his experience—unique in the way she made him feel. Why shouldn't they make a habit of this? She should come to his island and stay there.

And he needed a complication like that?

No. But when Leila nestled into the crook of his arm, she was so alluring he had to remind himself forcibly that he'd seen the damage relationships could cause firsthand—the boredom setting in, the unreasonable ties people put on each other, the tragedy of children no one had planned and no one wanted. To see those children shunted back and forth, never really spending time with their parents, but just living their lives with a series of childminders and nannies—

'Raffa?'

'I'm still with you,' he confirmed with a wry smile.

Seeing Leila resting so trustingly in his arms with her eyes full of concern for him prompted him to drop a kiss on the tip of her nose. It was hardly the prelude to a night of wild sex, but, for once in his life, he wasn't sure that was what he wanted, though he had never wanted a woman more.

What was he thinking? Leila had no place in his highly engineered existence, a life that he had polished to his liking over all his adult years. He had created the world's largest chain of fine jewellery stores, with offices across the world, and thousands of people depended on him to get it right. He couldn't afford to squander time on a woman, any woman, even if that woman was Leila Skavanga—especially Leila, who was so young and trusting, and who had her whole life ahead of her. So whatever he imagined he was feeling for her at this moment, he had to remember that his heart was an engine to power his body and nothing more. There was no room in that heart for feelings let alone a self-indulgence like Leila Skavanga. But before he had chance to think about the consequences of involving his emotions, Leila surprised him again and he sucked in a sharp breath as her small hand found him, guided him. Where was his much vaunted self-control now?

'Are you sure?' He felt bound to ask her.

'I've never been more certain of anything in my life,' she said, her gaze steady on his.

He had never been more careful in his life. He wanted Leila to enjoy every moment, and stopped immediately when she whimpered, to ask if she was all right.

'Yes,' she confirmed, moving in a way that drew him deeper.

He wanted to savour the incredible sensation, but Leila was impatient, and, cupping her buttocks, he positioned her. 'Still okay?' he murmured, moving deeper.

'Is it supposed to be this good?'

'I guess,' he whispered against her mouth, 'or why would everyone want to do it?'

'With you?' Her eyes flicked wide open.

'There are other men.'

'Are there?' she gasped, half laughing on a shaking breath as he began to move. She clung to him, her face flushed, her lips parted to drag in air. 'I had no idea it would be this good,' she admitted when he paused to enjoy being so deeply lodged inside her. 'I feel—'

She didn't get chance to tell him how she felt before falling off the edge of the cliff with a wail of surprise, and as she bucked convulsively it took all his ingenuity to keep her beneath him so she could enjoy the experience to the full.

'Incredible!' she exclaimed, panting as she came down. 'You're amazing—'

He laughed as he nuzzled her neck with his stubble. 'And you're a very hungry woman, Leila Skavanga.'

'You noticed?' she said, starting to smile as he dropped kisses on her mouth.

His answer was to move again. As far as he was concerned, it was Leila who was amazing.

'More,' she insisted when they'd been in bed so long dawn was starting to streak the sky with silver.

'I should get up.' He said this reluctantly, conscious of the long flight ahead of him. 'I have to pack before I leave. And I have to file a flight plan before the wedding.'

'Show-off,' she teased him groggily.

He only had to look into Leila's eyes to want to change his mind and postpone his flight. *Dios!* She made him want to postpone the rest of his life to be with her.

'Stay,' she said softly, sensing this hesitation in him. 'Stay with me in Skavanga, Raffa. Why not?'

'I'd love nothing more, but—'

'But you can't,' she said with resignation.

What could he say? He had a life to get back to, as did Leila. 'When you come out to the island—'

Reaching up, she silenced him with her fingertips on his lips. 'Don't say it, Raffa. I know. You have your life and I have mine. This was one very special night—but that's all it is. When I come out to the island I'll be visiting for business and for nothing else. You can rely on me to keep my side of the bargain, as I hope I can rely on you to respect the professional relationship between us. And at the wedding, I'd rather we just kept it light, if that's all right with you. I don't want my sisters getting upset—not today of all days. I must have Britt onside, as technically Britt employs me to run the museum for the Skavanga mining company, so it's important she takes my visit to the island as seriously as I do.'

'I understand.' She'd made it easy for him, which perversely only made him feel worse.

Leila was lying back on the pillows staring blankly ahead, being brave about this as she had been brave about so many other things in her life. How many times had he spent the night with a woman and felt nothing but relief when she left him in the morning? That was most decidedly not how he felt now. 'Go— Go and have your shower,' he prompted. 'Don't make yourself late for your sister's wedding.'

It was over, Leila reflected as she swung out of bed. Their incredible night was over.

'You're still coming to the island?' Raffa confirmed as she reached the door.

'Of course,' she said steadily. 'Nothing's changed.'

But it had and they both knew it.

CHAPTER FIVE

EVERYTHING IN HER life had changed since meeting Raffa. Take this flight to his island. Britt had bumped her up to business class for the first leg of the journey, which had always been one of Leila's ambitions, but the space and pampering only gave her too much time to think about Raffa, and how much she'd missed him.

And how much she had to tell him.

Shifting restlessly in her seat, she took her thoughts back to the wedding. They'd hardly spoken during the day. She'd been busy with bridesmaid's duties, while Raffa had been forced to leave early to make his flight. Some internal warning system had alerted her to the moment he left, and the dreadful sinking sense of loss she had experienced then had never left her. Maybe it never would. Professional relationship? Just the thought of the pledge they'd made to maintain a professional relationship between them seemed like so much nonsense now. Perhaps Raffa could accept it, but then he didn't know—

'It's time to fasten your seat belt, Señorita Skavanga.'

Jolted out of her troubled thoughts by the friendly young flight attendant standing at her side, Leila apologised and quickly fastened her seat belt. 'I didn't see you there. I was…' Daydreaming, Leila silently supplied.

'Welcome to Isla Montaña de Fuego, *señorita.*'

The Island of the Mountains of Fire. How appropriate. Staring out of the small window, she experienced a huge and extremely inconvenient swell of love for Raffa.

And had to mask those feelings. Raffa must know she was completely in control when they met up, and that meant no lingering glances, no longing, no nothing.

To dull the ache inside her, she turned her attention to the view outside the window as the plane came in to land. Seen from this height, Raffa's island retreat was surprisingly lush and green. A deep ivory band of sand bordered a bright blue sea on one side of the island, while on the other coastline an angry sea lashed a range of dramatic black rocks. The contrast was glaring. The young cabin attendant explained that they would be landing in the north of the island. 'The south is softer, and has fabulous golden beaches,' she went on, dipping her head to follow Leila's gaze out of the window.

Leila instantly pictured Raffa's fortress home being in the north, where it would be well barricaded from the world between forbidding mountains and a ferocious sea. 'Why don't you sit with me for landing, Elena?' There was so much more she wanted to know about the island and about the man who lived here...the man with whom, quite incredibly, she was expecting a baby.

'Where exactly is the castle?' she asked as soon as Elena was safely buckled in.

'Don Leon's home is in the south of the island.'

When Leila expressed surprise, Elena explained. 'The reasoning in the old days was that because of the treacherous rocks in the north, that part of the island was impregnable and could take care of itself, while the south was soft and vulnerable. So that's where Don Leon's ancestors built their castle.'

It made perfect sense, which was more than could be said for Leila's current state of mind.

'The castle is absolutely stunning,' Elena went on. 'Don Leon has been working so hard on it for years. Have you seen it yet?'

'No, I haven't.' Leila looked at Elena with renewed interest. The young girl was very pretty.

And why was she behaving like a jealous lover? It was time to put this pointless longing for Raffa Leon out of her head for good.

But how could she ever cut him out of her life now?

Elena interrupted Leila's thoughts with some more information about the castle. 'It's not forbidding at all. Don Leon has done so much of the work himself and he invites his staff each year for a party so we can see how the work is progressing. He's such a generous man.'

So much for the press dubbing him ruthless. Turmoil at the thought that this was the man Leila had always dreamed of fathering the child she had always longed for, combined with the guilt she felt at not having been able to locate Raffa before she arrived to let him know she had just discovered she was pregnant, was making her edgy and frustrated.

'I believe Don Leon's design studios are over here on the island?' she babbled, as if she didn't know they were, in a hopeless attempt to take her mind off the man and the consequences of their one night of passion.

'We'll fly over them soon. Is that where you'll be working?' Elena asked pleasantly.

Thankfully, Elena couldn't know about the turmoil in Leila's mind. 'Most probably.'

She couldn't even be sure of that. She had sent repeated mails to Raffa's headquarters in an attempt to contact him, and had finally introduced herself to his team via HR, but when she explained her ideas for an exhibition in Skavanga, she was told Don Leon would decide her agenda. But where was he? No one would tell her, and her tireless investigations had drawn a blank.

'And there he is,' Elena exclaimed, shocking Leila back into the present.

As the jet touched down and screamed along the runway Leila had the briefest glimpse of an unmistakeable figure. Lounging back against a Jeep, Raffa Leon, exactly as she remembered him: powerful, hard, self-avowed bachelor by preference, a man who had no intention of having children to disturb his smooth-running life.

If only he'd sent a driver so she could have had some time to compose herself. She longed to see him again, but dreaded this first meeting. She dreaded what she might see in Raffa's eyes. Nothing would be terrible. Intuition would be worse. She had to tell him her news before he could find out for himself.

And what would Raffa see in her eyes? Guilt? He would want to know why she hadn't told him the moment she knew she was pregnant. Why she hadn't emblazoned it in the sky. 'I had to speak to you in person' would sound lame in the face of the shock he was going to get.

Pausing at the top of the aircraft steps, she braced herself for their first encounter. 'How often are these flights?' she asked the young flight attendant as Raffa closed the distance between them in a few long strides.

'We fly whenever Don Leon sends for the plane,' Elena explained. 'There is no other way off the island. No ferries could possibly dock in the north. As you've seen, the coastline is too rugged. And the south is all helicopters and private yachts—most of which belong to Don Leon, or to his company.'

So she was stuck on Raffa's island, with no way off, other than with his permission. Why hadn't she thought ahead about this, and arranged to meet him on neutral ground?

'Leila…'

Too late now.

The familiar voice washed over her, the rich, deep tones disarming her and making her forget everything except seeing Raffa again, though she registered now that his manner was carefully judged and disappointingly neutral.

'Raffa…'

Coming down the steps, she extended her hand to greet him, matching his businesslike manner with a cool air of her own. 'It's good to see you again.'

'And you, Leila.'

He ignored her hand and removed his sunglasses.

That penetrating stare… Those incredible eyes could search her soul. Could he see the truth?

She looked away, but not before she noticed the speculation in his stare. Raffa missed nothing. He could read the smallest shift in body language and never took anything for granted. He was scanning her now for any sign of emotion to suggest she was a clinging vine who might make demands on him after what had happened between them at the party.

Composing herself, she lifted her chin to meet his gaze. Britt had mentioned the fact that Raffa's questing nature had contributed massively to his success, and that he was unparalleled when it came to spotting things other people missed, and that this was what kept him so far ahead of the pack. She would do well to remember that.

'You're well, Leila?'

Her cheeks flushed red at that simple question. Well? She was blooming. 'Yes, very well, thank you. You?'

He nodded briefly.

Raffa looked amazing, in nothing more than a pair of worn jeans and a dark, close-fitting top. She inhaled a faint tang of his cologne. He was standing so close she could see the amber flecks in his sepia eyes and feel his familiar power warming her. It was impossible to forget what had happened between them, or the consequences of their one night together.

'Let me carry your case,' he said, reaching for her bag.

'I can manage, thank you.'

'You don't have to manage, Leila.'

Raffa sounded faintly impatient and she couldn't blame him as she thought back to the last time they'd seen each other—glimpsed each other, really, across a crowded ballroom at Eva's wedding. She'd been too busy to speak to him, and yet the night before she'd been lost in his arms—wild in his arms. And now the consequences of that night, consequences that Raffa didn't know about yet, would have to be brought out into the open and discussed. There was an awkward time ahead of them, to say the least.

She followed him to the Jeep, determined she would keep her head, but once the doors closed and they were contained in the small cab she was all too aware of the tension swirling round them.

'You're very quiet,' Raffa remarked as he started the engine. 'Don't you have any news for me, Leila?'

'About the museum?' Her throat tightened on the question.

'Of course about the museum.' Slipping his sunglasses on, Raffa put the vehicle into gear and released the brake.

Of course. What else could they possibly have to talk about? The conversation between them was so stilted and awkward, she wasn't sure she could rescue the situation. Bracing her arm against the dashboard as Raffa bumped the Jeep over the rutted track that led to the highway, she glanced at his rugged face in profile. There was no softness in his expression. 'Did you see the mail I sent you?'

'Mail?' He frowned, his swarthy features more forbidding than ever. 'What mail?'

'The mail I sent to your company in advance of my arrival here. The mail I sent to introduce myself to your team. I copied you in.'

Raffa's frown deepened.

No one got under her skin as he did, and far from being the peacemaker, her usual role back home, she was screaming inside and had to say something. 'Were you ever going to read it?'

Pulling his head back, Raffa flashed a glance across at her. 'If it's in my inbox I'll get round to it.'

'Raffa, you disappeared off the face of the earth. Where've you been?'

'Tied up, looking after my grandmother. She hasn't been well recently.'

She went hot with embarrassment for misjudging him so badly. 'I'm so sorry. I hope she's feeling better now.'

Guilt flashed through her as Raffa responded with a curt nod of his head. With her own concerns banging in her brain, she hadn't paused to think why he might be off radar.

There had been a stack of mail waiting for him, but with his mind on Abuelita he hadn't even glanced at it.

His grandmother was supposed to be indestructible. She wasn't supposed to get sick. That wasn't Leila's fault, but there was something about Leila making him edgy. She'd changed. He couldn't put his finger on it yet, but he would. He reasoned that seeing her again had thrown him badly. He had thought he could handle it, but now he wasn't so sure.

'In future, I'll make certain your mail hits the top of the stack,' he offered for the sake of building a working relationship.

'Thank you, Raffa.'

Even that bland response made him suspicious. Leila was too mild—so mild she made him curious as to why. The Leila he knew was quiet, but she stood up for herself, and was feisty and fun. This Leila was guarded and distant. Keeping up a business front couldn't account for such a complete change in anyone.

Keeping up a business front wouldn't be easy for either of them, he conceded. It was hard for him to find a comfortable operating zone with a woman who had been his lover and who was now a colleague. It would have been easier with anyone other than Leila, because most women didn't want what she wanted from him; they were far more calculating. But Leila had always been quite open about wanting the whole nine yards: the happy ending, the home, the children—not quite sure about the doting husband, though she deserved nothing less. But none of that was in his gift. He was a confirmed bachelor who had learned to curb his feelings from a young age.

'Seeing as you haven't received my mail, I hope you won't think my ideas for the exhibition too ambitious, Raffa.'

Again he detected tension in her voice and wondered at it. 'Nothing you ever did could surprise me, Leila.'

She looked away, when he had only been trying to lighten the atmosphere. Now he was certain she was hiding something. 'Twenty minutes and we'll be there,' he said, wondering which of them longed to reach their destination more.

She was here to work, Leila reminded herself firmly. Raffa didn't have to be the man she remembered. She didn't expect him to be. And she would have plenty of chances while she was on the island to tell him she was pregnant. If they were going to work together she had to put things back on track before she tackled anything personal.

'I'm looking forward to learning more about your gems.'

Dipping his head briefly to register the fact that he'd heard her was Raffa's only response.

She couldn't leave it at that. She had to straighten things out between them. 'I realise you're far more sophisticated than I am, but—'

'Let me put you out of your misery, Leila.' He said this coolly, not even glancing at her as he concentrated on the road ahead. 'You're here to work and so am I. I'm not on your agenda and you're not on mine. Not in the personal sense, anyway. Does that reassure you?'

Her stomach clenched at Raffa's words. He couldn't have made it any plainer that he didn't want any reminders of their brief and passionate encounter. 'I am reassured,' she lied, her mind full of the baby. How could she tell him now?

She had to find a way to tell him. It was as simple as that.

They drove in tense silence for quite a time. She

stared blindly out of the window, but the incredible view finally pierced her sombre mood. Raffa's island home was beautiful and she couldn't remain immune to it. The jet hadn't flown over this part of the island. The agricultural land was lush and well cared for, and on the fringes of the rolling fields immaculately maintained farmsteads slumbered in the sun. He drove on through quaint villages, where white villas nestled in companionable groups on tree-cloaked hills, until finally he turned to her and said, 'This is the village where I live.'

She looked with interest at the cobbled streets and a tiny market square, where stalls selling fresh produce from outlying farms were bustling with activity. As they passed through the village they drove on along a clifftop road where she could see the bright blue sea glinting far below them. 'This is lovely,' she exclaimed impulsively, relaxing for the first time since she'd arrived.

'Wait until you see the castle. There—on the top of the hill.'

Seeing their destination loom in front of her made all of Leila's fears return. If only Raffa already knew about the baby, and they could celebrate her pregnancy together—not that he was ever likely to celebrate, with his thoughts on the subject.

She turned to look at him as he launched into a brief history of the ancient building he was working so hard to save, and found herself wishing she didn't have any secrets from him so she could relax and enjoy this trip to the full.

Her biggest surprise was when they drove beneath the imposing stone archway that led through from the outer walls of the castle into the inner courtyard. Instead of closing around her as she had expected, being inside the ancient fortress actually lifted her spirits. The castle might have been built with the sole intention of defending the island from invaders, but it felt more like a friendly giant than a glowering monster.

'Everyone says the same thing,' Raffa agreed when she commented. 'I think it's the angle of the sun on the stone that makes it glow and seem so welcoming.'

At least they were talking, Leila registered with relief. If she could keep that going, maybe the tension between them would relax. Build enough of a bridge and she could have a proper discussion about the baby.

'The same building beneath the steely skies of Skavanga might struggle to look as attractive as this,' she admitted, turning to him.

'You're probably right,' Raffa agreed. 'I hope you're not too disappointed when we go inside, as I only live in a small part of the castle. I'm gradually turning the rest into a museum.'

'Museums are becoming a bit of a theme between us,' she remarked as he switched off the engine. She stopped there, seeing something in Raffa's eyes that warned her off. It said there were no common themes between them.

'I've housed you in one of the guest turrets,' he said as they got out of the Jeep. Shading his eyes with his hand, he stared up to where the crenelated battlements were decorated with flags.

'Like Rapunzel,' she suggested lightly.

'Like someone I thought might enjoy the view.'

'I'm here to work, not to stare out of the window all day,' she reminded him, working hard to keep the conversation between them going. And you're not scrambling up my hair any time soon, she thought as Raffa glanced at her.

'I'll get my housekeeper to help you settle in.' He pulled away as if he was impatient to go.

His housekeeper? The castle, Raffa's whole way of life, only served to emphasise the gulf between them, and she had yet to broach the subject of his child.

'Leila?'

Having climbed the broad flight of stone steps, they had stopped in front of a huge arched entrance door peppered with iron studs. 'Yes?'

She turned, but whatever had prompted Raffa to say her name had died on his lips. She was glad when the door swung open and a smiling motherly woman greeted them.

'This is Maria, my housekeeper, Leila. Maria, may I present Señorita Skavanga.'

'Please, call me Leila,' Leila insisted as the older woman nodded and smiled.

Raffa excused himself almost immediately. 'I have building work to attend to,' he explained.

'Thank you for picking me up—' She turned around to say this, but he was already jogging down the steps.

'May I show you to your room, *señorita?*'

'Thank you, Maria.' She was glad of the housekeeper's friendly smile. She had never felt quite so isolated, or quite so far from home.

Leila's apartment in the turret was like the setting for a fairy tale. Exquisitely furnished in delicate French Empire style, it boasted the most astonishing views over the beautifully manicured grounds to the lush green fields beyond, and on to where a bank of trees faded to a misty purple in the shadow of the rolling hills. Leaning out of the open window, she dragged greedily on the blossom-scented air, but this was no time to be daydreaming. She had to settle in and then find Raffa so they could have that talk. She had never even been late before, and she hadn't even been sure that the strange feeling that had come over her was significant in any way, until finally she went to the chemist and took a test…several tests. And there was no doubt. She was pregnant.

The phone rang, distracting her. It was Raffa. Her heart bumped at the sound of his voice. The knowledge inside her made her feel so guilty, but she couldn't tell him over the phone.

'Can you be ready in half an hour?'

'I'm ready now.' Did that sound too eager?

Of course it did.

Remembering the marble-lined bathroom stocked with fabulous products, she quickly built in time to take a shower. 'Actually, half an hour should be fine,' she managed coolly.

It was only when she replaced the receiver that she realised she hadn't even asked where they were supposed to meet. She would have to sharpen up her wits if she was going to face Raffa with her news. She couldn't imagine he would take it well, and she had to be ready for the fallout.

The rest of the day went better than she had expected. Raffa picked her up in the Jeep and took her to one of his showrooms on the island, but he brought a co-worker with him, so once again she couldn't tell him her news. Would the moment ever arrive? She was keyed up every second of the tour and could hardly concentrate.

The laboratories were as clean and as sterile as Raffa's behaviour towards her. They were bright and filled with light and staffed by uniformed technicians. It was that small space thing again, Leila told herself firmly, glancing at Raffa as they travelled down to one of his vaults in a small steel lift. *Relax*. He can't hear your heart beating.

Raffa escorted her into an air-conditioned room with little furnishing other than a table on which sat a mirror, presumably so his most favoured clients could try on the jewels they wished to buy in absolute privacy. She felt confident, having prepared well in advance of her visit. 'I know many of your jewels have history, and I've read up about quite a few of them.'

Raffa inclined his head as if they were two strangers doing business together, which indeed they were—or they were supposed to be.

He laid out an incredible collection in front of her. 'This can be worn a number of ways,' he explained as he took apart one of the elaborate necklaces. 'These detachable drops can be worn as earrings, for example...'

As he held them up to her face, his hands brushed her cheeks and her skin blazed with awareness. 'Very nice,' she said, turning away so she couldn't see Raffa's face reflected in the mirror behind her.

'And these...' he showed her a string of milky pearls '...can be worn as a long necklace, or fastened with this diamond clasp and worn as a collar...'

He had to hear her sharp intake of breath when his hands brushed her collarbone and the cool pearls met her overheated skin, but when he glanced into her eyes he gave nothing away. The cool of the pearls, the warmth of his touch...

'Leila?'

She blinked and refocused on the tutorial she was supposed to be here for.

'I'm going to put the pearls back in the vault again. If you've finished with them?'

'Yes.' Her throat was dry, her voice hoarse. She could

see Raffa standing behind her, staring down. This was the moment—

'Shall I list the pearls as going to Skavanga?'

Raffa was already turning away as he asked the question, placing the priceless jewels in their velvet nest. The walls of the vault seemed to close around her, sucking all the available air from her lungs and her intention to tell him about the baby with it.

'Yes. Please put them on the list,' she managed faintly.

His preference would have been to strip Leila naked, drape her in jewels and have her on the table, but that was the wolf in him talking, and Leila was a lamb, vulnerable and far too honest for her own good. He had seen the longing in her eyes the moment she arrived on the island. He had finally deciphered what had made him edgy around Leila back at the airstrip, and it was that. And now he knew he couldn't lead her on. They'd had one passionate night and that had been a mistake, a mistake he had no intention of repeating. Leila deserved someone better than he could ever be, someone without his baggage. She had tempted him, but that was over now and she was here to do a job. He would respect that. His father had used women as if they were nothing more than disposable toys, and he had no intention of becoming that man.

'We've done enough for today,' he said, his mind still lodged in the past.

He'd done enough for today. He'd spent enough time with Leila, and he needed space from her now. Seeing her again had been a warning to him that, far from fading, his feelings for Leila Skavanga had only grown while they'd been apart.

CHAPTER SIX

THE NEXT FEW days passed quickly and things evened out
between them. Their history was too complex for them
to remain at daggers drawn for ever. Close proximity
led to them swapping confidences and swapping jokes,
but whether it was the intimate, confiding tone Raffa
used to explain the provenance of one of the jewels, or
whether it was simply his passion for his chosen subject and his vast store of knowledge, Leila had no idea.

Perhaps it was the way he looked into her eyes in
search of the same enthusiasm he felt for the treasures
he was showing her, she really couldn't say. She only
knew she was losing her heart to him all over again,
though they went to bed separately each night, and she
slept fitfully, wondering if Raffa did too.

As each day dawned she felt more and more convinced that if she could just hold on a little longer, the
golden moment would arrive when she could tell Raffa
about the baby and they'd both be happy about the news.
Being pregnant was such a life-changing event she
wanted to be sure she picked the right moment for him
too. As she was dealing with a man for whom family
life was anything but an attractive prospect, she wanted
to make sure she didn't blunder into the announcement.

She hadn't been expecting for them to work so closely

in the physical sense. There were times when tension seemed to surge between them, and she wondered if they were both fighting off desire, and other times when she told herself not to be so stupid. Sometimes she found herself studying Raffa instead of the jewels... Diamonds or his sexy mouth? A polished emerald, or the gleam in the depth of Raffa's eyes when he turned to confide some new fact, especially when he allowed his gaze to linger?

'What are you staring at?' he said one day, smiling.

She'd always been a sucker for eyes that crinkled at the corners. 'You,' she admitted bluntly. 'I was just thinking how different you are from the press you receive.'

'We all have different faces we show the world,' he said as he collected up the jewels for the night.

'And you have more than most?' she queried, laughing to make light of it.

'Here's one that might surprise you,' he said as he closed the vault. 'I'm immune to the charm of diamonds. I admire them. I admire the craftsmanship. And I know a good stone when I see one. But I prefer the simple things in life—like honesty and loyalty. I value those qualities far more than any hard, cold stone. Diamonds are just a means to an end for me. I make money out of them that allows me to support the causes I'm interested in.'

Honesty and loyalty, she thought as Raffa called the elevator. Where would Raffa think she stood where honesty was concerned if he knew about the baby?

'The exhibition you're planning in Skavanga will be good for both of us,' he said as they waited for the lift to arrive. 'I almost threw my first diamond away— After you.' He stood back as the doors slid open. He stabbed the lift button and they soared upwards. 'My father, who wasn't noted for his tolerance, brought a particularly big stone back from India. I didn't know the value of this dull-looking rock and kept it in my bedroom for over a week before he found it.'

She laughed, but it sounded forced. She would rather have been talking about the subject closest to her heart, until Raffa said, 'My father was always mad with one child or another.' His eyes narrowed as he thought back, remembering. 'We children hadn't been factored into his life plan. We were more of an inconvenience to him than anything else. An inconvenient consequence of his own reckless actions—'

Her heart shrank as she listened to him. They'd both been reckless, but if she had anything to do with it their baby would be anything but an inconvenient consequence. It would be a much-loved child.

'My family isn't close like yours is, Leila,' he went on. 'I don't have a great role model to look back on, hence no wife, no children and no intention on my part of ever changing the status quo.'

'So you don't want children?' Her question echoed in the small steel cab.

'No. I don't,' Raffa said flatly. 'I've told you things I haven't told anyone before,' Raffa admitted wryly as they walked outside into the brilliant sunshine. 'Must be your honest face.'

'I'll respect your confidence.' Her stomach churned at the thought of her less than honest relationship with Raffa.

'I'm sure you will. And I apologise if I sounded short down there. I didn't mean to.'

'The past kicks back sometimes. Raffa, there's—'

He broke off to speak to one of the technicians walking across the car park. They were all coming out for lunch now, and when he turned back to her the moment had gone.

'I trust you, Leila Skavanga. I can't say that about many people.'

This was getting worse by the moment. 'I trust you too,' she said on a dry throat, only wishing she could turn the clock back and blurt out the truth about their baby the moment she walked down the steps of the aircraft.

'Let's get back,' he said. 'I'm hungry, aren't you?'

'Starving.'

'Then I have to get back to my building work. I hope you've learned enough this morning to keep you busy planning.'

'Absolutely,' she confirmed. Raffa telling her about his past had explained so much about him. He was obsessive about his work at the castle, the ruin he was rebuilding brick by brick, perhaps as an exercise in pushing the memories of his crumbling childhood behind him. This was not the time to raise the subject of a child, however much it would be loved, that was going to be born as the result of yet another reckless coupling.

'We've got a fair moving into the grounds of the castle tomorrow,' he revealed as they approached the Jeep. 'I'll be up early sorting that out—so have breakfast without me.'

'Don't worry about me,' she said as he opened the door for her. 'I can entertain myself. Is the fair part of your plan to open more of the castle to the public?'

'That's right,' Raffa said as he swung into the driver's seat beside her.

This was better than being at daggers drawn with him. She would find a way to tell Raffa about the baby, but it would be a way that wouldn't pour more acid on the wounds he'd brought with him from his past. Perhaps friendship was the only way forward for them, she thought wistfully, flashing a glance across, but, as she'd always been wary of expecting too much out of life, wasn't it better to settle for less and be contented?

She woke the next morning feeling warm inside. The baby made her feel this way. Nothing could dilute her joy, not even the guilt inside her. She could already picture the infant with Raffa's curly black hair and his slanting smile. If it was a boy he would eat her out of house and home, and scare her rigid with his pranks. If it was a little girl...

It was to be hoped she had more sense than her mother.

Planning to have a family without factoring a man into the equation was all very well in theory, but she couldn't see Raffa being the type to quietly stand by when she told him about the baby and then let her get on with it. She would tell him today. She couldn't leave it a moment longer. Her heart had grown to encompass a new and very special kind of love and she wanted Raffa to know that joy too. There hadn't been a good time to tell him, so she would make an opportunity. She was confident he would be thrilled—once he got over the shock.

Frantically finger-combing her hair into some sort of order, she hurried out of the room, having decided that the best place to find Raffa was in the courtyard where he had said the fair was setting up.

The courtyard was bustling with shoppers from all over the island, and noisy with stallholders calling out to advertise their wares. She walked around it several times, but there was no sign of Raffa, and so she started to take a more active interest in the stalls. One geared specifically towards baby clothes drew her attention right away. The tiny, hand-stitched garments were so adorable that before she knew it her arms were full.

'Leila?'

She paled as Raffa took in everything at a glance. 'I didn't see you there.'

'Clearly.'

Her heart sank. Of all the opportunities she'd had, this was the worst possible moment. Her guilty face gave everything away and she could feel anger coming off him in waves. 'Raffa, I—'

'Let me get those,' he interrupted. Turning his back on her, he spoke to the woman manning the stall, reverting to Spanish as he completed the transaction, effectively cutting Leila out so all she could do was stand back, feeling useless.

Feeling worse than useless. Everyone on the island loved Raffa. They trusted him. He had said he trusted her. How did he feel about that now? What would these people—Raffa's people—think of her? She only had to watch the way they responded to Raffa to know they loved him. He'd done so much for them, creating employment and bringing the island to life again. And she was a nobody carrying his child, a child she didn't even have the guts to tell him about.

'Thank you,' she said automatically when Raffa swung around with her purchases. 'I'll give you the money.' She held out her hand with a bundle of notes, but Raffa ignored them and directed a hard, knowing stare into her eyes instead.

'Have you had some happy news from one of your sisters?' he suggested in an icy tone. 'Or a friend, perhaps?'

Her shocked look answered everything he wanted to know.

'You're ominously silent, Leila. Are you buying baby clothes with an eye on the future?'

Her throat was in knots. It should be so easy to tell him her news, but she'd left it too long to do so.

'Well?' Raffa prompted coldly. 'Don't you have anything to say to me?'

This was so far removed from how she had imagined it would be when she told Raffa about the child they were expecting. She had intended to tell him quietly, confidently, with the aim of reassuring Raffa that she expected nothing from him.

'Well, it's a very nice gift, anyway,' he said, hoisting up the bags up so they met her eyeline. 'A very generous gift, in fact—so many outfits.'

'I need to talk to you, Raffa. Can we go inside?'

A brief dip of his head was Raffa's only response.

Was this the friend she'd thought she'd made, the tender lover who had helped create the child inside her? She had taken far too much for granted. She hadn't known Raffa was overshadowed by his past, or what had gone into the construction of his new life. No children, he'd said. No children he'd meant. But as she planned to bring up their child alone, she was sure she could make things right between them—if only he would give her the chance to explain.

Cold anger filled him. He had trusted Leila. He had confided in Leila as he had never confided in anyone before. And now this greatest truth of all and she had shut him out. How long had she known about the baby? When they'd been laughing and growing closer as they worked together, had she known then? Had she known before she came to the island? He always took precautions, and had assumed—

Assume nothing. This was not the time to curse his uncharacteristic lack of caution. He had to know the truth. The thought that Leila might be scheming to trap him into some sort of arrangement tore him apart. Surely, she couldn't have planned this, but could he trust his own judgement when wanting Leila was a madness he couldn't control? He'd seduced her shamelessly, only to discover she had more passion in her than any woman he'd ever known. He'd lit that fire. And now he must live with the consequences.

A baby. His child. Incredible. Why hadn't she told him before now?

He could hardly wait until he'd shut the world out of his study before rounding on her. 'You must have known you were pregnant before you came here.'

'You make it sound as if I planned this.'

'Well, didn't you?' Crossing his arms over his chest, he leaned back against the desk to view her from his great height, but instead of shrinking from him Leila grew in stature and took him on.

'There's no plan here. I was waiting for the right time to tell you.'

'The right time,' he echoed. 'Tell me, Leila—when is the right time?'

'Don't,' she warned him. 'I'm not asking for anything from you. I'm quite capable of bringing up a child by myself.'

'I don't doubt it. Wasn't that your intention all along? Didn't you tell me when we met at Britt's party that you wanted children, but you didn't want the man?'

'That was just talk and you know it.'

'Was it, Leila? How do I know it was just talk when

I don't know you? I thought I was coming to know you, but I was wrong. Most women are open about what they want from me—'

'And I'm not?' she cut in.

'They ask—they get—they tell me what they're prepared to give me in return.'

A shudder ran through her. 'I feel sorry for you, Raffa, taking part in such cold-blooded transactions.'

'Grow up, Leila! We had sex. It was one night. It was never meant to be a lifetime commitment—'

'But there was always that possibility—'

'A possibility you hoped for.'

'No!'

'A possibility that could certainly have been avoided if you'd kept your legs closed—'

'And you'd kept your pants on,' she fired back. Launching herself at him, she tried to wrestle the bags from his hand. 'Give them to me and I'll happily go—'

'Go where?' he derided, holding them out of her reach. 'Are you going to swim home?'

'I'll find some way to leave your island,' she assured him, face tense, jaw clenched, her lips white with rage.

'We've got a few things to sort out first, Leila—'

'There's nothing for you to sort out. I wanted to tell you. I wanted to explain gently—'

He laughed in her face. 'What? So you could help me to get over the shock? I don't even know if it's my child!'

'Of course it's your child! I was a virgin—'

'What?'

Raffa's reaction stunned her. Hand over his face as if he couldn't bear to look at her, he was clearly appalled.

'What did you say?' Lowering his hand, he stared at her in disbelief.

'I was a virgin when I met you, and there's never been anyone else.'

She'd never known Raffa lost for words, but the way he looked now, bemused and drained of all emotion, was more frightening to see than any anger or derision of his could ever be.

'You lost your virginity with me,' he said, staring at her intently as if he had to get this fact set absolutely firm in his mind.

'Yes.' Her voice wavered. Her eyes filled with tears. The air around them was like a void, a black hole in space. And there was no way across that void, no way at all.

This was his worst nightmare come true. He had stolen the most precious gift Leila had to give without even knowing it. And now a child would be born as a consequence of his actions. Parents at war on opposites sides of an unbridgeable divide was his worst nightmare.

Consequences were a daily concern for him in business. He never made a move without planning forward first, but he had never had to factor such an almighty screw-up into his thinking before.

'Don't look at me like that,' Leila begged him. 'This isn't what you think, Raffa.'

'What do I think?'

'I don't know.' Leila searched for the right words to say. 'Maybe you think I planned this? With your wealth and title I can understand—'

'I thought that would raise its head at some point,' he said angrily, though deep down he knew Leila cared nothing for his wealth and title, but he was too shaken up to stop. Nothing rocked him, nothing touched him, but this had. She had.

Pressing her lips together in despair, she shook her

head. 'That's just it, Raffa. Your status doesn't mean anything to me. I care about you, Raffa. I care about you—Raffa—the man. I even fooled myself into thinking we were growing close, could become friends—'

'How convenient!' He wanted to slam his hands over his ears so he didn't have to listen to any more of this. 'What form would this friendship take, Leila? Was it designed to butter me up before you told me you were expecting my child?'

'I haven't engineered any of this, Raffa—'

'So you say.' Leila's voice had deepened with emotion and the expression on her face shamed him, but his circuit board was overloaded and what he needed most of all now was time and space away from her to think.

'I can't make you believe me, Raffa. I know the truth, and that will have to be enough for me. I must focus on my child. And right now?' Heaving a sigh, she shook her head. 'I'm not sure I want you to be part of my child's life.'

'That's not your choice to make, Leila.'

'Don't look at me like that,' she begged him quietly. 'I won't stand here and take your contempt, Raffa. I might not be anything special, but I'm not a piece of dirt attached to your shoe either.'

'How should I behave towards you, Leila?' His head was still ringing with everything she'd told him. 'Like the love of my life? Like a woman I've known for years and have planned to have a baby with? Or a woman I slept with once, who gets herself knocked up?'

The slap came out of nowhere.

Seizing her wrist an instant before her hand connected with his face, he held her motionless in front of him as a bolt of fury flashed between them.

'I don't expect either of those things,' she assured

him in a low, cold voice. 'I expect you to treat me with the respect due to the mother of your child, and nothing more. I don't expect anything from you in the material sense. I never have, and I never will.'

'Really?' He almost laughed.

'Don't mock me, Raffa. And don't judge me by the standards of anyone else you might have known. Whatever you think of me, I won't allow you to ride rough-shod over me.'

'So what do you want, Leila?'

'Nothing. Not from you,' she assured him with icy calm. 'I'm going to keep this baby and be a single mother like so many other women, and I'll get by.'

'Without me in the picture?' He laughed. 'You *are* naïve.'

'Naïve, Raffa? Or does the fact that I don't need you hurt your pride?'

He ground his jaw as a very real and primal fear rose up inside him. Reason had no part to play in that fear and it was centred around the birth of his child, and the safety of the woman in front of him. 'I don't remember you consulting me about any of this,' he said as blood pounded in his head.

'I don't need to consult you, Raffa. I'm not your employee. This is my body and my baby.'

'Our baby,' he shot back. 'There's a very good reason for my not wanting children—'

'Well, why don't you tell me what it is?' she exclaimed.

No. He could never do that. The guilt haunted him. It disabled him. 'All you need to know is that I don't want children. I never have and I never will, and this little surprise of yours hasn't changed anything.'

'Can't you explain why you feel so strongly?' Leila begged him.

As she reached out to touch him he pulled away. 'You have no idea what you've done.'

Shaking her head slowly, Leila raised her wounded gaze to his face. 'So what are you suggesting, Raffa?' she asked him quietly. 'Are you asking me to get rid of this baby?'

He reeled mentally at Leila's mistaken interpretation of his words. 'What type of man do you take me for?'

'That's just it, Raffa. I don't know what kind of man you are. I thought I did, but I was wrong. I don't understand why you're so set against having children. Is it me?'

'No, it's…'

'I can't understand why you're so horrified at the idea of me giving birth,' Leila exclaimed with frustration when he fell silent. 'And if you won't tell me—'

'I won't tell you, because it's none of your damn business. I've told you more than enough already.'

'Because we trust each other,' she insisted, staring up into his rigid face. 'Or we did.'

'Trust takes time to build, Leila, and can be lost in a heartbeat.'

'Is that what happened to us, Raffa?'

'What do you think?'

Raffa's words were like a series of slaps hitting her in the face. By the time they both fell silent her head was reeling with confusion and hurt. This was the last thing she had wanted when she told Raffa about the baby. They had shared so many things, and they had grown close while she'd been on the island; that wasn't an illusion. Friendship might have taken over from passion, she was quite prepared to admit that, but both were dead now.

And she had so wanted this to be a special and tender moment between them. If only she could get to the bottom of Raffa's horror at the thought of her giving birth. If only she could bring him back to her. His behaviour was so unreasonable there had to be something more eating away at him, but unless he was prepared to tell her, they would never be close again.

Her hand moved instinctively to cover her stomach, as if she could protect the tiny life from all the emotion swirling round it. 'The last thing I had intended was to upset you, or shock you. I kept waiting for the right moment—the perfect moment, but it must have passed me by. Please forgive me.'

He didn't reply. He couldn't reply. He was empty inside. He closed off from feeling because he didn't know any other way. He had lived behind emotional barricades since he was a child. How could he ever be a fit parent? His life didn't allow for children. He was always driving forward to seize the next opportunity, or to close the next deal.

'Parents at war are my worst nightmare,' Leila said, echoing his own thoughts on the subject. 'But perhaps we can be friends, Raffa. And if you really don't want any part in this, wouldn't it be better for me to return to Skavanga without any more fuss?'

'Fuss?' Repeating the word, he tossed it around in his mind. He wanted all the fuss in the world to surround Leila on the day she gave birth. 'And you want to go back to Skavanga?' he said distractedly, already making plans to appoint the top people in their field to attend her—but here. Here on the island.

'In your current mood,' she said quietly, 'I'd be relieved.'

He was slowly coming out of the dark tunnel into the

light, from the past to the present, and now he was fully focused on Leila he couldn't believe how controlled she was, how calm. But Leila had always been the one fixed point in a turbulent sea of siblings.

And the child had changed her. It had given her a new inner strength. No more the mouse in the shadow of her siblings, Leila had emerged as a warrior in defence of her child. But if she thought she could keep this baby away from him and disappear out of his life for good, she was wrong, though he would never promise her more than he was capable of giving. 'I accept full responsibility, of course, but that doesn't change anything between us.'

'I don't expect it to, Raffa.' Leila's gaze remained unswerving on his face. 'I'm quite capable of handling this on my own. I have a duty to tell you, and that is all.'

'How sensible of you.'

'And how cold of you,' she countered, staring at him with concern in her eyes. 'We're talking about a child, Raffa, and yet your manner is so distant we might be discussing a deal you may or may not want to buy into. I'm not sorry this happened. However inconvenient a baby might be for you, I can't wait to hold my first child in my arms. And I will *never* regret being pregnant.'

He held up his hand. 'I promise you that you have nothing to worry about. As far as all the practicalities are concerned I'll have my lawyers draw up a contract between us.'

'A contract?' Leila shook her head. 'That's your answer to everything, isn't it, Raffa? Get the lawyers to deal with it—delegate, distance yourself, don't engage your emotions in any way. The stroke of a pen is far easier and much safer than risking your heart.'

'You don't know what you're talking about. I pay lawyers to handle my problems.'

'But this isn't a problem,' Leila insisted with a sad laugh in her voice. Embracing her stomach, she added softly, 'This is a baby, Raffa.'

'I delegate so I can get on with the job of keeping thousands of people employed,' he informed her with biting calm. And now he needed space and time to plan. Walking around her, he headed for the door.

'That's right, Raffa—run away!'

He returned in a stride and stood staring down at her, but instead of recoiling she reached out to him. 'I wish I could help you, Raffa.'

'Help me?' He speared a glance at her hands and she lowered them to her sides.

'Perhaps you expected me to be more sophisticated,' she said, stopping him at the door. 'Perhaps you expect me to treat this lightly, to smile prettily and move on, accept a large cheque each month in lieu of your attention, as if I've scored a double—a baby and a wealthy patron.'

'I expect you to be honest with me. Is that too much to ask? *Dios,* Leila. You've been on the island how long?'

'I swear to you—I was trying to choose the right moment, and I thought I'd found it. I was coming to find you, but then I saw the stall selling baby clothes and I was distracted. I couldn't resist—'

She stopped and her eyes filled with tears. He knew then that the tiny clothes were innocent reminders to Leila of the small child who would wear them and as such they were more than baby clothes, they were Leila's promise of the future. He wanted to embrace her, to tell her it would be all right, but, unlike Leila, the thought of an impending birth filled him with dread. He had the additional concern of being responsible for a child when his own father had ruined so many lives, and, even if he could do better, how could he balance

his responsibilities of running a multinational corpora-
tion with being a father?

'I've handled this badly,' he admitted. 'I keep things
simple so I don't end up with children who are farmed
out to their grandparents, because their parents have
better things to do.'

'Is that what happened to you, Raffa?'

He could do without the compassion on her face. He
didn't need anyone's pity, and, with an impatient gesture, he turned away.

'You already told me that your grandmother brought
you up—'

'And made a damn good job of it,' he said quietly.

'So your parents didn't want children—'

'Please,' he said. 'Please stop before you make things
worse.'

'You'll see,' she said confidently. 'In a few months'
time our baby will be here and you'll feel differently.'

The irony of their role reversal struck him, as Leila,
speaking with such confidence about the birth, left him
racked with fear for her. She couldn't know what lay
ahead of her, and this new Leila was frightened of nothing and no one—would listen to no one, not even him.

'I'm only concerned for your safety, and for the baby's
safety,' he assured her. 'But if you want to hear that I'm
the by-product of too much sex and too little love, then
you would be right.'

'So where does that leave us, Raffa?'

'All you need to know is that love was never a factor.
Not once. Not ever—'

He was still back in the past, talking about his parents, but then he noticed that Leila's face had turned
ashen. She thought he was talking about them.

'Well, if nothing else,' she said gamely, 'I understand you better now.'

He should have known she would find some good amongst the debris. As the ghosts bore down on him he shook his head. 'I doubt that somehow.'

The mother he'd never known was dead. And his father—a man he hadn't spoken to for years—was currently sunning himself with the latest in a long line of teenage girlfriends in Monte Carlo. His grandmother had saved him, and it was Abuelita who had restored his faith in human nature.

Leila put her hand on his arm, and he was sure they both felt the shock of the physical contact. 'I should have found some better way to tell you,' she said. 'But at least you know now. Perhaps it would be better for all concerned if things are handled formally between us by a third party as you suggested. I'll return home as soon as you can make arrangements for me to leave.'

No, was his first reaction. She couldn't leave. For a whole raft of reasons, not least of which was Leila herself, fast followed by his concern over the birth of her child. There must have been something of this in his eyes as he turned to look at her, and she lifted her hand as if to ward him off. Moving her hand aside, he dragged her close.

'Don't do this, Raffa. Please…'

She knew it was hopeless to resist just as he did. The passion between them was so easily ignited and it had been far too long for both of them. As Leila reached up to link her hands behind his neck, he kissed her hungrily, and, lifting her into his arms, he carried her across the hallway and up the stairs into his apartment. Kicking the door shut behind him, he crossed the room and laid her down on the bed. Undoing the buckle on his jeans, he lowered the zipper and freed himself. Lifting Leila's skirt, he dispensed with her thong and settled over her. Driving a thigh between her legs—

He stopped.

Massively erect and hideously frustrated, he stopped. Pulling back, he swung off the bed.

'What?' she said, reaching for him.

'I can't do this, Leila.' Raking stiff fingers through his hair, he asked himself, what had he become? And then he swung round to find Leila crying.

Dios! What a mess this was.

CHAPTER SEVEN

LEILA CRYING SHAMED HIM. She wasn't the type to use tears as a weapon, or even as a last resort. Leila had never been quiet and ineffective. She possessed an inner strength. Even now she wasn't making a fuss as she straightened her clothes with a gentle grace that made him feel more of a brute than ever.

'Thank you,' she whispered, sensing his gaze on her.

'What the hell are you thanking me for?'

'You stopped,' she said as if that were obvious. 'You knew when to stop.' She looked up at him. 'And you could stop, Raffa.'

'Of course I could stop.' He frowned. 'I can't imagine why that should surprise you.'

Unless...

'Perhaps we both have issues from the past we're still working through,' she said, confirming his worst suspicions. 'I wanted you with a madness that drove everything else from my mind, and I think you wanted me.'

'You only think?'

'But you realised it wasn't the right time for either of us, and so you stopped.'

'Of course I stopped.' He shook his head, trying to make sense of something that made no sense. He lifted his shoulders in a shrug. 'I had to stop.'

His world might be very different from Leila's, according to her, but trust between a man and a woman when they were having sex was a given. He wondered now what she was hiding, and suddenly he dreaded hearing her answer to the question he had to ask. 'Have you been assaulted, Leila?'

'No.'

She spoke so quickly he believed her, but there was still a haunted look in her eyes.

'But there is something?'

He waited, but she said nothing more.

'I would never hurt you. I hope you know that.'

She didn't answer. She wasn't ready to talk to him yet. He knew something of Leila's family history from the press reports, and now his imagination was working overtime. The thought of what she might have seen at home chilled him. 'Can you tell me what's wrong?' he pressed gently.

'Not now, Raffa.'

She would tell him, he hoped, but it would be in her own time. 'Will you be all right in here if I leave you for a while?' He sensed she needed space; he did too.

'Of course I'll be all right, Raffa.'

There was such a mix of emotion in her eyes when she looked up at him, he guessed neither of them had an answer for the heat that had flared between them.

'Come and find me when you're ready,' he suggested. 'Have a rest—or don't have a rest. Do whatever you think best.'

'Thank you. I will,' she assured him quietly.

She waited until all the rattling atoms in the room had settled like dust, and then, standing up, she brushed herself down as if brushing away the ghosts of the past. It was time to tell Raffa everything. She wanted to help him, and if she confided in him perhaps they could re-build their trust. It was time to open up in the hope that he would do the same.

She guessed she'd find him in the courtyard. He was chatting with some of the older men who had come along to help him organise the fair. Sensing her arrival, he turned to look at her long before she reached him.

'Good—you're here,' he said. 'Let's go for that walk.' He introduced her and then explained their intentions in Spanish to the group of elderly men, who smiled broadly at her and, like everyone else on the island, instantly made her feel a very welcome part of their community.

'The gardens?' Raffa suggested as he escorted her through the line of stalls.

'Perfect,' Leila agreed.

The gardens surrounding the castle were ordered and tranquil, and she couldn't think of anywhere better to say the words she had never shared with anyone, not even her sisters or her brother, Tyr.

The scent of the recently watered grass combined with the heady scent of the roses in the flower beds was both intoxicating and soothing, and when they stopped beside a fountain she dabbled her fingertips in the cool-ing pool.

'My father beat my mother. Not once, but many times.' Her voice was flat, devoid of expression.

'*Dios,* Leila.'

'My mother knew I'd seen what had happened,' she continued without looking at Raffa. 'It was our unspo-ken pact. We both knew my father would never dare to touch her in front of my sisters, let alone in front of Tyr. She explained away the bumps and bruises as her own clumsy fault. I suppose that's why my mother's last wish was that I didn't live scared because of what I'd seen.'

Gathering Leila into his arms, he held her close. 'You are strong,' he whispered fiercely against her hair. 'Your mother would be proud of you, Leila. You're stronger than you know.'

'How can that be when I've done everything wrong?' she whispered.

'What have you done wrong?' he demanded, pulling back to look at her.

'I tried to become the woman my mother always wanted me to be, and look what a mess I've made of everything. I should have told you about the baby the instant I knew.'

'If you could have found me,' he reminded her. 'I'm good at disappearing.'

'Like my brother, Tyr,' she mused.

His loyalty to Tyr made him ignore that comment. 'And as far as dealing with the ghosts of the past is concerned, I'd say you've coped a lot better than I have.'

'What do you mean by that, Raffa?'

He shrugged it off. 'Whatever else this baby means to you, Leila, it can't form part of your self-improvement plan.'

'That's just it. I never planned to have a baby with you, Raffa. I never sleep around. I never have. And I certainly wouldn't use you to have a baby.'

'But now you are pregnant I must help you.' His heart lurched at the thought that Leila might say no. His plans to control every aspect of this birth were already taking shape in his mind.

'Don't look so haunted, Raffa. I'm healthy and I'm young, and I'll do everything I can to give our child the best possible start in life.'

'You have to allow me to worry about you. I always plan ahead, but still things can go wrong.'

'Nothing's going to go wrong, Raffa.'

As far as she knew. He was prepared to cut Leila all the slack in the world after what she'd told him, and he would try his best to calm his raging concern where the actual birth of the baby was concerned, but, where Leila's life and the life of their unborn child was concerned, he refused to take any chances.

'So what's your solution, Raffa?'

'We take things one step at a time. I'll have my doctors check you over and then we can move forward with more confidence to the next stage.'

She flashed him a reproachful glance. 'You mean you want your doctor to make sure it's your baby?'

'No. My only concern is that you and the baby are healthy, Leila. I'm suggesting you have a scan, to establish how far the pregnancy has progressed, so you know that everything's progressing normally.'

'You should be there for the first scan. A friend showed me a picture once. It's...' She stopped and smiled at him. 'There are no words.' Leila's face was rapt.

'That may not be possible. I have...commitments.' Commitments he couldn't discuss with Tyr's sister.

'Oh,' she said softly, masking her bitter disappointment behind a brave face and a determined chin.

'And we have to decide where you'll live,' he said, moving on.

'In Skavanga, of course.' She frowned.

'With my child? So I can look forward to seeing my son or daughter—what? Every six weeks or so?'

She couldn't meet his gaze.

'I don't think so, Leila. When we have a clearer

picture of when the baby's due, I'll draw up a visitation plan—'

'You'll draw it up?'

'In consultation with you.'

'You make it sound so cold. You can't just drive through what suits you best, Raffa. I'll take care of our child, and not with you looking over my shoulder to see if you approve.'

'And how will you do that on the salary you currently earn?'

'I have shares in the mine and, when your consortium has completed its investment and everything is running at full capacity, I've been led to believe I should be paid a healthy dividend.'

'You will benefit,' he agreed, 'but not enough. You're a very small shareholder, and my child—'

'Ah,' she interrupted. 'So now we come to it. Any child of yours will have different needs from every other child in the world. If it's a boy it will inherit a dukedom, and either sex will inherit a fortune. Where I come from, love and food and warmth and safety are the primary requirements for a child.'

'That's where we differ, Leila, because I don't see any separation between me and the rest of the world.'

'Just a few billion.'

'That doesn't make me special. I got lucky, that's all.'

'And you work hard,' Leila remarked in her equal-handed way.

'Yes, I do, and I don't want you working all the hours God sends in order to support our baby. This is my responsibility too. I'm just trying to make things easier for you, Leila.'

'But you live in such a different world.'

'It's warmer,' he agreed wryly.

'You know what I mean,' she insisted, but thankfully he had succeeded in lightening the atmosphere, and now she was trying not to smile.

'As far as I'm concerned, we live in the same world, Leila. You want to work. I want to work. If a child enters my life I want that child to enjoy the benefits I can provide for it. Otherwise, what the hell am I working for?'

If he could brush aside his fears for Leila for only a second he could see that with a child in his life there would be real purpose to the drive that carried him forward so relentlessly. He worked to help others, but to be able to do that and have a child of his own to do things for...

'I would never stop you seeing the baby, Raffa.'

He refocused on Leila's face, wondering what had prompted that remark. 'Custody is a long way from being decided yet.'

'But a child should live with its mother—'

'Don't you trust me, Leila?'

'Yes...'

No, he thought as she fell silent. Leila didn't trust him with something as precious as her child. Why should she when she hardly knew him? Leila only wanted to be a good mother. She would never forget that her own mother had been killed so tragically when she was so young, or what a sense of loss she had felt since then.

'We'll decide this together. Perhaps we should continue this discussion when you're feeling less emotional.'

'In around a couple of years' time?' she suggested, her amused glance flashing up to meet his.

'Whenever you're ready,' he said gently.

There was a long silence and then she said, 'I think I'm always going to be influenced by the letter my mother wrote to me before she died. I think she was trying to prepare me for the big things in life, like this.'

'A letter?'

'I had to promise to be bold…take life by the scruff of the neck and forge my own path, rather than allowing the past to haunt me and hold me back.' She smiled. 'I was trying to get the balance right and went overboard on the night of the party.'

They both had, he remembered, thinking back. Before that night he guessed Leila had made do with dreams, because dreams were safe and available to everyone, even the quietest of sisters. 'We will work this out, Leila, and while we do there's something you could do for me.'

She looked at him and raised a brow. 'What could I possibly do for you, Raffa?'

His grandmother's illness had really thrown him. Leila's news had really thrown him. Perhaps if he brought the two of them together… 'There's someone I'd like you to meet.'

'Who?' she said suspiciously.

'My grandmother. You did say you'd like to meet her.'

'I would. But how does that help our situation?'

'I don't know. Maybe it won't,' he admitted. 'But I think we should tell her you're expecting her first great-grandchild, don't you?'

CHAPTER EIGHT

RAFFA WANTED TO introduce her to the matriarch of his family? Maybe he was right and she was blinkered. Seeing herself as the small-town girl and Raffa as somehow inhabiting a different world was blown to smithereens when he had exactly the same concerns she had: family, and the people who depended on him.

'But what can I tell your grandmother?' The last thing she wanted was to upset an old lady who had been sick recently. 'I'm pregnant with your child, but I'm going home to Skavanga, so she may never see her great-grandchild. Perhaps it's better if we don't meet.'

'I won't force you to meet her.'

'Your grandmother has been ill and I can't imagine that meeting me is going to make her feel better.'

'You'd be surprised.' A glint of amusement brightened his eyes. 'You'd give her hope.'

'I don't see how.'

'She's given up on me becoming any type of family man.'

'So you parade me in front of her? How's that going to work? I don't doubt your grandmother longs for you to settle down and give her a great-grandchild, but please leave me out of it.'

'I would never attempt to mislead my grandmother. I would tell her the truth as I always do.'

'That's sure to cheer her up.'

'It's better than nothing.'

A flicker of humour crept into Leila's gaze. 'I don't think you know the first thing about women, Raffa.'

Raffa drew back his head in surprise. No doubt he considered himself an expert on women.

'Introducing the mother of my child to my grandmother is the right thing to do,' he said stiffly.

'And I'd love to meet her,' Leila confirmed, 'but I refuse to suggest that our relationship is anything more than it is.' That was a platonic working relationship between two people who just happened to be expecting a child.

As Raffa inclined his head in agreement she knew she'd have to watch him. Raffa Leon was used to having everything his own way, and for once in his life he would have to accept that that wasn't going to happen this time.

Raffa's grandmother's house wasn't close to the castle, as Leila had imagined, but about an hour's drive away, up in the hills where it was cooler. Raffa drove them up the switchback road in an open-topped bright red Maserati, and, apart from the thrill of riding in a sports car with a man who knew what he was doing, the view over a vine-crammed valley on one side, and a neon-bright sea on the other, went a long way to soothing her tension at the thought of finally meeting his grandmother.

It was a lovely day, with a breeze laden with the scent of blossom, and would have been a perfect day had it not been for the man at her side making her jittery. Raffa was wound up like a spring. This visit clearly meant a lot to him. The excess energy he was burning was as potent as any aphrodisiac, which was inconvenient on a day when her aim was to appear strait-laced and sensible, the type of girl who might make a mistake once in the heat of the moment, but who would never make the same mistake twice.

'My grandmother appreciates her own space,' Raffa explained as he turned off the main road onto an impressive tree-lined drive.

'And who could blame your grandmother for wanting to get away from you?' Leila said dryly. 'Or for wanting to live here?' she breathed, taking in the magnificent surroundings.

The picturesque drive boasted a shady avenue of lush green trees that led the way to a quaint sprawling manor house built of stone. With a cheery red front door and dozens of mullioned windows twinkling a welcome, the picture-postcard setting was made complete by a chorus line of colourful songbirds perched on the gabled roof. The manor house was one of the prettiest buildings Leila had ever seen, and was set off to perfection by the banks of flower beds in front of it, and the spray of cooling fountains in the yard.

'It's like a fairy dell,' she said, glancing around.

'My grandmother works hard on the gardens, but so far no sighting of fairies.' Pushing his sunglasses back on his head, Raffa opened the car door for her with a slanting smile.

'Just before we go in...' Leila turned to face Raffa beneath a porch extravagantly swagged with peach-coloured wisteria. 'What exactly have you told your grandmother about us?'

'That I'm bringing a very good friend to meet her. That is what we agreed, isn't it?'

She confirmed this tensely with a nod. She wouldn't

have believed it possible for any woman to have a platonic friendship with Raffa Leon, so it appeared she had achieved the impossible.

Wearing jeans and a tight-fitting top that clung to his sculpted muscles with loving attention to detail, rugged, too handsome for his own good, Raffa exuded raw, animal sex, and it was impossible to stand this close to him without imagining being intimate with him. It didn't help that she had some rather compelling memories to draw on.

'You look fine,' he said as she fiddled with her dress.

She'd chosen it carefully, thinking Raffa's grandmother had enough to contend with today without a fashion crisis hitting her between the eyes. It was a pretty dress with a floral pattern, a respectable neckline and a knee-length skirt.

'My grandmother speaks fluent English, though no Scandinavian languages,' Raffa explained, 'but as you're both fluent in English…'

'We'll be fine.'

Raffa was such a distraction she was careful not to look at him and it was a relief to hear footsteps inside the house coming closer. There was one brief moment when her concentration lapsed as Raffa eased onto one hip and her pulse jagged, but she quickly turned her thoughts to meeting his grandmother and everything settled down again.

The housekeeper's welcome was warm. Her apple cheeks were split by a wide smile as she embraced Raffa, proving he was clearly a popular visitor. The rest of the staff seemed excited by his arrival as they walked through the exquisitely furnished house, and Leila was conscious of attracting quite a bit of interest too.

'The dowager duchess is in the garden,' the housekeeper explained as she led them through a light-filled orangery.

The dowager duchess. Leila's heart began to pound. The title alone made Raffa's grandmother sound quite formidable.

Far from being a grande dame, as Leila had feared, the dowager duchess turned out to be a dainty, bird-like woman, with silver hair twisted into a casual bun on top of her head with a moth-eaten straw hat crammed on top of it. Wiry and upright, she was dressed in wide-legged linen trousers and a serviceable, long-sleeved blouse. A multi-pocketed gardening apron in a nondescript dun colour, out of which protruded an assortment of stakes, recent snippings and secateurs, completed her outfit. She was very much in charge of a squad of gardeners, whom she was directing as briskly as a sergeant major around her park-sized garden.

Leila only had to glance at Raffa to know how he felt about this woman. They adored each other, she realised, standing back as the giant of a man and the tiny woman embraced each other. When Raffa stood back to introduce her, she discovered that his grandmother had been well briefed in advance of her arrival.

'I hear congratulations are in order,' she exclaimed, drawing Leila into a hug. 'I'm so happy for both of you.'

Leila's gaze found Raffa's, and she wondered now if he'd told his grandmother some cock-and-bull story regarding their relationship.

He shrugged and his eyes were full of amusement as if to prove that Raffa Leon answered to no one.

'Come with me, Leila,' his grandmother invited warmly, unaware of the tension between her grandson and her guest. 'We'll have tea in the garden. I think

Rafael has got your message,' she added with amusement. 'You have the most expressive eyes.'

'I'm sorry if I've offended you,' Leila said as they sat down.

'Please don't apologise. I know Rafael, and I always make up my own mind, whatever he tells me.'

A table draped with a delicate lace cloth and an array of fine china had been set out for them beneath the generous shade of an ancient frangipani tree. Following Leila's glance across the manicured lawn as Raffa headed back to the house, his grandmother leaned forward to remark, 'Don't look so worried, Leila. The Dukes of Cantalabria have always been notoriously unscrupulous when it comes to choosing a bride.'

'A bride?' No amount of good manners could hide Leila's feelings. 'I'm not sure what Raffa has told you, but I've no intention of marrying him.'

'Of course not. Please forgive me. Seeing the two of you together takes me back to my own youth.'

'I'm afraid ours is not a lasting relationship.'

'With a child between you?' the dowager queried. 'I'd say there's a lifetime's commitment between you. Milk or lemon, my dear?'

'Lemon, please.' Leila's voice took on a new intensity. 'I just don't want to mislead you in any way.'

'How are you misleading me?' The old lady frowned as she passed Leila a delicate porcelain cup and saucer. 'Any fool can see my grandson is head over heels in love with you.'

Leila almost laughed out loud, but, in deference to Raffa's grandmother, she killed the impulse in favour of being frank with her. 'Raffa's not in love with me. All we shared was a moment of—'

'Pure passion,' his grandmother supplied with a nod

of her head. 'Don't look so surprised, Leila. I was young once. And please…I don't want you to feel awkward around me. I can assure you, it would take a lot more than your pregnancy to shock me. I'm only surprised Rafael can be so calm about it.'

'Calm?' Leila tensed.

The old lady started as if she had been jolted out of revisiting memories from the past.

'Forgive me, Leila. I knew this day would come. I just wasn't sure how Rafael would cope with it. It's great credit to you that he's taken it so calmly. I'm delighted for him—for both of you.'

Far from being reassured, Leila was doubly anxious, and determined to get to the bottom of Raffa's mysterious past. 'Is there some family problem I should know about?'

'You're thinking genetic problems,' the dowager observed shrewdly. 'Let me reassure you right away, it's nothing like that, Leila. I'm thrilled you're having a child, and there's no reason to suppose your baby won't be perfectly healthy.'

'But is there something more I should know?'

'What *do* you know?' The dowager stared at her levelly.

'Only a little,' Leila admitted, hoping the old lady would fill in the gaps.

'Drink your tea before it gets cold, dear,' the dowager said, dashing Leila's hopes.

'I'm glad I've had this chance to meet you,' Leila said to break the sudden silence. 'It meant a lot to Raffa.'

'And I'm delighted to meet the mother of my first great-grandchild.' There was a pause, and then the dowager covered Leila's hand with hers. 'Forgive me, Leila, but there are things that cannot be discussed over tea. I'm sure Raffa will explain.'

'Yes. I'm sure he will,' Leila agreed without much conviction, her anxiety levels rising by the minute as she wondered what Raffa's grandmother could mean.

'How long are you staying?' The dowager's shrewd gaze met Leila's over their teacups.

'Not long,' Leila said honestly. 'Just long enough to choose some gems to display in Skavanga.'

'At the museum you're in control of,' the dowager said with interest, putting down her cup. 'Perhaps I'll pay you a visit one day. Now where is my grandson?' she said, turning in her chair. 'Perhaps he's choosing some gems to show you. We keep some of the very best in an armed vault in the house,' she added with a touch of the familiar family steel.

Leila's tension eased into a smile. 'You are so like Raffa.'

'Stubborn? Driven?' the old lady suggested, meeting Leila's gaze. There was a twinkle in her eye as she leaned forward. 'Fiercely determined to have our own way? Something tells me you're just like us, Leila Skavanga.'

CHAPTER NINE

'TALK OF THE DEVIL!' the dowager exclaimed as Raffa appeared in the doorway of the house.

The mellow sunshine and the beautiful garden provided a deceptively soft frame for a hard man. A hard man with a mysterious past, Leila now knew, determined she would get to the bottom of the mystery.

Would she always feel this way when she saw him? Leila wondered as Raffa strode towards them. Yes, she realised as he flashed a quick smile. And this was her chance, maybe her only chance to find out what his grandmother had meant when she talked about Raffa's concerns regarding Leila's pregnancy. As soon as he was within earshot she sprang up. 'Could we have a walk round your beautiful garden?' she asked the dowager.

'Of course. Rafael, please escort our guest.'

The heady scent of the flowers was intoxicating, but that was nothing compared to standing close to Raffa, only inches away…feeling his gaze on her back as she bent down to smell the roses, or feeling his breath brush her neck when she straightened up.

'So, what's this about?' he said as they walked towards a small bridge across the stream that ran through the garden. 'What did you want to talk about that you can't say in front of my grandmother?'

Pausing in the middle of the bridge, Leila leaned back against the worn balustrade with her arms resting on the warm, smooth wood. 'Your grandmother said she was surprised that you could take my pregnancy so calmly. She said there were things it wasn't possible to discuss over tea. She reassured me that there were no genetic problems in your family to worry about, so I wondered—'

'My grandmother said too much.'

He hadn't meant to snap. Or turn his back. Or lean over the bridge lost in his thought, but the guilt he had lived with for so long was curdling inside him. He had to take several deep breaths before he could control the emotion. Feelings that had been buried for so long had a way of running wild. They had threatened to ruin him as a youth, but he had mastered them as an adult, and control ruled him now. Leila must think him distant and aloof from her, but she was wrong. He was intensely focused on the only thing that mattered to him now, which was Leila's safety when she gave birth to their child.

'Raffa?'

'What?'

'Have I said something to upset you? I didn't mean to be intrusive or to probe into your past.'

'I know.' He still didn't turn around. It would have been easier for both of them if he had kept Leila at a distance, stopped her coming to the island, but his head had been full of her, and he doubted now that any amount of work or distraction could shake her out. He couldn't have known she was carrying his baby, or how that would make him feel. He could never have anticipated the old ghosts from the past coming back to taunt him with the guilt he'd lived with all his life.

Following Raffa's gaze down the busy stream as it

rushed and bubbled on its way to the sea, she could feel the barricades rising around him. Raffa's self-imposed isolation was a shield to keep her and the world at bay, and whatever had made Raffa withdraw into himself, it was something he had kept hidden for years, so he was hardly going to blurt it out now. But her impulse was to reassure him, and there was nothing to stop her doing that.

'Your grandmother cares very much about you, Raffa. She didn't break any confidences. She wouldn't tell me anything.'

Straightening up, he turned to face her, and his expression had not mellowed as she'd hoped. 'Is that what this walk is about?' There was suspicion in his voice, even hostility. 'Do you expect me to reveal all now?'

'No,' she said, holding Raffa's burning gaze steadily. 'Of course I don't. I just wanted you to know you're not alone.'

'It's you we're supposed to be sorting out, Leila.'

'I don't need sorting out. And you shouldn't be so proud that you can't admit that you do.'

'What?' he said softly.

'I'm sorry, but someone has to tell you. Your grandmother is one of the strongest women I've ever met, but she loves you so much she has spent her whole life tiptoeing around you, and whatever it is that makes you feel so guilty. And I won't do that.'

Drawing back his head, Raffa stared down at her in disbelief.

Even now, even with Raffa glowering down at her, her only wish was to reach out to him and hold him until the ghosts had no strength left. He was a pent-up powerhouse of outraged affront, which increased the force of his physical appeal tenfold. She felt it as a primitive and very earthy response to him, and Raffa felt it too. Just the smallest change in those hostile dark eyes told her exactly how Raffa Leon would like to resolve this situation. Perhaps the combined force of their passion would be enough to banish all their ghosts in one fell swoop, she reflected wryly.

'Shall we say goodbye to my grandmother?' Raffa suggested in a neutral tone.

'Yes,' she agreed in the same careful manner.

'Seat belt,' Raffa reminded her as they slid into the car.

Before she could reach for it, he had leaned across to help and his considerable weight pressed against her breasts. The catch clicked into place and still they remained motionless. Glancing into Raffa's eyes, she saw the heat in them and felt an answering tug.

Settling back into the driver's seat, he reached for his sunglasses and switched on the engine, by which time the aching need inside her had grown to a pulsing urge to mate. Would she ever find an answer to her obsession with this man?

Her life had changed completely since meeting Raffa. She had changed completely, Leila realised as he gunned the engine and released the brake. She glanced at Raffa's harsh profile, and then on to assess his impossibly powerful frame like a trainer at the stockyard picking out the king of the herd, a magnificent wild stallion to mount, to tame, to ride.

If that was all that lay behind the attraction, perhaps she could forget her principles for one day, slake her lust and go home, but there was so much more to Raffa Leon. She was compelled to stay so she could enjoy more of his passion, his humour and his whip-sharp mind, and uncover all those secrets his grandmother had hinted at.

She had never been a quitter, Leila reflected as Raffa floored the accelerator and G-force thumped her in the back.

He drove the car to its limits. There was something hot about a woman carrying his child that made Leila irresistible. He had to have her right away. She was sending him all the same messages and he was drowning in pheromones. He could never have anticipated the way Leila's pregnancy would make him feel—protective, yes, possessive too, but in a good way, a way that made him want to stake his claim over and over, so he could hear her cries of pleasure.

'What are you smiling at?' she asked him.

'Am I?' he retorted innocently. He was remembering the way she'd stood up to him—challenged him. He couldn't remember anyone doing that. Leila was right about his grandmother tiptoeing around him, but it wasn't just his grandmother who did that. When it came to his past, no one trespassed. But Leila had, and, though she had jolted him out of the status quo, it only made him think more of her. There was nothing weak about Leila beneath that peacemaking manner, and he liked that.

The visit with his grandmother had been a success. He had hoped they would like each other. He just hadn't realised how much. With his *abuelita* as an ally Leila had no reason not to stay on the island to have her baby. He had already appointed her doctors, and the support staff was on standby. Leila might have amused him by standing up to him, but control over this birth was all his.

'Why are we stopping?' she said as he pulled off the road.

'We're stopping because some things can't wait.'

'Like what?' she said, her voice shaking with excitement as she feigned innocence and gazed around.

'Like the view is spectacular?' He raised a brow. The view was spectacular, but they both knew that wasn't the reason he'd stopped the car.

'You can't,' she protested when he removed his seat belt. 'Raffa—what if someone drives past?'

'So that isn't a flat no?' he said, curbing a smile. 'You have an urge. I have an urge. Let's do something about it.'

'How do you know I have got an urge?'

'Your eyes are darkening... Your lips are swelling... Your nipples are—'

'Stop,' she said, sucking in a fast breath. 'You are so bad.'

'Would you have me any other way?' As he angled his chin he saw the answer in her eyes. Reaching across, he very gently stroked the swell of her belly and a sigh escaped her.

'You're a very bad man, Raffa Leon.'

'I make you angry?'

'Yes, you do.'

'Then please allow me to soothe you,' he suggested, tipping his sunglasses down his nose. Drawing her into his arms, he lazily brushed her lips with his.

She was only wearing a tiny thong beneath the dress. No bra. She didn't need one. Her breasts were glorious, firm and full, while her nipples were engorged and pressing urgently against the fine, summer-weight fabric, in serious danger of being chafed unless he freed them.

'What are you doing?' she demanded in a husky whisper.

'Feeding,' he growled, laving her nipples with his tongue. 'Hmm. You taste different.'

'Soapy?' she suggested.

'No. Womanly and—'

'Pregnant?'

'Maybe.' He gave a crooked smile as he gazed up into Leila's eyes.

'No maybe about it,' she said, breaking off to gasp when his hand stroked her thigh.

'Nice?' he asked, trailing his fingertips over her.

Leila's answer was to arc towards him, making herself more available. 'Not sure I can bear being teased,' she warned him. 'Being pregnant seems to have made me…'

'Mad for sex.'

'How do you know?'

'I know everything about you, Leila Skavanga. And it's been far too long.'

Removing her thong, he slipped down from his seat and went to kneel in the well of the car. 'Rest your legs on my shoulders and your feet on the dashboard.'

'Really?' she said, glancing around.

'Really,' he confirmed.

'How do I explain this if a tractor drives past?' she managed between hectic breaths.

'Just say you've got a cramp and I'm doing the best I can to distract you—'

'In Spanish?'

He grinned as he freed himself with one hand and positioned her with the other.

'Don't stop,' she begged him when he got busy with his tongue. 'Don't you dare stop… Oh, this is so good…'

He teased her again with just a fraction of his length.

'I want all of it,' she insisted.

'Greedy must wait—'

'Who says?' she demanded, thrusting forward.

It was his turn to groan. She was so tight, so hot and wet, and such an unbelievably perfect fit for him. And this was a really great position. Leila was at the perfect height for him so all he had to do was rock back and forth. It felt so good, so necessary, and it was only a matter of moments before they both lost it.

'Again,' she demanded, still pulsing round him.

Leila hadn't been joking when she said she was mad for sex, but then they'd always been mad for each other. There was some special chemistry between them that reason had never played a part in. 'I think you like that,' he murmured as she groaned.

Leila's answer was to grip him with her internal muscles and tell him fiercely, 'I love it!'

Binding his buttocks close with fingers of steel, she rubbed herself against him until he was almost in danger of losing control, and it was only when they heard the sound of an engine in the distance that they stopped. He tried to find Leila's thong, but a search under the seats proved futile and he was forced to give up.

'The heat between us must have vaporised it,' she said, trying not to laugh.

He secured their seat belts and they sat bolt upright, looking respectable just in time for the local bus to drive past.

'Well, that must have been quite a shock for them,' Leila said, whipping her thong off the dashboard, where it had been all this time. 'I guess our secret is out.'

'Looks like it,' he agreed, looping his arm around her neck to drag her close for a kiss.

Resting his forehead against Leila's, he wanted this moment to last. Maybe this could work. Maybe he could persuade Leila that there would be benefits beyond her imagining if she agreed to live in Spain with their child.

'Do you always get your own way?' she murmured against his mouth as if reading his thoughts.

'Always,' he said confidently.

'Then I think you might just have to get used to me saying no, Raffa Leon, because I can be difficult—and stubborn. Just ask my sisters.'

Unconcerned, he reached across, and, lifting her into his arms, he positioned Leila on his lap. 'Say no,' he invited.

CHAPTER TEN

THINGS HAPPENED FAST in his world and even faster in Leila's, it turned out. He had left Leila on the island for a brief twenty-four hours to attend a meeting in London, and by the time he got back she had introduced herself to his staff, drawn up a schedule of training visits to help improve her insight of the retail diamond industry and booked an appointment with her own doctor in Skavanga.

'You'll go to my doctor, Leila.'

'Don't you trust me to handle this, Raffa?' She didn't even trouble to raise her head from the latest academic paper on heat treatment of gemstones she was reading.

'I have engaged the foremost obstetrician to guide you through this birth. If he's good enough for the British royal family, he should be good enough for you.'

She gave him a direct look over the top of the cute little spectacles she wore for close work. 'And I have arranged to speak to my family doctor, a woman who has known me all my life. I don't need the foremost man,' she added. 'Birth is a natural process, Raffa. I'm not ill. I'm pregnant.'

'You'll do as I say.'

'Really?' she said mildly. Standing up to confront

him, she added, 'I think you'll find that this is my body, my baby and my decision to make.'

'This is our baby and I won't take any chances with either of you.'

As Leila stabbed a look at him he reined back. She was sitting on top of a hormonal volcano. He should remember that.

'You're going to be a father, Raffa.'

Yes. He was going to be a father...

He tried to feel something.

He felt nothing but the customary throb of anxiety. He envied the contented smile on Leila's lips. Knowing she was going to be a mother had lit her up from the inside out, while all he could do was dread the birth.

'No,' he argued flatly, forgetting everything he had vowed to do and say. 'You will not be having your baby in Skavanga. You will have your baby here on the island, where I can keep you safe.'

'But I've never suggested anything different other than having my baby in Skavanga,' Leila protested, frowning as she looked at him as if he'd gone mad. 'I can't understand why you're making such a fuss about it. We have a state-of-the-art hospital in Skavanga and excellent specialists, most of whom I know.'

'I have no doubt that you have every confidence in them,' he said, 'but I have appointed the best.'

'Oh,' she mocked him. 'I forgot for a moment that your money can buy anything, including guaranteed, trouble-free birth.'

He swung away so she couldn't see the expression on his face. 'It can provide a substantial buffer against any unpleasantness for you,' he said, turning slowly round to face her. 'And yes, in my experience, my money does buy the best.'

'But it can't buy me, or my agreement to your plan. Are you seriously suggesting a doctor who has known me all my life would let me come to any harm?' she pressed him.

He shook his head. 'I'm not prepared to take that risk.' This wasn't up for discussion.

'Well, I'm not going to London,' she said, holding his stare unblinking.

'Did I say anything about London?'

She frowned. 'No, but I thought—'

'You'll stay here on the island. The specialist and his team will come to you. You'll have the finest midwife, nurses, and a paediatrician especially appointed for the baby. And as far as the accessories are concerned, you can order anything you want online.'

'The accessories,' she echoed as if mystified. 'You make our baby sound like this season's fashion must-have.'

'Don't be so ridiculous, Leila.'

'But you don't show any more involvement than that, Raffa.' Leila's face was tense with disappointment.

'Imagine having a nursery at the castle,' he pressed on. 'I know how much you loved your turret room, and you can speak to my decorators, have the nursery decked out any way you want. The top stores will provide cribs and toys and clothes and strollers, and any other baby equipment you might need. You'll have a completely free hand, Leila—'

'But I'll be a prisoner,' she said with horror.

He shook his head wryly. 'I thought we'd got past that Rapunzel thing. You'll be free to come and go as you like.'

'After the birth.'

'Well, obviously.'

As he gazed around the room Leila had been using as an office he should have known that a carefully preserved sixteenth-century citadel with a sheikh's ransom in antiques and furnishings would cut no ice with her. He was right. Those hormones hadn't gone anywhere; they were merely slumbering, waiting to explode.

'You can't keep me trapped on your island when I want to go home.'

'Just think carefully before you make any rash decisions. Think about what you want, and then think about what's best for the baby.'

'Don't patronise me, Raffa,' she said quietly. 'I don't need to think about what's best for my baby. What's best for both of us is for me to return home to Skavanga and my life there.'

'I'm not trying to patronise you. I'm trying to do everything I can to help you.'

'Then let me go.'

Her voice was barely above a whisper, but the expression in her eyes as she held his gaze was absolutely determined.

'At least agree to sleep on it.'

She stood up, ready to go. 'I will,' she promised without much enthusiasm.

By this time they were mere inches apart. 'What are you doing?' she said.

'I'm kissing you into compliance.' Brushing her lips with his mouth to a lazy rhythm he felt her soften in his arms.

'Get off me,' she warned, starting to laugh as he continued to tease her. 'You can't get around me like this.'

'Can't I?' His hands had moved down to cup the swell

of her buttocks, bringing Leila into contact with the best argument he'd got.

'You're unscrupulous.'

'Yes, I am,' he agreed.

'And a very bad man,' she added with a shuddering sigh.

'We've already established that,' he confirmed, rasping the tender skin below her ear very lightly with his stubble. 'Shall we continue this discussion in the morning?'

'I'm not going to change my mind,' she insisted, turning to stare into his eyes.

But she wasn't going to discourage Raffa from trying his absolute best to convince her he was right either, Leila concluded as he swung her into his arms.

Raffa shouldered the door to his bedroom and carried her inside, kissing her across the room before lowering her gently onto the bed, where he stripped off her dress and tossed it aside. As it floated to the floor she remembered the incident with the thong, and warned him not to lose her dress. 'I don't want to walk through the castle naked to find it.'

'These walls must have seen a lot of excitement in their time. Perhaps I should send the staff home and let you do just that.'

'Then you should strip off too,' she insisted. 'Why don't I help you?'

She lingered over every glorious inch of him, peeling back his top slowly so she could appreciate the bronze map of hard muscle...the flat stomach...the impossible width of his shoulders, tapering down to the washboard waist—

'Let me help you,' Raffa offered when she fumbled with his belt.

Swinging off the bed, he freed the tine. His jeans and boxers followed, and she was glad of her ringside seat as Raffa turned his back to stretch like a big cat. Every inch of him was bronze, and his thighs were towers of muscle, his legs so lean and long. His calves were powerful, and even his naked feet were sexy. She loved his naked feet. But most of all she loved his hard-muscled buttocks, those twin engines of pleasure—

She had to stop thinking about twin engines of pleasure, or she would lose it right now.

'What?' Raffa said, swinging round to stare her in the eyes.

'Nothing—'

'Liar. I can see what you're thinking in your eyes—' Sweeping her into his arms, he kissed her. 'And I'm right, aren't I?'

'This won't change my mind,' she insisted as he dropped kisses on her mouth. 'I'm going back to Skavanga just as soon as we've finished our business here.'

He laughed. 'I'm not even going to ask what type of business you're referring to.' Lowering her onto the bed, he hummed with appreciation as he kissed his way down her body. 'You do taste different.'

'Better?'

'Different,' he argued, stretching out his length against her. 'Rich and full—'

'Like a carton of cream?'

'Like pregnant—'

Making love with Raffa was different this time. He didn't tease her as he usually did, and there was a new intensity in the way he looked at her, the way he touched her, and it was a dangerous development in their relationship that made her want to stay with him for ever and not just for the birth.

He was totally devoted to Leila as he made love to her. They had never been so relaxed with each other, or so intimate. He'd never felt so close. Yes, they'd had sex many times, but nothing like this. This was reassurance from him to her, his pledge to Leila that whatever happened in the future the child they'd made would always be a bond between them. He took her slowly and with infinite care, but these slow, careful thrusts were as potent as their wildest sex had ever been, and she lost control almost immediately, her fingers biting into him as she screamed his name until he soothed her down.

'Remind me to teach you some control,' he teased her when she quietened.

'Must you?' she teased back.

'Do you think I'm going to let you glut yourself every time?'

'Why not?' She smiled, and there was mischief in her eyes. Then, lacing her fingers through his hair, she brought him close again for more.

How could he resist this woman? Thrusting deep, he took her over the edge again, and again. He never tired of watching Leila lose control in his arms. It was the best; it was a sign she felt safe with him. And he would keep her safe. He would keep the baby safe too. However accommodating Leila might think him, nothing had changed. She would give birth to their child at a place of his choosing, which meant here on the island. He would not risk Leila's life.

Abuelita was right when she said they were well matched for stubbornness, but where the birth of a child and the life of a mother were concerned he would take no chances, so, whatever Leila thought, in this instance history proved he did know best.

He cemented the growing closeness between them with a visit to his inner sanctum. Leila had already toured the cutting and sorting rooms in his laboratories on the island, as well as the design studio, but now he wanted to show her some of the world's greatest treasures. As well as being a businessman, he was an avid collector of gems with an interesting history. These remarkable items had only been seen by his grandmother, along with a handful of sheikhs, sultans and assorted potentates, who appreciated the chance to view collections similar to their own.

Lights flashed on automatically as they entered the vault. The walls and floor were black marble, while the display cases were formed from blast-proof glass. He wasn't surprised to hear Leila gasp. The lighting had been specifically designed to startle the visitor with a blaze of refracted light from the jewels from the moment they entered the chamber.

'I thought that first vault you showed me was incredible, but this is something else,' she murmured as he led her forward.

He started the tour by explaining the difference between a diadem and a tiara. 'The tiara is more of a semi-circular headband, while the diadem is like a crown.' And when Leila expressed her preference for an elaborate diadem set with removable emerald pendants, he suggested she try it on.

'Will you help me?'

'It would be my pleasure.'

'Mine too, I'm sure.' She laughed as he pushed

back her hair and settled the priceless masterpiece on her head.

And somehow her clothes found their way to the floor and the sight of Leila, naked, seated on one of the display tables, wearing only a diamond crown, was a sight he knew would be branded on his mind for ever. It certainly added a frisson to their lovemaking, as she had to sit very straight and still, so the crown didn't fall off her head.

'What happens when I—?'

'No extravagant movements,' he warned.

'I'm not sure about that,' she wailed.

'You have to keep still, Leila, or I'll have to stop—'

'Don't you dare stop!' she warned him as he moved steadily back and forth.

Basking in sensation, he watched her closely, listening to her breathing quicken so he knew exactly when to hold her still.

'Thank goodness you caught the crown,' she panted out a good time later.

'No problem,' he said, settling the priceless diadem back on its stand.

'This is your playroom, isn't it?' she challenged him as she slipped down from the table and moved to inspect the next display case in line.

'But you're the first playmate I've brought in here. And the last,' he assured her when she shot him a mock-warning look.

'I'm pleased to hear it,' she murmured as she leaned over the glass. 'What do we have in here?'

'Some of the world's most valuable coloured diamonds,' he said, more interested in stroking the lush curve of her buttocks as he moved behind her.

'They're amazing—' She gasped as he moved in close and his hands found her breasts.

'Pale blue diamonds like your eyes,' he murmured, weighing her breasts appreciatively. 'And bright pink diamonds like your nipples—'

'Just don't suggest canary yellow like my teeth,' she warned him, starting to laugh.

'I don't generally deal in pearls, except that link I showed you, but if I did, your teeth would certainly compare.'

'Cheese—'

He silenced her in the most obvious way. 'Lean over a little more,' he coaxed. 'Take a closer look inside the case.'

'A much closer look,' Leila agreed, gasping with pleasure as he settled deep.

'Hold on,' he warned. 'The display case is bolted to the floor, so it can take some hammering,' he added reassuringly.

She laughed, but was eager to do everything he asked to increase her pleasure.

'The diamonds light up the room,' he murmured, continuing to move steadily. 'Would you like me to tell you where some of the most famous pink diamonds in the world are found?'

'Are you kidding me? I couldn't concentrate if you offered me a dozen on a plate.' Standing on tiptoe, she gasped for breath as she thrust her buttocks towards him, giving him better access.

'East Kimberley in Western Australia—Leila, I really don't think your mind's fully on this tutorial—'

'Oh, it is,' she assured him, arching her back so he could see what he was doing.

Forget the diamonds. Taking firm hold of her buttocks, he enjoyed her, and, from the sounds she was making as he moved fast and hard, Leila was enjoying him too.

'So? What did you think of the visit?' he asked when they finally left the facility.

'Thrilling,' she admitted dryly.

Linking his fingers through hers as they strolled to the car, he pulled her close. 'One day the Skavanga mine will produce diamonds as fine as those I just showed you.'

'Then I'd better make sure the display cabinets in the museum are securely bolted to the floor.'

His gaze warmed with amusement. 'It would be a wise precaution,' he agreed.

'Can we display some of those treasures you just showed me in the museum?'

Raffa narrowed his eyes. 'We are still talking about the diamonds, bad girl?'

'Of course we are. I'm not sharing you with anyone.'

He was as sure as he could be that he had overcome all Leila's arguments when it came to the birth of the baby. The way she was resting her head on his shoulder, the way her arm was locked around his waist. He'd never felt closer to anyone, and Leila was giving every signal that she felt this way too. It wasn't a triumph, it was an enormous relief for him, and when they reached the car, he pressed her back against it and whispered in her ear, 'I want you again.'

'What shall we do about it?' she said, pretending surprise.

'Get home fast?' he suggested.

'Why not here?' she challenged, glancing around.

'Because everyone will be pouring out of work soon, and I don't want to frighten them.'

'Here in the shadows quickly?' She was looking over her shoulder at a handy covey of trees.

'Better still, in the car quickly. I love an element of danger, don't you?'

'Yes, I do,' Leila agreed with her mouth very close to his lips. 'It's far more exciting.'

'And you're the quiet sister?'

'That's what they call me.'

'Then they are mistaken.'

'Thank goodness for that,' she said, shooting him a wicked look as she climbed into the car.

He followed and knelt in the footwell, pulling Leila forward to the very edge of the seat.

The next week was highly charged at night, and hectic by day. They shared bed, bath and every available surface in his apartment at the castle, while in their working hours he took Leila through each department in turn so she could understand the process of turning polished gems into priceless works of art. She was an able student on both sides of the divide, and inevitably they grew even closer, sharing humour, facts and preferences, and learning more about each other every day. He was confident she'd stay on. Why would she leave the island when she had everything she could possibly need right here?

He was feeling upbeat when he went to collect Leila for supper, and when he knocked on the door of her turret room, she called, 'Come in…'

'What the hell?' There had been nothing in her voice to give him the slightest clue that he would find her packing a suitcase.

'Your grandmother rang to say she was taking the jet to London tomorrow,' Leila explained cheerfully, shaking out a dress. 'She asked if I'd like to hitch a lift with her.'

'She did what?' he interrupted softly.

'She didn't tell you?'

'What do you think, Leila?' Impulsive trips were right up his grandmother's street, but why had she asked Leila along? And why the hell had Leila accepted her invitation. Why was Leila leaving?

'Why didn't you tell me? When were you going to tell me, Leila? When you got back to Skavanga?'

'Don't be angry with me, Raffa. We both knew I couldn't stay here for ever.'

'That's news to me.'

'No,' she said firmly. 'I always said I'd be going back to Skavanga to have the baby. I never misled you. I told you several times.'

She had, but he had thought she would come round— that she had come round.

'I need to get back before I'm too far down the road with this pregnancy, so I can start planning the exhibition.'

'The exhibition?' he echoed with disbelief. 'Can't you leave that to someone else?'

'No. You know how I feel about the museum and I thought you would be keen for me to get on with the work as we'd planned.'

'Without telling me first that you were going?'

'I knew you were busy today, so I was going to tell you tonight.'

'In bed or out of it?'

'That's not fair, Raffa. I was going to tell you as soon as I saw you. It was a last-minute thing—I had no idea your grandmother was going to London, and the connections to Skavanga are excellent from there.'

He was beyond fury, beyond words. He shook his head as he struggled for control. 'You could at least have done me the courtesy of speaking to me before leaving the island with our unborn child. But then I suppose you've got everything you want out of me now, so it's time for you to go—'

'No!' Leila's face was a mask of outrage as she interrupted him. 'That's never been the type of relationship we have. Please be reasonable, Raffa.'

'Reasonable?' What place did reason have to play where the birth of his child was concerned? 'You're not going anywhere, Leila.'

'Don't be ridiculous!' she said as he moved to bar the door. 'You can't stop me leaving. Short of locking me in and making sure I miss that flight, I'm going home tomorrow. It's time for me to leave. You won't share your hang-ups with me, so we've gone as far as we can. I told you everything, Raffa.' Looking disappointed in him, she shook her head. 'And you've told me precisely nothing. You want to control everything without giving me any reason for why you must do so—and if I can't understand you, what chance have we got? I wouldn't just walk out without saying anything. I was going to thank you before I left—'

'You were going to thank me?' he echoed, leaning back against the ancient door. 'Am I supposed to be grateful for that?'

But everything Leila said was right. He couldn't open up to anyone, not even Leila, but he had been utterly convinced that she would stay.

'Raffa, please,' she said, closing the lid of her suitcase. 'It's all arranged. My onward ticket's booked. It's not as if I'm disappearing as you and my brother so often do. You know where I am. You can come visit any time you want.'

Leila was dictating terms now? '*Dios*, Leila! You're having my baby. You can't just walk out like this.'

'Were you planning to hold me prisoner on the island until I gave birth?'

The silence hung between them and then she laughed without humour. 'You were,' she whispered incredulously.

'I only want to keep you safe.'

'There you go again—I don't understand why this obsession with keeping me safe when I'm just as safe in Skavanga. You can't micromanage the birth, as if it were a business, Raffa.'

Leila couldn't know the depth of his fears for her, and as he couldn't tell her they had reached stalemate.

'I'm leaving the country, Raffa,' she stated firmly. 'But I'll only be a plane ride away, so please don't be angry with me.'

'Am I to suppose my grandmother called you up out of the blue?'

'Well, yes, she did, actually.'

He had to confess, it would hardly be the first time his grandmother had acted impetuously. She was probably visiting her own doctor in London when she thought of Leila, and had wanted some company on the flight.

There was a wistful look in Leila's eyes that told him she wished things could be different, almost as if she wished he would beg her to stay. He had been so fixated on the birth, he hadn't given much thought to the future. He supposed now he had imagined Leila getting on with her life as he got on with his after the birth of their child. They would live separate lives, and only meet up when they handed their child over for a visit—

Dios! Just the thought of that made him sick. The idea of handing a child back and forth, like a parcel—

Leila's eyes were full of tears as if she was waiting for him to say something that would make things right between them, but his life had been built on objectivity, not emotion, and he didn't have any answers she'd want to hear.

'You always knew we had to get on with our lives at some point, Raffa. I haven't even had my first scan yet.'

'Well, you can have that here.'

'I've already booked one in Skavanga. I could send you a photograph.'

Shaking his head, he said a flat, 'No.' Why bother? What use was a photograph to him?

Leila deserved stability, security and a storybook ending with a man who could feel emotion. He couldn't offer her that. As always when emotions threatened, ice had already closed around his heart. And even if he let her go, he could still control every aspect of the birth, but from a distance.

'*Bon voyage,* Leila,' he said coolly. 'As you so rightly say, you'll only be a short plane ride away.'

CHAPTER ELEVEN

SHE HELD OUT until Raffa left the room and then she crumpled. So much for self-determination. Someone should have warned her how much it sucked. Did Britt feel like this after one of her storming tirades? Did Eva fold like a wilting leaf with ice flowing through her veins instead of blood? When her sisters acted steely, was it all a sham?

The temptation to return to being the quiet little mouse was overwhelming. She might have done, had it not been for the child growing inside her, the child who depended on her to get things right. There was never going to be a good time to leave Raffa. And she'd learned a lot while she'd been here. She'd changed, discovered her own seam of strength. Maybe it had always been there, but quietly.

Raffa, with all his talk of the 'top men for the job', wanting to control every element of the birth, had put everything in perspective for her. She had grown to love him, and now she couldn't love him more, but she had no expectation of him loving her back. She doubted Raffa even had the capacity to love. His reaction when she had offered to send him a photograph of the scan had been proof enough of that.

It was that thought that broke her, and, like a wounded

animal, she buried her head in her arms and bayed her frustration into the empty, uncaring room. But even that was an indulgence. She had to be strong for the baby, and so standing up she faced the brutal truth. Would an aristocrat like Don Rafael Leon seriously consider progressing a relationship with Leila Skavanga, a small-town girl who worked in a mine beyond the Arctic Circle, whose father had been a drunk and whose mother had been his punchbag?

The thought of her mother made her cry again. Be bold in all you do. Was she being bold, or was she being stubborn?

It wasn't always easy to be strong, Leila concluded, even with a baby to consider. There were times when she missed her mother with a huge aching pain, and this was one of those times, but she wasn't going to throw her mother's wishes to the four winds. She was going to take them and make them count for something. She would turn the Skavanga Diamond exhibition into a talking point around the world. And she would write Raffa a note before she left, setting him free, and at the same time promising not to cut him out of their baby's life. It had taken two to make this precious child, but she would bring it up, and she would give birth in Skavanga, without fuss or the 'best man for the job' standing over her.

At last the call connected. By which time he was almost jumping out of his skin with frustration. 'Grandmother. What the hell are you doing?'

'Why, Rafael,' his grandmother tempered, slowing down his heated oratory at a stroke. 'This must be a serious call for you to give me my Sunday title.'

'You know it's serious. How could you do this to me?'

'How could *I* do this to you, Rafael?' There was a pause. 'Maybe I'm saving you from yourself by taking Leila with me.'

He gave a short dismissive laugh. 'Destroying me would be closer to the truth. Don't you know how much it means to me to keep her here so I can supervise the birth?'

'Don't you know how much I love you, Rafael?'

He let the silence hang. 'You know I do,' he growled at last.

'Then trust me, Rafael. I do know what I'm doing.'

'I hope so.' It was a fight to keep the anger from his voice, but he had always respected his grandmother too much to lose control when he was speaking to her.

'I know you think you should be doing something more, Rafael, but you can't control everything.'

'I can try.'

'You certainly can't force Leila to obey you. She has a mind of her own, that one.'

'There's no need to sound quite so pleased about it.'

'If you trap a wild bird, Rafael, it will die.'

'And if you set it free?'

'Time will prove me right or wrong,' his grandmother insisted calmly. 'Well? Aren't you going to wish me *bon voyage,* grandson?'

Gritting his teeth he managed, 'Safe journey, and a speedy return home, Abuelita.'

Being on the private jet with Raffa's grandmother was informal and fun—or it could have been if the aircraft hadn't been taking Leila away from the man she loved.

'There's no shame in a little fear when the plane takes off,' Raffa's grandmother said briskly, handing over a wad of tissues.

Leila had no fear of flying. Her only fear was losing Raffa, who had brushed her off so easily.

'Better now?' the dowager enquired once they were airborne.

Tipping her head with a wry smile, Leila nodded. 'Much better, thank you.'

'We're survivors, you and I, Leila. Nothing gets us down for long. We're like corks that bob up again, and we learn from setbacks, don't we?'

Leila nodded wryly. 'Promise you'll come and see me in Skavanga when the baby's born.'

'Try and keep me away. But I'm going to ask something of you in return.'

'To visit you?' Leila guessed.

'Correct.' The old lady's gaze was unwavering as she offered Leila her hand to seal the pact.

'Deal,' Leila agreed softly.

'And now I'm going to tell you some things about Rafael that he would never tell you himself. I didn't tell you before because I've always kept my grandson's confidence, but I can't sit back and watch Rafael destroy the best thing that's ever happened to him—that's you and your baby, in case you're in any doubt, Leila.'

Deep down, Leila supposed she had always known that this particular old lady never did anything by chance, and the flight to London was the perfect opportunity for them to have a one-to-one.

'Rafael reminds me of his grandfather so much. Although—' The dowager made a whimsical gesture with her hands. 'Rafael has his reasons for being the way he is, while my husband had no excuse.'

'But you loved him?'

'I adored him,' Raffa's grandmother corrected her. 'Who wants a weak man? Not me. You were crying because of Rafael when we took off, and not some fear of flying.'

'I was very sad to leave the island,' Leila confessed guardedly.

'And that's not all,' the dowager said briskly. 'I don't think you're frightened of anything except your own heart, Leila Skavanga. You're certainly not frightened of flying, though you've got every reason to be after your parents' accident.'

'Strangely it's never affected me that way.'

'Because the crash was no accident?' the dowager suggested when Leila hesitated. 'The press suggested your father was drunk at the controls.'

The dowager's frankness was refreshing and it tempted Leila to unburden thoughts that had plagued her for years. 'Or maybe my mother seized control because she'd had enough.'

'And sent them both plummeting to their deaths.'

'Being controlled isn't pretty,' Leila agreed.

'But you would never allow yourself to be controlled by anyone. And if I tell you that Rafael's mother died giving birth to him, then perhaps you can understand his fears for you a little better.'

Oh, no. Oh, no. Oh, no.

'I had no idea.'

'And Rafael wouldn't want you to know. He wouldn't want to frighten you, so he would never tell you, which is why I wanted this opportunity to have you to myself. Your safety is driving him crazy, Leila. That's why Rafael feels he must control every aspect of this baby's birth.'

He found the note right away. Leila had left it on his pillow. He ground his jaw and seriously considered tear-ing it up. What could it tell him that he didn't already know? Leaning back against the wall, he opened the envelope. There was one sheet of paper inside. The short note might as well have begun 'Dear John'.

It was a polite, emotion-free deed of separation. It was a reasonable and considered application to remain friends. It was an offer of complete access to his child at any time of his choosing—providing that access took place in Skavanga. Leila didn't want anything from him—no child support, no help with housing, no money, nothing. Though she promised to keep him in the loop—so kind of her. Thanks to him and his excellent introduction to the diamond industry, she intended to pursue her studies and take a Masters degree in Gemology—in Skavanga, of course. It was at that point he ripped the note to shreds and tossed it in the bin. Leila had rocked his world with her abrupt departure. If it hadn't been for the baby—

He would never see her again?

But there was a baby, and that baby had to be born and he had to know Leila would come through that birth safely. It wasn't enough for him to write the cheques and pull the strings. He had to *know*. This was as much a part of his nature as stubbornness was part of Leila's character. He had to see for himself that she survived the birth, for as much as he resented the way Leila had cut herself free he would happily die rather than harm her in any way.

The dowager had fallen asleep, leaving Leila to mull over her incredible revelation. Knowing Raffa's mother had died in childbirth explained so much about him. Now she knew why he wanted to control the birth of their child. It wasn't to exert his authority over her, as she had supposed, but simply to keep her safe.

And what had she done?

She had cut all ties with him, leaving no loose ends. There was no way back. She had always believed a clean break was for the best, having been used to radical change in her life from a very young age. But had she tried to get to know him—really tried? She felt like curling into a cringing ball at the thought of how selfish she'd been.

'Have you, dear?'

Leila blinked, realising she must have spoken out loud. 'I'm afraid I've only been thinking about myself.'

'I've been saying the same thing to Rafael for years,' his grandmother remarked. 'If you ask me, it's time both of you took your blinkers off.'

It seemed so long since she had left the island, and her personal world had been spinning in the wrong direction ever since. Wrong, because it never brought her any closer to Raffa. As far as her work was concerned, it couldn't have been better. Preparing the site for the exhibition was going well, but there hadn't been a word from Raffa, who had thrown all his considerable resources behind Leila to make sure she had all the help she could possibly need for her work from his team. And why should there be any word from Raffa, when she had made it quite clear in her letter to him that it was over between them for good?

But now she'd had her scan she had to talk to him as a matter of urgency. She'd had some really big news. She'd tried all the various numbers she had been given for him, including his PA, who was cagey about Raffa's whereabouts, and even his grandmother. Sharif and

Roman might have been able to tell her, but she didn't want to get into the inevitable conversation with them, and so she called Britt.

'Who knows?' Britt said, yawning as if she had just woken up. 'We haven't heard from him.'

Leila could hear Sharif murmuring in the background and realised they must be in bed together. She couldn't get off the phone fast enough. She thought about ringing Eva, but didn't want to be subjected to the third degree.

What did Leila know about Raffa Leon? She didn't even know where he was, or how to contact him. How she longed to be in his arms now, confiding in him, but she'd made too good a job of driving him away.

'The babies are doing fine, thank you,' she informed the empty air. 'Our twins are doing fine, Raffa.'

To hell with control! To hell with all Leila's protestations that she was fine and could live without him, and her sisters' insistence that Leila needed space. He'd given her long enough and the birth of their child was imminent. He'd kept a watching brief on her from a distance. She attended check-ups regularly. She ate sensibly, worked reasonable hours and got plenty of rest. She was the model of a modern working mother-to-be. He should be satisfied with that, but he wasn't about to leave her to go through the birth alone.

'You're clear to go, Romeo-Lima-two-five-eight—'

'Roger, Control.' Opening the throttle on the twin engines, he released the brakes.

For a time he was content to let his spirit soar with the jet. Every second took him closer to Leila and the answers he could only find when they were together. She'd got under his skin. Leila Skavanga had invaded every part of him. Life was vivid Technicolor with her.

Without her it was a dull, stormy grey. Levelling off, he handed over the controls to his co-pilot.

'Coffee, Tyr?'

'No milk,' the powerfully built Viking reminded him.

Removing his headphones, he left the cockpit. Both he and Leila had secrets. His was possibly the hardest to keep. Leila's brother was back in her life. She just didn't know it yet, but it wasn't up to him to break the news. Tyr would let his sisters know he was back when he was ready.

The flight attendants jumped to attention as Raffa walked into the galley.

'I'll sort myself out,' he told them as politely as he could and they quickly made themselves scarce. It was a rare beast that challenged him when he was in this mood. Leila would challenge him, but Leila wasn't frightened of anyone.

He went through the mechanics of assembling two strong cups of coffee. Why the hell did he miss her so much? It wasn't as if Leila was easy. She was quiet but she challenged him constantly, and was possibly the strongest woman he had ever known.

And now it was coming up to Christmas and she shouldn't be on her own. Her sisters and their husbands were away for the holidays, and he couldn't bear to think of Leila alone.

With a shrug and a smile he reached for the satellite phone.

CHAPTER TWELVE

SHE WAS STILL working and intended to carry on until the museum closed its doors on Christmas Eve. She'd be back in the new year if she hadn't given birth by then.

She was all organised. The cards were written, the presents were wrapped, the fire was lit and the house was glowing. Christmas was going to be great. She was going to decorate the nursery over the holidays, and finish the baby shawl she had painstakingly knitted, unpicked and knitted again, until she got it—well, almost right. She had baked too, taking round little pies and cakes as gifts to her neighbours, so the house smelled great. The baby stuff was piled in a corner waiting to be set out in the nursery—the best part—the reward for all her labours. She only had a short time to go now. The doctor had said she might deliver early, as it was twins.

There was only one thing missing from her Christmas preparations, Leila reflected as she sat on the rug, hugging her knees in front of the fire, and that was this man… Picking up the newspaper, she stared at the ridiculously handsome face before reading the banner headline. Bite-sized pieces of the text jumped out at her: *Don Rafael Leon… Famous Spanish billionaire… Strikes gold again… Battles a sandstorm in Kareshi… Risking his life—*

Her heart stopped. Clenching the newspaper, she wished Raffa would stop risking his life. Why did he have to do that? Why couldn't he slow down for once?

Why couldn't he be here?

Why hadn't she heard from him? Rubbing her face on her hands, she thought back to how determined she'd been to handle this birth alone, and how reluctantly Raffa had granted her wish. Now she understood why he was so concerned and why he had his people watching out for her—her own doctor had told her about the regular calls from Raffa's doctor, taking the opportunity to reassure Leila that professional confidence between doctor and patient extended to everyone, even other doctors. Her doctor had even taken calls from Raffa, though he never left a number, but why would he, when Leila had told him in that letter not to get in touch?

That wretched letter! Why had she left it for him in the first place? To be fair? To be fair to Raffa? Sanctimonious twaddle! What was that about? What had she been thinking? Hormones had been thinking for her, obviously. Why couldn't he be here? Where was he? Was he even safe? Why did two of the best men in her life have to disappear? Was she jinxed?

She wanted to tell him she understood everything now. She wanted to hold him and be strong for him. Pressing her head into her knees, she fought back tears, knowing she had to be strong for their babies. Lifting her chin, she straightened out the newspaper and read on: *Raffa Leon, bringing back more fabulous gems to be set with the now famous Skavanga Diamonds.*

Raffa and his colleagues in the consortium had made Skavanga a household name. When she'd been on the island with him and had asked the secret of his success, he'd said good product and publicity, along with a unique selling point, adding that, yes, there were fabulous gems on show in his underground vaults, but his most valuable stock was kept in an underground cave guarded by gryphons and dragons...

The tears were back when she remembered how they'd laughed. They'd been in bed at the time—

No. Bed. Thoughts.

Not now. Not ever. Finished. Done with. Bed thoughts—specifically sex thoughts of any kind, especially those involving intimate moments between them—were absolutely forbidden. Raffa's humour and his tender asides—those were forbidden too. She had to stop thinking about him, or she'd never ease this ache inside her.

So, what was he doing for Christmas?

Leila stared round her cosy home. Would he be somewhere nice like this, or in some sterile hotel? With the glow of the fire, and the red ribbons and candles she had brought down from the box in the eaves, it looked so warm and welcoming. There was just one thing missing...

Oh, if this wasn't the biggest pity party of all time. She'd be dressing up in a red robe, sticking cotton wool to her cheeks and giving herself gifts out of a trash sack in a minute. She was well organised, with plenty of food. She was safe and warm. What more did she want?

Don't even think the name.

That lasted all of five seconds.

She'd posted Raffa's card early, along with a special card for his *abuelita*. She had kept Raffa's card carefully neutral. 'Wishing you a wonderful Christmas and the very best New Year ever. Leila x'

That wasn't thinking his name. That was running a mental checklist to make sure she hadn't left anyone off her list. She'd sent Raffa the type of card she would send to a close friend—a friend close enough not to need an update on her status, because he already knew enough about her life, and yet distant enough to suggest she was back in harness in her old life, and quite happily getting on with it.

Except for the yawning great crater in her chest where her heart used to be.

She wasn't going to think like that…

Was the house always this quiet?

She looked at her phone and then remembered she'd turned it off. Her sisters were driving her mad by email, saying it was too close to the birth of the baby and she should turn her phone on. But she didn't want to speak to anyone—unless that someone was Raffa. And as he wasn't about to call…

Glancing out of the window at the fat flakes of snow tumbling down, she smiled wistfully at the thought of Raffa becoming a local hero. He'd certainly helped to put Skavanga on the map again. The Skavanga Diamond brand was already famous across the world, and the people of Skavanga loved him for it.

The town had been failing for so long, with Britt battling tirelessly to keep everything afloat, and then the consortium came along, and now it was like Christmas every day. They'd all worked hard to make Skavanga a success. There was a café at the museum now, as well as a playground for the children, and film installations showing diamonds in production from rocks to sparkling gems…

Ho hum…

The fire crackled, the snow pattered lightly against the window. Now what should she do?

Oh, come on! She'd eaten supper. It was almost bed-time. Wasn't this the time she looked forward to the most? Not just for sleep and oblivion, and a chance to dream, but to get out her small hoard of baby stuff...to touch it, to fold it, to hold it to her face...

She could spend some time thinking about the twins before she went to bed. What could be better than that?

The twins Raffa didn't know about yet.

Hugging her enormous belly, Leila bit her lip anx-iously. Why couldn't anyone tell her where Raffa was? He had to be the most elusive man on the planet. Should she leave him to enjoy the festivities in peace? Or should she keep trying those numbers Britt had told her to try? She didn't want to bother her sisters again so close to Christmas. She looked at her phone. Small. Silent. Off. Described it to a tee.

But there was nothing to stop her trying those num-bers one more time. If Raffa was busy at least he'd know she'd been trying to get hold of him. Picking the phone up, she stared at it for a few tense seconds, and then, closing her eyes, she held down the button to turn it on—

And jumped when it rang immediately.

'Leila? Is that you?'

Raffa!

'Where the hell have you been, Leila?'

'Ha...aa...'

'Is that any type of answer?'

Paralysed with surprise, she could hardly speak. Hearing Raffa's voice had shocked her rigid. Hugging the phone so close to her face it must have left an imprint in her skin, she drank in the sound of his voice. He could have said anything— He could have ordered pizza and she would still have tears running down her face. Just to hear him... Just to know he was safe.

She had to pull the phone away from her ear for a moment to draw a deep, shuddering breath and compose herself, before she could manage a steady, 'Hello, Raffa... What a surprise...'

'If you say it's nice to hear from me, I'll find you and spank you, pregnant or not. Why have you had your phone turned off?'

'Erm...I couldn't sleep. So I turned it off and forgot to turn it on again.'

'I saw all your calls listed and was worried to death. I've been trying to call you non-stop.'

'Sorry...' She caressed the phone. He'd been trying to call her. Lovely phone. She'd never turn it off again. Ever.

'I spoke to your sisters, and all they'd say was you'd gone to ground, and that maybe you needed some space. The way they said it made it sound like space from me, so...'

'So you were speaking to Eva, I'm guessing,' Leila supplied as her head began to clear.

'Maybe,' Raffa agreed wryly.

He didn't want to get her sister into trouble. That was nice.

'And did you? Do you?' he pressed urgently. 'Need space, I mean. Talk to me, Leila. I need to hear your voice.'

Raffa needed to hear her voice. She looked around the room as if the furniture would be good enough to confirm that she was actually awake and this wasn't one of her nightly Raffa dreams. 'I'm fine now. I don't need space now,' she added in case he thought he should ring off. Better release her death grip on the phone before her fingers dropped off. She couldn't hold him on the line by strangling the receiver.

'So you're well, Leila?'

She was now with Raffa's voice rolling over her like honey. 'Quite well, thank you.'

'Quite well.' He laughed at the prim expression. 'Your doctor wouldn't tell me anything—apart from the fact that I shouldn't worry as you were in good health and the pregnancy was progressing as planned.'

'Doctor-patient confidentiality,' she agreed, silently thanking her lucky stars that Raffa hadn't heard the news about their twins yet. She couldn't bear him to hear that from anyone else. And she wasn't about to tell him over the phone. 'So, where are you now?'

'Outside your door.'

What?

'Did you hear me, Leila?'

'You're as bad as my brother.' She flared as her heart went crazy. When Tyr disappeared they never knew when he was coming back. 'Sorry…' She composed herself—just about. 'I heard you.'

'Well? Aren't you going to let me in?'

Like a runner off the blocks she catapulted into action, or rather she used her unusual weight distribution as leverage to stumble forward and up, slowly straightening until she was upright. Turning full circle, which was harder than it sounded when your belly took up half the room, she hardly knew where to begin. Heading for the door by a circuitous route so she could plump cushions and straighten throws as she went, she couldn't help wonder how a wood shack would stand up to a castle.

Cosy. It was cosy. And she loved it and lived in every inch of it, that was how.

The door was the only thing between them now. She could sense Raffa standing behind it as she stretched out her hand and wrapped it around the handle. Taking one steadying breath, she flung the door wide.

He looked amazing.

Never mind that. Forget the impulse to fling herself into his arms with relief. Raffa had been out of contact for months. The right thing to do was to stand back and be cool with him—

To hell with that!

Flinging her arms around his neck, she hugged him as if her life depended on it. 'Raffa!' The air was cold and frosty, and his stubble-roughened cheek was cold, but he smelled warm and delicious, and he was every bit as solid and fabulous as she remembered. 'How wonderful to see you.'

'You too, Leila,' he said quietly.

Untangling herself, she stood back, feeling rather stupid. That was a ridiculous greeting to give someone she hadn't seen for months, and now she couldn't gauge Raffa's reaction to her overly excited puppy act. He was taking his time to look her up and down as her cheeks fired with embarrassment. 'Won't you come in? Please, come in out of the cold…' And give me chance to compose myself, she thought as she turned her back on him.

Closing the door once Raffa was inside, she turned around. Muffled up in a heavy dark jacket and jeans, he looked insanely handsome. And she loved him so much that was crazy too, especially as her love had no basis in hope or reality. She couldn't help herself. She was nuts about him. And would have to hide it, if this wasn't going to be the most embarrassing encounter of all time.

'Nice,' he said, glancing round the cabin.

There was genuine warmth in his voice and she relaxed a little, enough to tell him, 'The cabin has been in our family for generations.'

'You're very lucky, Leila—to have such a history. And such a strong bond with a place.'

Unlike Raffa, she thought, remembering what his grandmother had told her about his youth. 'Yes, I am,' she agreed as he continued to look around.

What a lot of space he took up, and the little that was left was filled with his energy. She'd never think of the cabin the same way again, she realised as Raffa absent-mindedly shrugged off his jacket in response to the cosy heat. She took it from him. It was still warm from his body and she tucked her hands inside it as she went to hang it up.

'When you said you lived in a cabin, I had no idea what to expect,' he admitted, 'but you've made such a lovely home here. And the surroundings... The lake, the trees, the mountains, the drive here—it's all spectacular.' The sexy mouth pressed down as he shrugged. 'No wonder you never want to leave Skavanga.'

Never leaving Skavanga suddenly seemed an unreasonable penalty for leaving the rest of the world and Raffa Leon behind. 'Skavanga's lovely, but it's nice to get away from here too.'

'To the island?'

'Your island is beautiful, Raffa.'

'Yes, it is.'

His gaze lingered, warming her face. It was as if they were both reading each other, searching for clues, looking for changes. Just hearing Raffa's voice in her home was like having the most beautiful soundtrack to a romantic film playing. It wasn't so much the words he used, but the timbre, the pitch—

And was this a good idea? she wondered as they continued to stare at each other. There was so much to catch up on, so much to work through.

'Sit, Leila. You look tired.'

She sank into a chair with relief, while Raffa went to examine some of the old sepia prints on the wall. Just seeing him had exhausted her. Emotional overload, she reasoned, combined with pregnancy hormones on red alert.

'We used to come here for holidays with our grand-parents,' she explained as he moved down the row of photographs, scrutinising each one in turn. 'This was the first prospectors' hut, but we've improved the cabin over the years—'

She stopped as Raffa flashed an amused glance at her. 'So you have inside facilities now?'

'Can you seriously imagine Britt using a bucket?'

They both laughed and the tension eased a little. Maybe this visit would turn out okay after all.

'As the mine took off a lot of other people started to build cabins in the vicinity,' she explained as Raffa peered out of the window.

'Sorry—I'm expecting a van to turn up, and I don't want to keep the men waiting outside in the cold.'

'A van?'

'With supplies.'

'Oh...'

Her brain refused to compute this, but she must have frowned, because Raffa shrugged. 'If you don't want them, send them back. But there's food too, so let's have supper first.'

She smiled. 'You're hungry.'

'No time to eat,' he confirmed. 'Long flight, long drive, but worth it.'

As Raffa fell silent she realised he was trying to see the newspaper she'd been so avidly reading with his pho-tograph prominently displayed. She should have closed it up before she opened the door and heeled it under the seat now. 'Would you like to sit down?'

'Why? Do I make the place look untidy?' he suggested, turning to shoot a wry smile at her.

No. You make it seem small.

Pulling back from the window, Raffa turned to face her, and, leaning back against the wall with his arms folded across his chest, he smiled, the flash of strong white teeth showing in stark contrast to his burnished skin. 'It's good to see you again, Leila.'

'You've been in the desert—'

Raffa waved an admonishing finger at her. 'I told you no questions.'

'Not where Tyr's concerned,' Leila agreed. 'So have you two been working together?'

'Tyr will tell you when he's ready to tell you. So this is the original prospector?' he said, changing the subject as he turned to examine one of the framed photographs on the wall. 'This one here?'

Like Tyr, Raffa was expert at keeping a confidence, Leila realised. She'd get no more out of him. 'That's right. That's my ancestor, the first Skavanga.'

'You don't look a bit like him.'

'I decided in the end that a beard doesn't suit me.'

His cheek creased in a smile. 'You should have this shot hanging in the museum.'

'I'm ahead of you, Señor Leon. A copy's already hanging in the entrance hall.'

'I might have known it, Ms Efficiency.'

She blushed as Raffa's gaze swept her belly. 'How many months are you now, Leila?'

'A month or so to go.' This conversation was so back to front. Her brain was sluggish thanks to pregnancy hormones and still she hadn't got round to telling him about the twins.

'I thought you had longer than that. By my calculations—'

'Your calculations are off.'

'Oh?'

'There are things you couldn't possibly know about, Raffa.'

'Such as?'

Even with that suspicious look on his face Raffa made her heart turn over. Taking a deep breath, she told him, 'Such as, I'm having twins.'

'Twins?' Raffa's voice dropped an octave, and for once he seemed at a loss. Dipping his head, he said, 'Two babies?'

'That is the usual count,' she confirmed, trying to appear light-hearted as she waited for his reaction. Double the expected tally could hardly light up the heart of a man who didn't want children.

Raffa's face lit, then darkened dramatically. He might have frightened her if she hadn't known why. His surprise at what she'd told him had been replaced in an instant by dread at the thought of her giving birth to two babies.

'Your grandmother explained why you feel the way you do,' she said quickly. 'Please don't be angry with her, Raffa,' she added as he glanced at her. 'She only did it because she loves you, and because she knows I love you too.'

There. She'd said it. Her feelings were laid bare before him for him to stamp on if he chose to, but this was too important for her to hold anything back.

Raffa's face revealed nothing. Why should it when he had been hiding his feelings all his life, and when she had brought up a past he would rather forget? 'Your grandmother told me that your mother died giving birth to you,' she said carefully, feeling it was better to get everything out in the open now. 'Apart from your feelings when you were old enough to understand what had happened, she also told me that your father and siblings never allowed you to forget what had happened...'

Reaching out when he still remained silent, she let her hand fall back. Raffa wasn't ready for sympathy. He never had been. That was why he held his feelings close and why he repelled others, especially those with a claim on his emotions.

'Twins,' he murmured. His eyes cleared as he looked at her. 'Really?'

'Really.' She couldn't tell what he was thinking, but at least he was thinking, rather than expressing some knee-jerk reaction. She'd give him more time. She'd give him all the time he needed. 'I haven't asked you if you'd like something to eat or drink,' she said, striving for normality.

'Sorry, Leila— Have to go. The van's just arrived. You stay where you are.' Raffa's hand on her shoulder was gentle and insistent. Crossing the small room, he shrugged on his jacket. 'Baby supplies.' He frowned, as if realising he would have to rethink his plans completely. 'I didn't know how you'd be fixed, so, like I said, I brought food too. We can have a picnic.'

'Sounds like fun.' Or it might have been if Raffa hadn't been so distant.

His mind was fixed on other things. He was still getting over the shock, she reasoned. And who could blame him?

'Relax, Leila. There's no agenda here. Just two friends playing catch-up.'

Of course. She sank back. Hopes crushed. She was so emotional at the moment there was no grey, only black and white. Maybe he didn't want two babies. Raffa hadn't exactly enlisted the town band to herald the first. Why couldn't she tap into calm Leila, the girl who was such a thoughtful, sensible mouse? Why was she sitting here with her heart thumping and her thoughts flying in every direction?

She started with alarm when the door opened and Raffa came in carrying a huge carton. 'No, you stay there,' he insisted when she moved to help him. 'I can manage.'

He didn't want any involvement, she reflected as she hauled herself out of her chair. Going to stare out of the window, she watched him directing the men. After so long apart every glimpse was a gift. And though she had categorically stated she didn't want anything from Raffa, and that she didn't need anything, it made her heart soar to think he'd gone shopping for her.

And she should make him feel welcome in return.

Lumbering into action, she fetched dishes from the cupboard, and soup and salad from the fridge, just in time before he blazed back into the house.

'Coffee on?'

'Yes,' she murmured, belatedly accepting in some part of her pregnancy-scrambled brain that she would have to turn the coffee machine on for coffee to happen. And now the sheer size of Raffa dominating her compact living space—his energy, the sheer power blazing off him—

'Here, let me get that for you—' Reaching across, he took charge of coffee production, and when he pulled back he brushed her body so that now her hands were shaking.

'I've got something to show you,' she blurted.

'Oh?'

Raffa was too busy making coffee to pay much attention.

'Yes...' She looked at him hopefully.

'Good.'

Tears pricked her eyes. She had to remind herself that he didn't have a clue what she was talking about, and that the pregnancy was making her overly emotional. But if he could only show some interest—give some reaction—

It might help if you actually showed him what you're talking about?

Okay, she would. And if he was still aloof and distant when she showed him, at least that was proof she was on her own. And wasn't that what she had always wanted? The babies without the man? Remember that?

What a sad idea that seemed now.

'You all right?' he asked with concern as she sucked in a fast breath in lieu of a sob.

'Yes,' she said, more to convince herself than Raffa.

'Good. Then I'll go and help the men get the rest of the stuff out of the van, so they can get off. You can handle the rest of this? Yes?' he pressed.

'Yes,' she said on autopilot.

It wasn't just food Raffa had brought with him—or even one box of supplies. It was a vanload of baby equipment: baby clothes, toys, a stroller, a Moses basket, a cot, a playpen—the last two flat-packed, requiring assembly, so the last items to make it into the house, courtesy of Raffa and two burly men from the store, were a toolkit, a stack of decorating sheets and a workbench.

'Raffa, please... No more. Stop. It's too much. I can't let you do this—'

'Do what?' he said, paying off the men with a generous tip as he turned to stare at her. 'There's everything you could possibly need—'

'That's just it.'

'What is?' he demanded impatiently.

'I don't need anything.'

'Oh, not that again. You clearly do.' Raffa's gaze swept the room. 'In fact, I'll have to get more stuff on order. Come on, Leila,' he insisted when she began to protest. 'How are you going to hoist a couple of cots up the stairs in your condition?'

'I'll get them delivered and pay to have them assembled, if I have to.'

'And the playpen?'

'I don't need one yet. And when I do I'll assemble it with the instruction sheet laid out in front of me.'

Raffa wasn't even listening. And before she knew it they were staring at each other daggers drawn, arguing about who was in control. 'You can't just walk in here and take over, Raffa. This is my house, my pregnancy—'

'And our children. Never mistake me for a man who could be satisfied with making the odd guest appearance on significant days after the birth, Leila. I'm going to be involved from day one, so get used to it. I'm not trying to compete with any preparations you've made. These are our children. Aren't I entitled to be excited too?'

Raffa, excited? You wouldn't know it from his face. As always, he was perfectly under control. 'Yes, of course you are. And if you'll just stop pacing for a moment, there's something I really want to show you.'

CHAPTER THIRTEEN

'What is it, Leila? What are you going to show me?'

'I wanted to send it to you,' she said as she heaved herself up. 'But you're as good at disappearing as Tyr, and I didn't know when you'd get it—if you'd get it. And I couldn't risk it getting lost in a heap of mail on your desk.'

'Like your email.'

'Like my email,' she confirmed dryly.

'So, what is it? What are we talking about?'

Shrugging her shoulders, she smiled. 'Wait and see.'

He glanced at Leila's swollen stomach as she made her way across the room to a bureau and felt his heart clench. 'You'll need a bigger house,' he murmured, thinking out loud as she rooted through some papers. 'I'll have to order twice as much equipment—'

'I don't need anything, Raffa.'

'You'll trip over that pride of yours one day, Leila. You do need things. Let me help you. These babies are my responsibility too.'

She shrugged and appeared to consider this, but then she turned to him and her face was as open as he remembered when they'd first met. 'I panicked when no one would put me in touch with you—' She was holding something behind her back. 'I was worried about you,

Raffa. I don't think you or Tyr has the slightest idea how many people care about you, or how they worry when you go off radar. For God's sake,' she exclaimed, tears welling in her eyes, 'I've already lost a brother. Do you seriously think I could bear to lose you?'

'You haven't lost Tyr, and you haven't lost me, Leila. I could never reach you when I rang, and I tried I don't know how many times.'

She thought about this for a moment. 'Eva must have told Reception not to put you through. It's the type of thing she does when she's trying to protect me and doesn't realise she's only making things worse. But you're right. I should have tried harder— I should have found some way to tell you—'

'No. I'm just as much to blame,' he agreed. 'Now, show me what you've got behind your back.'

She handed him an envelope.

'What's this?' His guts twisted as he remembered the last time he'd read a letter from Leila.

'I started to write to you, then realised that was about as pointless as putting a letter up the chimney for Santa. And if I sent it to the office, I didn't want it lying forgotten on your desk. It's too important for that. Why don't you open it, Raffa? Please…'

Opening the envelope, he pulled out a small black-and-white photograph. He stared at it in silence. It was an image from the latest scan. Twins. Two little people…one blowing bubbles, while the other sucked his or her thumb.

'Our babies, Raffa,' Leila said gently. 'Your children… and mine.'

Wave after wave of emotion crashed over him. Feelings he'd bottled up for years ran riot inside him. Tears sprang to his eyes, and he had never cried. He could never have predicted that seeing his children would affect him like this.

'Raffa…'

He couldn't speak yet. He couldn't think coherently. All he wanted to do was to stare at the image on the tiny piece of paper.

'Please don't disappear again, Raffa. I was so frightened for you.'

Still holding the scan, he turned slowly to look at Leila. He doubted he could ever bear to be parted from this small piece of evidence, let alone give it back to her.

'Raffa?' she said again.

Shaking himself round, he went to kneel at her feet, and, taking her hands in his, he held them tightly. 'Leila… Look at me. I'm so sorry. I should never have left you. I should never have listened to you and your ridiculous notion that you needed space, or to my own stubborn belief that who I am is cast in stone. We're both far too stubborn, you and I.'

A small smile crept onto her face. 'How could I have contacted you if I needed you? Never do that to me again, Raffa. We're not alone any more. We have these two to think about.'

As she spoke Leila stroked her hand over the curve of her belly, and as his grip tightened on the scan he knew his life had changed for ever. And for the better by far.

She laughed softly. 'It would probably be more convenient for everyone if I were still Leila the peacemaker, the sister who goes along with what everyone else wants for the sake of a quiet life—'

'Strange. I've never seen you like that, Leila—'

She huffed with amusement. 'Whether you have or not, I can't be like that ever again, because I'm going to be a mother and I've got these two to think about.'

Her face lit up. 'Two babies at one time! Who'd have thought it?'

'I would. And you've never been the mouse you think you are. Your sisters always turn to you for advice—can't you see that? They trust you to be cool and calm when you consider a problem.'

'Like now?' she said dryly.

'There's a difference between keeping your voice down, and being quiet and retiring, and the fact you don't shout the odds as loudly as your sisters doesn't mean you can't be heard. In fact, yours is the voice we all remember.'

Wrapping his arms around her, he drew Leila close so he could rest his face against her belly. His heart filled with love the moment he felt movement beneath him. It made him laugh; it made him smile. It was a miracle and he was part of it. Even more of a miracle was the fact that the babies and Leila had allowed him to feel after so many years of denying that pleasure. Thanks to them he could let loose his emotions and experience every life-changing moment to the full from now on. Reaching up, he drew Leila into his arms and kissed her, but what began as a tender expression of his love for Leila, and for their children, soon grew in passion. 'I'll never leave you again,' he pledged fiercely.

'Even if I want you to?' she challenged with a smile against his mouth.

'Even then.'

'Except for when you have to be away on business,' she guessed.

'I've only got a couple of appointments before Christmas and then I'm going to devote myself to you and the babies.'

'Really?'

'Give me your shopping list,' Raffa murmured.

'Most of what I want can be found right here,' she whispered. 'But if you're serious…'

'Absolutely.'

She could taste her tears on Raffa's mouth, but she could see her happiness reflected in his eyes. Like him, she had smothered her emotions, fearing them, but they had freed each other and she felt a settling and a peace inside her that she had never known before.

'I've never seen you like this,' Raffa said as she sniffed and laughed.

'You've never seen me this pregnant before.'

Raffa's sexy mouth slanted in a smile that warmed her through. 'I must admit two babies does account for some extra hormonal activity.'

Leila was just content to relish the strength of his arms and the sense of being safe.

'It's so good to be home finally, Leila.'

'And so surprising to want both the man and the baby,' she teased Raffa gently as he rested his brow against hers.

'Babies,' he reminded her wryly. 'What?' he queried lazily, brushing her lips with his.

'I thought we were going to have something to eat?'

'We are,' he confirmed. 'But not yet.'

'How am I supposed to resist you?'

'You're not.'

She held him off for a moment with both hands flat against his chest. 'Seriously. How can it ever work between us, Raffa, when we're worlds apart?'

'We're worlds colliding,' he argued, still teasing her lips with his.

'Why won't you admit I'm right?'

'Because I'm always right.'

She gave a small growl of warning to this, which made him smile. Leila was a passionate mother-to-be, high on hormones, which made her more beautiful than ever to him. She was like a lioness that, having tested her boundaries, had found them infinite, and had made the leap to freedom from a self-imposed cage. Quiet Leila had been temptation enough for him, but this new, bold version of the same woman was more than enough for him.

'You'll be a wonderful mother, Leila, but right now that's not uppermost in my mind.'

'How can you want me when I'm heavily pregnant, wearing my brother's cast-off work shirt?'

Her mention of Tyr threw him for a moment, and he longed to put her mind at rest, but a pledge was a pledge, and his honour was non-negotiable too.

'On you it could only be high fashion,' he teased, drawing a veil over the confidence he had sworn to keep for Tyr.

His body ached for Leila, and when he kissed her he felt a tremor of need run through her. Drawing back, he tested his theory. 'Still mad for sex?'

'What sort of question is that, Raffa? Of course I am.'

Losing no more time, he swung Leila into his arms. 'Your bedroom?'

'Under the eaves.'

'Perfect.'

It was perfect. Leila's bedroom was a warm, safe nest. If only he'd been able to think of her here while he'd been away, he wouldn't have worried about her half as much. No wonder she had wanted to come home to Skavanga. With the snow tumbling down outside the big windows that framed the lake, the mountains and the heavily snow-laden trees, it was paradise outside, and paradise inside. This was one haven he would never want to leave.

'Watch out! The room's too small for you,' she exclaimed as he ducked his head to avoid a beam.

'The room's perfect for me, Leila,' he said as he lowered her carefully onto the bed, kicked off his boots and lay down beside her.

'Mind reading's never been one of my many skills, but I do have others,' she said, toying with the buttons on his shirt.

'I remember them well,' he said as he started to undress her.

'Why are you smiling as you kiss me, Raffa?'

'You taste so good.'

'Anxiety and pregnancy taste good to you?'

'What are you anxious about, Leila?'

'That I can still do this—I mean, with this mega-sized bump.'

'We'll find a way,' he promised, kissing his way from her neck to her breasts. 'I was right—no anxiety here,' he confirmed, circling her nipples with his tongue before tugging on them gently.

'They're bigger.'

'They're lush and full and beautiful. Every part of you—'

'Is pregnant,' she said.

'Like I haven't noticed?' he murmured contentedly, kissing his way down to her belly.

'Will you stop that? I'm ugly—'

'A pregnant woman could never be called ugly. And you are particularly beautiful,' he insisted, nudging his way between her thighs.

'You can't—'

'I think you'll find I can...'

'Oh, yes… Oh, Raffa… Please—'

'Don't stop?' he queried with amusement, lifting his head. 'I've got no intention of stopping. You taste too good to stop—'

'Oh… I— Now! I can't hold on,' she wailed, lacing her fingers through his hair to keep him close.

'Let it go, baby— Just let it go—' He held her firmly. His tongue did the rest.

'That was amazing,' she managed, still convulsing as he kept her going with his hand.

'More?' he suggested.

'A lot more…'

'You've been missing this, I think,' he murmured, turning her so that now Leila had her back to him.

'So much—'

He laughed as he curled his body round her. 'Hang on,' he whispered, lifting her leg over his.

'How long do I have to hold on?' She gasped as he found her with his hand. 'I'm not sure I can—'

'Any time you like—'

She screamed her next release before he had even finished the sentence. He was gentle as he entered her—so gentle. It was good for him this way—like all the best sensations in the world woven together. Leila had curled up to allow him the best possible access and she was so ready for him—so warm, so tight, so wet. 'Tell me if I'm hurting you.'

'I'll tell you if you stop,' she growled.

He laughed softly, while Leila gasped out loud. He rocked into her gently, at the same time sheathing himself completely, maintaining the same steady rhythm with his hand while she thrust backwards onto him, dictating both the pace and force he was using. It wasn't long before she was on the edge again. He could feel the sudden tensing in her body—the awareness shimmering through her—the realisation that pleasure was on its way.

'Enjoy, baby,' he murmured. The slightest adjustment to the pressure and speed at which his finger was working was all it took to make it impossible for her to hold on, and as she let go with a series of wild cries of relief he increased the force and pace of his thrusts to prolong her pleasure for as long as he could.

They slept wrapped in each other's arms. Their discussion did not continue, as Leila had insisted it must do, straight after lovemaking—not that night, nor the next morning, or the next.

They lived the dream—the dream for both of them. Closeness without complications—without thought for the future. They were pushing difficult decisions aside, like where to live, and how to combine their two very different lives. They were together and that was all that mattered. They were getting to know each other better too. They were growing closer because of the sex, whereas in the past, sex had been an end in itself.

They padded around barefoot—sometimes even naked. Leila would cook something on the stove while he stood behind her with his hands loosely linked around her belly. Her calm essence healed him, while the food she cooked fuelled their lust. They took meals to bed—left others forgotten to grow cold as they feasted on each other.

He couldn't remember a time when he had ever been so happy, or so relaxed. And he couldn't bear to let this go. He couldn't envisage a time without Leila. He wasn't prepared to contemplate a future without her. But this timeless idyll had to end. They both knew it. He still had business commitments to fit in before everything closed down for Christmas, while Leila had insisted on working until the very last minute, and so, with less than a week to go before Christmas Day, he dropped her off at the mining museum on his way to the airport.

'We'll talk when I get back from New York. There's plenty of time,' he said confidently. 'The babies aren't due yet, so—'

'Plenty of time,' Leila confirmed, standing on tiptoe to kiss him goodbye.

If this past week of indulging themselves had achieved anything, it was to establish a new level of trust between them. They could do this. They were both strong individuals who could handle a long-distance relationship, and they would make sure their children didn't suffer because of it.

At least that was how he felt until he woke up one morning in an anonymous hotel somewhere in the world to find it was snowing, which reminded him of Skavanga. He could have been anywhere in the world. A luxury hotel was a luxury hotel and when he was away from Leila everywhere looked the same to him. He found himself longing for a small wood cabin on the shores of a lake, and a woman who for him had no equal. His meetings were over and all he could think about was Leila facing the run-up to their twins' birth on her own. It didn't have to be this way—for either of them.

He'd never had so much fun shopping. He'd never had fun shopping. It wasn't the type of thing he did, but today was different, and wherever he went his happiness was infectious. He had discounts pushed on him, encouraging him to buy ten times more than he had intended. He got back to the hotel, filed a flight plan for Skavanga and was airborne by late afternoon. He rented a Jeep at the airport and drove out to the cabin. He hadn't called Leila.

He hadn't warned her he was coming back. The feelings inside him didn't allow for half measures. This was either the biggest surprise she'd ever had or it was a dud.

She heard the engine and was hanging out of an upstairs window when he arrived. 'Raffa?' She sounded ecstatic. 'What are you doing?'

'Visiting a friend,' he called up, holding his feelings of elation on the shortest rein. 'I hope that friend hasn't been up a stepladder, decorating?' He tried and failed to adopt a stern tone. He was just so excited to see her—to hold her—to kiss her again.

'Your friend's been getting the nursery ready. What do you think?' She glanced over her shoulder, where he could see a set of ladders with tins of paint jostling for position on the top step.

'I think I'll have to paddle her backside, if that's what my friend's been up to—'

'Excellent,' she called down. 'Can't wait. The door's open—let yourself in.'

'You don't even lock the door round here?'

'I don't have too many barbarians calling—you're the first.'

She flew into his arms before he even had chance to step inside the house. 'Did you run down those stairs?' he demanded sternly, holding Leila at arm's length so he could stare into her eyes.

'No, I waddled down them—'

He didn't care how she got down the stairs, just that she had got down them safely and was in his arms again. Dragging her close, he kissed her. If this was what it felt like to come home, he was coming home every day from now on.

'I've missed you so much,' she exclaimed, searching his eyes as she gripped him as if her life depended on it.

'I've only been away a few days—'

'Too long,' she interrupted him fiercely, resting her cheek against his heavy jacket.

'Come on,' he said, wrapping her inside the jacket. 'Let's go inside before you catch cold. It's freezing out here.'

'You think?' she demanded cheekily, staring up at him. 'I'm really hot.'

'So you are.' He acted surprised, and then dragged her close as he ushered the woman he loved into the house.

CHAPTER FOURTEEN

'NO. YOU DON'T do anything, Leila. This is a time for you to rest, so I do it all,' he insisted, having stripped down to his top and jeans after bringing all his booty into the open-plan living room.

'You do it all?' Leila demanded cheekily as he rifled through the bags. 'Haven't we been here before?'

'But never at the cooker—'

She laughed. 'Can you cook?' she demanded, planting her hands on her hips.

'I can,' he said as he slammed a cookery book written by a hot chef on the scrubbed pine table. 'All I have to be able to do is read and keep a handle on the time.'

'Multitasking?' She looked dubious.

'I'm not your typical man—remember?'

She laughed. 'So you're definitely promising something more than tins and fries?'

'No tins. No fries,' he confirmed. 'Just really great organic food direct from the market for the mother-to-be—'

'And you're going to do *everything* for me?' Leila confirmed as if she needed this in writing before he stood a chance of making her believe him.

'*Señorita*—' He made her a mock bow. 'I'm going to make Christmas for you.'

'And what do I have to do?' She lifted a brow.

'You have to stand there and look pretty—'

'Pretty fat? Pretty awful?'

'Pretty pregnant,' he argued, dragging her into his arms. 'And you've got paint on your nose,' he murmured, brushing her lips with his.

'Sorry—'

'Don't be.' He held her at arm's length. 'Have you been eating while I've been away?' She looked pale, he thought.

'Of course I have.'

'Not convinced, Leila. But I'm going to make it right. Break out the beer for me, the juice for you—'

'And you'll get cooking?' Her smile lit up her face. 'This I have to see.'

His heart soared as she laughed. 'This you're going to see, *señorita*. And while we're on the subject of making Christmas—you haven't done too badly yourself. You've added some more decorations.'

'Do you like it?' she said, glancing round at the traditional Scandinavian ornaments. 'I haven't overdone it?'

'Are you kidding?' He grinned. 'Christmas can never be overdone.'

There was a big pine tree festooned with tiny bells and flags to one side of the crackling fire, and while many of the decorations appeared to be recently homemade, others were a bit battered, and obviously much loved after many outings. There was a lot of red and white fabric, which looked great against the pine walls of the cabin. The hems of the curtains, the cushions, the throws, were all heavily embroidered with dainty, though intricate, cross-stitch.

'My grandmother's work,' Leila explained, seeing

him looking at it. 'They don't come out very often, but I changed them especially for you.'

There were hearts and bells and Santa and Mrs Claus on the window ledges, and on the table an arrangement of candles, moss and berries. It was a homely setting and one that warmed him through. 'This is quite something to live up to,' he observed as he rolled up his sleeves. 'I'd better get cooking—'

'Yes, you better had. Would you like a glass of egg-nog to go with that beer?'

'I think I should keep a clear head, don't you?'

Before she could answer him, he dragged her into his arms. 'Happy Christmas, Leila Skavanga. Do you have any idea how much I love you?'

'You love me?'

'Yes, I do. Of course I do!'

She smiled cheekily at him. 'Then I hope you can prove it again and again.'

'In so many ways,' he promised softly. Staring deep into Leila's eyes, he sank into her calm, loving expression. He'd missed her so much.

'Your last Christmas without babies,' he commented wryly, pulling back to start cooking. 'Make the most of it—it's sleepless nights from here on in.'

'I can't wait.'

'It will be hard work.'

'I'm looking forward to that too.'

And he wanted to be part of it—now more than ever.

He surprised himself with the array of tempting dishes he produced, and there was Christmas Day to come yet. 'Who knows what miracles I can conjure up, now I've hit my stride.'

'Modest as always, Raffa—but I have to admit, this is delicious.' Leila laughed as she tucked in.

He hummed and adopted a thoughtful look. 'Maybe I should take cooking up as a profession?'

Cocking her head to one side, Leila disagreed with this proposition. 'You can't do that. We need you down at the mine.'

'Then I'll take over the café.'

'Oh, no, you won't.' She worked a frown. 'Stealing my customers from the museum? We'd never get the women out of there if you were running it.'

'And while we're on the subject of *your* museum, Señorita Skavanga,' he interrupted, seizing his chance. 'You have to stop working there soon.'

'When the babies come, I'll stop.'

'Take care you don't give birth during one of the tours. It would give a whole new meaning to "If you'd like to follow me…"'

'Bet no one would take me up on that one.'

'Here—Leila. Taste.'

'Hmm—delicious,' she exclaimed, but quickly returned to her chosen subject. 'I'll know when it's right to stop working, Raffa. I'm a good couple of weeks away.'

'Don't I have any say in this? Oh, yeah, wait a moment, I do,' he drawled as Leila tipped up her chin to challenge him. 'And if I say you stop work right after we celebrate Christmas, so you can put your feet up over New Year—'

'You've got it all worked out, haven't you, Raffa?'

Bringing their plates to the table, he laid them down with a flourish. 'I usually do—'

'And so do I,' Leila assured him, her lips set in a stubborn line. 'And I am going to stop work when my body tells me it's time to stop work, and not a moment sooner.'

'Are we playing whose will is stronger?' he suggested as he spooned some of the deliciously aromatic paella onto her plate.

'That's easy—I win,' she assured him. 'This is delicious, by the way.'

'So you accept I can multitask?'

'I accept you're an exceptional man, Señor Leon—but that doesn't mean I have to do everything you say—'

'In bed or out of it?'

'That's a loaded question from a very bad man.'

'Yes, it is,' he agreed. 'More paella?'

'I could never get enough of this.'

'Excellent—fill your mouth and be quiet for a second, because I've got a very important question to ask you.'

'What are you doing on your knees? Did I drop some food on the floor?'

'Señorita Skavanga…Leila…will you do me the honour of agreeing to become my wife?'

She froze and stared at him. And then had to chew double fast and swallow before she could exclaim, 'Are you serious?'

'Would I be down here on the floor for any other reason?'

'It does seem unlikely,' she agreed, shooting him a wicked look. Then sliding off the stool, she joined him on the floor, kneeling in front of him, which was no small feat in Leila's condition. Linking fingers with him, she stared into his eyes. 'Raffa Leon, will you do me the honour of becoming my husband?'

'In the interest of harmony and equality? Yes.'

'I love you very much,' she whispered as he kissed her hands.

'And I love you, Leila Skavanga.' Leaning very far forward indeed so he could reach past the bump, he kissed the woman he loved again…and again.

EPILOGUE

It started without warning. One minute Leila was sitting across from him telling him some crazy anecdote from her childhood, and the next her face was frozen with shock.

'Leila?' He was out of his seat and round her side of the table in a heartbeat.

'The babies—' She panted the words out. 'Raffa— Call an ambulance!'

'I'm taking you to the hospital,' he stated calmly. 'I'll call ahead to warn them we're on our way—'

'Raffa— Raffa! I can't—'

Grabbing a couple of throws from the sofa, he wrapped them around her. Lifting her, he picked up his keys on his way across the room, but by the time they reached the front door it was clear they weren't going anywhere.

This was one time neither of them could control the situation. Plucking the phone out of his pocket, he called the emergency number, trying to subdue his fears. He'd faced guns and knives in the course of his travels when he was searching for gems in some of the world's wildest places, but he had never known fear like this in his life. The thought of losing Leila—

He might as well be dead too. He would do anything,

anything to keep her safe, but the babies weren't going to wait for his team of experts.

'Stay on the line,' he told the paramedic as he shouldered his way into Leila's room. 'I might need you to talk me through this.'

Not only couldn't he control the speed of this birth, he needed help. And where Leila was concerned, he was grateful for every word of advice they could give him.

He laid her down on the bed. She reached for his hand and kissed it. 'I'm so glad you're here with me, Raffa.'

'I won't leave you for a second—unless the paramedic tells me I have to go fetch something,' he qualified, realising that for once in his life he really didn't know best. The thought of Leila giving birth alone to twins in an isolated cabin, however cosy and safe she might think it, racked him with guilt. What if he hadn't been here? He should have insisted she move to town. He should have hired help— Damn it to hell! He should have arrived in Skavanga sooner—

'Raffa?'

'Sorry—' His cursing had been both forceful and eloquent. 'I don't think the twins can hear me yet.'

She managed a laugh. 'You're going to make a terrible father if you swear all the time.'

'I'm already a terrible partner. I don't know what I was thinking leaving you here on your own so close to the birth.'

'We thought we knew when the babies were arriving. I was stubborn. I told you to go. I was so certain I knew exactly when they were coming.'

The babies cut her off again before she could say anything more. Like him, they were impatient—impatient to be born. He listened closely to the advice the paramedic was giving him. 'I've got to grab a few things, but I'll be right back—'

'I'm not going anywhere, Raffa.'

Leila was smiling bravely, but all the ghosts from the past hit him at once as he stared down at her. If he failed her— If he failed her now—

No chance. There was no chance that would happen. He recited the list so she could tell him where to find everything. 'Here—take the phone and keep speaking to the paramedic,' he suggested, already halfway out of the door. 'They're on their way—'

Her face turned anxious. 'They might not get here soon enough, Raffa.'

'But I'm here,' he reassured her, 'and the local medics are flying in by air ambulance, so they won't take long.'

As she sank back on the pillows he realised Leila had turned his life upside down. And he thanked God for it.

He thanked God even more heartily when the sound of rotor blades drowned out the sound of the kettle boiling. He would walk on hot coals for Leila, but the thought of risking her life or those of the twins by making some beginner's mistake during the delivery was a calamity he refused to consider. One baby, maybe. But two? He'd do it. Of course he'd do it, but knowing medical assistance was on its way had lifted his spirits and made it possible for him to look forward to the birth of his children with excitement and happiness, rather than the dragging fear that had dogged him since he had first learned Leila was pregnant. Scrawling a note for the medics, he attached it to the wreath outside the front door.

He took the stairs two at a time. So much for his relief at the quick response of the medical team! The first baby was already on its way. There was no mistaking the father of this impatient, strong-willed boy. He was wrapping the youngest member of the Leon dynasty in a towel and placing him in Leila's arms as the paramedics joined them in the room. He stood back immediately to let the professionals do their job.

'Raffa, you're wonderfully calm,' Leila managed on a shaking breath as the second twin made her noisy entrance into her world. 'I couldn't have done any of this without you.'

'You could probably have done all of it without me, but I'm glad you didn't have to. You shouldn't have to,' he murmured, studying the face of his firstborn as the paramedics checked his son's tiny baby sister over. 'And I don't think either of us had a choice. These babies were coming when they decided the time was right, with or without our agreement.'

'Happy Christmas, Raffa,' she murmured as the paramedics loaded her onto a stretcher.

'Happy Christmas, mouse.'

The look they exchanged was full of love and peace, and the promise of a happy future together with their children, though Leila was no more a mouse these days than he was a restless adventurer. She had given him the home he'd always longed for, while he had only to stand back and watch Leila grow in confidence, he reflected with amusement. Leila had turned out to be every bit as feisty as her sisters. Like Britt and Eva, she was a true Skavanga Diamond, but, as far as he was concerned, Leila was the jewel in the crown.

* * * * *

'I was a virgin!'

'How was I supposed to know that? You're a twenty-six-year-old woman.'

Pepe thought virgins of that age were extinct. It was a thought he kept to himself. Cara's skin had gone as red as her hair. He didn't particularly fancy being on the receiving end of a slap in front of his entire family, even if she would need a stepladder to reach him.

'You used me,' she said. 'You let me believe you were serious and that we would see each other again.'

'When? Tell me? When did I say we would see each other again?'

'You said you wanted me to come to your new house in Paris so I could advise you on where to place the Cannelotti painting you bought in the auction.'

He shrugged. 'That was business talk. You know about art and I needed an expert's eye.'

'You said it while dipping your finger in champagne and then placing it in my mouth so I could suck it off.'

'What's done is done. I've apologised, and as far as I'm concerned that's the end of the matter. It's been four months. I suggest you forget about it and move on.'

With that he stalked away, striding towards Luca and Grace, ready to tell them he was leaving.

'Actually, it's not the end of the matter.'

Something in the tone of her voice made him pause.

'It's impossible for me to *"forget about it and move on"*.'

THE IRRESISTIBLE SICILIANS

Dark-hearted men, with devastating appeal!

These powerful Sicilian men are bound by
years of family legacies and dark secrets.
But now the power rests with them.

No *man* would dare challenge these hot-blooded Sicilians…
But their women are another matter!

Have these world-renowned Sicilians met their match?

Read Luca Mastrangelo's story in:
WHAT A SICILIAN HUSBAND WANTS
March 2014

Read Pepe Mastrangelo's story in:
THE SICILIAN'S UNEXPECTED DUTY
April 2014

And look out for Francesco Calvetti's story
coming soon!

THE SICILIAN'S
UNEXPECTED DUTY

BY
MICHELLE SMART

Published in Great Britain 2014
by Mills & Boon, an imprint of Harlequin (UK) Limited,
Eton House, 18-24 Paradise Road, Richmond, Surrey, TW9 1SR

© 2014 Michelle Smart

ISBN: 978 0 263 24569 1

Harlequin (UK) Limited's policy is to use papers that are natural, renewable and recyclable products and made from wood grown in sustainable forests. The logging and manufacturing processes conform to the legal environmental regulations of the country of origin.

Printed and bound in Spain
by Blackprint CPI, Barcelona

Michelle Smart's love affair with books began as a baby, when she would cuddle them in her cot. This love for all things wordy has never left her. A voracious reader of all genres, she found her love of romance was cemented at the age of twelve when she came across her first Mills & Boon® book. That book sparked a seed and, although she didn't have the words to explain it then, she had discovered something special: that a book had the capacity to make her heart beat as if falling in love.

When not reading, or pretending to do the housework, Michelle loves nothing more than creating worlds of her own featuring handsome, brooding heroes and the sparkly, feisty women who can melt their frozen hearts. She hopes her books can make her readers' hearts beat a little faster too.

Michelle Smart lives in Northamptonshire with her own hero and their two young sons.

Recent titles by the same author:

WHAT A SICILIAN HUSBAND WANTS
  (The Irresistible Sicilians)
THE RINGS THAT BIND

Did you know these are also available as eBooks?
Visit www.millsandboon.co.uk

This book is dedicated to Adam, Joe and Zak,
my gorgeous Smarties.

CHAPTER ONE

PEPE MASTRANGELO HELPED himself to another glass of red wine from a passing maid and downed it in one. His aunt Carlotta, who had taken it upon herself to shadow him since they'd arrived back at his family home, was blathering on in his ear about something or other. Probably parroting her favourite inanities about when he, Pepe, was going to follow in his older brother's footsteps and settle down. Namely, when was he planning to get married and have babies?

Aunt Carlotta was not the only guilty party in this matter. The entire Mastrangelo clan, along with the Lombardis from his mother's side, all thought his private life was a matter of public consumption. Usually he took their nosiness in good part, knowing they meant well. He would deflect their questions with a cheeky grin, a wink and a quip about how there were so many beautiful women in the world he couldn't possibly choose just one. Or words to that effect. Anything but admit he would rather swim in a pool of electric eels than marry.

Marriage was for martyrs and fools, and he was neither.

He'd almost married once, when he'd been young and foolish. His childhood sweetheart. The woman who'd ripped his heart out, torn it into shreds and left an empty shell.

Now he considered that he'd had a lucky escape. Once bitten, twice shy. Only complete idiots went back for a second helping of pain if it could be avoided.

Not that he ever shared that little titbit of information with people. Heaven forbid. They'd probably try to talk him into something ridiculous like therapy.

Today though, his usually quick repartee had deserted him. But then, he wasn't usually fielding these questions with a pair of almond-shaped green eyes following his every move. To make it even harder to concentrate, those same eyes were drilling into him with pure loathing.

Cara Delaney.

He and Cara had been appointed his niece's godparents. He'd been forced to sit next to her in the church. He'd been forced to stand by her side at the font.

He'd forgotten how pretty she was—with her large eyes, tiny nose and small heart-shaped lips, she looked like a ginger geisha. Although *ginger* was the wrong word to describe the red flame of hair that fell down her back. Today, wearing a red crushed-velvet dress that showcased her curvy figure yet barely displayed an inch of flesh, she looked more than pretty. She looked incredibly sexy. Under normal circumstances he'd have no hesitation in spending the day in her company, flirting with her, plying her with drinks, maybe seeing if a repeat performance could be on the cards.

Being in the presence of his ex-lovers was not usually a problem, especially as his 'emotionally needy' detector was so acute. As a rule, he could spot a 'looking for marriage and babies' woman at ten paces and avoid her at all costs. As such, meeting up with an ex-lover was usually no big deal.

This time was different. Under normal circumstances he hadn't last seen them when he'd sneaked out of the hotel suite, leaving them sleeping in the very bed they'd just made love in. And usually he hadn't stolen their phone.

As soon as the date for the christening had been set a month ago, he'd known he would have to see Cara again. It was inconceivable that she wouldn't be there. She was his sister-in-law's best friend.

He'd expected the loathing that would be pointed his way. He really couldn't blame her for that. What he hadn't expected was to feel so... The word that would explain the strange sickness churning in his stomach wouldn't come. Whatever the word, he did not like it at all.

A quick glance at his watch confirmed he would have to endure her laser glare for another hour before he could leave for the airport. Tomorrow he'd be taking a tour of a profitable vineyard in the Loire Valley that he'd heard through the grapevine—pun intended—was being considered for sale. He wanted to get in there and, if viable, make an offer before any competitor started digging around.

'I *said*, she's beautiful, isn't she?' Aunt Carlotta's voice had taken a distinctly frosty tone. Somehow, in between her non-stop nattering, she had managed to acquire Lily without him noticing. She held the baby aloft for his perusal.

He peered down at the chubby face with the black eyes staring up at him, and all he could think was how like a little dark-haired piglet she looked. 'Yes, beautiful,' he lied, forcing a wide smile.

Seriously, how could anyone think babies were beautiful? Cute at a push maybe, but beautiful? Why anyone raved about them was beyond him. They were the most boring of creatures. He quite liked toddlers though. Especially when they were getting up to mischief.

He was saved from having to fake any more enthusiasm by a great-aunt barging him out of the way so she too could coo at the poor child.

Using this momentary lapse of Aunt Carlotta's attention, he sidled away.

Was this the way people acted at all christenings? From the way his relatives were behaving, anyone would think Lily had been conceived from a virgin birth. Having not attended a christening in nearly fifteen years, he wouldn't know. Given a chance, he would have got out of this one too. But there'd been no way, not when he'd been made godfather. Luca, his brother, would have strung him up if he'd tried to avoid it.

He wondered how long it would take for Luca and Grace to try again. No doubt they would keep trying until a boy was born. His own parents had struck gold from the outset, the need for an heir immediately satisfied with Luca's birth. Pepe's own conception was more along the 'spare' lines and to give Luca a playmate.

Was he being unfair to his parents? He didn't know or care. He'd been feeling out of sorts all day, and having the red-headed geisha glaring at him as if he were the Antichrist was not helping his mood.

Forget it, he thought, reaching for another glass of red from a passing maid. No one would notice if he left earlier than was deemed polite...

'You look stressed, Pepe.'

He muttered an expletive under his breath.

He should have known he wouldn't be able to escape without her collaring him. There had been something too determined in that expression of hers.

Plastering another fake smile on his face, he turned

around and faced her. 'Cara!' he exclaimed with bon-homie so fake even Lily would see through it. Grabbing her shoulder with his free hand, he pulled her into him and leaned down to kiss both her cheeks. She was so short he almost had to double over. 'How are you? Enjoying the party?'

Her dark coppery eyebrows knotted together into a glare. 'Oh, yes. I'm having a marvellous time.'

Pretending not to notice the definite edge to her voice, he nodded and raised the wattage of his grin. 'Fabulous. Now, if you'll excuse me, I have—'

'Running away again, are you?' Her Irish lilt had thickened since he'd last seen her. When they'd first met, here in Sicily three years ago, her voice had contained only the lightest of traces; by all accounts she'd left Ireland for England when she was a teenager. When he'd seduced her in Dublin four months ago, he'd noticed her accent had become more pronounced. Now there was no doubting her heritage.

'I have to be somewhere.'

'Really?' If an inflection could cut glass, that one word would have done the trick. She nodded her head in his sister-in-law's direction. 'She's the reason you stole my phone, isn't she?' It wasn't a question.

He drew in a breath before meeting Cara's stony glare. The last time he'd been with her, those eyes had been brimful of desire. 'Yes. She's the reason.'

Cara's geisha lips always drew a second glance—her bottom lip was beautifully plump, as if it had been stung by a bee. Now she drew it tightly under her teeth and bit into it. When she released it, the lip was a darker, even more kissable red. Her eyes had become a laser death stare.

'And was it my phone that led Luca to find her?'

There was no point in lying. She already knew the answers. Lying would demean them both. '*Sì.*'

'You came all the way to Dublin, to the auction house where I work, spent two million euros on a painting, and all to get hold of my phone?'

'*Sì.*'

She shook her head, her long copper locks whipping over her shoulders. 'I take it the whole "I've always wanted to visit Dublin, please show me around" thing was also deliberate?'

'Yes.' He held her icy gaze and allowed the tiniest of softening into his tone. 'I really did have a great weekend— you're an excellent tour guide.'

'And you're an unmitigated...' She buried the curse beneath a deep breath. 'But that's by the by. You seduced me for one reason and one reason only—so you could steal my phone the minute I fell asleep.'

'That was the main reason,' he agreed, experiencing the strangest tightening in his chest. 'But I can assure you, I enjoyed every minute. And I *know* you enjoyed it too.'

Cara had come undone in his arms. It had been an experience that still lingered in his memories and his senses, but an experience he ruthlessly dispatched from his head now.

All he wanted was to get away from her, get away from this claustrophobic party with all the talk of *babies* and *marriage*, and find himself a few hours of oblivion.

Her cheeks coloured but her jaw hardened. 'What's *enjoyment* got to do with anything? You lied to me. You spent a whole weekend lying to me, pretending to enjoy my company...'

He flashed his most winning smile. 'I did enjoy your company.' He certainly wasn't enjoying it now though.

This conversation was worse than the frequent visits to the headmaster he'd endured as a schoolboy. Just because he deserved someone's censure didn't mean he had to enjoy it.

'Do I look like I was born yesterday?' she shot back. 'The *only* reason you hooked up with me was because your brother was so desperate to find Grace.'

'My brother deserved to know where his wife had gone.'

'No, he did not. She's not his possession.'

'A lesson I can assure you he has learned. Look at them.' He nodded over to where Luca had joined his wife, his arms locked around her waist. Fools, the pair of them. 'They're happy to be back together. Everything has worked out for the best.'

'I was a virgin.'

He winced. He'd been trying his best to forget that little nugget. 'If it's an apology you're after then I apologise, but, as I explained at the time, I didn't know.'

'I told you...'

'You told me you'd never had a serious boyfriend before.'

'Exactly!'

'And as I told you before, not having a serious boyfriend does not equate to being a virgin.'

'It does—did—for me.'

'How was I supposed to know that? You're a twenty-six-year-old woman.' He'd thought virgins of that age were extinct, a thought he kept to himself. Cara's skin had gone as red as her hair. He didn't particularly fancy being on the receiving end of a punch in the face in front of his entire family, even if she would need a stepladder to reach him. There was something of a ferocious Jack Russell about her at that moment.

'You used me,' she said, almost snarling. 'You let me believe you were serious, and that we would see each other again.'

'When? Tell me, when did I say we would see each other again?'

'You said you wanted me to come to your new house in Paris so I could advise you where to place the Canaletto painting you bought in the auction.'

He shrugged. 'That was business talk. You know about art and I needed an expert's eye.' He still needed one; he'd bought his Parisian home to showcase his art collection, but the entire lot was still in storage.

'You said it while dipping your finger in champagne and then placing it in my mouth so I could suck it off.'

A flare of heat stirred in his groin. That particular moment had been during their last meal together, shortly before she'd agreed to join him in his hotel room and spend the night with him.

He cut his thoughts off the direction they were headed. The last thing he needed at that moment was to remember anything further about that night. It was becoming uncomfortable enough in his underwear as it was.

'Why didn't you steal my phone from the outset? Why string me along for a whole weekend?' Her eyes were no longer firing hostility at him. All he saw in them was bewilderment.

It had been easier dealing with Aunt Carlotta's jabbering mouth than with *this*. Okay, he got that Cara felt humiliated—he hardly recalled his actions that weekend with pride—but surely it was time for her to get over it?

'I couldn't steal your phone because you keep your handbag pressed so tightly to you I knew it would be impossible to steal.' Even now, she had the long strap placed diagonally over her neck and across her chest, the bag itself tucked securely under her arm.

'I'm surprised you didn't arrange for someone to mug me. I'm sure between you and your brother you know enough shady people to do the job. It would have saved you wasting a weekend of your precious time.'

'But you could have got hurt,' he argued silkily. A strange shiver rippled through his belly at the thought, a feeling dismissed before it was properly acknowledged.

He'd had enough. He'd behaved atrociously but it had been necessary. He wasn't prepared to spend the rest of the evening apologising for it. He'd never told her an actual lie—how she'd interpreted his words was nothing to do with him. 'You share a house with three other women, which made breaking into your home too risky, and you keep your phone on you when you're working. If you'd left your handbag unattended just once throughout that weekend, I would have taken it, but you didn't—you didn't let it out of your sight.'

'So now it's *my* fault?' she demanded, hands on hips.

Cara had to be one of the shortest people he'd ever met, certainly on a par with his great-aunt Magdalena. In the four months since he'd last seen her, she'd lost weight, making her seem more doll-like than he remembered. Yet, whether it was the long flaming hair or the ferocity blazing from her eyes, she stood tall and unapologetic before him, as if a tank would not be enough to knock her down.

He bit back another oath. 'What's done is done. I've apologised and as far as I'm concerned that's the end of the matter. It's been four months. I suggest you forget about it and move on.'

With that, he stalked away, striding towards Luca and Grace, ready to tell them he was leaving.

'Actually, it's not the end of the matter.'

Something in the tone of her voice made him pause.

'It's impossible for me to *"forget about it and move on"*.'

A shiver of something that could be interpreted as fear crawled up his spine...

Cara watched Pepe's back tense and all the muscles beneath his crisp pink shirt bunch together.

Only Pepe could get away with a pink linen shirt, unbuttoned at the neck, and snug-fitting navy chinos for his own niece's christening. The shirt wasn't even tucked in! Yet he still oozed masculinity. If she could, she'd rip all the testosterone from him—and there must be buckets of it—and flush it down the toilet. Standing next to him in the church, she had been acutely aware of how overdressed she looked in comparison, and had fumed at the unfairness of it all—*he* was the one underdressed for the occasion. With his long Roman nose, high cheekbones, trim black goatee covering his strong chin and his ebony hair quiffed at the front, Pepe looked as if he'd stepped off a catwalk.

She'd truly thought she'd been prepared. In her head she'd had everything planned out. She would be calm. She would politely ask for five minutes of his time, explain the situation and tell him what she wanted. Above all else, she would be calm.

Under no circumstances would she let him know of her devastation when she'd awoken alone in his hotel suite, or her terror when the stick in her hand had turned pink.

She would be calm.

All her good intentions had been thrown by the wayside when she'd taken one look at his handsome face and wanted to knock his perfect white teeth out.

The whole time she'd been next to him at the christening, even while they were making their respective promises as Lily's godparents, all she could think was how much she wanted to cause him bodily harm. She'd even found herself gazing at the silver scar that ran down his cheek, wishing she could track the culprit down and shake his hand. Or her hand. She'd asked Pepe about the scar during their weekend together but he'd evaded the question with his customary ease. She hadn't pushed the matter but it had tugged at her. All she'd wanted to do was trace a finger down it and make it magically disappear.

Who, she'd wondered, could have hated him enough to do such a thing? Pepe was charm personified. Everyone adored him. Or so she'd thought.

Now it wouldn't surprise her in the least to discover a queue of people wishing to perform bodily harm on him.

The violence of her thoughts and emotions shocked her. She was a pacifist. She'd attended anti-war demos, for cripes' sake!

She'd spent the past four months castigating herself for being stupid enough to fall for Pepe Mastrangelo's seduction. She should have known it wasn't her he was interested in. After all, he'd never displayed the slightest interest in her before. Not once.

On her frequent trips to Sicily to visit Grace, they would often make a foursome for evenings out. Luca had terrified her, had done from the moment she'd met him. Pepe, on the other hand, had been fun and charming. After a few dates she'd been able to converse with him as easily as she could with Grace. Tall and utterly gorgeous, he was the type of man females from all generations and all persuasions would pause to take a second look at.

However much she'd liked his irreverent company, she'd always known he tagged along on their evenings out as a favour to his big brother's wife. He would flirt with Cara as much as the next woman, fix his gorgeous dark blue eyes on her and make her feel as if she were the only woman in the world—until he fixed those same eyes on another woman and made her feel exactly the same way. His blatancy had made her laugh. It had also made her feel safe. He was not a man any woman with a sane mind could take seriously.

Well, more fool her for falling for it. She would *never* make the same mistake again, not for him, not for anyone.

Hadn't she always known that sex was nothing but a weapon? Hadn't she witnessed it with her own eyes, the devastation that occurred when grown men and women allowed their hormones to dictate their actions? It ripped lives and families apart.

Pepe was a man who positively revelled in allowing his hormones to lead the way. He thrived on it. To him, she, Cara, had been nothing but a means to an end, the sex between them a perk of the task he had undertaken. His brother had wanted his wife back and Cara's phone had contained the data with which to find her. The fact that she was a human being with real human feelings had meant nothing. When it came to his family, Pepe was a man without limits.

And that lack of limits had come at a price.

'I can't *"forget about it and move on"*, you feckless, irresponsible playboy, because I'm pregnant.'

CHAPTER TWO

CARA DIDN'T KNOW exactly how Pepe would react to her little statement, but when he finally turned to face her, his wide smile was still firmly in place.

'Is this your idea of a joke?'

'No. I'm sixteen weeks pregnant. Congratulations. You're going to be a daddy.'

His eyes bored into hers but his smile didn't dim, not by a single wattage. All around them gathered his family. She could feel their curious gazes resting on them. Resting on *her*.

It was too late to wish she could hide behind Grace as she had done so many times since her teenage years. Whenever she was in a new social situation she would let Grace hold court until her nerves were silenced and she felt capable of speaking without choking on her own tongue. Grace had understood. Grace had protected her.

But Grace had married and moved countries. Grace had also disappeared for the best part of a year, forcing Cara to get her own life in order. She couldn't keep living her life through her best friend. She needed a life that was her own.

And she'd been getting there. She'd moved back to Ireland, landed a job she loved, albeit at the lowest rung, but it was a start, and even made some new friends. She had truly thought she'd found her own path to some kind of fulfilling life.

Pepe hadn't just blocked the path, he'd driven a ruddy great bulldozer through it and churned it into rubble.

He'd left her alone, scared and pregnant, with a future that loomed terrifyingly opaque.

Eventually he inclined his head and nodded at the door. 'Come with me.'

Relieved to get away from all the prying eyes, relieved to have a moment to gather her wits together, she followed him out and into the wide corridor.

Pepe leaned against the stone wall and ran a hand through his thick black hair.

A maid appeared carrying a fresh tray of canapés, which she took into the vast living room.

No sooner had the maid gone when a couple of elderly uncles came out of the same door, laughing between themselves. When they saw Pepe, they pulled him in for some back-breaking hugs and fired a load of questions, all of which Pepe answered with gusto and laughter, as if he hadn't a single care in the world.

The minute they were alone though, the smile dropped. 'Let's get out of here before any more of my relatives try and talk to me.' He set off in a direction within the converted monastery she'd never been in before.

'Where are we going?'

'To my wing.'

He made no allowances for her legs being half the length of his, and she struggled to keep up. 'What for?'

He flashed her a black look over his shoulder, not slowing his pace for a moment. 'You really wish to have this conversation in front of fifty Mastrangelos and Lombardis?'

'Of course not, but I really don't want to have it in your personal space. Can't we go somewhere neutral?'

'No.' He stopped at a door, unlocked it and held it open. He extended an arm. 'I'm getting on a flight to Paris in exactly two hours. This is a one-off opportunity to convince me that I have impregnated you.'

She stared at him. She couldn't read his face. If anything, he looked bored. 'You think I'm lying?'

'You wouldn't be the first woman to lie over a pregnancy.'

Throwing him the most disdainful look she could muster, Cara slipped past him and into his inner sanctum.

Thank God she had no hankering for any sort of future for them. He was a despicable excuse for a human being.

Pepe's wing, although rarely used, what with him having at least three other places he called home, was exactly what she expected. Unlike the rest of the converted monastery, which remained faithful and sympathetic to the original architecture, this was a proper bachelor pad. It opened straight into a large living space decked with the largest flat-screen television she had seen outside a cinema, and was filled with more gizmos and gadgets than she'd known existed. She doubted she would know how to work a quarter of them.

She stood there, in the midst of all this high-tech luxury, and suddenly felt the first seed of doubt that she was doing the right thing.

'Can I get you a drink?'

'No. Let's just get this over with.' Of course she was doing the right thing, she castigated herself. Her unborn child deserved nothing less.

'Well, I need one.' He picked up a remote control from a glass table in the centre of the room and pressed a button.

Eyes wide, she watched as the oak panelling on the wall behind him separated and a fully stocked bar emerged.

Pepe mixed himself some concoction she didn't recognise. 'Are you sure I can't get you anything?'

'Yes.'

He tipped it down his neck and then fixed his deep blue eyes back to her. 'Go on, then. Convince me.'

Pursing her lips, she shook her head in distaste. 'I'm pregnant.'

'So you've already said.'

'That's because I am.'

'How much?'

'How much what?'

'Money. How much money are you going to try and extort from me?'

She glared at him. 'I'm not trying to extort anything from you.'

'So you don't want my money?' he said, his tone mocking.

'Of course I do.' It gave great satisfaction to watch his ebony brows shoot up. 'You have lots of money. I have nothing. I am broke. Boracic. Poor. Whatever you want to call it, I am skint. I'm also carrying a child whose father can afford to pay for a decent cot and wardrobe and a decent place for him or her to live.'

He sucked in air through his teeth. 'So you *are* trying to extort money from me.'

'No!' Clamping her lips together, Cara opened her handbag and took out a brown envelope, from which she pulled a square piece of paper. She handed it to him. 'There,' she said tightly. 'There's your proof. I'm not trying to extort anything from you. I'm sixteen weeks pregnant. You *are* going to be a father.'

For a moment Pepe feared he would be sick. His stomach was certainly churning enough for it to happen. And his skin…his skin had gone all cold and clammy; his heart rate tripled.

And no wonder.

If this were a forgery, Cara had done an excellent job.

The square piece of paper clearly showed a kidney bean. Or was it that alien thing he had watched as a child? E.T.? Either way, this was clearly an early-stage foetus. He studied it carefully. There was the name of the Dublin hospital on it, her name, Cara Mary Delaney, her date of birth and the due date of the foetus. He did the maths. Yes. This put her at sixteen weeks pregnant.

It had been sixteen weeks since he'd been to Dublin…

'You don't look very pregnant.' She looked thinner than he had ever seen her. She'd never been fat as such, more cuddly. While she hadn't transformed into a rake, she'd lost some of her, for want of a better word, *squishiness*.

'I've been under a lot of stress.' She gave him a tight smile. 'Unexpected pregnancy can do that to a woman. But the baby's perfectly healthy and I'm sure I'll start showing soon.'

He looked again at the scan picture. Cara was a smart woman but he doubted even she could forge something of this standard. The resolution on this picture was more clearly defined than the one he had held and gazed at for hours on end over a decade ago, but everything else was the same.

Cara was pregnant.

He looked back at her, realising for the first time that she was shaking. It took all his control to keep his own body still.

Dragging air into his lungs, he considered the situation as dispassionately as he could, which was hard. Very hard. His brain felt as if someone had thrown antifreeze into it. 'Congratulations. You're going to be a mother. Now tell me, what makes you so certain I'm the father?'

She opened her mouth, then closed it, then opened it again. 'What kind of stupid question is that? Of course you're the father. You're the only man I've been stupid enough to have sex with.'

'And I'm supposed to take your word on that, am I?'

'You know damn well I was a virgin.'

'I am not disputing that you were a virgin. What I am questioning is my paternity. I have no way of knowing what you got up to after I left. How do I know that after discovering all you'd been missing, you didn't go trawling for sex—?'

Her hand flew out from nowhere. *Crack*. Right across his cheek, the force enough to jerk his face to the side.

'Don't you dare pull me down to your own pathetically low standards,' she hissed, her face contorted with anger.

His cheek stung, smarted right where her hand and fingers had made contact. She might be small but she packed a proper punch. He could feel her imprint burrowing under his skin. He raised a hand to it. Her finger marks lay on the long scar that had been inflicted on him when he'd been eighteen. There were still times when he could feel the blade of the knife burn into his skin.

'I will let you do that this one time,' he said, speaking carefully, controlling his tone. 'But if you ever raise a hand to me again you will never see me or my money again.'

Her breaths were shallow. 'You deserved it.'

'Why? Because I pointed out that you are expecting me to take you at your word? Trust me, I take *no one* at their word, especially a woman purporting to be carrying my child.'

'I *am* carrying your child.'

'No—you are carrying *a* child. Until the child is born and we can get a paternity test done, I do not want to hear any reference to it being mine.' After what Luisa had done to him, he would never take anything to do with paternity at face value again. Never.

Only fools rushed in twice.

Cara itched to slap the arrogance off his face again, so much so that she dug her nails into the palms of her hands to find some relief.

If she could, she would leave. But she couldn't. She hadn't been exaggerating about the state of her bank balance. Paying for the return flight to Sicily had left her with the grand total of forty-eight euros to last her until payday, which was still a fortnight away. It was one thing living on baked beans on toast when she had only herself to support, but it was quite another when she would soon have a tiny mouth to feed and clothe. And she needed to find a new home, one that allowed children.

When she'd first discovered she was pregnant, her fear had been primitive, a cold, terrifying realisation that within her grew a life, a baby.

Jeez. A baby. She couldn't remember ever even *holding* a baby.

That real terror had morphed when the freeze in her brain had abated and the reality of everything that having a child meant had hit her.

A child would depend on her for *everything*. Love. Stability. Nourishment. Of the three, came the sharp knowledge that she would only be able to provide the first.

At that precise moment, even more so than when

she'd taken the pregnancy test, her life had changed irrevocably.

What stability did she have living in a shared rented home that banned children? What nourishment could she provide when she barely earned enough to feed herself? Nappies alone cost a fortune on her salary. Maybe if this had all happened a few years down the line, when she'd scaled the career ladder a little higher and was earning more, things would have been more manageable. But they weren't. At that moment she had nothing.

'So that's it, is it?' she demanded, fighting with everything she had to keep her tone moderate, to fight the hysteria threatening to take control. 'What do you want me to do? Give you a ring in five months and tell you if it's a boy or a girl?'

He speared her with a look. 'Not at all, *cucciola mia*.'

Cucciola mia: the endearment that had appropriated itself as his pet name for her during their weekend together. Curiosity had driven her to translate it on the same phone he had stolen from her. She had been more than a little chagrined to learn it meant something along the lines of *my puppy*. The way he said it though…in Pepe's thick Sicilian tongue it sounded tantalisingly sexy.

Momentarily distracted at the throwaway endearment, it took a second before she realised he was studying the scan picture.

'I notice this was taken a month ago,' he said, referring to the date of the scan shown clearly on the corner.

'And?'

'And it's taken you all this time to tell me. Why is that?'

How she hated his mocking scepticism, as if he were looking for a conspiracy in every little thing.

'I didn't tell you any sooner because I don't trust you

an inch—I wanted to be sure I was too far gone for you to force an abortion on me.'

Pepe's firm, sensuous lips tightened and his eyes narrowed, lines appearing on his forehead. After too long a pause, he said, 'Why would you think that?'

She almost laughed aloud. 'You have loved and left so many women it's become a second career for you. What do you, Playboy of the Year, want with a child?'

His features darkened for the split of a second before his usual laconic grin replaced it. 'It might make a nice accessory for pulling more women.'

She would have believed he was serious if the granite in his eyes hadn't said otherwise. She gave an involuntary shiver.

'Do you think I was oblivious to the disparaging comments you made about babies?' she demanded. 'Do you think I didn't notice you rolling your eyes whenever Grace and Luca discussed having kids?'

'So that's proof I would demand an abortion, is it?'

'You made it perfectly clear that kids are not and never will be on your agenda.'

A tiny pulse pounded on his jawline. After a loaded pause, he said, 'Say a paternity test proves it is mine. What do you expect from me? Marriage?'

'No!' She practically shouted her denial. 'No. I do not want to marry you. I don't want to marry anyone.'

'That's a relief,' he drawled, heading back to his bar to pour himself another glass of his concoction. 'But in case you're only saying what you think I want to hear, know marriage will never be on the cards, whatever the outcome of the paternity test.'

Had he drugged her? For a moment she actually considered the possibility. She could hardly credit she had allowed him to seduce her so thoroughly.

She looked back on their weekend together. It was as if she had been under some kind of drug that allowed the hormones so prevalent in the rest of society to actually work in her. For the first time in her life she had experienced desire. It had been the headiest feeling imaginable.

She had *wanted* to believe he was serious about her.

She had *wanted* to believe they could have a future together.

An image of her parents flashed in her head. Was this what it had been like for them? Especially her father, who'd hooked up with a new woman on a seemingly weekly basis. With all the affairs he'd had and all her parents' fights and making up, had they constantly experienced that same headiness? Was that what had caused their monstrous selfishness?

She blinked the image away. She would *not* be like her mother and think only of her own needs. Her unborn child's needs would always take priority, whatever the personal sacrifice.

'I'm glad you think that way because, believe me, I have no intention of marrying you.' She'd rather marry an orang-utan.

'Good. People who marry for the sake of the baby are fools. And I am not a fool.'

She glared at him. 'I can think of many a choice word to describe you but *fool* isn't one of them.'

'Then we are on the same page,' he mocked.

'About marriage, then yes, but, Pepe, I need help. Financially, I am in no position to support a child.'

'So you thought you would come to me.' He tipped his drink down his neck in one swallow.

'If you think for a second I like the idea of having to beg you for money then you have a very twisted view of me. I've come to you for help because this is your responsibility...'

'You're going to pin the blame for this on me?'

'I'm not the one who got carried away,' she countered pointedly. Warmth spread inside her as she recalled lying in his arms after they'd made love for the first time. Pepe's usual languidness had gone. A more serious, reflective side of his nature had come to the fore, a side she'd never seen before. As they'd talked and his face had come closer to hers, she'd found herself staring at his lips. And he'd been staring at hers. And even though they had made love barely ten minutes before, the heat he had created inside her and she in him had flared back to life, and he'd rolled on top of her and kissed her—devoured her—and before either of them had been fully aware of it, he'd been inside her. If she'd thought having him inside her the first time had been something special...this had been indescribable. For what had felt an age, they had simply lain there, gazing into each other's eyes, before he had reluctantly withdrawn to get a condom.

That one stolen moment had been enough to create a life.

'I hardly think that was enough to make a baby,' he said, his tone becoming grim.

'Well, it was. You used me, Pepe. Whether you like it or not, you are responsible.'

It sickened him to know she could be right.

You are responsible.

Despite the playboy image he had cultivated—an image he exulted in—Pepe couldn't remember the last time he'd been so reckless.

Actually, he could remember. The last time he'd made love to a woman without using a condom he'd been eighteen. Young and believing himself to be in love. A lethal combination.

It hadn't been a conscious decision to enter Cara unsheathed. At the time it had felt like the most natural thing in the world. Not that he'd been thinking properly. He'd been reeling from the discovery that she was—had been—a virgin. He'd also been struggling to understand everything going on inside *him*.

Usually he would make love to a woman and get back into bed, have a fun conversation, drink a glass of wine or whatever, maybe make love again and then leave without a second thought or a backward glance. He'd never got back into bed with a churning stomach and a tight chest before. He could only assume it was guilt he'd been feeling. Guilt at her virginity or guilt at what he'd had to do, he did not know.

Guilt or not, he'd *never* got back into bed with a woman and needed to make love to her all over again. Not straight away. For all his reputation, Pepe thought with his brain, not the appendage between his legs. At least he had until that night with Cara.

But he hadn't been inside her for long enough to make a baby. It had been a minute at the most. But *caro Dio*, he'd had to force himself to withdraw and get that condom. Being inside her without a barrier…

His groin twitched as more sweet memories filled him.

For that one minute inside her, he'd felt a sense of sheer wonderment and belonging…

'I need a coffee,' he muttered. He wanted another drink—a proper drink—but knew it was time to stop. A plan was formulating and he needed to think clearly. 'Can I get you anything?'

Cara shook her head. She was leaning against the wall, arms folded, chin jutted up, looking ready for a fight.

By the time he'd made a quick call to the kitchen, his plan was fully developed. Cara could like it or lump it. If she wanted a fight, she had to learn it was one she would never win.

CHAPTER THREE

'SIT DOWN.'

It was a definite command.

Cara tightened her arms around her chest and pressed harder into the wall, which was the only thing keeping her upright—her legs were shot. Not that she could trust the wall. For all she knew, it might be hiding a secret bathroom. The only saving grace was that her dress was long enough to hide her knocking knees.

But even if her legs could be trusted to behave, there was no way she would obey. She didn't care how rich and powerful Pepe was in his world, she would not grant him power over her, no matter how petty. Not without a fight.

'Suit yourself.' He lowered himself onto one of the oversized chocolate leather sofas, stretched out his long legs, kicked off his shoes and flashed a grin.

Her knees shook even harder.

How she hated that bloody grin. It was so...fake. And it did something ridiculous to the beat of her heart, which was hammering so hard she wouldn't be in the least surprised if it burst through her chest.

'I can see you are in a difficult predicament,' he said, hooking an arm behind his head and mussing his hair.

She inhaled slowly, getting as much oxygen into her lungs as she could. 'That's one way to describe it.'

'I have a solution that will suit us both.'

Her eyes narrowed.

'It involves sacrifice on both our parts.' He shot her a warning glance before displaying his white teeth. 'But I can assure you that if I am the father of your child as you say, the sacrifice will be worth it.'

What the heck did Pepe Mastrangelo know about sacrifice? His whole life revolved around nothing but his pleasure.

She nodded tightly. 'Go on.'

'You will live with me until the child is born. Then we shall have a paternity test. If it proves positive, as you say it will, then I will buy you a home of your choice. And, of course, support you both financially.'

'You want me to live with you until the baby's born?' she asked, certain she had misheard him.

'Sì.'

'Why?' She couldn't think of a single reason. 'All I need from you at the moment is enough money to rent a decent flat in a nice area, and buy some essentials for the baby. Obviously you'll have to pay child support when the baby's born.'

'Only if the baby proves to be mine. If it isn't, I won't have to pay you a single euro.'

Cara spoke through gritted teeth. 'The baby is yours. But seeing as you're proving to be such a disbeliever, I'm happy to sign a contract stating I have to repay any monies in the event the paternity test proves the Invisible Man is the father.'

He gave a quick shake of his head and turned his mouth down in a regretful fashion. 'If only it were that simple. The problem, for me, is that there exists the possibility that the child you carry inside you *is* mine. I cannot take the risk of anything happening to it.'

'I told you I delayed telling you about the baby so you couldn't force me into an abortion. I'm four weeks too late for one in Sicily and it's completely illegal in Ireland.' She blinked rapidly, fighting with everything she had not to burst into angry tears. She would not give him the satisfaction of seeing her cry. She would not give him the power her mother had given her father.

She might have no choice but to throw her pride at his feet but she had to retain some kind of dignity.

'I never said anything about an abortion,' he pointed out. 'What does concern me is your health. You're clearly not taking care of yourself if your weight loss is anything to go by, and by your own admittance you don't have enough money to support a child. Or so you say. For all I know, you could be on the make, using this pregnancy as a means to help yourself to my bank account.'

It was Cara's turn to swear under her breath. 'Do you have any idea how offensive you are?'

He shrugged, utterly nonchalant. He clearly couldn't care less. 'Finances aside, if that *is* my child growing inside you then I want to make damned sure you're taking care of it properly.'

'I am taking care of myself as best I can under the circumstances, but, I can promise you, our child's welfare means more to me than anything.' Her unborn child meant *everything* to her. Everything. Its well-being was the only reason she was here.

Did Pepe think she *wanted* to throw herself at his financial mercy?

He shook his head in a chiding fashion and stretched his arms out. 'My conditions are non-negotiable. If you want me to support you during the rest of the pregnancy then I will. But I will not give you cash. All you have to do is move in with me, travel where I travel, and I will feed and clothe you, and buy anything else you may need. If paternity is established after the birth, then I will buy you a house in your name, anywhere you choose, and give you an allowance so large you will be set up for life.'

He made it sound so reasonable. He made it sound as if it were such a no-brainer she wouldn't even need to think about it.

And there she'd been, worrying for months against telling him because she'd convinced herself he would demand an abortion.

'You see, *cucciola mia*, I am not the baby-aborting monster you thought I would be,' he said chidingly, reading her mind.

A sharp rap on the main door to the wing provided a moment's relief for her poor, addled brain.

At Pepe's invitation, a maid entered the room carrying a tray with a pot of coffee, a pot of tea covered by a tea cosy and two cups.

'It's decaf,' he explained when it had been placed on the glass table and the maid left.

'I told you I didn't want anything.'

'You need to keep your fluid levels up.'

'Oh, so you're a doctor now? Or have you an army of illegitimates scattered around the world that's made you a pregnancy expert?'

He quelled her with a glance.

She refused to bow to its latent warning. 'Sorry. Am I supposed to believe this is the first time you've had a paternity suit thrown at you?'

His eyes were unreadable. 'I always use protection.'

'And you're expecting me to take you at your word for that?'

His features darkened before his lips gave a slight twitch and he bowed his head. 'A fair comeback.'

He really was ridiculously handsome.

She castigated herself. As far as she was concerned, Pepe's looks and masculinity were void. She would *not* let her hormones create any more havoc.

It was unfair that she was the one standing yet it still felt as if he, all chilled and relaxed on the sofa, had all the advantage.

A whorl of black hair poked through the top of his shirt. She remembered how that same hair covered his chest, thickening across his tightly defined pecs and down the middle towards his navel, and further down... She'd always assumed chest hair would be bristly, had been thrilled to find it as soft as silk. It was the only thing soft about him; everything else was hard...

She swallowed and pressed the tops of her thighs together to try to quash the heat bubbling within her.

Her throat had gone dry.

Damn him, she needed a drink.

Lips clamped together, she moved away from the wall and poured herself a cup of the steaming tea before carrying it to the sofa opposite him. She only intended to perch there but it was so soft and squidgy it almost swallowed her whole. She sank straight into it, her legs shooting out, the motion causing her to spill the tea all over her lap.

Cara cried out, kicking her legs as if the movement would stop the hot fluid seeping through her dress.

Immediately Pepe jumped to his feet and hurried over, snatching the cup from her hand. 'Are you okay?'

In too much pain to do anything more than whimper, Cara grabbed the hem of her dress and bunched it up to her thighs, flapping it to cool her heated skin. Making sure to keep the dress up and away from the scald, she yanked the tops of her black hold-ups down.

'Are you okay?' he repeated. For some silly reason,

the genuine concern she heard in his voice bothered her far more than the scald.

The milky white of her left thigh had turned a deep pink, as had a couple of patches on her right thigh. She took a deep breath. 'It hurts.'

'I'll bet. Can you walk?'

'Why?'

'Because we should run cold water over it.'

Her thighs—especially her left one—were stinging something rotten, so much so she didn't even think of arguing with him.

'Come, we'll run the shower on it.'

Wincing, she let him help her to her feet.

Her legs shook frantically enough that she almost fell back onto the sofa, only Pepe's grip on her hand keeping her upright.

He frowned and shook his head, then, before she knew what he was doing, lifted her into his arms, taking great care not to touch her thighs.

'This is unnecessary,' she complained. She might be in pain but she didn't need *this*. Besides, she was vain enough to know she must look ridiculous with her dress bunched around the tops of her thighs, her modesty barely preserved. Her stupid black hold-ups had fallen down to her knees like the socks of a scatty schoolgirl.

'Probably,' he agreed, heading through the living area and into a narrow corridor, carrying her as if she weighed little more than a child. 'But it's quicker and safer than you trying to walk.'

The position he held her in meant her face was right in the crook of his strong, bronzed neck. A compulsion to press her face into it almost overcame her. Almost. Luckily she still retained some control. But she'd forgotten how delicious he smelt, like sun-ripened fruit. Her position meant her senses were filled with it and she had to use even more restraint not to lick him.

Pepe's bathroom was twice the size of her bedroom and resembled a miniature black, white and gold palace. She had no time to appreciate its splendour.

'You're going to have to take your dress off,' he said as he carried her down some marble steps and carefully sat her on the edge of the sunken bath.

'I jolly well am not.'

'It will get wet.'

'It's already wet.'

'Suit yourself.' He knelt before her and placed a hand on her knee.

She tried not to yelp. 'What are you doing?'

'Taking your stockings off.' He tugged the first one down to the ankle. While she hated herself for her vanity, Cara could not help feel relief that she'd remembered to wax her legs a few days ago.

'They're hold-ups,' she corrected, breathing deeply. The trail of his fingers on her skin burned almost as much as the scald.

'They're sexy.'

'That's inappropriate.'

His lips twitched. 'Sorry.'

'Liar.'

Hold-ups removed and thrown onto the floor, Pepe helped manoeuvre her into the empty bath before reaching for the shower head that rested on the gold taps.

He held it over his hand then turned it on. Water gushed out, spraying over them both.

Adjusting the pressure, he smiled with a hint of smugness. 'Still happy to keep your dress on?'

'Yes.' She would rather suffer third-degree burns than strip off to her underwear in front of him.

'I've seen you naked before,' he reminded her wickedly, turning the shower onto her thighs.

'Not under bright light, you haven't.'

The cold water felt like the greatest relief in the world. Cara closed her eyes, rested her head back and savoured the feeling, uncaring that the cold water spraying off her thighs was pooling in the base of the bath, sloshing all around her bottom. It was worth it. Slowly, wonderfully, her tender skin numbed.

It was only when she opened her eyes a few minutes later that she realised her dress had risen higher and that her black knickers were fully exposed.

One look at the gleam in Pepe's eyes and she knew he'd noticed.

'I think that's enough now,' she said, leaning up and yanking her sodden dress down to cover herself.

Pepe screwed his eyes shut to rid himself of the image. It didn't work.

The image of Cara's soaking knickers and the memories of what they hid burned brightly, almost as brightly as her flushing cheeks.

His trousers felt so tight and uncomfortable it was hard to breathe.

He gritted his teeth and willed his erection to abate.

He turned the tap off, replaced the shower head and crouched back next to her, making sure to look at her face and only her face. 'Your thighs should be okay—it doesn't look as if they're going to blister—but to play safe I've got some salve in the medicine cabinet you can put on them. I'll get it for you and then you can get changed—where's your change of clothes?'

'I didn't bring any.'

'Why not?' Whenever Cara came to Sicily she always came for at least a week.

'I only came for the day.'

'Really?' He'd arrived from Paris with barely twenty minutes to spare before the christening started, avoiding the inevitable for as long as humanly possible. He hadn't imagined Cara had done the same.

'I didn't want to risk spilling the beans to Grace before I'd had a chance to speak to you.'

'That was good of you,' he acknowledged.

'Not really.' Her face tightened. 'I was worried she'd be unable to keep it from Luca and that Luca in turn would tell you.'

Upon reflection, Pepe was certain that if his sister-in-law had known she would have tracked him down at the earliest opportunity and given him hell. 'I'll ask Grace if she has any clothes you can borrow…'

'You jolly well won't.' Cara glared at him.

'You're right. Bad idea.' If he sought Grace out he'd have to explain why her best friend was sitting with scalded thighs in his bath, and then everything about the baby would become common knowledge… 'Have you told *anyone* about the baby?'

'Only my mother, but she doesn't count.'

'Good,' he said, ignoring the tightening of her lips as she mentioned her mother. He had enough to think about as it was.

'Why's that, then? Worried all those doting Mastrangelo aunts and uncles will try and marry us off?'

'They can try all they like,' he answered with a shrug. Given a chance, they'd have him and Cara up the aisle quicker than it had taken to impregnate her.

That was if he *had* impregnated her.

He didn't care that she'd been a virgin, he didn't care that the dates tallied—until he saw cast-iron proof of his paternity he would not allow himself to believe anything. 'I bow to no one.'

'Well, neither do I. Your suggestion that I move in with you is ridiculous. How the heck would I be able to get to and from work if I have to travel all over the place with you? You work all over Europe.'

'And South America,' he pointed out. 'You'll have to give up your job.'

He noticed her shiver and remembered she'd just had a cold shower pressed against her for the best part of ten minutes.

'Let's get you out of the bath. We can finish this argument when you're dry and warm.'

'I'm not giving up my job and I'm not moving in with you.'

'I said we can argue the toss when you're dry.'

He could see how much she hated having to use him for support. Not looking at him, she allowed him to help her to her feet. He held her arms and kept her steady while she climbed out of the bath.

She looked like a drowned rat. Even her face was soaked.

Too late, he realised it was tears rolling down her cheeks.

'You're crying?'

'I'm crying because I'm angry,' she sobbed. 'You've ruined my life and now you want to ruin my future too. I *hate* you.'

He took a large, warm towel off the rack and wrapped it around her shaking frame before taking a deliberate step back. 'If you're telling me the truth then your future is made. I'll give you and the baby more money than you could ever hope to spend.'

'I don't want to be a kept woman. I just want what *our* child is entitled to.'

'You won't have to be a kept woman. The option will be there for you, that's all. If your child is mine, you'll have enough money to do whatever you want. You can hire a nanny—hell, you'll be able to hire an army of them—and return to work.'

Her teeth clattered together. 'But I won't have a job to go back to.'

'There are other jobs.'

'Not like this one. Do you have any idea how hard it is getting a foot on the ladder in the art world without *any* contacts?'

'There are other jobs,' he repeated. Deep inside his chest, a part of him had twisted into a tight ball, but he ignored it. He had to. He could not allow any softening towards her, no matter how vulnerable she looked at that particular moment.

Luisa had shown her vulnerable side numerous times. It had all been a big fat lie and he had been the sucker who had fallen for it. Every day he looked in the mirror and saw the evidence of her lies reflecting back at him. He could have had surgery to remove his scar. Instead he had chosen to keep it as a reminder not to trust and, more especially, not to love.

'You don't have to move in with me,' he said. He drew the towel together so it covered her more thoroughly and forced himself to stare into her damp eyes. He refused to break the hold, no matter the misery reflecting back at him. 'You can catch your flight back to Ireland and carry on eking out an existence. Or you can stay. If you stay, I will support you and we can take the paternity test as soon as the child is born. But if you leave now, you will not receive a single euro from me until my paternity—or lack of it—has been proven. And if you choose to leave, you'll have to go through the courts to get a DNA sample from me. That's if you can find me. As you know, I have homes in four different countries. I can make it extremely difficult for you to get that sample.'

He knew how unreasonable he must sound but he didn't care.

He could not afford to allow himself to care.

If Cara really was carrying his child then he must make every effort to protect its innocent form, and the only way he could do that was by forcing her into a corner from which the only means of escape was his way. Short of tying her up and locking her in a windowless room, this was his best chance of keeping her by his side until the birth.

He would not risk losing another child.

CHAPTER FOUR

CARA DIDN'T THINK she'd ever felt as self-conscious as she did at that moment, and she'd had plenty of experience of feeling awkward and insecure.

Pepe's blue shirt came to her knees and she'd rolled his trousers over so many times to get them to fit length-ways that it looked as if she had two wedges around her ankles. All she needed was a pair of extra-long shoes and she'd make the perfect clown.

Following him up the metal steps and into his jet, she forced herself to return the smiles and friendly greetings given by the glamorous cabin crew. Not one of them batted an eyelid at her presence. Most likely because strange women accompanying Pepe on his travels was par for the course, she thought snidely.

The jet was a proper flying bachelor pad, all leather and dark hardwood panelling. A steward showed her to a seat for take-off. She was nonplussed when Pepe took the seat next to her.

'You have ten seats to choose from,' she said, glaring at him.

'So do you,' he pointed out in return, strapping himself in and stretching his long legs out. He looked at the cheap mobile phone in her hand. 'Who are you contacting?'

'Grace.'

'What are you going to say to her?'

'That her brother-in-law is a feckless scumbag with the morals of an amoeba.'

He cocked an eyebrow.

She sighed. 'I wanted to write that but until we've got the finances sorted I'm not prepared to risk her ripping your head off.'

'That's decent of you,' he said drily.

She speared him with another poisonous glare then hit send. 'I've apologised for leaving the christening without saying goodbye. I've also told her I cadged a lift off you to the airport. Someone was bound to have seen us leave together.'

'Are you worried people will talk?' Pepe didn't sound worried. If anything, he sounded bored.

'Nope.' Let them think what they liked. The truth would come out. It always did. And when the truth came out, people would see that, beneath the charming, affable exterior, Pepe Mastrangelo was a horrid specimen of a man. 'I don't want Grace worrying, that's all.'

It crossed her mind, not for the first time, that she should have gone to Grace for help. In normal circumstances Cara *would* have gone to Grace, but when she'd found out she was pregnant, Grace had been in hiding, going through her own troubles. So, she'd told her mother, but her mam was going through yet another of her new husband's infidelities and so hadn't been particularly interested other than on a superficial level. Not that Cara had expected anything else from the woman who had given birth to her.

But then Luca had tracked Grace down and now the pair of them were madly in love and in a bubble of happiness. It would have been the perfect opportunity to ask for help.

Grace would have given her money and anything else she needed, no questions asked. But Cara wouldn't have been able to keep it contained and the whole sordid story would have come out, and then God knew what would have happened.

In any case, her child was not her friend's responsibility. It was Pepe's.

And this mess was not of Grace's making. This was all on her, Cara. And the feckless playboy, of course.

It was too late to go to Grace for help now. Pepe would undoubtedly turn to Luca, who in turn would put pressure on his wife not to give Cara any financial help. Grace was so loved up at the moment she would probably comply. At the very least it would cause friction between them.

Thanks to Pepe, she couldn't turn to the one person she needed.

The steward, who was still making checks and pretending not to listen to their conversation, finally disappeared into a separate cabin.

'How are your thighs?' Pepe asked. If he was fazed about anything, he had yet to show it.

'Not too bad.' The salve he had given her had been bliss to apply. He'd also given her a wrap that resembled cling film to place on it too. He'd been so... *Concerned* was the wrong word but it was the closest for the way he'd treated her wounds. Not that he'd treated *her* with the same consideration.

How could someone be so gentle and at the same time be so horribly uncaring? That was part of what had tipped her over the edge and set the waterworks off.

'You should take the trousers off. I'm sure it can't help with the material rubbing against it.'

'They're fine.' No way was she taking any of her clothes off within a ten-mile radius of him ever again.

The plane began to taxi down the runway. Cara turned to look out of the window, a lump forming in her throat.

This was utter madness.

'Pepe, please, let me return to Dublin, just for a couple of days to get things in order.' It was an argument they'd had three times in the past hour.

'Impossible. I have a full day of business tomorrow and a business dinner in the evening.'

'Yes, but I don't. I'm supposed to be at work!'

'You will attend my meeting with me.'

She took a deep breath. Her blood pressure really didn't need any more aggravation.

'As I have made you more than aware, the week ahead is filled with appointments.'

'I have to wait until the weekend to go back home?' she said, horror-struck.

'I'm afraid a trip back to Dublin is not on the schedule for the foreseeable future.'

'You're kidding me?'

'You can make any necessary arrangements via other means.'

'So I have to hand in my notice by text or email?'

He shrugged. 'It's entirely up to you how you want to handle it.'

'I'd like to handle it by *not* giving up my job,' she stated angrily. 'But seeing as I *do* have to quit, I'd prefer to tell my boss in person.'

He almost looked sympathetic. 'I appreciate this is an inconvenience but if, as you say, the baby is mine, you will be well recompensed for any aggravation.'

'And my housemates? Will they be *recompensed* too?' His brow furrowed.

'I'm leaving them in the lurch. If you won't let me go

to Dublin, I can't clear my room out and they can't find another housemate to take my place.'

'That is not a problem. I can send someone over to clear your room for you.'

'You will not!' There was no way she wanted some stranger rifling through her knicker drawer. Closing her eyes, she slowly expelled a lungful of air. They had been so busy arguing she'd barely noticed the jet increase in speed. Suddenly her stomach lurched and she was leaning back.

The jet became airborne.

She took another deep breath. 'If I contact my housemates and ask them to get all my stuff together, can you send someone to collect it?'

'Of course.'

'Can they get it to me for tomorrow morning?'

'Why so soon?'

'Because I have nothing on me apart from my handbag and a stick of mascara. I need my stuff.'

'I've already made arrangements for new clothing to be delivered to the house first thing for you.'

Of course he had. For such a languid person Pepe was proving surprisingly efficient.

'I want *my* stuff.'

'And you will have it. Soon.'

'How soon?'

'Soon. And I will ensure your housemates get adequate compensation from your missed rent.'

'Good.' She would not say thank you.

Her stomach rolled again and she breathed in deeply through her nose.

'Are you okay?'

She did *not* want to hear any concern from him. 'I'm pregnant. My child's father is refusing to acknowledge paternity without a blood test yet still thinks it's acceptable to make me give up my job—a job I love—and leave my housemates in the doodle to follow him around the world like some sort of concubine. Plus I have no clothing or toiletries on me. So, yes. Everything is dandy.'

His gorgeous blue eyes darkened further and crinkled with amusement. 'My concubine, eh? Do you know what a concubine is?'

She felt her cheeks go scarlet. 'It was a statement of my unhappiness not a statement of fact.'

'A concubine is, in essence, a man's mistress.'

'I'm well aware of that.'

'A man pays for all his concubine's bills, buys property for her—'

'Basically a concubine is there for a man's pleasure when he's bored of his wife's company,' she interrupted. 'But seeing as you have no wife, I can't be your concubine.'

A gleam came into his eyes. 'Ah, so as I have no wife, does that mean you are going to be the main source of my pleasure?'

'I'd rather eat worms.'

'I'm sure I can think of something better for you to e—'

'Don't go there. I feel sick enough as it is.'

He laughed. 'That's not how I remember things.'

'Watch it or I will vomit.' But not through the memories of their night together.

Those memories moved her in wholly different ways.

Nope, the queasiness in her belly was solely due to motion sickness. She scrunched her eyes closed and took a long deep breath.

Pepe twisted onto his side to stare at her. Cara really

was incredibly sexy, even with her face contorted into a grimace.

But he would not go there again. Flirting with her was just asking for trouble. They had enough problems to get through.

She opened one eye. 'What?'

'Sorry?'

'You're staring at me.'

'Can't a man stare at a gorgeous woman?' Okay, so flirting was asking for trouble, but Cara really did look beautiful when she was angry, as clichéd as he knew that was.

'I'm pregnant,' she spat.

'You're also incredibly sexy. A man would have to be dead from the waist down not to desire you. But have no fear—I'm not going to make any unwanted passes at you.' All the same, he felt a tightening in his groin and almost groaned aloud at the incongruity of it all.

Cara despised him. No matter how much he might still desire her and, he suspected, she still desired him, he preferred his women to not loathe the very sound of his name.

And sex between them…nothing good could come of it. It had got him into enough trouble as it was, just as he'd always suspected sex with Cara would—why else had he kept such a distance from her sexually before?

In the world in which he mixed, sex was freely given with no real commitment assumed by anyone. Pepe liked it that way. It saved messy entanglements and even messier goodbyes. Everyone knew where they stood, no one got hurt, and everyone was happy.

'Well, that's good to know,' Cara said sarcastically. 'Let me guess—now that you don't need anything from me, there's no need to pretend any more.'

'What do you mean?'

'You never desired me before you needed to get hold of my phone.'

'On the contrary, *cucciola mia*, I've always found you incredibly attractive.'

'I'm pretty sure you find any woman with a pulse attractive. I'm saying you never desired *me* in particular.'

'I did, but I'm terrified of my sister-in-law. She would have tied me naked to a tree if I'd tried anything on with you.'

Despite herself, Cara snickered. Pepe was the cause of all her stress yet somehow he was able to soothe much of it away. The git. 'I would have loved to have seen that.'

'Don't worry—if the baby does turn out to be mine then I'm sure you'll get your chance when Grace finds out.'

'There's no *if* about it. This baby is yours.'

'Time will tell.' A black eyebrow shot up, a quizzical groove appearing in his forehead. 'If it *is* my child, will I also have to worry about your angry father beating at my door?'

'Seeing as he's not around, that's the last thing you'll have to worry about.'

He straightened in his seat, consternation replacing his amusement. 'Oh. I'm sorry. I didn't realise you'd lost your father too.'

It occurred to her that this was the closest Pepe had come to showing genuine contrition all day.

'My father isn't dead,' she quickly clarified, recalling being told his own father had died over a decade ago.

He looked confused. 'Then surely he will want to rip my head off and play football with it?'

She couldn't help the wry smile that formed on her lips, although she experienced the usual sickening churn in her belly she felt whenever she thought of her father. 'I'm sure there's a lot of fathers out there who would love nothing more than to cause you actual bodily harm, but I can assure you my dad's not one of them.'

'Why not? A father's job is to look out for his child.'

'My dad never bothered to read the job description.' Only years of faux nonchalance on the subject kept the bitterness from her voice, yet the churning increased, a situation not helped by the roils in her belly from the motion of the jet. Talking about her father always made her feel so *raw.* 'Believe me, if he were to meet you, the closest he would come to touching you is putting a hand on your shoulder and insisting on buying you a beer.'

For all of Pepe's antics and reputation, he knew damn well that if he had a daughter and some man lied to her and impregnated her, then he would certainly want to rip that man's head off.

Not that he was admitting to having impregnated Cara. Not yet. Not until the DNA test proved it beyond any doubt. And until that DNA test proved it, he would not allow himself to think of that child as being anything but a foetus. After what Luisa had put him through, this was an essential act of self-preservation.

He thought back to a time over a decade before when he had been looking at a scan of a foetus, trying to discern a head and tiny limbs from what was little more than a kidney bean. The emotions provoked by looking at that scan were the strongest he had ever experienced. Totally overwhelming. He had felt fit to burst. He could only imagine the strength of his feelings if that little life had been allowed to develop and allowed to be born.

But that little life had *not* been allowed to develop and be born, a fact that resided inside his guts like a vat of poison…

All the same, he could not imagine having a child and being so disassociated from their feelings that he didn't care if they were used and hurt. He might only be the 'spare' of the family, but he had never doubted his parents' love for him.

It was their respect he'd always failed to achieve.

He could well imagine how his brother would react if anyone were to hurt Lily. That person would likely never walk again.

Cara must have seen the way his thoughts were going because her features contorted into a grimace. 'Do you know, now I think about it, you and my father are incredibly alike. He's a charmer, just like you. Maybe I should introduce you to him—you can exchange shagging tips.'

It took every muscle in his face to keep his smile fixed there. 'Why do I feel I have just been insulted?'

'Because you're not as stupid as you look?' Before he could react to this latest insult, she stood up. 'If it's all the same to you, I'm going to curl up on that sofa and get some sleep. I assume one of the stewards will wake me before we land?'

She *did* look tired. So tired he bit back any further retort and any further questions about her father. Like it or not, she was pregnant and, now that he'd admitted her into his life, her health was his responsibility. Her already pale face was drained of colour.

He experienced a twinge that could be interpreted as concern. 'Are you feeling all right? Physically, I mean,' he added before she could bombard him with another long list of all the wrongs he had done.

'I'm feeling a little icky. But don't worry—it's not bad enough that you have to worry for your upholstery.'

He watched as she made her way to the sofa, holding on to something fixed for stability with every step.

A tap on the door broke through Cara's slumber.

There was none of that 'where am I' malarkey often

experienced when awaking under a new roof. Before she even opened her eyes she knew exactly where she was.

Pepe's house. Or, to be more precise, in a guest room in Pepe's Parisian house.

She'd pretended to sleep for the rest of the flight back to Charles de Gaulle airport. It certainly beat talking to him.

She'd ignored him as they'd gone through Customs, blanked him on the drive back to his house and pretended to be deaf when they arrived at his home, a five-storey town house in an exclusive Parisian suburb. She'd also pretended to be mute. She'd had to clamp her lips so tightly together when she was shown to her room that she'd pretended they'd been superglued. It was either that or have him witness her wonder at its sheer beauty. For a house purported to have been bought to showcase Pepe's art collection—and it was every bit as huge and glamorous as she'd expected—it had a surprisingly homely charm to it.

But she wouldn't tell Pepe that. She didn't want him to think she liked anything about him, not even his beautiful home.

It was talking about her father that had done it.

Her father, the arch charmer, the man who could make a woman forgive him over and over, make a woman believe his faults were in fact *her* faults.

Pepe's charm had always felt different from her father's. He had none of her father's seediness. Or sleaze.

But one thing he did have was the ability to make her *want* to believe in him. She'd wanted to believe Pepe saw her as more than a one-night stand. On his jet she'd felt herself thawing towards him, his gorgeous, easy-going smile slowly melting the edge of her defences. More than that, though, had been the unexpected depths she'd seen in his eyes. For a few moments she could have sworn she'd seen pain in them, something dark, something that hinted there was more to him than what he wore on the surface.

She'd thought she'd seen more to him that weekend in Dublin when he had seduced her so thoroughly. And it had all been a lie. Just as everything that came out of her father's mouth was a lie.

Pepe was of the same mould. Something she would do well to remember.

She sat up and rubbed her eyes.

Another knock at the door.

'Mademoiselle Delaney?' came a muffled female voice.

'I'm awake,' she called back, slipping out of the bed. Much as she hated to admit it, that had to qualify as *the* most comfortable bed she had ever slept on.

The handle turned and a middle-aged woman carrying a tray of coffee and croissants walked in.

Cara remembered her from their arrival, was certain Pepe had introduced her as Monique, his housekeeper.

'Good morning,' said Monique, heading straight for a small round table in the corner of the room and placing the tray on it. 'Did you sleep well?'

'Yes, thank you,' she answered in a small voice, forcing a smile. She always felt so...*noodley* when with strangers, as if her tongue had loosened, then tied itself into knots.

'Your deliveries have arrived,' Monique told her, drawing back the heavy full-length curtains to reveal a small balcony.

Morning sunshine filled the room.

Cara cleared her throat. 'What deliveries?'

'From the boutiques. I will bring them to you now.

Monsieur Mastrangelo has requested that you be ready to leave in an hour.'

Her heart sinking, Cara remembered a trip to the Loire Valley was on the day's agenda.

Her spirits lifted a fraction when Monique, assisted by a young woman, brought the boxes of clothes in to her, and a hand-case of toiletries.

'If there is anything else you require, please let me know,' Monique said before leaving the room.

Putting her half-eaten croissant to one side, Cara began going through the boxes, her spirits sinking all over again as she fingered the beautiful fabrics and accessories.

Why couldn't Pepe have ensured the clothing he'd ordered for her was inappropriate and gross? Here was an entire wardrobe for her and there was not a single item she wouldn't have selected herself if money had not been an object. Simple, elegant, casual clothing with an innate vibrancy. Even the nightdresses he'd ordered were beautiful.

When she opened the hand-case she wanted to scream with both joy and despair. Enclosed was every lotion and potion a woman could want, and make-up selected especially for her colouring. Worst of all was that it was all brands she coveted. She would walk past their counters in department stores and gaze at the beautiful items, promising herself that she would buy them when she earned enough money.

Shouldn't she be pleased she had them roughly five years ahead of schedule? Maybe she should but she couldn't muster up the necessary sparkly feelings. She didn't want to feel any gratitude towards Pepe. Wasn't that how Stockholm syndrome started? Not that she'd been kidnapped, not in the traditional sense of the word.

In the 'really not been given any other option' sense of the word then she had been.

She gathered all the toiletries together and took them into the en suite. Before stepping into the shower, she examined her thighs. Pepe's ointment was a marvel. The only discernible sign of injury was a slight pink mark. No pain *at all*.

The shower itself invigorated her. The gel smelt so utterly gorgeous and the water pressure and heat were so marvellous that she washed herself twice.

Well, that certainly beat the pathetic excuse for a shower she had in her shared bathroom in Dublin.

Wrapping a large fluffy white towel securely around her, she wandered back into her bedroom. She needed to select something to wear, which in theory shouldn't be a problem, but when one was confronted with a dozen beautiful outfits it became one.

For the first time in her life she had a problem selecting what to wear.

Just as she'd decided on a pair of designer black jeans and a cherry-red cashmere jumper, there was another knock on her door.

'Come in,' she called, expecting to see Monique standing there.

Her welcoming smile turned into a scowl when she found Pepe there instead.

CHAPTER FIVE

'WHAT DO YOU WANT?'

'Good morning to you too, *cucciola mia*,' he replied with a flash of his straight white teeth. He was wearing a grey suit with a white shirt and a black cravat. Yes. A cravat. Pepe wore a cravat that should look ridiculous but instead...

He looked far too gorgeous for sensibility.

'We need to leave shortly.'

Cara shrugged. 'If you want me to come with you, then you'll have to wait. I'm not ready.'

'Monique told you to be ready in an hour. That was an hour ago.'

'I don't wear a watch and my phone's out of battery, so I have no way of knowing what the time is. I would charge my phone but the charger's in Dublin,' she added pointedly.

'Is no problem,' he said, brushing his way past her and perching on her bed. 'As you suggested, I will wait for you.'

'Not in here, you won't.'

'And you are going to stop me how?' he asked in a chiding fashion.

She speared him with the nastiest glare she could muster.

He laughed softly, which made her scowl all the more.

Still laughing, he rummaged through one of the boxes and held up a pair of skimpy black lace knickers. 'Are you going to wear these?'

She snatched them from him, knowing her cheeks had turned a deep red to match her hair. 'Get out and let me get changed.'

'I would but I have a feeling you will get ready quicker if I'm in here with you.'

Calling him every nasty word she knew under her breath but loud enough for him to hear, Cara gathered her selected outfit and swept off back into the en suite, letting the door shut with a bang.

For a moment she was reluctant to take the towel off. She had no fear he would barge in on her—where that certainty came from, she could not say—but it wouldn't surprise her in the least to learn he had X-ray vision.

The thought made her feel distinctly off-kilter, in a way that was completely inappropriate.

The thought of Pepe staring at her naked body while she was oblivious should *not* make her breasts feel heavy...

Swallowing away moisture that had suddenly filled her mouth, she pulled her knickers on, too late recalling them being the same pair Pepe had just fingered.

This was how he'd been able to seduce her so easily.

For some reason her testosterone-immune body re-acted to Pepe and became pathetic and weak-willed around him.

By the end of their weekend together she had been like a lust-filled nympho.

What was it about him?

And what was so wrong with her that she still reacted to him, even after everything he had done? Not forgetting that she was pregnant—shouldn't pregnancy act as a natural form of anti-aphrodisiac? If it didn't, it jolly well should.

Pathetic. That's what she was.

Dressed, she went back into the room. Pepe had moved to an armchair in the corner, his long legs stretched out, doing something on his phone.

His eyebrows rose when he saw her. 'Are you going to be much longer?'

'I'm good to go.'

'Your hair's still wet.'

'It's a bit damp, that's all.' She'd towel-dried it as well as she could.

'It's cold outside.'

'My hairdryer's in Dublin.'

Pepe was fast beginning to recognise the look Cara threw at him as her 'if you'd let me get my stuff as I've asked you repeatedly, I wouldn't have this problem, ergo, this problem is *your* fault' look.

'I will ensure a hairdryer is here for you when we return from the vineyard.'

'I'm hoping my hair will be dry by then.'

'Hmm.' He gazed at her musingly. 'I would say sarcasm doesn't suit you but it actually does.'

She scowled. 'Funnily enough, it's only when I'm around you that my sarcastic gene comes out.'

'I will have to work hard to eradicate it,' he said, getting to his feet and leaning over to swipe her nose. She did have the cutest nose. 'And I'll work hard to eradicate the evil looks you keep throwing at me.'

'The only way that's going to happen is if you find *your* reasonable gene and let me return to Dublin.'

'You're welcome to return to Dublin any time you

like,' he said, smiling to disguise his irritation. 'I have made it clear what the consequences will be if you do so.'

'Like I said, you need to find your reasonable gene. Find it and I might lose my sarcastic gene.'

'I have already found my reasonable gene. It is unfortunate it differs from your definition of *reasonable* but there you go—you can't please everyone.' He expanded his hands and mocked a bow. 'Now, my fiery little geisha, it is time for us to leave.'

'What did you call me?' The look she gave him was no mere scowl. If looks could turn a man to stone he would now be made of granite.

'So touchy.'

'Calling me a geisha is pretty much on a par with calling me a concubine.'

'Not at all—a concubine is a permanent fixture in a man's life, there to give pleasure. A geisha is a hostess and an artiste. It is rare for a geisha to have sex with a male client.'

She didn't look in the slightest bit mollified. If anything, her scowl deepened.

'I can see I have my work cut out with you,' he said with a theatrical sigh. 'Maybe it is a good thing you will be with me for five months—I fear it will take me that long to get a smile out of you.'

Cara sat upright as they drove into a heliport, or whatever the name was for a field with a great big white helicopter with red Mastrangelo livery on it, and an enormous hangar right behind it.

Her stomach turned over at the sight of it. 'Please tell me we are not travelling in that thing?'

'It's either an eight-hour round trip to the vineyard by car, or we can do it in a quarter of the time in this beauty.'

'I vote for the car.'

'Sorry, *cucciola mia*, but I vote for the chopper. An hour there, an hour back.'

'It's a split vote.'

'It's my time and money.'

'Do I *have* to come? Can't I just wait here?'

'Yes, you do have to come.' For the first time she detected an edge to his voice. 'I'm not arguing with you again. I assure you, the ride will be perfectly safe and comfortable.' To prove his non-arguing point, he opened his door and got out.

She stuck her tongue out at his retreating form, watching as he joined a trio of men standing by the helicopter, all wearing black overalls. She guessed they were the flight crew.

The interior of the helicopter settled her nerves a touch. It was much less tinny than she had thought a helicopter would be. If anything, it was rather plush. She climbed aboard and sat down on a reclining white leather seat. Pepe showed her where all the big-boy-with-too-much-money gadgets were located on the seat, including a foldaway laptop.

'Aren't you sitting with me?' she asked, perturbed when he went to climb back out.

He grinned. 'One of us has to fly the thing.'

Before she could react, he'd jumped out and slid the door closed. In less than a minute he had opened the door at the front and made himself at home with the controls.

'Very funny, Mastrangelo,' she said, speaking over the low partition dividing them. If she wanted she could lean over and prod him. Which she was seriously considering doing if he didn't stop buggering about…

'Where's the pilot?' she asked, desperation suddenly lacing her voice.

He didn't look back, simply continued doing whatever he was doing with the range of knobs and buttons and thingies before him. 'Ladies and gentlemen, this is your captain speaking,' he said, amusement lacing his deep voice. 'For your own safety, Air Mastrangelo asks that you keep your seat belt fastened at all times and refrain from smoking for the duration of the flight.'

'You are having a laugh.'

He put some headphones on then turned his head back to look at her. 'Put your belt on, Cara—I promise you are in safe hands.'

'What about the men you were talking to? Aren't they going to fly it?'

'They were the maintenance crew.'

It was only when he turned the engine on that she truly believed Pepe was going to pilot it.

'Please,' she shouted over the noise of the propellers—who would have known it would be so *loud*?—'tell me you're only joking.'

'Belt on.' He started speaking into the mouthpiece of the headphone, talking in fluent French, his whole demeanour altering, adopting a serious hue.

'You can really fly this thing?' she asked when he'd stopped speaking and was doing stuff on the dashboard—was it even called a dashboard?

'I really can.'

'You're really qualified?'

'I really am. Have you got your seat belt on?'

'Yes.'

'Then we are good to go.'

And just like that, they were airborne.

And just like that, Cara's stomach lurched. She actually felt her half-eaten croissant and decaf coffee move inside her.

Slowly, the helicopter rose. At least it seemed slow, their ascent high above the heliport gradual.

Nothing was rushed. Everything in the cockpit was calm. And, as she watched him concentrate, watched him fly the beast they were in, her fears and nerves began to subside.

She'd ridden on planes many times, was used to the smoothness and almost hypnotic hum of the engines. This was different on so many levels.

There were so many things she wanted to ask him, not least of which was how did playboy extraordinaire Pepe Mastrangelo have the discipline to get his pilot's licence? His intelligence was not in doubt, but this was a man with the attention span of a goldfish—at least with women. She might know next to nothing about flying a helicopter but she knew for certain there was a lot more involved than learning to drive a car.

Surely it was something he would be proud to tell people? Never mind all the double dates they'd shared with Luca and Grace; they'd spent practically a whole weekend together, discussed all the vineyards he owned with his brother, discussed all the travelling he did between those vineyards as his brother liked to base himself on the family estate in Sicily, and not once had he mentioned flying his own helicopter. He hadn't even hinted at it.

As she looked at him now, relaxed but alert, clearly in his element…it was as if he'd been born to fly.

She wanted to bombard him with questions but, despite the unexpected smoothness of the flight—a smoothness she knew without having to be told came from the skill of his piloting—the nausea in her stomach was spreading, reaching the stage where all her concentration had to be devoted purely to breathing and swallowing the saliva that had filled her mouth.

'Everything okay in the back?' he called out to her.

'All dandy. Thank you.' She inhaled deeply and closed her eyes.

'There are sick bags in the side pocket of your chair,' he said after a few moments of silence had passed.

All she could manage was a grunt.

It was Cara's *thank you* that alerted Pepe to something being wrong. He'd guessed on the jet to Paris from Sicily that she was suffering from motion sickness, had kept a close eye on her sleeping form in case she awoke and needed attention, but nothing had come of it.

He'd piloted enough people in the past decade to know when someone was suffering from it. Right then, he could hear in the deepness of her breathing that she was one of the unfortunate ones. He didn't imagine she would extend politeness towards him under any other circumstance.

'There's a neck pillow in the side pocket too,' he called out over his shoulder, pressing the button to turn the air conditioning on. 'If you put it on it'll help keep your head stable. Find a fixed point in the horizon to focus on. I promise I will make the ride as smooth as I can. The conditions out there are good.'

He received another grunt in return.

If there was one thing he had learned it was that those afflicted by motion sickness were never in the mood for idle chit-chat. All he could do to help on any practical level was concentrate on the job in hand and do his best to keep the craft in as straight a motion as he could. He regretted not taking the 'doors off' approach, but at the time had thought it would probably terrify her if she was alone in the back.

Every now and then he would ask if she was okay and

get a grunt in return. He didn't hear any sound of retching or vomiting, so that was a plus.

By the time he landed on the field a few miles from the vineyard he was thinking of purchasing, all was silent.

When he climbed over the partition to help her out, he almost did a double take. He had never seen anyone turn that particular shade of green before. Except, maybe, the Incredible Hulk.

She'd taken his advice with the neck rest, but apart from that she'd clearly dealt with her malady in her own way, reclining her seat as far back as it would go and keeping her eyes scrunched closed. Her hands gripped an empty sick bag, her knuckles white.

He slid the door open to let the air in then went back to her. He crouched down and placed a hand lightly on her shoulder. 'We're here.'

Cara opened one eye and peered at him. Or was it a glare? He couldn't quite tell. 'I know. We've stopped moving.'

'Can you stand?'

'I'll try in a minute.' She snapped her eye shut again then sucked in a breath and swallowed loudly. 'By the way, if you try and carry me out of here, I will sock you one.'

'Just breathe.'

She filled her lungs.

'That's it. In through the nose and out through the mouth.'

'I do know how to breathe. I've been doing it all my life.' Her snappy retort was said with teeth that weren't so much gritted as sucked.

'That's a very clever trait to have,' he said gravely. He had to admit that, despite her green hue, there was something incredibly sexy about the way she sparred with him. 'I will give you five minutes for your body to right itself and if you're still not capable of walking I *will* carry you to the car.'

His threat did the trick as when he returned exactly five minutes later Cara was sitting upright with her eyes open.

She looked at him. 'I think I need your help getting to my feet.'

'You must be bad.' If he hadn't already seen with his eyes that she was unwell, her clammy skin would have definitely given the game away. Her hand gripped his wrist so tightly her neat but short nails dug into his flesh.

She leaned into him, allowing him to half drag her to the open door.

'It'll be easier for you to get out if you sit down—it's a bit of a gap at the best of times.' Not waiting for an argument, he helped her sit her shaky frame to the floor and dangle her legs out of the overhang.

Then he jumped down.

'Can you get down or do you need my help?' If it was anyone else he'd just pull them down the last few inches.

Her green eyes pierced into him. He could see how much it pained her to have to say, 'I need your help.'

He placed his hands on her waist. 'Put your arms around me.'

'Do I have to?'

'No. It'll probably be safer for you though.'

This time she gritted her teeth for real.

Tilting her head to the side and away from his gaze, she looped her arms around his neck, taking care not to touch him in anything but the loosest of fashions.

Deliberately, he closed the small gap between them, felt her heavy breasts crush against his chest. Not for the first time that day he felt a flicker of excitement stir inside him. It was nice to know he wasn't dead from the waist down as he'd been fearing in recent months.

As it was such a short distance for her feet to reach—although if she'd been a few inches taller she would probably have reached the ground from the sitting position—it was a simple matter of tugging her down onto terra firma.

She swayed into him, her cheek coming to rest against his chest, her arms dropping from his neck like deadened weights.

'I'm sorry,' she muttered.

'I'm not.' He slipped his arms around her waist to support her limp form, and enjoyed the feel of her soft curves pressing against the contrasting hardness of his body. She really was incredibly cuddly. She was also clearly unwell. 'Can you walk?'

'Yes.' There was a definite air of defiance in her affirmation, a defiance aimed at her own legs rather than him. 'Do *not* carry me.'

'Come. The car is waiting for us.'

Half dragging her, Pepe somehow managed to manoeuvre Cara the ten metres or so to the Land Rover.

Christophe Beauquet, the vineyard's current owner, was behind the wheel waiting for them. He made no effort to get out and welcome them and made only the briefest of grunts when Pepe helped Cara sit down in the front.

Pepe leaned over to strap her seat belt on, trying to ignore, again, her gorgeous scent. He could hear her furious swallowing, knew she was doing her best to keep back what her body was so desperate to expel. Her hand still clutched the sick bag.

'She needs to look forwards,' he explained before jumping into the back of the four-wheel drive.

Christophe didn't even try to hide his disgust. 'All this fuss for a short air ride?'

The hairs on Pepe's arms lifted. It took him a moment to realise it was his hackles rising. 'She's pregnant,' he answered shortly, leaning back into his seat and clamping his mouth into a firm line. He did not like the Frenchman's tone. He didn't like it *at all*.

CHAPTER SIX

WHEN CARA AWOKE it was dusky. Unlike when she'd awoken that morning, she didn't have the faintest idea where she was. The last thing she remembered was pulling up alongside a pretty farmhouse. Oh, and she remembered Pepe practically yanking her door open so she could vomit. How he knew she was waiting until the car stopped moving before giving in to it, she didn't have a clue. But he did know. And as she'd vomited out of the car and into the paper bag, he was by her side, rubbing her back and drawing her hair away from the danger zone.

It was support of a kind she'd never expected from him, and remembering it made her belly do a funny skip.

She patted her body, relieved to find herself fully dressed. She felt better. A little woozy, but on the whole much better.

When she sat up, she found her shoes, a gorgeous pair of flats from a designer brand she had coveted for years, laid neatly by the double bed she had been placed in.

She guessed she should get up and find Pepe. He was around somewhere, in this picture-book home.

It didn't take long to find him.

She shuffled out of the room and into an open landing. Below, she could hear voices. Walking carefully, she made her way down the stairs and followed the murmurs into a large kitchen.

Sitting around a sturdy oak table was Pepe, the man she remembered as Christophe and a tiny, birdlike woman. So small, the woman was inches shorter than Cara. It was like looking at Mrs Pepperpot come to life.

Mrs Pepperpot spotted her first and bustled over, taking Cara's arm and leading her over to join them, all the while gabbling away in French.

Pepe rose from his chair. 'Cara,' he said, pulling her into an embrace and kissing her on each cheek. 'How are you feeling?'

'Much better,' she mumbled.

'Good.' He stepped back and appraised her thoughtfully. A half-filled glass of wine lay before him. 'You are still a little too pale but you no longer look like the Incredible Hulk.'

'That's a bonus.' She sat on the chair he'd pulled out for her and budged it close to his. No sooner had she sat down when Mrs Pepperpot put a steaming bowl of what looked like a clear broth in front of her and a basket of baguettes.

'*Mangez,*' she ordered, putting her hands to her mouth in what looked like an imitation of eating.

'Cara, this is Christophe's wife, Simone,' Pepe said by way of introduction. 'She doesn't speak any English but she makes an excellent consommé.'

Cara gave Simone a quick smile. 'Thank you—*merci.*'

The consommé smelt delicious. Her starved belly rumbled. Loudly.

'*Mangez,*' Simone repeated.

'She's been waiting for you to wake up,' Pepe said. 'It's also thanks to her that the doctor made an impromptu home visit.'

Vaguely she remembered a heavily scented woman sitting on her bedside and prodding her with things. 'I thought I'd dreamt that.'

He laughed softly. 'You're four months pregnant. It seemed prudent to get you checked over in case you were suffering from something more serious than motion sickness.'

For all his jovial nonchalance, she knew she hadn't dreamt his concern. A strange warmth swept into her chest, suffusing her blood and skin with heat.

She turned her face away. 'I've suffered from motion sickness since I was a little girl. Pregnancy has just made it worse.'

'Even so, I've made arrangements for my family doctor to fly to Paris tomorrow to check you over. The doctor you saw here had concerns about your blood pressure being too low.'

'It's always been low,' she dismissed with a shrug.

'It is better to be safe. You have a child inside you that is dependent on your good health for its survival. I was going to get my doctor to check you over anyway, so I've just brought it forward by a few days.'

'Steady on, Pepe. You almost sound like a concerned father.'

His eyes flickered but the easy smile didn't leave his face.

Luckily any awkwardness was interrupted by Simone placing a jug of iced water in front of her and pouring Cara a glass.

'Why does she keep staring at me?' Cara muttered under her breath a few minutes later so only Pepe could hear. Simone kept nodding and beaming at her, unlike her surly husband, who did nothing but cradle his glass of wine. The Frenchwoman might not speak English but

Cara would bet Christophe knew more than enough to get by.

'Because you're pregnant and she wants to make sure you're getting the nutrition you need. You need to eat.'

'How can I eat when everyone's staring at me?'

For a moment she thought Pepe was going to make a wisecrack. Instead, he drew Christophe and Simone into conversation and, while the talk between them was of a serious tone, it worked, diverting their attention away from her.

Pepe was right about the consommé. It was delicious. Along with a still-warm bread roll, it filled her belly just enough.

It was at the moment she put her spoon in her empty dish that Christophe laughed at something Pepe said, downed his wine and held out a beefy hand. Pepe rose from his seat to take it and, leaning over the table, the two men shook hands vigorously, Christophe gripping Pepe's biceps.

'Is this a new form of male bonding?' Cara said in an aside to Pepe.

To her surprise, it was Christophe who answered. 'It is always good to formalise a deal with a shake of the hand.'

'You're buying the vineyard?' she asked Pepe.

'I would say it's more that Christophe has agreed to *sell* me the vineyard.' Pepe raised his glass in the Frenchman's direction. 'You drive a hard bargain, my friend.'

'Some bargains deserve to be hard fought.' Christophe lifted the wine bottle and made to refill Pepe's glass.

Pepe held out a hand to stop him. 'Not for me. I will be driving back to Paris shortly.'

'Driving?' Cara asked hopefully.

'*Sì.* I got some staff to bring a car over for us.'

'Where are they?'

'They've taken the helicopter back. Don't worry—
I got the flight crew to come. They left about half an
hour ago.'

For a moment she just stared at him, incredulous. 'Seriously? You got your pilots to drive all this way to drop
off a car and then fly back?' How long had she been
asleep? Five hours? He must have got the wheels in motion the second her head had hit the pillow.

He shrugged as if it were no big deal. 'They weren't
doing anything else. It gave them a day out.'

'Did you do this…for *me*?'

'The helicopter's not long been reupholstered. I didn't
want to risk you ruining it by upchucking everywhere.'

Somehow, she just knew Pepe could not give a flying
monkey about upholstery.

'I thought we were going to a business dinner tonight?'

'I'm sure they can survive without our company for
one night,' he said drily. 'I am not so cruel that I would
force you to spend another hour in a craft that makes you
violently ill for the sake of a dinner party with a handful
of the most boring people in all of Paris.'

A compulsion, a strange, strange desire, tingled through
her fingers to lace themselves through his.

Quickly she fisted her hands into balls.

So what if he'd displayed a hint at humanity?

It didn't mean she had to hold his hand.

It didn't change a thing.

By the time they left the vineyard, the sun had set and
the Loire Valley was in darkness. The roads were clear,
the drive smooth, but still Pepe was aware that Cara's
breathing had deepened.

'Are you feeling all right?' he asked, turning the air
conditioning up a notch.

'I think so.' Her head was back against the rest, her eyes shut.

'Open a window if it helps.' It was too dark to see the colour of her complexion, but he'd bet it had regained the green hue.

Cold air filtered through the small opening she made in the window, and she turned her face towards it, breathing the fresh air in.

'You say you've always suffered from motion sickness?' he said a few minutes later when he was reasonably certain she wasn't going to upchuck everywhere.

'As long as I can remember. Boats are the worst.'

'Have you been on many boats?'

'A couple of ferry crossings from England to Ireland when I was a teenager. I spent most of those hugging the toilet.'

'Sounds like fun.'

'It was—tremendous fun was had by all.'

He laughed softly. If there was one thing he liked about Cara it was her dry sense of humour.

He slowed the car a touch, keeping a keen eye out for any potholes or other potential hazards. The last thing he wanted was to do anything to increase her nausea.

'How long have you flown helicopters?' she asked.

'I got my licence about ten years ago.'

'I had no idea.'

'It's no big deal,' he dismissed.

'Sure it is. I assume it's more involved than passing a driving test?'

'Slightly,' he admitted, recalling the hundreds of flying hours he'd put in and the unrelenting exams. He'd loved every minute of it. And, he had to admit, his mother's pride when he'd received his pilot's licence had been something to cherish. Her pride was generally reserved for Luca.

'Are you going to make me fly in one again?'

'No.' He knew if he insisted, she would—ungraciously—comply. As he was fast learning, keeping Cara Delaney attached to him was proving trickier than first thought.

'So you're going to buy the vineyard, then?' she said, changing the subject.

'I am. It's a good, established business and the soil is of excellent quality.'

'How did you get Christophe to agree to sell it to you? He looked like he'd rather be wrestling bears than dealing with you when we arrived.'

'I think surliness is his default setting,' Pepe mused. 'He's one of those men who feel they have to prove their masculinity by puffing out their chest and pounding on it.'

He heard what sounded like a snigger. For a moment it was on the tip of his tongue to share how he'd been on the verge of telling the Frenchman that he could forget the sale, so incensed had he been by Christophe's attitude to Cara's nausea. If his wife, Simone, hadn't been such a welcome contrast, soothing Pepe's ruffled feathers and chiding her husband's surliness away, he would have refused to even take a tour.

Dealing with ultra-macho men was nothing new—he was Sicilian after all. Most men there drank testosterone for breakfast. Today, for the first time, he hadn't wanted to play the macho games such men demanded. He never gained any gratification from them. His own power was assured. There was no need to beat his chest or play a game of 'mine is bigger than yours'. Without being arrogant, he knew that went without saying—in *all* circumstances. But men like Christophe expected those games to be played. Today, for the first time, Pepe had refused.

He'd wanted to look after Cara.

His fingers tightened on the steering wheel as he recalled the way his stomach had clenched to see her so obviously unwell. Yes. A most peculiar feeling. Maladies did not normally bother him. People became ill, then, as a rule, people recovered. A fact of life.

Pregnancy was also a fact of life. As was motion sickness. Cara's suffering really shouldn't bother him beyond the usual realms of human decency.

Yet it did. It was taking all his self-restraint not to lay a comforting hand on her thigh. Saying that, if he were to lay a hand there, comforting or otherwise, she'd likely slap it.

'Are you going to run the deal by Luca first?' Her soft Irish lilt broke through his musings.

'No.' He spoke more sharply than he would have liked. 'No,' he repeated, moderating his tone. 'This is my domain. *I* run our dealings outside Sicily.'

'I thought Luca was in charge.'

'What made you think that? Is it because he's the older brother?'

'No. It's because he's the more steady and *reliable* brother.'

Even in the dark he knew his knuckles had whitened.

'Your brother might be as scary as the bogeyman but at least he conducts himself with something relatively close to decorum and thinks with more than his penis.'

Any minute and his knuckles would poke through his skin. 'Are you deliberately trying to pick an argument with me?'

'Yes.'

'Why?'

'Because I don't like it when you're nice to me.'

'Does driving you home constitute me being *nice*?'

'As opposed to you flying me back in that tin shack, then yes; yes, it does. And incidentally, you're not driving me *home*. You're driving me back to your house.'

'My home is your home until your baby is born.' Although, at that particular moment, he would take great pleasure in stopping the car, kicking her out and telling her to walk herself back to Paris.

Impossible, ungrateful woman.

Impossible *sexy* woman.

There was no denying it. Cara Delaney was as sexy as sin, and as much as he tried to keep his errant mind on the present, it insisted on going back sixteen weeks to what had been, in hindsight, the best weekend of his life.

'Would you prefer if I spent the next five or so months being horrible to you and having no consideration of your needs?'

'Yes.'

He cocked an eyebrow. 'Really?'

'The only niceness I want from you is my freedom.'

'You have your freedom. You are here under your own free will. You are welcome to leave at any time.'

'But for me to leave would mean a life of poverty for our child. Or at least, the start of its life would be full of poverty unless you do the decent thing and give me money to support him or her.'

'I will give you money to support our child when I have definitive proof that it *is* our child. I will not be played for a fool.'

He heard a sharp inhalation followed by a slow, steady exhalation.

'I really don't get it.'

'Get what?'

'Your cynicism.'

'I am not cynical.'

'You impregnated a virgin yet you refuse to believe your paternity without written proof. If that's not cynical, then I don't know what is. And I don't get why you are that way.'

'There is nothing to get. I do not take anything at face value. That's good business sense, not cynicism.' Much as he tried to hide it, a real edge had crept into his voice. He'd thought she would be grateful he was rearranging his schedule to drive her back to Paris, had assumed a little gratitude would soften her attitude towards him. But no. For all the softness of her curves and her bottom lip, Cara Delaney was as hard as nails.

From the periphery of his vision, he saw her straighten.

'Grace and I used to talk about you,' she said.

'Why doesn't that surprise me?'

'We used to wonder why you were the way you were.'

'I haven't the faintest idea what you're talking about.'

'You come from a loving family. You had two parents who loved and supported you and encouraged you...'

'That is what you used to say about me?' he interrupted with a burst of mocking laughter.

'Your mother dotes on you,' she said coldly. 'By all accounts your father doted on you too. You have a closer relationship with your brother than most siblings can dream of. *That's* what I mean about coming from a loving family.'

'*Sì,*' he conceded. 'My parents loved me. Luca and I are close. It is normal.'

'I have two stepsisters who hate me only fractionally less than they hate each other. I have a bunch of half-siblings scattered around Dublin whom I have never met. I have a mother who doesn't care a fig that I'm pregnant. I have a father who is unaware he's going to be a granddad, but that's because he's had no involvement in my life for over a decade.'

For a moment he didn't know what to say to that unexpected outburst or how to react to the raw emotion behind it. 'You haven't seen your father in ten years?'

'Thirteen years. My parents split when I was eleven. Mam and I moved to England when I was thirteen and I haven't seen him since.'

'My father died thirteen years ago.' Something in his chest moved as he thought of Cara going through her own personal trauma while his own life was shattering, first by the death of his father and then by Luisa's vile and ultimately devastating actions.

'I'm sorry.' Her voice softened. 'I've seen pictures of your dad—you look just like him.'

'*Sì*. He was a very handsome man.'

This time she did laugh. 'Oh, you are so full of yourself.'

'You can be full of me too if you want.'

'Are you trying to make me sick again?'

He chuckled, glancing over at her, certain there was the trace of a smile playing on her lips.

Mind out of the gutter, he chided himself. He needed to keep his attention focused on the road before him, not on memories of burying himself inside her tight sweetness.

All the same, he took a sharp breath in the hope it would loosen the tightness in his groin.

'Did your mother stop your father from seeing you after she left him?'

'No. He stopped himself from seeing me. It was too much hassle for him to go across the Irish channel and see his eldest child. We exchange Christmas cards and that's it.'

For a moment he thought she was going to say something else, but when he glanced at her, he saw her eyes were closed and she was massaging her forehead. For all her bitterness there was a definite vulnerability about her when she spoke of her parents.

'Did you miss him?'

'My father?'

'Yes. It must have been a hard time for you.'

She laughed, a noise that sounded as if it were being done through a sucked lemon. 'If anything, it was a relief. My father is a serial shagger. He cheated on my mum so many times I think even *he* lost count.'

'Were you aware of this at the time?' Surely her father would have been discreet?

'I've always known, even when I was too young to understand. They never bothered keeping it a secret from me. I caught him out twice—once when I was going to the park with my friends and walked past the local pub and saw him through the window draped over some woman.'

'He was with another woman in your local pub?' Even Pepe, who was not easily shocked, was shocked at this.

'You think that's bad?' Her tone rose in pitch. 'The next time I caught him out, which couldn't have been more than six months later, I found him in the marital bed with another woman—a different woman from the woman he was with in the pub.'

'You caught him in the act?'

'No, thank God. They were lying in bed. I remember my dad was smoking a cigarette. I don't know what shocked me the most—I'd no idea he was a smoker.'

And Cara had no idea why she was sharing all this with Pepe of all people.

It had been the same over the weekend they'd shared together. He was such an easy person to talk to and had such an unerring ability to make the person he was with—namely her—believe that every word she uttered was worth listening to, that it was quite possible to spill your guts to him without even realising. He'd done it then, listened to her rabbit on for hours about her love of her job, her hopes for the future.

No one had ever made her feel like that before.

He'd made her believe she was special.

It would be all too easy to believe it again.

She opened the window a little further and practically stuck her nose out of it, inhaling the cold air gratefully. It compressed the anger and pain of those horrible memories back down to a manageable level.

Silence sprang between them, a silence that was on the verge of becoming uncomfortable when Pepe said, 'What did you do? Did you tell your mother?'

She sucked in more cold air before answering. 'Yes. Yes, I did. He didn't even bother to deny it. She threw him out for all of two days before taking him back. She always took him back.'

Her stomach twisted a little more as she recalled hearing them 'make up'. They hadn't cared that their ten-year-old daughter was in the house. They'd never cared.

Her entire childhood had revolved around her father's affairs and her mother's reactions to them. Those reactions had never been about Cara. Their daughter had been secondary to everything in their sick marriage where sex was a weapon used to hurt each other in the most cruel and demeaning ways.

'I always swore I'd never get involved with a man who was like my father, so more fool me.'

'What do you mean by that?'

'You,' she practically spat. 'How else do you think

my dad was able to pull so many women and use them so badly? He's a charmer, just like you are.'

'I am *nothing* like your father.' His vehemence was the most emphatic she had ever heard him.

'You use women for your own gratification with no thoughts of them as real people.'

'That is utter rubbish. I have never cheated on anyone. Ever.' An ugly tone curdled his words. 'I despise cheats.'

'You still use women.'

'I do not use women. I am never anything but honest with my lovers. Do not kid yourself into believing they are in my bed under false pretences.'

'You used me. I thought you wanted me in your bed because you wanted *me*. I had no idea you wanted to get your hands on my stupid phone and not my body.'

It was Pepe's turn to suck in a breath. 'I accept that I used you, Cara. I am not proud of what I did but it had to be done. My brother was a man on the verge of a breakdown. It doesn't change the fact that I found you as sexy as hell. I still do. I wanted to make love to you regardless of the circumstances.'

'You still used me. You can tell me until you're blue in the face that you're nothing like my father but I know better. You're two of a kind. You make love to women and then dump them, leaving them to deal with the emotional fallout. And the unwanted after-effects. Like babies,' she couldn't resist adding.

A screech of brakes and a swerve of the wheels as he brought the Mercedes to a shuddering halt on the verge.

Pepe turned the engine off, his breathing ragged.

Cara took little consolation that she had finally pierced his charming armour.

For long moments the only sound was their breathing.

'I am going to start driving again in a moment,' he

said grimly. 'Unless you want me to leave you to make your own way back to Paris, I suggest you do not speak to me, other than to say if you're feeling ill.'

From the tone of his voice, she knew he meant every word.

CHAPTER SEVEN

IT WAS NO USE. Sleep really had no intention of coming. She could count as many sheep as she liked but they might as well be blowing big fat raspberries at her for all the use they were at getting her off to slumber.

Cara climbed out of bed and reached for her new robe, which was more of a kimono. However much she might tell herself that she was itching to get her well-worn flannelette dressing gown back, there was no getting around the fact this scarlet silk kimono was utterly gorgeous and felt like liquid on her skin.

After three days in Pepe's Parisian home she still wasn't as familiar with the layout as she should be, but she knew her way to the kitchen.

She hadn't seen much of him since their drive back from the Loire Valley. Instead of keeping her chained to him, he'd had a change of heart and now insisted she be chained to Monique the housekeeper instead. Okay, maybe that was a slight exaggeration. What he had actually said, when they'd arrived back at the house after almost three hours of ice between them, was that all his meetings for the rest of the week were in Paris and that she was free to stay at home if she would prefer. Just as she'd thought he was becoming a more reasonable human being, he'd qualified it with, 'Monique is around during the day. She can accompany you if you need to go anywhere.'

'Where is there for me to go?' she'd shot back. 'I don't speak the language and I don't have any money to do anything. Parisian prices are stupidly high.'

He'd shrugged without looking at her. 'I have a swimming pool and spa—you're welcome to use them whenever you wish. Besides, if the paternity test proves your child is mine then you'll have more money than you know how to spend.'

She'd responded by calling him a name that would have made the nuns from the convent she'd attended before moving to England blush.

The following morning he'd made matters even worse by having a top-of-the-range laptop, smartphone and e-reader delivered to the house for her. The e-reader had, from what she'd been able to ascertain, unlimited credit installed. She'd taken a perverse pleasure in downloading as many books as she could, all featuring the most unheroic, misogynistic protagonists that she could find. Hopefully Pepe would receive an itemised bill with all the titles listed for him.

She hated that he would do something thoughtful. It was the same as when he'd driven her home rather than make her fly back in the helicopter. She didn't want him to be *nice*. She wasn't going to be like her mother and forgive deplorable behaviour because of a stupid gift.

Making her way down the winding staircase, she headed for the kitchen. The house was in darkness but for the dim glow of night lights that were strategically placed throughout.

She switched on the main light of the kitchen, blinking several times as her eyes adjusted to the brightness.

It felt strange being in there, in a kitchen as large as

the house she'd grown up in, feeling as if she were an intruder. She had no idea where anything was but found the fridge easily enough—seeing as it was a whopping American-style fridge large enough to use in a mortuary, it would have been hard to miss.

What she really wanted was some warm milk. Grace's mother, Billie, would make it for them when she went for one of her frequent sleepovers there. It was comforting. Now, if only she knew where to even begin searching for a saucepan…

The whisper of movement froze her to the spot. Her hand gripped the plastic milk carton.

'You're up late, *cucciola mia,*' a deep Sicilian drawl said from behind her.

She spun around to find Pepe striding languorously towards her. 'You scared the life out of me,' she snapped. Or, at least she tried to snap, but her mini-fright had left her a little breathless. Seeing all six feet plus of semi-naked Pepe also did something to her pulse-rate, but there he was, muscle-bound and gorgeous, and wearing nothing but a pair of low-slung jeans that perfectly accentuated his snake hips and showed his taut, olive chest to perfection. The silky hair that ran from his chest and down in a thin line over his toned stomach, thickened where the buttons of his jeans were undone…

His hair was tousled, black stubble breaking out along his jawline, almost as thick as his trimmed goatee.

Sin. That was what he looked like. A walking, talking advertisement for sin. And temptation.

'I didn't mean to scare you,' he said, not looking the least apologetic. 'I heard noise and came to investigate.'

'I couldn't sleep.'

His deep blue eyes held hers, meaning swirling in them. 'Nor could I.'

She broke the lock first, aware of warmth suffusing more than just her face.

'What brings you out of hiding?' he asked, standing a little closer than she would have liked.

She took a step back. 'I've not been in hiding.'

'You've barely left your room in three days. Monique says you've been no further than the dining room.'

'This isn't my home. I don't feel comfortable roaming around as if I belong here.' She felt especially uncomfortable now, but in an entirely different way, in a 'sexy half-naked man in front of me' kind of way.

She must be delirious. Sleep deprivation could do that.

'You *do* belong here. While you are under my roof, this is your home. You are free to treat it as you wish.'

'Except leave it.'

'You are always free to leave.'

She bit back the comment that wanted to break free. What was the point? It would only be a rehash of all their other arguments regarding her freedom.

'I was after some warm milk,' she muttered. 'I thought it would help me sleep.'

'I thought I heard you thrashing about in your bed.' At her quizzical expression, he added, 'My room is next to yours.'

'Oh.'

'You didn't know?' His lips quirked into a smirk.

'No. I didn't.' It shouldn't matter where Pepe slept. He could sleep in a shed for all she cared. But the room next to hers...?

Why the thought should heat her veins, she had no idea.

The playful, sensuous expression in his eyes softened a touch. 'I make a mean hot chocolate.'

It took a moment for her to realise he was offering to make her some. 'Thank you.'

He started busying himself, opening doors and rifling through drawers.

She suppressed a snigger and hoicked herself up on the kitchen table. 'You don't know your way around your kitchen any better than I do.'

'Guilty as charged.' He knelt down and leaned into a cupboard, giving her an excellent view of his tight buttocks straining against the denim. 'I employ housekeepers so I don't have to know my way around my kitchens. When I'm home alone, take-out is my best friend.'

Oh, the blasé way he pluralised *kitchen*! Cara thought of the poky galley kitchen she shared—*had* shared—with three other women. It would probably fit in Pepe's fridge.

When he reappeared he had a milk pan in his hand. 'It would be quicker to microwave it but my mother always taught me it was sacrilege to make a hot chocolate like that.'

'I thought you had a fleet of staff when you were growing up?'

'We did,' he said, matter-of-factly. 'But making our nightly hot chocolate was a job my mother always liked to do herself. She used to sit Luca and I on the kitchen table—much as you're sitting now—while she made it.'

'It sounds wonderful,' she said with more than a touch of envy. Evenings in the Delaney household had normally consisted of her mother fretting about where her father was.

He cocked his head while he thought about it. A glimmer of surprise flittered across his features. 'Yes, it was.'

Pepe added the expensive cocoa powder to the warming milk before spooning some sugar into the mixture, whisking vigorously as he went along.

Looking at his childhood from Cara's perspective, he could see it had been idyllic. His feelings about being spare to Luca's heir were not something that had developed until he'd hit his teenage years, but Luca had always been the good one, whereas he'd always been the naughty one. Looking back, it was as if his parents' expectations of him had been lower from the start.

Or had it been that their expectations of Luca had been set too high? His brother had been groomed to take over the family business. He'd had responsibility thrust upon him from the womb. For Pepe, the only responsibility he'd had—and it was a self-imposed one—was to make his serious big brother laugh.

He whipped the milk pan away from the heat right before it reached boiling point, then poured it into the two waiting mugs.

When he turned to pass Cara her drink, his chest compressed.

Her short legs dangled from the table, hovering inches above the floor, and she was chewing on her bottom lip.

He wondered if she knew the top of her robe had parted a touch, giving him a tantalising glimpse of that wonderful cleavage his senses remembered so well. The first time he'd buried himself in those glorious breasts he'd thought he'd died and gone to heaven.

During the intervening months the wonder of that night was something he had suppressed with a ruthlessness he'd never before had to employ. But it had always been there, hovering in the periphery of his memories, taunting him, tantalising him. Often it would catch him unawares, a visual memory or a familiar scent, always with the same end result, a burst of need that would shoot straight to his groin and clutch at his chest. The same burst of need he was currently experiencing. The same need that had been a semi-permanent ache since he'd stood next to Cara at the font at Lily's christening.

Under normal circumstances, that one night wouldn't have been the end of them. He would have gone back for more. Hell, he might even have brought her here to Paris as he'd insinuated, but not for the sake of his art collection. No, he'd have brought her here so he could devour that delectable body over and over until he was finally spent and there was nothing left for him to discover and enjoy.

As she reached out a hand to take the mug, her kimono strained against her breasts, moulding them for his hungry eyes, and the need in his groin tightened, straining against the denim he wore.

The hem of the kimono barely covered her knees.

Was she wearing *anything* beneath it?

'What are you doing?' Cara's voice was a husky whisper.

Without even realising it, he'd closed the gap between them. One more step and he'd be able to part her creamy thighs and slip between them...

Cara's heart thumped so strongly she could hear it pound against her ribs.

'I asked, what are you doing?' How she managed to drag the words out, she didn't know. Pepe was so close he'd sucked all the air from her lungs.

His large warm hand closed over hers and removed the mug, placing it on the table, out of her reach.

And then he was cupping her cheeks, forcing her to meet his stare. 'I'm going to kiss you.'

'No!' It was more of a whimper than a refusal. She tried to wrench her face free from his clasp but his hold was too strong. And, somehow, too gentle.

'*Sì.*' He brushed a thumb over her bottom lip. 'Yes, *cucciola mia*. I am going to kiss you.'

She didn't want to respond. God alone knew she didn't want to respond.

Yet when his lips slanted onto hers and held there for long moments before prising her mouth apart, and when his thick tongue slipped into her mouth, the only word revolving around and around in her head was *yes*. Yes. Yes. Yes.

The only answer her body gave was yes.

The hands she tried to ball into fists fought back, tracing up his bare biceps and clinging to his shoulders, her nails digging into the smooth flesh.

And still she tried to fight. Desperately she fought against the growing rip tide of need pulsating through her blood, fought against the moisture bubbling in her most intimate area.

But mostly she battled for her head, a fight she was so far from winning she…

His hand was cupping her breast.

When had that happened…?

It felt so…good. Wonderful. His touch…

But it wasn't enough. The silk of the kimono was too restrictive.

Pepe must have read her mind because he slipped a hand beneath the thin material and spread it whole against a breast so sensitive, the relief of him finally touching it—touching her—made her gasp into his hot mouth.

And then she was kissing him back, her lips moving against his with no conscious thought, her tongue dancing against his, her whole body alive to his touch, the heat from his mouth and the taste of *him*.

Roughly he tugged her kimono apart, exposing her

naked flesh. He snaked an arm around her waist and pulled her flush to him, crushing her breasts against his chest, crushing her mouth with an ever deepening kiss, his other hand trailing up her back, up the nape of her neck and then spearing her hair, gently tugging at it, before trailing back and reaching down to take her hand, which he placed on the front of his jeans. His fingers curled into hers as he pressed her hand tight to him. Even through the thick denim she could feel the length and weight of his erection. She could feel the heat emanating from him.

It was a heat her starved body revelled in.

Because it had been starving.

It had been starving for *him*.

He had brought her to life, given her an appetite she hadn't known she had, and then he'd left her. Alone. And pregnant.

'See, *cucciola mia*,' he said, breaking his mouth away and dragging kisses across her cheek and down her neck. 'This is how badly I want you. Enough that I think I might explode if I don't have you.'

His words, the sound of his voice, were things the small part of her shrieking at her treacherous body anchored onto, using them to bring her out of this erotic stupor he had put her in.

Somehow she managed to wedge her hands between their meshed chests—and, God, her body really didn't want her to; her lips ached for just one more kiss, the apex of her thighs begged her to let him continue—and, using all the strength she could muster, pushed him away.

'I said *no*.'

He almost reeled back.

Pepe's chest heaved as he stared at her with eyes that penetrated, almost as if he were reaching into the deepest recess of her mind. 'Your mouth said no. The rest of you said yes.'

Although his words were nothing but the truth, she shook her head, her shaking hands frantically wrapping the kimono back up, tying it as tightly as was physically possible. 'When a woman says no, then the answer is no. No, no, no. You have no right to help yourself to me.'

His face contorted and he took another step back. 'Do *not* imply that I am some sort of rapist. You wanted me as much as I wanted you. You kissed me back. You enjoyed every minute of it.'

The savagery of his words made her flinch.

To compound it all, she felt hot tears sting the backs of her retinas. 'I don't care how much I *enjoyed* it,' she said, forcing the words out, aware her words were hitched. 'This is not going to happen. Unlike you, my brain is in control of my actions.'

His lips curved into something that was supposed to resemble a smile. 'You think? Well, *cucciola mia*, you will learn that my control is second to none. Have no worries—I will not touch you again. Not without a written contract from you saying yes.'

With that parting shot, he strolled out of the kitchen, leaving her rooted to the table she was still sitting upon.

CHAPTER EIGHT

PEPE GROWLED AT the screen before him. The words of the contract could be in gobbledegook for all he cared.

There was no point lying to himself. He was angry. Angry at Cara. Angry at the situation they had been forced into. Angry at himself.

But especially angry at her.

He'd never forced himself on a woman in his life. Never. He despised men who did such things, thought castration too mild a punishment for such deeds.

Had he really misread the situation so badly?

No. Absolutely not.

Cara had the most expressive face of any woman he'd ever known. They said that eyes were windows to the soul. With Cara, her eyes were windows to her emotions. If she was angry, happy, tired or ill, her eyes were the signposts for him to follow.

How had he become an expert on her *emotions*?

He shook his head briskly and rubbed his eyes. He probably wouldn't feel so crummy if he'd managed to get any sleep. But how was a man supposed to sleep when his body ached with unfulfilled desire?

One thing he was not, though, was hurt. His ego might be a touch bruised but, on a personal level, it made no difference if Cara was willing to share a bed with him or not. There were plenty of women out there who were. And in reality, it was probably better that they didn't resume a sexual relationship, especially as she was of a completely different mindset from his usual lovers.

He doubted there would ever come a time he would be able to bump into Cara at a party, sidle over to her, maybe give her bottom a cheeky pinch, and then catch up on old times.

The animosity would always be there.

In any case, if her baby did prove to be his, then he had to concede she would be a huge part of his life...well, for the rest of his life. If the baby was his then they would be for ever united, even in the most cerebral fashion.

An image of a tiny baby with a shock of Cara's flamered hair came into his head, an image he blinked away along with the nagging voice that kept piping up, asking him if he really wanted nothing more than to be a part-time father.

He clenched his hands into fists.

He didn't want to think that far ahead.

He didn't want to imagine how he would feel if Cara really was carrying his child.

Once, a long time ago, he'd been caught up in the magic of pregnancy, the unmitigated joy and wonder of knowing he had shared in the creation of life and that soon he would be a father. The child had been no more than a foetus but already he had loved it, had thought of the future that child would have with him and Luisa, and the family they would create together.

His child would never have felt second best.

His child never got the chance to feel anything, least of all second best.

Luisa had ripped that chance away from him.

Cara was nothing like Luisa.

Cara was like no one he'd ever met.

But what did he know of her *really*? He'd known Luisa pretty much all of his life but he'd never guessed she was capable of ripping his heart out and stamping on the remnants.

He would never trust another woman. He couldn't. There was only so much pain one man could take and he'd reached that limit before he'd even finished his teenage years.

Only when Cara's baby was born and the paternity test established that he truly was the father would he allow himself to think properly of the future.

Only then would he allow himself to think of what it truly meant to have a child.

Until that time came, his life would continue as it was. Except with a houseguest. A fiery, sexy houseguest.

Suppressing a yawn, he checked his watch. It was time to call it a day. There was a party he had to attend, a party he'd been looking forward to until approximately five days ago, being hosted by a good friend who was celebrating his first wedding anniversary. Not feeling in the mood to drive, he got his driver to take him home, all the while trying to shake himself out of the melancholic mood that had crept under his skin.

By the time he arrived back at his home he felt no better, but, with practised ease, slipped his old faithful smile on and strolled into the house.

'Where is Cara?' he asked Monique, who had hurried out to greet him.

'In her room.'

'Has she left it today?'

'Only for her lunch and a late afternoon snack.'

'Did she eat any breakfast?'

'A croissant and an apple.'

He headed to his room, refusing to reflect on his need to monitor Cara's eating habits. It was simple concern extended towards a pregnant woman, nothing more.

As he passed, Cara's bedroom door opened. Her eyes widened to see him and she took a step back, would no doubt have shut the door in his face if he hadn't stuck a foot in the doorway to prevent her.

'Good evening, *cucciola mia*. How has your day been?'

'Long and boring.'

'Then it must be a source of comfort to know we are going out tonight.'

She pulled a face but opened the door properly and leaned against the door frame, hugging her arms around her chest. 'It's getting late. Do I have to go?'

'Yes.'

'Can't I stay here with Monique?'

'Monique goes home at weekends—aren't you lucky? You can have me all to yourself.'

Her cheeks coloured and she scowled. 'How thrilling. Can't you get another babysitter for me?'

'It's too short notice. Besides, I don't think I could afford to pay anyone else to put up with you.'

'I'm no bother. I just stay in my room. It's like baby-sitting a five-year-old.'

Anyone listening in on them would be amused at the dryness of their conversation. If they were to scratch a little under the surface it would be a whole different story. The second her door had opened, Pepe's heart had begun to thunder, the weight in his gut twisting and clenching. The half-smile on his face could have been drawn on.

As for Cara…her beautiful lips were pulled in and tight, while her green eyes spat fire at him.

He wanted to touch her. He wanted to pick her up and

carry her across the room, lay her on the bed and make love to every inch of her.

After the way she had reacted in the kitchen in the early hours, it would be a long day in hell before he touched her again. She would have to get down on her knees and beg before he would even consider making love to her.

All the same, he couldn't resist reaching out a hand and tapping her cute little nose. 'We leave in an hour, *cucciola mia*. Cocktail dress. Be ready or I'll come in your room and help you.'

'You wouldn't dare.'

'Is that a challenge?'

'No!'

'In that case, be ready on time. I need to shower—see you in sixty minutes.'

Exactly one hour later, Pepe knocked on Cara's bedroom door. He half hoped she *wasn't* ready.

Forget the good talking-to he'd given himself earlier about not resuming their sexual relationship; just three minutes sparring outside her bedroom had laid waste to those good intentions.

There was something so damn sexy about his red-headed geisha.

If only she really were a geisha. Or better still, his own personal concubine. He was pretty sure bitching at her master wasn't part of either's job description. Geisha or concubine, all the woman concerned herself with was her master's pleasure. Seeing as it was pleasure of a sexual nature he wanted from Cara, he would much rather settle with concubine.

He was certain she did it deliberately, but she made him wait a full sixty seconds before opening her door.

The wait was worth it.

The quip he had ready on his lips blew away as his mouth fell open.

Pepe was used to dating beauties. He shamelessly used his wealth, charm and looks to pick the cream of the crop. Yet Cara outshone all of them.

Dressed in a richly red silk floor-length dress that showed off her curves, the sleeves skimming her shoulders to leave her arms bare, her glorious hair piled into a sleek chignon, she looked stunning. In her ears were heart drop crystals that shimmered under the light, and on her feet were shoes that had the same shimmering effect. Her make-up was subtle bar the lipstick, a rich red that perfectly matched her dress and made her kissable lips infinitely more so.

'*Mio Dio,*' he said appreciatively. 'You are beautiful.'

'It's amazing what money can do,' she said tartly, although her cheeks flamed to match her hair, her dress, her lips...

'You are Hestia come to life,' he breathed.

'That's appropriate seeing as the Vestal Virgins get their name from her Roman counterpart.'

A smile escaped his lips. 'She was also the Roman Goddess of the Hearth—of fire.'

'And I bet you see yourself as Eros—wouldn't you just love to get your hands on the Vestals?'

His smile tightened. 'Actually, no. I've found virgins too needy for my taste.'

It was a low blow and one he wished he could take back as soon as it escaped his lips. There was something about her spiky tongue that he reacted to. Her barbs penetrated him like no one else's.

Cara's eyes narrowed but she raised her chin and pulled the door shut behind her, her movements releasing a cloud of her perfume. 'Then we are better suited than I believed. I've always found lustful men too immature for *my* tastes.'

'How are you going to introduce me to your friends?' Cara asked as they sat in the back of the blacked-out Mercedes through the dark Parisian evening. The city twinkled with what seemed a million lights, giving it a magical quality that enthralled her.

'As my companion.'

'Is that how you introduce all your lovers?'

'I wasn't aware that you were my lover,' he responded easily, the coolness he'd displayed since she'd made the jibe about him being immature having dispersed. She much preferred it when he was cool towards her. It made it much easier to hate him.

'I suppose you can always introduce me as your pregnant one-night stand who you're waiting to give birth so you can get a paternity test to prove that you're the daddy.'

She felt him tense, knew that beneath his tuxedo his frame had tautened.

'Why are you happy to dress in a suit for business and wear a DJ for a party, but refuse to make an effort for your own niece's christening?' she asked, blurting out one of the many questions that played on her mind.

'I wasn't aware I hadn't made an effort for it,' he answered coolly.

She shrugged. Pepe's choice of attire was none of her business. 'So where is this party?'

'In Montmartre.'

Now he mentioned it, the lights of the sprawling hill that comprised Montmartre gleamed before them, the white Basilica of Sacre-Coeur sitting atop, almost surveying all beneath it. As they drove into the bustling arrondissement, she pressed her face to the window to take in the beautiful architecture, ambling tourists and nonchalant locals.

'How are you feeling?' he asked. 'Any nausea?'

'So far so good,' she confirmed.

'That is good.' Not trusting the casual tone to his voice, she looked at him and found him holding a paper bag aloft. He winked. 'Just in case.'

Despite herself, she laughed, the action loosening a little of the angst in her chest.

He moved closer to her and pointed out of the window. 'Through those gardens is the Musée de Montmartre. It is reputed to be the oldest house in Montmartre.'

'Didn't Renoir live in it?' she asked, wholly aware of his thigh now pressed against hers.

'Not quite—there is a mansion behind it that he lived in for a while. Maurice Utrillo lived there though.'

As they snaked their way through the cobbled streets, he pointed out more features of interest, his words breathing life into the ancient buildings, especially from the Impressionist era. He knew so much about the district, had such lively knowledge, his heavy Sicilian accent so lyrical it was a joy to listen to him.

Cara hid her disappointment when the driver came to a stop in a narrow street lined by a terrace of white-washed five-storey homes, cafés and shops. She could have happily continued with their tour.

To her surprise, they went into a packed poky café that smelt strongly of coffee, body odour and illicit cigarettes. Pepe greeted the staff personally with his usual enthusiasm, shaking hands and kissing cheeks, before leading her through the back and out into a small court-yard.

'Ladies first,' he said, waving his hand at a flimsy-looking iron staircase that led all the way to the top floor. 'Don't worry,' he added, clearly reading her mind. 'I assure you it is safe.'

'Aren't there indoor stairs?' She was in no way mollified by his assurance.

'There are, but as you have seen, the café is busy, and if all tonight's guests were to use them, we would get in the way of the staff.'

'So why go through the front entrance? Why not get your driver to drop us off at the back?'

'Because the staff would be most put out if they knew I had been here and hadn't dropped in to say hello.'

'You do have a high opinion of yourself,' she muttered.

His smile dropped a wattage before the teeth flashed. 'Forgive my modesty but I am a good employer.'

Her brow knotted.

'I own the building,' he clarified.

'I thought you owned vineyards.'

'I do. Didn't you know variety is the spice of life?'

She sniffed pointedly, and hugged her wrap closer around her chest, wishing she had worn the thick designer coat Pepe had bought her. 'I'm surprised you haven't turned it into a high-tech hotel.'

He pulled a face. 'And rip it of its charm? This street is old-style Montmartre, unaffected and barely known by the tourists that have infected much of the rest of this glorious place. I intend to keep it that way.'

'You own the entire street?'

He inclined his head in affirmation then looked back to the iron stairs. 'Shall we?'

'I don't know...'

'Do you suffer from vertigo?'

'No.'

'Then where's your sense of adventure?'

'I've never had one.'

'Liar. You spent a year travelling Europe with Grace, so don't tell me you have no sense of adventure.'

'I'm pregnant.'

'Are pregnant women not able to climb stairs?'

'Don't be silly.'

His features softened. 'Cara, I promise I would never allow anything to happen to you or your baby. This staircase is only a couple of years old—I oversaw its construction myself. I'll be right behind you—I promise you'll be safe.'

Much as she knew she must be a fool to believe him, she found herself putting a foot onto the bottom step, half expecting the whole thing to come crashing down on them.

It was a lot sturdier than she anticipated. And, she had to admit, knowing he would be there to catch her if she should trip was…comforting. Pepe's strength and assurance were more than a little comforting.

'Which floor are we going to?' she asked, turning her head to look at him.

The grin that spread across his face made her stomach flip over. 'You and I, *cucciola mia*, are going all the way.'

Her cheeks burning at the suggestion in his tone, she climbed up, slowly at first until she became aware that Pepe, being a couple of paces behind her, had an excellent view of her derrière. Yep, knowing he had a face full of her backside certainly acted as rocket fuel and she reached the top in no time.

She had no idea what she'd been expecting: from the general dilapidation of the café below, she'd half assumed Pepe had made her dress up as a joke, but she certainly hadn't been expecting *this*.

The party was being held in a loft conversion. Except it was nothing like any loft she'd ever been in. Extremely large and airy, simply decorated with what she would refer to as faux shabby chic, it must have covered the length of the entire terrace.

'So do you own this loft too?'

He raised a brow.

'I know; a silly question. But this place...' Her voice trailed off.

'A little different from the café on the ground floor?'

'Yes. Exactly.'

'The café is a fixture in Montmartre. I didn't want to make any changes other than have it fitted with a kitchen that wasn't liable to catch fire at any moment. This loft, on the other hand, was begging to be converted into a proper work and living space.'

'Is it a studio?' There might be so many people crammed into the space that she couldn't see any art paraphernalia, but she'd recognise the smell of turps anywhere—with an artist for best friend, that was a given.

'*Sì.*' He nodded at a diminutive man holding court to a large crowd of glamorous people. 'That is the tenant, Georges Ramirez.'

'I know him,' she said, awed. 'Well, I know *of* him. We've auctioned his work before.'

'He's an old friend. The loft was designed with him in mind.'

As he spoke, Georges looked in their direction and spotted Pepe. His little gang looked too and in the click of a finger two dozen pairs of eyes had widened and two dozen sets of lips had curled into smiles. A few people, including Georges and the pretty woman clutching his hand, broke from the crowd and headed towards them.

In a whirl of French and English, and some Italian and

Spanish, Pepe presented her to people who were clearly his friends, introducing her simply as Cara with no further explanation. Names were thrown at her, hands shaken and embraces exchanged—well, embraces with Pepe were exchanged. All the while she stood there wishing the floor would open up and swallow her, whisk her away to somewhere familiar and calming.

Her hands had gone clammy, her pulse racing. 'I need to use the bathroom,' she whispered for Pepe's ears only, trying to keep any trace of panic from her voice.

He stared at her with a quizzical expression before inclining his head. 'The bathroom is through that door on the left of the bar,' he said, pointing at a long table pushed against a far wall, piled high with all manner of alcohol and soft drinks. 'Go through it and then it's the second door on the right.'

The door by the bar led into another enormous, brightly lit space. Canvases and sculptures were crammed inside, protected by a large stand-up sign that read 'Any Person Found Touching The Work Will Be Chemically Castrated'. An unexpected giggle escaped from her mouth.

Luckily the bathroom was empty and gave her time to collect herself.

She hated crowds. Hated large parties. Especially hated crowds and large parties where she didn't know anyone. It was that *new girl* feeling all over again, the knowledge that everyone was already acquainted with their own little friendship bands. Outsiders were most definitely *not* welcome. Outsiders on the arm of the man who was definitely the alpha male of the pack were as welcome as anthrax.

When she finally left her sanctuary, a tall brunette with the most amazing hazel eyes blocked her way. 'Ah, so *you're* my replacement,' she said with a dazzling smile.

CHAPTER NINE

'SORRY?' CARA DIDN'T have the faintest idea what she was talking about.

'I was Pepe's original date for the evening,' the beauty said without the slightest trace of rancour.

Cara didn't know what to say, could feel herself shrinking from the inside out.

'It is not a problem,' the beauty assured her. 'We used to date but it was over a long time ago. I'm sure we'll hook up again some other time when he's back on the market and in need of a semi-platonic date for the evening. In the meantime, you should enjoy him while you have him.'

Cara searched for signs the woman was having a joke at her expense but saw nothing but open friendliness in those hazel eyes. She swallowed and forced her rooted tongue to work. 'What does *semi-platonic* mean?'

'Oh, you know—what is the English expression?' Her eyes scrunched up as she thought, then another beaming smile broke out on her spectacularly pretty face. 'I know—it means "friends with benefits"!'

'Friends with benefits,' Cara echoed weakly, her stomach roiling at the thought.

That friendliness turned to consternation. 'Have I spoken out of turn?'

'Not at all,' Cara said, knowing as she said the words that they sounded weedy and pathetic.

The woman slapped her own forehead. 'I have a very big mouth—forgive me, I meant no harm. I didn't know you were serious about him.'

'I'm not.' Cara strove to affect nonchalance. From the pity in the other woman's eyes, she failed miserably at it.

'I must use the bathroom now,' the woman said, shuffling to the door. 'Please, forget what I said. I didn't know—'

'I'm not serious about him,' Cara interrupted, her horror at the woman's assumptions trumping her innate shyness. 'I'm well aware Pepe has the attention span of a goldfish.'

'That is a little unfair,' the woman said with a slight crease in her forehead. 'To goldfish.' With a quick wink she entered the bathroom and shut the door behind her.

Taking rapid breaths, Cara rejoined the party, trying desperately to contain the nerves that threatened to overwhelm her.

As she sought out Pepe she could feel people staring at her, feel their curiosity about this stranger in their midst. For this was no social-networking occasion, this was a proper party for friends to mingle, catch up on each other's lives, drink too much alcohol and behave indiscreetly. She couldn't even have a glass of wine to calm her nerves.

Eventually she found him chatting to a couple of women, a tall glass of beer in his hand. Walking towards them, she almost came to a stop when she saw one of the women cup his buttocks and give them a squeeze. How Cara's feet carried on moving, she had no idea, but it felt as if a million hot pins were being poked into her skin.

Pepe laughed and grabbed the wandering hand. He

brought it to his lips. Whatever he said as he kissed it made the wandering-hand woman burst into laughter.

'Cara,' he called, spotting her and beckoning her over. When she reached him, he placed an arm around her waist, his hand gripping her hip. The same hand that just moments earlier had held another woman's hand so he could kiss it.

'I don't think I've introduced you—this is Lena and Francesca. Ladies, this is Cara.'

The two women looked at her with unabashed interest. Wandering-hand lady held her hand out. Much as she wanted to refuse, Cara forced herself to shake it, all the while thinking, *This hand just squeezed Pepe's butt. This is* another *of his ex-lovers.*

How many of them were here?

The hot pins poking her skin were now strong enough to make her brain burn.

'Ladies, look after her for me while I get her a drink.' With that, Pepe disappeared into the crowd.

Francesca, the non-wandering-hand woman, an adorably plump blonde who had squeezed herself into a black dress that gave her a cleavage like two pillows, was the first to speak. 'I don't think we have met before, *non*?'

Cara shook her head.

'How did you come to meet Pepe?'

At least it was a question she could answer. Even so, it took two attempts for the words to form. 'His brother is married to my best friend.'

Francesca's eyes gleamed. 'Ah, Luca. Now that is one fine specimen of man,' she said, turning back to Lena.

The two Frenchwomen spoke in their native language before Lena addressed Cara. '*Je regrette un... non* English.'

'Lena doesn't speak English,' Francesca said apologetically. 'I am translating.'

Even if Cara had actually paid attention in her senior school French classes, there was no way she would have been able to keep up with the speed with which the two women spoke.

As Cara stood there like a spare wheel while the two women conversed loudly before her, that same dreadful outsider feeling doused her all over again.

'I need to find Pepe,' she whispered, backing away, horribly aware her cheeks were flaming.

Slipping back into the crowd, she spotted him easily enough, standing by the bar with what looked like a glass of orange juice in his hand. It came as no surprise to find him talking to a woman. This woman's hand was playing with the lapel of his tuxedo jacket.

If her brain could burn much more it would boil. Everything inside her felt taut, as if it had been wound into a coil. Perspiration broke out on her skin.

'Where are you going?' Pepe caught hold of her wrist as she passed him.

She hadn't even realised her legs were moving.

'To the bathroom.' She said the first thing that came into her mind.

'Again?'

'Yes.'

His eyes narrowed slightly as he studied her. 'You're very pale. Are you all right?'

'Yes.' She tugged her wrist out of his hold. 'Excuse me. I'll be back in a minute.'

The lapel-fingering woman said something to him in French, looking at Cara as she spoke. No doubt she too was asking if Cara was his latest lover. The latest in a long, long line.

Taking advantage of his momentary distraction, Cara slipped out of the door. This time the adjoining room was full of partygoers all talking and laughing loudly. A small queue had formed by the bathroom.

She didn't want the bathroom. She wanted to escape. She wanted to get as far away from Pepe and all the women who had shared his bed as she could.

As she stood there, feeling helpless, not knowing what to do, the opportunity for escape presented itself.

A door in the far corner flew open and a latecomer, dressed in a long coat and carrying a box of champagne, burst into the room. This was clearly someone who hadn't bothered to observe the rule of using the outside entrance.

Screams of laughter greeted the newcomer's entrance. Cara took her advantage and skirted her way past the crowd to the door.

Bingo.

The staircase was dimly lit and narrow, but she easily made her way down the first few flights until she reached the first floor. There, she shrank back to avoid a couple of bustling waitresses exiting large swing doors to the left, expertly carrying plates of steaming food.

Making sure no other member of the café staff was waiting to use the swing doors, she carried on to the ground floor and found herself in the centre of the café, right next to the bar.

A young man pouring a bottle of lager into a glass spotted her. *'Je vous aider?'* he said, openly appraising her.

Not having a clue what he'd just said, she grappled for the right words in a language she hadn't spoken in over a decade. *'Un téléphone, s'il vous plaît?'*

'Un téléphone?'

'*Oui. Je voudrais un taxi.*' She couldn't hide the desperation from her voice. '*S'il vous plaît.*'

He appraised her a little longer than was necessary before nodding. '*Une minute,*' he said, then left the bar and walked to a table where four middle-aged men were loudly slurping coffee. They all turned to look at her.

'Hey, English,' one of them called to her.

'Irish,' she corrected, inching closer to them.

'Need taxi?'

She hesitated before nodding. She might be desperate to get out of this place but she'd heard every horror story going about single women getting lifts with strange men.

He pulled a wallet out of his back pocket and showed her his ID, proving he wasn't a mad axeman as her hackles feared. He was a taxi driver.

'You have money?' he asked, no doubt referring to her lack of a bag or clutch.

'It's at the house,' she said, thinking of her precious forty-eight euros. She gave him the name of the street where Pepe lived.

He looked her up and down, no doubt estimating the cost of her silk dress before inclining his head and getting to his feet. 'Wait here. I get car.'

She cast a nervous glance over her shoulder to the direction of the staircase. It wouldn't be long before Pepe noticed she was missing.

Actually, with all those women fawning all over him, it was likely he wouldn't notice she'd gone for hours. All the same, she didn't want to take the risk.

If she was to see him now, she had no idea how she would react.

'Is it okay to pay you when we get there?'

He slipped his jacket on and shrugged.

Taking the shrug as assent, she followed him out into

the cold night air, hugging her arms round her chest and wishing she'd had the chance to grab her wrap, which had been whisked away as soon as they'd walked into the loft. The taxi was parked around the corner, but she made no attempt to soak up her surroundings, her entire focus on getting back to Pepe's house, getting her passport and getting the hell out of there.

The journey back passed in a blur. The only thing she saw on the entire journey was those women's hands touching Pepe as if they owned him.

When they arrived on Pepe's street, she got the driver to crawl along until she recognised his distinctive red front door.

'Give me a minute to get my money,' she said, turning the handle. And then God knew what she would do. The fee was thirty euros.

To her disquiet, the driver also got out of the cab and followed her up the steps to the front door.

She rang the bell. And rang it again. Then banged on it. Then rang it again, all the while aware of the driver standing beside her impatiently.

She banged one last time before she remembered—Monique didn't work weekends. Pepe had told her just a few hours ago that she would be returning to her own home.

Despair was almost enough for Cara to hit her head against the unyielding door.

Eejit that she was, she'd run away to an empty house for which she didn't have a key.

Swallowing away the bile that had lodged in her throat, she tried to think. Nothing came. Her mind was a complete blank.

She didn't have a clue what to do.

'I can't get into the house.'

'I want my money.' The driver's tone was amiable enough but she detected the underlying menace in it.

'You'll get it.' She rubbed a hand down her face. 'Give me your address. I'll drop it over to you as soon as Pepe gets home and lets me in. I'll sign anything you want.'

'You don't pay?'

'I will pay. But I can't get into the house, so I can't get my purse.'

'You don't pay, I get police.'

'No, please.' Her voice rose. 'I promise, I will pay it. I promise. I'm not a blaggard.'

A meaty hand grabbed her shoulder. 'You pay or I call police.'

Her fear rising, she tried to shake him off. 'I *will* pay. Please don't call the police.'

His hand didn't budge other than to lock onto her biceps. 'Come, we go see police.'

'Get off me!' she cried. All the heat in her skin had been replaced by cold terror. The thought of being dragged into a police station and being accused of criminality was more than she could bear.

But the driver was clearly furious and had no intention of letting her go. Keeping a tight grip on her, he hauled her back down the steps to the cab.

Before she could open her lungs to scream for help, a large car sped around the corner, coming to a stop before them in a screech of brakes. The engine hadn't been turned off before Pepe jumped out of the passenger side and took long strides towards them.

'Take your hands off her *now*,' he barked, his anger palpable.

'She no pay,' the driver said, refusing to relinquish his hold, even though he'd turned puce at the sight of Pepe.

'I *said*, take your hands off her. *Maintenant!*'

Before Cara knew what was happening, the driver let her go and a slanging match between the two men erupted, all of it conducted in French, so she couldn't keep up. Her hands covering her mouth, she got the gist of it well enough.

If she weren't witnessing it with her own eyes, she would never have believed Pepe was capable of such fury. The menace came off him in waves of pumped-up testosterone, his face a contortion of wrath.

It ended with Pepe pulling a wad of notes from his pocket and throwing them at the driver with a string of words spat at him for good measure. A couple of the said words jumped out at her as she recalled how she and Grace had once made it their mission to learn every possible swear word in French. She was pretty sure Pepe had just used the very choicest of those words.

When he finally looked at her, the rage was still there. 'Get in the house,' he said tightly, sweeping past her and up the steps, unlocking the door.

'What the hell do you think you're playing at?' He slammed the door shut behind her.

'I'd forgotten Monique had the night off. Thanks for coming to my rescue.' Her breaths felt heavy, the words dredged up. She knew she should show proper gratitude towards him—if Pepe hadn't arrived when he did she would likely be bundled in the back of the taxi on her way to the nearest police station. But now they were safely ensconced in his home, her fright had abated a little but blood still pumped through her furiously. Forget the driver, all she could see were those overfamiliar women and Pepe's amused, arrogant self-entitlement as he accepted their attentions.

'I thought he was trying to rape you.'

'Well, he wasn't.' She was barely listening. She kicked

her crystal shoes off. 'He was trying to get me to a police station to have me arrested.'

'What did you run off for? You told me you were going to the bathroom! You humiliated me in front of my friends.'

'Oh, poor diddums,' she said, making no effort to hide her sarcasm. 'I couldn't stomach staying at that party a minute longer.' Turning, she hurried through the reception and up the spiral staircase.

'Are you feeling ill?' He kept pace easily. Too easily.

'Yes. I feel sick. Sick, sick, sick.' She practically ran to her room.

'Why didn't you say something instead of running off and leaving me like a fool waiting for your return?'

'Because *you're* the cause of my sickness. Now get lost.' Thus said, she slammed the door in his face.

Immediately he shoved it back open. 'What the hell do you think you're doing?'

'Leaving.'

Uncaring that he stood mere feet away, and uncaring that the dress she wore cost thousands of euros, she tugged it off and threw it onto the floor, unceremoniously followed by her matching designer bra and knickers. The clothing felt soiled, bought to satisfy his conscience.

'Like hell you are.'

'Like you can stop me.' Storming into the walk-in wardrobe filled with yet more clothing bought to satisfy his conscience, Cara rummaged through until she found the dress she'd worn to the christening. Her dress. Bought with *her* money.

In the back of her mind a voice piped up telling her to clad herself in as much of the designer clothing as she could before leaving. It would be something to sell online.

She ignored it. Sanity could go to hell. These expensive clothes, as beautiful as they were, made her feel cheap.

She found her original underwear, freshly laundered, and stepped into the knickers.

'Where are you going to go?'

'Home.'

'How are you going to get there? You don't have any money.'

She turned on him. 'I don't know!' she screamed. 'I don't know where I'm going to go or how I'm going to get there, but as long as I'm far away from you I don't care!'

'If you walk away you will never see me or my money again. Your child will grow up without a father. Is that what you want?'

'Why would I want our child to know *you* as its father? You'd be a lousy father just as mine was. Selfish.'

'I am *nothing* like your father.'

'So you keep saying and, do you know what, I think you're right. My father might be an utter scumbag but even he wouldn't hold his own baby hostage as you're doing.'

'I'm doing no such thing,' he said, his own voice rising, a scowl forming on his face. 'I'm trying my best under difficult circumstances to protect our child.'

'By holding your bank account and the promise of access to it over my head as a sick method of keeping me prisoner? That'll be a good story to tell the grandkids.'

'I will do whatever is necessary to ensure my child makes it into this world without coming to harm.'

'My child? Our child? So you're admitting paternity now, are you?'

'No!' He swore. At least she assumed he swore, given the word he spurted out in Italian contained real vehemence behind it. 'It was a slip of the tongue.'

'You're good at that,' she spat with as much vehemence as *she* could muster.

'And what do you mean by that?'

'Only that you must have slipped your tongue into half the women at that party tonight. How many of your exes were there? A dozen? More?'

His eyes glittered with fury before the visible anger that had seemed to swell in him dissipated a touch.

He leaned back against the wall and surveyed her. 'You're jealous.'

Her response was immediate and emphatic. 'Don't talk such rot.'

'You are.' He said it with such certainty she tightened her grip on the bra lest she punch him one.

'I am not jealous!' How dared he even suggest such a thing? Jealous because of *him*? 'I was humiliated. All those women acting as if they owned you, all pretty much spelling out what a great lay you are... Is it any wonder it made me feel sick?'

'See?' A half-smile played on his lips. 'I knew you were jealous.'

'For me to be jealous would mean I have to have feelings for you, and the only feelings I have for you are hate. Do you understand that, Pepe? I despise you.'

Turning her back on him, she stormed into her en suite and locked the door behind her.

She absolutely was not jealous.

No way.

For the first time she realised she'd been screaming at him with only her knickers on. Could her humiliation get any greater?

She tried to put the bra on but her hands shook so much she couldn't hook it together. And she'd left her stupid dress in the room.

Pepe banged on the door.

'Go away!' she screamed. 'Just leave me alone.'

'I'm not going anywhere.'

'Well, I'm not coming out until you're gone.'

'Then you'll be in there for a long time. For ever, if necessary. Because I am not going anywhere.' Now there was no amusement to be heard in his voice. Only a determined grimness.

Let him wait. Let him wait for ever. Let him…

Patience was clearly not Pepe's forte. 'You have exactly ten seconds to open this door or I will break it down. Ten.'

The fight began to seep from her. This was all too much. 'Please, Pepe, just leave me alone.'

'Eight.'

He was serious.

'Seven.'

The tears that had been fighting to break free for the past hour suddenly escaped. She could no more contain them than she could prevent him breaking the door down.

'Four.'

With salt water rushing down her cheeks like a mini waterfall and trembling hands, she unlocked the door and pulled it open.

CHAPTER TEN

ALL THE ANGRY emotion raging through Pepe's blood constricted when he saw Cara standing there sobbing, still clutching her bra, only her knickers on to protect her nakedness.

Something hot and sharp pierced through his chest.

Instinct and something deeper, something unquantifiable, made him close the gap between them and wrap his arms around her.

'Shh,' he whispered, resting his chin on her cloud of hair and raising his eyes to the ceiling. 'Please don't cry, *cucciola mia*.'

She didn't even attempt to fight, just clung to him and cried into his chest, sobs racking her frame. Her generous breasts compressed against him but for once he couldn't react to it. Cara's sobs hurt his heart too much for him to care about anything but soothing them away.

He'd spent the past five days doing his best to forget she was pregnant. He'd been so set on blocking it out that he'd completely failed to take *her* feelings into account. Cara was such a feisty woman it was easy to forget her vulnerabilities. But she was vulnerable. Pregnancy made her more so.

He remembered the first time he'd met her. It seemed so long ago that it could have been a different lifetime but in truth it had only been a few years. It was a few weeks before his brother had married Grace. Cara had gone to stay with them in the build-up to the wedding and Luca had talked him into going on a double date, pointing out Cara would feel like a gooseberry otherwise. As she was such an important part of his bride-to-be's life, Luca was determined Cara would find Mastrangelo hospitality second to none.

Pepe hadn't been impressed. He'd been used to strong, confident women; the only bit of vivacity he'd found on Cara had been the colour of her hair. Other than that, she'd been like a wallflower, practically gluing herself to Grace's side, talking to him and Luca only when spoken to and even then in monosyllables. He'd thought her surly and rude.

As the wedding had approached, slowly he'd seen a different side to her unfurl, until, by the day of the nuptials, when he had been best man and she the chief bridesmaid, she was happy to chat with him as easily as she could with Grace.

But no one else.

He'd come to realise she wasn't surly, just painfully shy. It took her a while to overcome her nerves with someone, but when she did, she was excellent company with a dry wit that delighted him. But…she'd been Grace's best friend. She would likely always be a part of his life. There was a vulnerability to her that none of his lovers had. Any attraction to her was quashed.

He would not involve himself with vulnerable women, no matter how sexy they were. All the same, he'd enjoyed her company, would happily return home to Sicily when she stayed there and go out on double dates. They always had the best of times together.

He'd known early on from Grace's disappearance that

Cara would hold the key to finding her. But he'd put it off. And put it off some more, always hoping Grace would turn up of her own accord or that Luca would find another clue to finding her. But as the months had passed with no word, he could not in all conscience stand idly by while his brother turned into an emotional wreck. So he'd swallowed that same conscience and sought Cara out. The one woman he'd sworn he would never seduce…

He'd spent the best weekend of his life with her.

He'd been haunted by memories of it ever since.

And now she was here, back in his arms. Her naked breasts crushed against him. Breasts that tasted like nectar…

His blood thrummed, deep and heavy, his senses reacting to the scent and feel of *her*, a primitive desire that came alive only for her.

He did not want to admit those brief moments of fear when he'd realised she'd gone from the party. Vanished into the night.

He did not want to think of the cold tightness that had clutched at his chest as he'd forced his driver to put his foot down through the dark Montmartre streets.

He did not want to think of his rage when he'd seen that oaf of a taxi driver manhandling her in such a callous manner.

Pepe despised violence. He'd grown up surrounded by it, not in his family, but in the associations his father had had until *he* had allowed his own conscience to lead him away from it.

Growing up, Pepe had vowed he would never allow his fists do the talking for him. Even when he'd felt the hot blade of the knife slice down his cheek he hadn't retaliated. He'd been so numb from the preceding events that it had almost been a relief to feel something.

Yet for all that, it had taken every ounce of restraint not to throw himself onto the taxi driver and pulverise him.

If that driver had hurt her in any way, he doubted he'd have been able to hold on to that restraint.

Cara had stilled. He could feel her breath, hot through the crisp linen of his shirt, tickling his skin.

'I...I need to put some clothes on,' Cara said, trying to break away. It was happening again, that almost liquid feeling in her bones, the slavish desire creeping through her every pore. She tried to pull away but Pepe was too strong.

'You're not going anywhere.'

She hated the thrill that surged through her at his unequivocal declaration.

All she could see were his women. Her head was crowded with them, all lined up and merrily waving at her, happy—proud even—to be used by him and, she had to admit, use him in return. There was no romance. Romance had nothing to do with Pepe's liaisons.

Eejit that she was, she'd once been proud of her immunity to him.

It had been one big fat lie cooked up by her pride because he had never shown the slightest bit of interest in her other than as a friend. He'd flirted with her the same way he'd flirted with every other woman on his radar, but not once had he tried it on. Not until he'd needed something from her.

She'd been *happy* believing his sexual ambivalence towards her was mutual. She'd felt *safe*. Look at the trouble she'd got herself into when she'd allowed herself to believe otherwise.

She didn't feel safe now. Not pressed against his broad frame with his arms wrapped around her so protectively, his hand snaking down her naked spine, marking her, his musky scent filling her senses…

Her tears had left her feeling raw. Exposed and hollow. Except the void inside her was filling with something else that she tried desperately to stop. Heat. Sweet, sweet heat that pushed the tormenting images away, until the only thing that filled her head and the hollow ache inside her was *him*.

'Those women meant nothing to me.' His gravelly tones whispered into her ear, his breath warm, sending tiny darts of pleasure skittling across her skin.

Her breath hitched. 'And I do?'

He clasped her cheeks with his big hands, tilting her head back so she was forced to look at him. His eyes were deep pools of lava.

'I don't know what you mean to me,' he said, his honesty stark. Brutal. 'You've been in my head for four months and I can't shift you from there. If I'd had the choice, I would have wanted more than one night with you. And you would have wanted more than one night with me.'

Before she had the chance to form a lie of denial, his head tilted and his lips moulded on hers.

Her response was stark and utterly shocking. All the sweet heat swirling inside her immediately converged into a pool of need so deep the intensity frightened her. It took all her strength not to react, not to move her lips in time with his.

She wanted to punch at him, but when she moved her hands to his shoulders to push him away, her fingers gripped onto him.

Pepe's lips cajoled and teased and still she resisted, fighting with the last of her will power until his tongue broke through the tight line of her lips and darted into the heat of her mouth.

Something inside her snapped.

Her grip on his shoulders tightened as she responded in kind, exploring his mouth and sensuous lips as if his kisses were the life raft to cling to, to stop her drowning.

His hands caressed away from her cheeks, one snaking round to gather her hair together and spear her scalp—she had no idea when it had escaped the confines of the tight chignon—the other making broad strokes down her back until it reached her bottom. He clasped it and pulled her tight to him so his arousal was stark against her belly.

Pure, undiluted heat rushed through to her core and an unwitting moan escaped from her throat.

'*Cucciola mia,*' Pepe groaned, breaking away to nip at her delicate earlobe. Unbelievably, he was already fired up enough to explode.

Thank God he was still dressed. If he'd been naked, he would have plunged into her the second that earthy moan had echoed into his senses.

Drums played loudly in his head, his heart thundering to the same rhythm.

The bed was only a few feet away but the distance could be as far as the moon.

Unwilling to break away from her delectable body for more than the fraction of a moment, he shuffled her to the bed then gently pushed her onto it so she was sitting on the edge.

'Don't move,' he ordered, drinking her in, her colour-heightened cheeks, her bottom lip plump and begging to be kissed, her green eyes bright and dilated, her breasts heavy and swollen, the pale nipples ruched.

'*Sei bella,*' he said thickly. And she was. Beautiful.

Jeez, his hands were trembling, his fingers and thumbs

disconnected from his brain, unable to work the buttons on his shirt.

Abandoning his quest to undress himself, he sank to his knees before her and gripped her hips, pulling her to him so she looked down at him.

There she sat, gazing at him with a heavy desire he recognised and which filled him with something that fizzed in his heated blood. Her fiery hair hung down and he reached for a lock of it, greedily inhaling the sweetness of its scent.

He straightened a little to kiss her again, gratified beyond measure when she responded in kind, kissing him back, her tongue playing with his, mimicking his actions while her small hands gripped his scalp.

He covered one of her breasts with the palm of his hand, thrilling to feel the soft weightiness of it, and rubbed his thumb over the nipple. Cara arched her back in response and dug her nails into his skull, deepening their kiss.

These kisses, no matter how delicious and rousing they were, were not nearly enough.

He wanted to see if she responded with the same wild abandon that had caused him to lose his head four months ago.

But first he wanted to taste *all* of her.

Trailing kisses down her neck, he reached her breasts and hungrily took one puckered nipple into his mouth.

She moaned and cradled his scalp some more, pushing him against her. Lavishing attention on her other breast, he then bent down lower, raining kisses over the softness of her rounded stomach and down to the black lace covering the heart of her.

Hooking the side of her knickers with his fingers, he tugged at them, looking back up at her as he pulled them down to her ankles. He could smell her arousal, a scent that hit him like an aphrodisiac cloud.

'Spread your legs.' Did that thick guttural voice really belong to him?

Colour heightened her cheeks and, for one heart-stopping moment, he thought she would refuse.

'Please,' she said through heavy breaths, 'turn out the light.'

He kissed her. 'It will be good. I promise.'

Understanding her shyness, he did as she requested, turning out the main light so the only illumination came from the landing, then returned to kneel before her.

He placed a hand on a trembling thigh. 'Lie back,' he said thickly.

She swallowed, before leaning back, her eyes not leaving his face until he gently pushed her thigh to one side.

Cara's eyes closed and her head rolled back, her chest rising and falling rapidly.

Moving the other thigh to expose her to his covetous eyes, he held her open to him. Even in the dim light he could see the moisture glistening from her, her arousal there for him to see, and as he pressed his mouth to the heart of her he was suddenly grateful to still be clothed. Unable to relieve his own tension meant there was no danger of embarrassing himself by coming too soon.

Dimly he remembered being on their hotel bed in Dublin and her refusal to let him go properly down on her. He'd placed a simple kiss between her spread legs before she'd pushed him away and clamped her thighs back together.

He hadn't pressed her on it, had simply thought she was as eager as he for him to be inside her. He'd never considered that she could be a virgin who had never been naked in front of a man.

Now he realised he'd got off lightly. If he'd been given a real taste of her arousal then, he doubted he would have slept in four months.

Cara's scent and taste should be bottled as an aphrodisiac.

Her tiny moans deepened and when his tongue found her clitoris she jerked and gasped, tried to move him off her.

'Relax,' he murmured, pressing a hand to her belly while slowly inserting a finger inside her. If he didn't already know how aroused she was, this would have proved it beyond doubt.

Relax? Oh, how desperately she wanted to. How Cara yearned to let herself go and lose herself in the wonders of what Pepe was doing to her, because it felt *so good*.

But she couldn't.

No matter how hard she concentrated on the magic of his tongue and fingers, no matter how much her body ached for release, the switch in her brain refused to turn off and just let go.

'Please, Pepe,' she murmured when she could not take any more. 'Make love to me.'

He looked up at her with hooded eyes, a wolfish grin spreading over his face. 'Say it again.'

'I want…'

He got to his feet. For one fearful moment she thought he was going to leave her there, exposed on so many levels.

Instead he unbuttoned his shirt, his movements deft. He cocked an eyebrow. 'You want…?'

She swallowed moisture away, staring dazedly at the magnificence of his body as he shrugged the shirt off and casually discarded it.

His trousers and underwear quickly followed, and all she could do was gaze at him with a catch in her throat.

Pepe's arousal was all too apparent, his erection jutting out in front of him, large and proud.

'You want?' he repeated, stepping between her still-parted legs. 'I want to hear you say it. I want to hear from your own lips that you want this.'

She understood why he was demanding this from her and in a way she couldn't blame him. Even if she did blame him it would make no difference. If he were to walk away right now the big deep pool she was swimming in would dissolve into a tiny puddle. 'I want this. *I want you.*'

His eyes glittered. 'Then you shall have me.'

He leaned down over her, barely touching her, the dark silky hair on his chest brushing against her sensitised breasts, tickling her. Slanting his lips on hers, he kissed her with a possessiveness that took her breath away, his hands kneading her thighs until he had her exactly where he wanted her.

And then he was inside, joyously, massively, deeply inside her, filling her completely.

'Ahh,' she moaned, pulling him down so his full weight was on her, adjusting herself slightly to accommodate him further, to allow him even deeper penetration.

Her body remembered the heights he'd taken her to before and, like a greedy child, was desperate to feel those same sensations again, to experience the same rippling pleasure that had blown her mind.

In and out he thrust, kissing her, squeezing her breasts, clutching her hips, penetrating to her very core until she felt everything inside her tighten.

As if he could sense that she was on the edge, Pepe

increased the tempo and ground even deeper into her. It was enough.

Her orgasm rippled through her in waves so powerful and beautiful that any form of coherence abandoned her and all she could do was ride it, catching every last swell.

Cara awoke with a jolt.

An arm was curved around her belly. Deep, heavy breathing sounded from the pillow beside her.

Swallowing, she opened her eyes.

Pepe was there beside her, fast asleep. Through the dusky light she gazed at the thick black lashes, the dark stubble across his jawline, the mussed hair, the trimmed goatee.

Her heart constricted then began to hammer. She swallowed again.

After they had made love for a second time, Pepe had gathered her into his arms and fallen asleep with her head resting on his chest. Sleep had come easily for him.

She, on the other hand, had lain awake for an age. She'd disentangled herself from his arms knowing she should wake him and insist he return to his own room. Instead she'd found herself gazing at him, much as she was staring at him now. He was just so beautiful, even in repose with his mouth slightly parted, that firm yet sensuous mouth that had brought her such pleasure.

In this ethereal morning light she couldn't find the energy to rebuke herself for being so stupid as to fall back into his bed.

Recriminations could wait.

All she could focus on at that moment was that sensual mouth.

Slowly she brought her face to his, close enough to feel his breath against her skin. Closing her eyes, she brought her lips to his, breathing him in. She raised a hand to his face and gently traced her fingers down his cheek and down the strength of his neck and over his broad shoulders. It amazed her that a body so hard could be covered with skin so smooth.

Slowly she explored him, dragging her fingers through the silky hair on his chest, circling the dark brown nipples, then tracing down the flat hardness of his belly. Her pale hand contrasted against the darkness of his olive skin. They were a couple full of contrasts, her yin to his yang.

Not that they were a couple, she reminded herself hastily. They were simply two individuals thrown together by circumstances with a chemistry that refused to be denied. If not for the life growing inside her, Cara would not be here. Pepe would likely not be here either, or if he was it would be in the arms of another.

Her stomach curdled at the thought and she squeezed her eyes shut to banish it.

Was that what her mother had done? How many times had *she* squeezed her eyes shut to banish the pictures of her husband with his other women?

Before the images could swamp her, Pepe's eyes opened and fixed on her, bringing her back to the here and now.

'You stopped,' he murmured, his voice thick with sleep. She hadn't realised her hand had stopped its exploration until he enfolded it with his own.

All memories dissolved as he pulled her down for a kiss, breathing in heavily.

Returning it, she closed her eyes and allowed him to guide her hand down to the thick mass of hair on his groin and the erection that had sprung from it.

Tentatively she encircled it, heat surging through her

as she felt its silky weight and length, felt it throb beneath her touch. When she rubbed her thumb over the tip she discovered the bead of moisture already there and felt a thrill like no other that this was for her. Even if it was only for now.

CHAPTER ELEVEN

WINTER SUN SHONE brilliantly through a gap in the heavy drapes right in Cara's eyes, waking her. She turned her head. Pepe had gone.

On legs that felt weighted, she climbed out of bed and padded over to the window, pulling the drapes open.

The room smelt of a familiar scent that she recognised from four months earlier. Sex. Their sex.

Air. That was what she needed. And plenty of it.

Firstly wrapping herself in the kimono, she unlocked the French door and stepped out onto the small balcony overlooking a large park.

The cold air hit her and she accepted it into her lungs, willing the frigid particles to douse her shame.

It did nothing of the sort.

She knew she didn't deserve to have her shame extinguished.

After everything she had been through and all the promises she had made her unborn child, she was no better than her mother.

Every time one of her father's affairs had come to light, which was a regular occurrence, her mother would vow to leave. Every time she changed her mind, too hooked on the highs and lows of her marriage to care about anything as basic as self-respect. Certainly too hooked to care about the effect it was having on her only child.

Her mother had been an addict. Her husband had been her fix. Not even his litter of illegitimates had made any difference.

And now here Cara was, well over a decade after her parents' marriage had finally done them all a favour and disintegrated, and she knew that unless she did something right now she would turn into an addict just as her mother had been.

Movement behind her caused her to turn.

Pepe stepped onto the balcony carrying two steaming mugs and wearing only a pair of faded jeans. There was something about seeing his feet bare that tugged at her in a manner that was entirely different from the effect his bare torso had on her.

'Good morning, *cucciola mia*,' he said with a lazy grin, handing her one of the mugs. Placing his own mug on the small table, he stood behind her and wrapped his arms around her waist, nuzzling into her neck.

'Please, don't,' she murmured, shaking her head. 'One accident with scalding tea is enough for anyone in a lifetime.'

He chuckled. 'In that case, drink up and we can go back to bed.'

She took a deep breath, planning to confess that she didn't want to go back to bed. Or, rather, that she did want to go back to bed with him. But she wanted it too much. That was the problem. She wanted it far too much.

Before she could speak he pressed a kiss into the small of her back then stood beside her at the balustrade.

'I owe you an apology,' he said, his light tone becoming serious. 'I'd forgotten how shy you are around strangers. I shouldn't have left you alone with anyone but me last night, not until I knew you were comfortable with them.'

Cara blinked in shock.

An apology was the last thing she'd expected to hear from Pepe's mouth.

She took a sip of her tea, determinedly looking out to the park, at the distant people walking their dogs, some carrying the morning's newspapers, life going on blithely regardless of her personal torment.

'I also should have warned you that a few of my ex-lovers would be there, but to be honest I never gave it a thought,' he continued. 'It's never been an issue. I should have taken into account that you are made from a different mould from them.'

The mention of his *ex-lovers* pierced like a lance into her skin. She forced herself to breathe, focusing on the park before her, allowing her attention to be captured by a young couple out for a bike ride, a toddler-sized child sitting in a special seat attached to the father's bike.

Pepe would never be a father in the traditional sense. He was too…free. Meeting his friends and the casual, bohemian intimacy they all shared had only confirmed everything she already knew.

And she, Cara, was of a *different mould*.

It hurt to admit it, but he was right. She could never be like those women. The scars of her childhood ran too deep. She could never share the man she loved. Just thinking of Pepe sharing intimacies with another woman made her skin go clammy and nausea swell inside her, and she didn't even love him.

Did she?

No, of course she didn't. Pepe might be able to reduce her to a quivering pulse of sensation but that didn't mean she was falling in actual love with him.

Did it?

'I need to leave,' she said, blurting the words out.

Whatever her feelings for him and whatever they meant, nothing could come of them.

Pepe stilled then cast an unreadable eye on her before getting his coffee. When he rejoined her at the balustrade he stood a good foot away from her.

'I'm going to appeal to your better nature to do the right thing and give me some money now so I can return to Dublin and find a home to raise our child in.'

'And if I don't?'

'Then I guess I'll have no choice but to stay. I know I was going to leave last night but I was so…' she almost said *devastated* '…upset that I wasn't thinking straight. I guess my hormones were playing up too, making everything seem ten times worse than it really was.'

Her hormones had had nothing to do with it. The white-hot jealousy she had experienced at the party had been all her own. She would rather chop her own ears off than admit it.

She took a deep breath before continuing. 'Even if I had been able to leave last night I would probably have come back like a dog with its tail between its legs. Nothing's changed. I'm still skint. My return ticket from Sicily is worthless here, so I have no way to get home until my wages from the auction house get paid into my account. But, Pepe, I can't stay here, especially not now.'

For the first time since joining Cara on the balcony, Pepe felt the chill of the air. He stared ahead at a young family who had been enjoying a bike ride. The parents had now dismounted and rested their bikes against a large tree, the father in the process of getting the toddler out of its seat.

Once he had dreamt of him and Luisa having such a family, had allowed his hopes and dreams to fill.

'Why are you so keen to get away from me?' he asked bitingly. 'Did I not satisfy you enough last night?'

'No, it was wonderful,' she said wistfully.

'Then what is the problem with staying here and sharing my bed?'

'Because we both know it won't be for ever. Chances are you'll be sharing it with someone else long before our baby is born.'

Imagining someone else in his bed drew a blank. It had drawn a blank since Dublin.

Until he and Cara were able to work through this strange desire that burned between them, he had the most sickening feeling he would never be able to move on.

'And what about you?' he asked more harshly than he would have liked. Something akin to panic was nibbling at his chest. 'How do I know you'll take care of yourself? How do I know you'll do what's right and what's best for the life inside you?'

He heard her take a sharp inhalation, but when she finally spoke her tone was a lot softer than he had been prepared for. 'What happened, Pepe? What happened to turn you into such a cynic that you believe me capable of harming our defenceless child?'

'Because it's happened to me before.'

He could feel Cara's eyes on him, could feel her shock. He kept his own eyes firmly fixed on the family in the distance. He had no idea where the parents had produced a ball from, but they were playing a game of what looked to be catch with their small toddler.

'I've not always been a cynic. I once believed in love and marriage. I was going to marry my childhood sweetheart.' He wasn't aware of the pained sneer that crossed his face. 'Once, just once, we failed to use contraception and Luisa fell pregnant. I was eighteen and she was seventeen.'

He could feel Cara's eyes still resting on him, took a small crumb of comfort that she didn't immediately start peppering him with questions.

His throat felt constricted. This was something he had never discussed before, not with Luca, not with anyone. But he owed Cara the truth, because somewhere, hidden deep inside him, was the knowledge that it *was* his baby she carried, a truth he dared not utter in case, by saying the words, it brought the whole thing crashing down.

'I was delighted at the prospect of becoming a father. I was…' He shook his head at the memory. 'At the time, my head was all over the place. My father had just died from a heart attack and I didn't know how to handle it. But then Luisa told me she was pregnant and suddenly there was proof that life *did* have meaning and that miracles did occur. Luisa and I had spoken of marriage many times and, to me, it made sense to just bring the whole thing forward. I wanted our child to be born a Mastrangelo with parents who shared the same name.'

Trying to collect his thoughts, he finished his now cold and tasteless coffee and finally allowed himself to look at Cara.

She stood with her back to the balustrade, her arms folded across her chest, staring at him.

His heart expanded to see the paleness of her cheeks and the undeniable apprehension ringing in her green eyes.

'I thought Luisa was happy too but as the weeks passed she became more and more withdrawn, refusing to let me tell my family or her family about the baby until the time was right. And then, the morning after the first scan, the day she had agreed we could tell the world of our joy, she confessed that she'd had a one-night stand. She'd slept with someone else while I'd visited Luca at his university for a weekend.' Now he didn't bother hiding his bitterness. 'She and her lover had forgotten to use contraception. She was so terrified I would find out she engineered things so that days later we too got so carried away we forgot to use contraception. That way, if she fell pregnant, she could pass the child off as mine.'

A low whistle escaped from Cara's lips. There was no apprehension in her eyes now. Only compassion. Which somehow made him feel worse.

'The only reason she confessed was because she couldn't live with the guilt.'

'What did you do?' Cara breathed.

He laughed cynically and shook his head. 'I said I didn't care. I told her it didn't matter. I told her I loved her enough that I would raise the child as my own even if there was doubt that it was mine. But that was a lie—it wasn't *her* I loved enough to do that for, it was my unborn child. Because that baby was *mine*. I had already committed my heart to it. I had pictured the boy or girl it would be, the teenager he or she would grow into. I had pictured walking my daughter down the aisle and I had imagined my grown son asking me to be his best man.'

Long-buried unspoken memories threatened to choke him but Pepe forced himself to finish his sordid story. 'At first she agreed. Then, a couple of weeks later, when she was fifteen weeks pregnant, she went away for a weekend to visit an aunt. That too was a lie. She had in fact gone to the UK for an abortion. Her lover—who, it transpired, she was still seeing—had given her the money to pay for it all.'

Silence hung between them, the air thick and heavy.

'Dear God,' Cara whispered. 'I am so sorry.'

'Sorry for what?' he snarled, his attempts to keep a leash on his emotions snapping. 'That I was deceived? That I was stupid enough to want to be cuckolded and by Francesco Calvetti of all people…'

'*He* was her lover?'

'You know him?'

She shook her head and curled her lip in distaste. 'I know *of* him.'

Of course she did. Luca, his brother, had gone into business with the bastard, an association that had recently ended. Grace, his sister-in-law, despised the man. 'When we were kids our parents used to force us to play together. He and my brother were once good friends.'

Cara placed a tentative hand on his arm. He guessed it was supposed to be a comforting gesture, but at that moment comfort was the last thing he needed. He felt too unhinged for that. Spilling his guts for the very first time was not the catharsis people claimed.

He especially didn't want comfort from her, the woman who made him feel more unhinged than he had felt in fifteen years.

Enfolding her hand, he raised it to his cheek and placed it on his scar. 'Luisa gave me this scar. I was so angry at what she'd done, I called her every nasty, vindictive and demeaning name I could think of. In return she slashed me with a knife from her mother's kitchen. I've kept the scar as a reminder never to trust.'

Cara's eyes were huge and filled with something that looked suspiciously like tears.

He dropped her hand. 'So now you know it all. I hope

you can now understand why I do not trust people and why I cannot give you the money you want, not until after our baby is born. It's not personal towards you. Please believe that.'

Cara dressed mechanically in a blue skirt, black roll-neck jumper and a pair of thick black tights, and tied her hair back into a loose ponytail. Her hands shook, her mind filled with him, with Pepe.

After their talk on the balcony he had disappeared, muttering about needing a swim. Wordlessly she had let him go, too shocked and heartsick at his story to even attempt to stop him.

Her heart stopped when she found him in the kitchen eating a *pain au chocolat*. He'd added a black T-shirt to his jeans, his black hair was damp and he'd had a shave.

He lifted his eyes to see her standing hesitantly in the doorway, and got to his feet. 'Please, help yourself,' he said, indicating the plate heaped with pastries in the centre of the table. 'I've made a pot of tea for you.'

Knowing he had gone out of his way to make the tea especially for her kick-started her heart. When he moved with fluid grace to pour a cup out for her and she spotted his bare feet, she had to blink back the sting of hot tears that burned in the backs of her eyes.

She reached for a plain croissant and placed it on the plate he'd laid out for her, then took the seat next to him. She broke a bit of it off and popped it into her mouth, all the while watching as he added milk to her cup before placing it before her.

'Thank you,' she whispered, breaking off another piece of croissant and nibbling at it. She wanted to touch him. She wanted to place her hands on his cheeks and kiss him.

'Do you know what I love the most about Grace?' she asked him when he'd sat back down.

He cocked an eye.

'Nothing. I love *everything* about her. When I moved to England at thirteen and started a new school, I was cold-shouldered by practically everyone. They all had their cliques. I was the outsider. But Grace took me under her wing. She would drag me into the art room at lunch breaks. She would drag me to parties at weekends and stay right by my side, making sure everyone included me. She introduced me to art. Even when it was obvious that I couldn't draw much more than matchstick men, she never put me down. I ended up practically moving into her home. She encouraged me to study History of Art at university because she could see that's where my passion lay. We studied different courses but we lived together and remained inseparable. I would give my life for Grace. She was more than a best friend. She was the one person who believed in me. My parents were so wrapped up in themselves they didn't care about me other than on the level of feeding and clothing me.'

Cara kept her gaze on Pepe as she spoke. If he could lay his soul bare then so could she.

'My father had so many affairs I lost count. Time after time, Mam would say she was leaving but every time she forgave him.' She shuddered. 'I would hear them having make-up sex. It was the most disgusting sound I've ever heard. Do you know what the worst part was?'

He shook his head, his face a mask.

'*He* left *her*. After all the affairs, the lies and the humiliation, one day he went to work and never came back. He'd found a teenage lover who "made him feel like a young man again". My mother was utterly devastated. I don't think she would ever have left him. She held on for two years in the hope that he would come back to her, but when he served her with divorce papers she finally accepted it was over and carted me off to England to start over.'

She popped the last of the croissant into her mouth. Unable to resist any longer, she stroked a hand down his smooth cheek and rubbed her thumb over the thick bristles on his chin. His deep blue eyes, which hadn't left her face, dilated, and his chest rose.

'Not long after we arrived in England, my mam started a new relationship with a man who was just like my dad. An unfaithful charmer. Everyone loves him but he is incapable of keeping his pecker in his trousers. And just like with my dad, she forgives him every time. I've spent my entire life feeling second best to my parents' libidos and hormones, and I'm terrified of turning out like them. Our child will *never* feel second best. Ever. I won't let it happen. Our child is innocent and deserves all the love I—and hopefully you—can heap on him or her.' She bit her lip. 'But, Pepe, I'm so *scared*.'

'Scared of what?'

'You,' she answered starkly. 'Until I met you, sex to me was tawdry and meant nothing but power and humiliation. I wanted none of it. But now I can understand why my mam let my dad treat her like a piece of rubbish and why she lets my stepdad treat her the same way, because I can feel it happening inside me when I'm with you. I woke up this morning and I knew I should leave but I was almost helpless to resist you. I'm scared that if I stay much longer I'll never want to go.'

CHAPTER TWELVE

PEPE COVERED CARA'S HAND, his eyes boring into her. 'Do you think you're falling in love with me?'

'No!' Her denial was immediate. Snatching her hand away, she wrung her fingers together on her lap and looked away.

'Good.'

She flinched.

He placed a finger under her chin and forced her to look up at him. 'I say "good" because there is a way to get through this without screwing either of us up. And without screwing up our child. I have never cheated on anyone in my life. After what Luisa did to me, it is not something I would ever put anyone else through. I like my affairs short and sweet. I admit, there are occasions when I will sleep with an ex, but never if either of us are involved with someone else.'

Pepe watched as she bit into her bottom lip. Learning the full truth of Cara's past explained so many things about her. His complaints about his own childhood seemed unbelievably petty in comparison. He'd never doubted his family's love for him.

'I have a proposal for you,' he said, thinking aloud. 'Will you hear me out?'

With obvious apprehension, she jerked her head.

'Let's see if we can make this work. We don't love each other but we do have a serious case of lust. Eventually it will work its way out of our systems.'

'Do you think?' She looked so hopeful he felt an incomprehensible stab of pain in his chest.

He nodded. 'For as long as we're together I can promise you exclusivity. Your mother lived in a vicious cycle of high emotion and denial, neither of which applies to us. We'll take it all one day at a time. When our desire for each other reaches its natural conclusion, we can go our separate ways—and hopefully we can go our separate ways as friends. We both want what's best for our child and that's for him or her to have parents who respect each other and can work together for their child's happiness. Our child will have two parents who are happy in themselves and have no antagonism towards the other.'

'So you do believe the baby is yours?'

He closed his eyes before inclining his head. 'Yes, *cucciola mia*. I believe the baby is mine.'

Pepe waited for a beat, just in case the world did come crashing down.

'Forgive me. Not trusting people is so hardwired into me that when you told me you were pregnant I went into denial. I think maybe I lost my head a little.'

'Make that a lot,' she said with a smile that lightened her features and lifted his spirits.

Cara was not Luisa. If there was one thing he knew about his flame-haired lover it was that she didn't have a selfish bone in her body. He could not in all good conscience make her continue to pay for Luisa's sins. And nor could he allow his child to pay.

His child.

He really was going to be a father.

His chest swelled with an emotion so pure it pushed all the oxygen from his lungs.

His child.

Their child.

'I think we should both promise to give this…thing a minimum of a fortnight to at least try and make it work.'

'No more being kept as a prisoner?'

'You are free to come and go as you please—I'll even give you your own set of keys. See, I *am* trying.'

'Very,' she agreed with a straight face.

He tapped her snub nose playfully, his spirits lifting even further. This could really work…

'If you give me your bank details I will deposit a sum of money into it which should go some way to recompensing you for your future loss of earnings with the auction house.'

'You do believe I'm not after your money?' she asked, suddenly looking anxious. 'All I want is for our child to be provided for.'

'And it will be,' he promised. Now that he had openly acknowledged his paternity it felt as if a great weight had lifted from him.

Deep inside, he had always known the truth. Cara was too…straight to tell anything but the most innocuous of lies. It was his own damaged pride that had refused to believe it.

A wave of something that felt suspiciously like guilt rolled into his guts.

He'd done the best he could, he told himself defiantly. Anyone who walked in his shoes would have reacted in the same way.

All the same, he knew he would have to go a long way to make it up to her.

And he knew the best way to start.

Reaching for her hips, he pulled her so she was sitting astride him.

'What are you doing?' she asked with a gasp.

'Celebrating our agreement.' Thus said, he tilted his head and kissed her.

'So this is how we celebrate?' she said when they finally came up for air.

He nuzzled into her neck, marvelling at the softness and the oh-so-heady scent. He was reminded of the way she had tasted on his tongue, could almost taste it anew. 'Can you think of a better way?'

She tilted her head back to give him better access and sighed. 'No. Nothing better. This is perfect.'

A fortnight came and went. It didn't even cross Cara's mind to leave.

Now that she was no longer a prisoner, life in general improved considerably. She could come and go as she pleased. She spent hours wandering around Paris's famous museums and galleries, including three days back-to-back at the Louvre, and spent many a happy lunch doing nothing but hanging out in Parisian cafés drinking hot chocolate.

Her personal belongings, including all her beloved art and history books, had finally been shipped over from Dublin and she had a marvellous time going through all her stuff. Most of it was put back in the boxes—she reminded herself on a daily basis that this was only a temporary arrangement and that it would not do to start thinking of it as permanent.

All the same, life with Pepe was good. More than good. Now that they had reached an understanding, all the antagonism had died. She knew that whatever happened between them, their child would not suffer for it.

He treated her like a princess. They'd gone for her twenty-week scan together, and to witness the adoration on his face was almost as thrilling as seeing her baby for herself. The money he'd put into her account—an amount that, if she were a cartoon character, would have made her eyes pop out of her head—had been happily spent that morning on baby furniture and other paraphernalia, with more than a little change left over. It was all now being stored in Pepe's humongous garage alongside his fleet of sports cars.

And now, back at the house, they were having a swim together in Pepe's underground luxury pool. Or, rather, she was lazing in the shallow end watching him swim lengths. He sped through the water like a porpoise, his strokes long and practised. There was something rather hypnotic about watching him, she mused. Who needed a book when one could watch Pepe?

After she'd counted him do approximately fifty lengths, he waded over to her, a large grin on his face. 'You should swim, lazybones.'

'I was admiring the view.'

His grin broadened and he swooped in for a kiss.

'Hmm,' she sighed, greedily kissing him back. It never ceased to amaze her how much Pepe wanted her. Or how much she wanted him. Already she could feel the stir of an erection in his swimming shorts, rubbing against her thigh.

'I've been thinking,' she said as he nuzzled into her neck, 'that I should really look at getting a driver's licence for when the baby's born.'

He stilled a touch. 'I can provide you with a car and a driver.'

'I'm sure you can,' she agreed drily. 'But it would be

nice to have the freedom to just…go, when the mood takes me.'

She had to think practically. She just had to. Thinking in detail about her and their baby's future kept her silly emotions in check. And if ever her stomach rolled at the thought of their future being without Pepe, she quashed it. After all, Pepe would always be an enormous part of their lives; they'd just be living under different roofs.

For the time being, things between them were magical, but she would *not* allow herself to think it could last for ever. Pepe didn't do for ever.

'Have you thought about where you'll want to live with the baby?' he asked, reading her mind.

'I was thinking maybe here in Paris,' she admitted. In the month they'd been together she'd travelled with him to his homes in Portugal and Spain. Of all the places Pepe called home, Paris was her favourite. There was something so wonderful about the city, the bustle, the chic women, the architecture, the art. Wandering the streets always evoked a feeling of contentment that was only surpassed at night when she would lie sated, wrapped in his arms, drifting off to sleep.

'Really? That's a great idea.' And it *was* a great idea, Pepe told himself. His stomach hadn't really cramped at the thought of Cara and their baby living away from him.

'It just makes sense, especially as this house is going to become your main base. It'll make it easier for the baby to be living in the same city as her mam and dad.'

He forced a smile. 'I was thinking of turning your old room into a nursery.'

'An excellent idea. You'll be right next to him or her then.' Her face scrunched. 'You'll have to move my boxes into another room though, at least until I move out.'

'Not a problem.' For practicality, they'd moved her

clothes and toiletries into his room, but all her other stuff was still in her old room, still in boxes from when he'd had it flown over from Dublin.

Cara was saying words that should have been balm to his ears. She'd not developed feelings for him that ran beyond a sexual level, and nor had she dropped any hints, subtle or otherwise, about making things between them permanent. Everything was proceeding exactly as planned. He was positive that any day soon his lust for her would start to abate. Any day.

So why did the thought of her living under a different roof from him make his chest feel so tight? Why did the thought of living without her make it hard to breathe?

After a long weekend in Sicily with Pepe's family, spent hanging out with Grace and deflecting her friend's worries about Cara and Pepe's relationship, Pepe left for a week-long trip to Chile, a distance they'd agreed was too far for her pregnant self to accompany him.

Alone in the house, Cara's mind kept drifting back to the talk she'd had with Grace, when her friend had tentatively voiced her concerns.

'Cara, you do know Pepe isn't a man for the long term? It's just that there's been no mention of marriage or anything—'

'Of course it's not permanent,' Cara had interrupted. 'We're just taking it a day at a time until it runs its course.'

'Do you know what you're doing?' Grace had asked with a furrowed brow.

'Of course I do,' she'd said defiantly. 'I'm getting to know my child's father properly. We're not going to have some fake marriage for the sake of the baby which only ends in misery for everyone. When our relationship runs its course we'll still be friends, which will only benefit our child. We don't want him or her being born into a war zone.'

She'd ignored her friend's worried face, pushed the image away now as she cast her eye around the huge space that was Pepe's living room.

Before leaving for Chile he had taken her to the huge vault storing his infamous art collection. 'I'm putting the hanging and placement of my collection in your hands,' he'd said solemnly.

Cara had been incredibly touched.

Pepe had left his multimillion-euro art collection in *her* hands, giving her carte blanche to hang and place them in his home as she saw fit. Trusting her.

Deciding where to place it all, overseeing the hanging—he'd insisted on getting professionals in because he didn't want her having to climb up and down stepladders when she was six months pregnant—had fulfilled her more than she had thought possible. It had been a project and a half, and one she had embraced with all the Irish enthusiasm that flowed in her blood.

Pepe had such an amazing and eclectic eye for art. Among the Old Masters were more modern pieces, including several by Georges Ramirez, one of which was a nude bronze whose torso she would recognise with her eyes closed using only her hands. The face was a blank but she would bet Pepe had been the model for it.

The only piece she disliked was the Canaletto. It brought back too many bad memories, serving as a reminder that Pepe could be ruthless when it came to getting what he wanted. She'd stuck that particular painting in a small guest room, all two million euros of it.

'Cara?'

Pepe's deep voice rang out from downstairs.

Quashing the urge to skip down the stairs to greet him, Cara forced her legs to move in a more sedate fashion.

'I'm right here,' she said, unable to hide the beam that spread over her face at the sight of him. It was the longest they had been apart and, despite the task he'd set her, she'd missed him dreadfully. Especially at night. The bed had felt empty without him. She would never admit it, lest he read too much into it, but on the second night she had given in and borrowed one of his shirts to sleep in.

After a long, knee-trembling kiss from him, she took his hand to give him the tour.

'Wow,' he said with open admiration as they stood in the main living area. 'You really know your stuff.'

Pepe was the first to admit he didn't know the first thing about art. The pieces he bought were never about investment—although that played a part in it—but were simply pieces that caught his eye and pulled at him.

Cara's own eye had placed them all exactly where they should be, the items selected for each room complementing the feel and décor of that particular room.

He'd smiled to see the portrait his sister-in-law had done of him hanging on the wall of his office. Grace had painted him as a Greek god but with a definite touch of irony and not a little humour.

'Are you happy to have that there, where anyone can see it?' Cara said, indicating the bronze by Georges Ramirez, which she had placed in the corner of the living room.

'You recognise it?' he asked wickedly.

'Of course I do,' she said with a frown.

With a jolt he realised she'd been living with him for two months. She knew him far more intimately than any other living person.

When, he wondered, would her allure no longer affect him?

He'd assumed they'd stay together for a few weeks, maybe a month, before he'd get her out of his system. He'd suggested a minimum of a fortnight, more to convey his sincerity in wanting to make things work between them than in any real hope.

Two months on and they were still together and he wanted her every bit as much as he had at the beginning. More so, if that was possible.

'Have you considered doing this professionally?' he asked, waving his hands around the room. 'I know plenty of people who would pay a small fortune to have their art collections displayed to their very best.'

'Not really,' she said with a shrug. 'Before Grace married Luca we often said we'd like to open our own gallery— she'd do all the art and I'd run it. But life takes over. I was very happy at the auction house.'

'Speaking of galleries, we've got a few hours to kill before we go to the exhibition tonight,' he said, referring to the opening of an up-and-coming new artist's work he'd promised they would attend. 'Shall we go for a swim?'

She pulled a face. 'My bikini line hasn't been done for weeks.'

'So? It's only me who's going to be looking.' He would be doing a lot more than looking. He'd be doing a lot more right now but for Monique bustling around in the kitchen, liable to barge into the living room at any moment.

A whole week without Cara had felt interminably long.

'I'd still feel self-conscious.'

'I can do it for you.'

Cara didn't trust the gleam that came into Pepe's eyes. 'Do what?'

'Your bikini line.'

'No way.'

'Why not?'

'Because…' Because she still wasn't comfortable with him being *down there*. Blame it on her Catholic upbringing—which was an irony in itself—or blame it on her reaching the grand old age of twenty-six before getting naked with a man, but, whatever the reason, she had a hang-up about her nether regions. Not Pepe's though. She adored *his* nether regions.

He arched an eyebrow. 'Because?'

She was stumped for a good answer.

She was still stumped for a good answer fifteen minutes later, sitting naked on a towel on the sofa in Pepe's bedroom.

'Relax, *cucciola mia*,' he purred, kneeling before her, having placed a jug of hot water on the floor beside him. He also carried a couple of razors and a tube of shaving gel. To make her feel less self-conscious he'd stripped off too. Or so he'd said.

'I need you to spread your legs,' he said, pouring some gel onto his palm.

Swallowing, she did as she was bid and parted her thighs.

'Further.'

She took a deep breath and exposed herself to him, resting her head back in a futile attempt to do as he'd suggested and *relax*.

'I won't hurt you,' he said with the utmost sincerity, before planting a kiss on her inner thigh. 'Trust me.'

Mixing the gel on his palm with a couple of droplets of the hot water, he rubbed his hands together to form a lather, then carefully swiped it over her bikini line, taking great care around the delicate area.

She closed her eyes. Happy to wax her legs, she'd always drawn the line at waxing her bikini area, preferring the less painful route of shaving.

Never in a million years would she have believed she'd allow someone else to do it for her.

When she finally dared look, she found his head bowed in concentration.

Trust me, he'd said.

With a jolt of her heart she realised that she *did* trust him.

She trusted him as she'd never trusted anyone other than Grace.

But this was a different form of trust. This was a deeper, more intimate trust, a trust she'd never expected to find with a man, with anyone.

'Okay?' Pepe's dark blue eyes were looking up at her.

She nodded and gave a half-smile. Her legs and torso were no longer tensed; indeed, her entire body had now relaxed.

'What do you think about Charlotte for a girl?' she said.

He looked up briefly, his lips pursing the way they always did when he was considering something. They'd already agreed on Pietro for a boy, in honour of Pepe's father. Choosing a girl's name had proved trickier. At first she'd thought he was being deliberately awkward when he dismissed the names she kept coming up with... until the penny dropped that he was, in his own subtle fashion, trying to avoid naming their child after any of his ex-lovers. Not all the names, thank God. A few he dismissed for other reasons, like thinking a particular name was 'wet'.

She'd now taken to throwing a name at him, watching him purse his lips and then shake his head, all the while hoping she never came across one of his 'friends' who shared that particular name.

This time, there was no shake of the head. Instead, a broad grin spread across his handsome face. 'That is perfect.' He nodded, still grinning. 'Charlotte Mastrangelo-Delaney. *Sì*—perfect.'

When he refocused his attention to his current handiwork, Cara tried to shake away the jealousy coursing through her blood, knowing she was being irrational. So what if Pepe had been prepared to marry Luisa so they and their child could all share the same surname? In those days he'd been little older than a child himself with romantic ideals that had no place in the real world.

Cara and Pepe had reached the perfect compromise when it came to naming their child, both reasoning that it wasn't his baby, or her baby, but *their* baby, and therefore should share both their names.

At least he was capable of compromise. Most of the time. He still had an unerring ability to get his own way on most things. Like now.

Before much more time elapsed, he leaned back and flashed a grin. 'See—that wasn't too bad, was it?'

'It was fine.'

'Stay where you are—I need to get some fresh water to clean you up.'

She watched him stride off to the en suite, not in the least bothered about his nudity, with a lump in her throat. No wonder so many artists clamoured to immortalise him in whatever medium they used. Pepe's strength and poise, mixed with his underlying good humour, were like nectar to a bee.

He returned with a fresh jug of water and a towel.

This time he didn't have to ask her to part her legs.

'Have you done this lots of times?' she asked, then

immediately castigated herself. His answer had the potential to lance her.

His eyes met hers, glittering with something she didn't recognise. 'Never.'

Her heart hitched.

For long moments neither moved. She wished she could read what was swirling in his eyes, but before she could catch it, he broke the hold.

Bowing his head, he placed a kiss on the area he'd just shaved. Then another kiss. And another.

His movements were so gentle and…reverential, that as he made his way to the very heart of her she forgot to feel embarrassed, lying back to rest her head on the back of the sofa and simply *feel*.

Pepe was such a wonderful lover, she thought dreamily. So tender yet so fantastically wild, and always wanting her. She remembered how he'd arrived back from an overnight stay in Germany. Within five minutes of getting home he'd had her bent over on the desk in his study. She'd been so desperate for him too that they'd been like a pair of rutting animals.

Heat from these gorgeous memories pooled into her core right at the moment Pepe found her clitoris. She moaned.

Her mind drifted off, her body a haze of sensation all circling around what this wonderful man was doing to her.

Oh, how she loved him. With every fibre of her being.

And as this realisation filled her, the pulsations that had been building inside filled too, and, with a cry, she felt the pulsations explode, rippling out of her in one long, continuous wave of sensation.

When she opened her eyes, Pepe was gazing up at her, his eyes hooded and glistening.

'That's the most beautiful thing I have ever seen,' he said hoarsely, before rising to kiss her. Pulling her into his arms, he lifted her off the sofa and carried her over to his sprawling bed.

His lips fused to hers, his hands gripping hers above her head, he entered her immediately. But, despite his impatience to be inside her, there was nothing hurried about their coupling. This was tender beyond her imagination.

With her body already fizzing from her earlier climax, she didn't think she was capable of another orgasm, but Pepe knew her so well, knew exactly when to increase the friction to bring her all the way back to the edge.

Clinging to him, she gloried in his fervent control, her heart singing in tune with her body. Pepe might not love her—might never love her—but in this moment he was making love to her as if she meant more to him than just the mother of his child and his lover for the moment. He was making love to her as if she were the most precious thing in his world.

When her climax finally erupted, he was right there with her, his face buried in her shoulder, groaning words in Italian as he drove himself inside her with a final thrust.

'You are crying?' he asked, long minutes later when he eventually lifted his head from her neck.

She hadn't even noticed tears were streaming down her face.

'Did I hurt you?'

She gave a quick shake of her head. 'Hormones' was the most she could utter.

How could she tell him she was crying because she'd done the one thing she'd sworn she would never do?

Far from living together as a couple sating the desire between them, it had shifted it into something deeper.

She had fallen in love with him, and she knew without a shadow of doubt that when the time came for Pepe to call it a day her heart was going to shatter into tiny pieces.

CHAPTER THIRTEEN

'Are you sure you're okay?' Pepe asked for the third time since they'd left the house. Cara seemed to have lost much of her colour and was much too quiet for his liking.

'I guess I'm a little apprehensive about this exhibition.'

Reaching for her hand, he pulled it over to rest on his thigh. 'I won't leave you alone for a second when we're there, I promise.'

She smiled wanly. 'I know you won't.'

'How did you cope when you worked at the auction house? You had to deal with new people on a daily basis.'

'That was different. It was work and so I could put my professional head on.'

'Maybe you should try that tonight,' he mused. 'If you see all the rich guests as potential clients for when you go back to work—if you go back to work—you might find it easier to cope.'

'It's worth a try,' she agreed non-committally.

Shifting gear, he drove into a street that was officially the beginning of Montmartre. Knowing how much Cara loved to hear about the arrondissement, he began pointing out places of interest, making a mental note to actually take her to them and not just drive past.

She looked so beautiful this evening. But then, she always looked beautiful. Tonight, she'd left her hair down, the red locks spread out over her shoulders like a fan. She was wearing a simple, high-necked, long-sleeved black dress with a wide red belt hanging loosely around the middle, resting on the base of her swollen belly. In the week he'd been away, her bump had grown. For the first time she actually looked pregnant. In his eyes she'd never looked more beautiful.

'Who's the artist exhibiting tonight?' she asked when he turned into the small car park at the back of the exhibition room.

'Sabine Collard. Have you heard of her?'

She shook her head. 'Sabine Collard,' she repeated. He loved the way she tried to pronounce her Rs the French way. It sounded so adorable coming from her Irish lilt.

The gallery was already packed.

Keeping a firm hold on Cara's hand, he guided her through the throng and towards the star of the evening.

When Sabine, a young, angry-looking young lady, spotted Pepe, she embraced him and planted kisses on his cheek.

'Let's stick to English,' Pepe said when Sabine began jabbering in French. He didn't want Cara unable to join in with the conversation.

Sabine gave a Gallic shrug. '*D'accord.* It is very good to see you. I have missed you at the studio.'

Had it been very long? With a jolt, he realised he hadn't visited the studio since Cara had moved in.

'Sabine shares a studio with a few other artists,' Pepe explained to Cara, whose grip on his hand had become vice-like. Casually he rubbed his thumb over her wrist in a wordless show of support.

'So modest!' Sabine exclaimed before addressing Cara directly. 'Your lover owns the studio. It is a *huge* building that was once a hotel. And it is not a "few" artists working and living there—we number fifteen! All living and working rent-free because your lover is one of the few patrons of the art who truly is a patron in all senses of the word.'

'It's not completely selfless,' Pepe hastily explained when Cara's eyes widened. 'I allow them to live and work there rent-free in exchange for a cut of any money they make when they sell their pieces.'

'Five per cent,' Sabine snorted. 'Hardly a big cut, especially when the most of us don't sell anything.'

'I can always raise it,' he warned with a grin.

A beatific expression came over her face. 'Oh, look, there is Sebastien LeGarde. I must socialise.'

Cara watched the chic Frenchwoman sashay away in the direction of a rotund man with the shiniest bald spot she'd ever seen.

Even if she'd been born French she would never have that certain élan Sabine carried off so effortlessly.

'No.'

She looked back at Pepe. 'No what?'

'No, I haven't slept with her.'

'I didn't say you had,' she pointed out primly.

'You were thinking it.' He reached out and gently stroked her cheek. 'There is a chance a couple of my exes will be here though.'

'There's always a chance we'll bump into your exes whenever we step out of the front door,' she said, more tartly than she would have liked.

She had no right to feel jealous. Ever since they'd agreed to make a go of some sort of semblance of a relationship, Pepe had treated her with nothing but respect. Whenever they went out he stuck to her side, his unspoken support worth more than all the money in the world.

He really was nothing like her father and she knew

with as deep a certainty as she'd ever known anything that he would never cheat on her.

All the same, she couldn't help the cloying sickness that unfurled inside her whenever she met his ex-lovers or even made the mistake of thinking about them.

There was a reason jealousy was oft referred to as the green-eyed monster. Thinking of Pepe with anyone else made her go green inside and made the monster within her want to scratch eyes out.

One day soon she would have to find a way to live with it.

She had no idea how she would be able to.

Pepe wanted them to part as friends?

She didn't think she'd even be able to cope with fleeting glances at him. How could *anyone* be strong enough to endure that, to love someone with all their heart and know the recipient would never feel the same way?

All she could do was hold on and hope for a miracle.

Miracles happened. Didn't they?

But even if they didn't, one thing she did know was that she would not behave as her mother had with her father. Whatever happened, Cara was confident her child would never witness the selfish behaviour that Cara had witnessed from *her* parents. Both she and Pepe were committed to that.

Any devastation would take place internally.

'I didn't know you owned a studio,' she said, quickly changing the subject away from something that could easily make her vomit. As she spoke, a sharp stab of pain ran down the side of her belly.

'Are you okay?' Pepe asked, noticing her reflexive wince.

Sucking in a quick blast of air, she nodded.

'You're sure?'

'Yes.' As she reassured him that all was well, it suddenly occurred to her that her back had ached all day. She'd been so excited about Pepe coming home after a week away that she hadn't thought much about it.

'I bought an old hotel a few years back,' Pepe said. 'I had it turned into a home for artists, a place where they could live and work. As you know from Grace, artists often work strange hours. The majority live in poverty.'

'What made you want to do it?' she asked, glad of the conversation to take her mind off irrational thoughts. Besides, she loved hearing anything that helped unlock the mystery that was Pepe Mastrangelo.

His mouth tightened a fraction before he answered. 'There is something incredibly *free* within the art world which I have always felt an affinity with. Growing up in Sicily...it was like living within a straightjacket. It's probably the reason I enjoy flying so much—it gives me a real sense of freedom. Many artists pursue their craft in defiance of their parents' wishes. I wanted to create a space for them to pursue their dream without having to worry about where the rent money was going to come from. Only artists who have been cut off financially from their families are eligible to live there. The only other stipulation is that the artist must have a genuine talent.'

'That's an amazing thing to do,' she said, genuinely touched.

'Not really,' he dismissed. 'It's an investment for me.'

She raised a brow. 'Five per cent?'

He suddenly grinned. 'Georges Ramirez started off in that studio.'

'Really?'

He nodded. 'He was only there for six months before a gallery owner I introduced him to gave him an exhibition and...the rest is history.'

'And does he pay full market rate on the loft?' she asked slyly.

'Near enough,' he said, grinning.

'You never cease to amaze me,' she said with a shake of her head. 'You're always trotting off from country to country on family business, yet you still invest your time as well as your money in the art community.' She gave him a crafty wink. 'How many of your artists have you dropped your kecks for in the name of art?'

His lips twitched. 'Half a dozen. Can I help it if I'm prime model material?'

She sniggered and reached for his hand, lacing her fingers through his. 'Do your family know what you do for the art world?' Somehow, she thought not. Grace would certainly have mentioned it.

He began scanning the room. 'I don't think they would be that interested. My life has never been that much of an interest to them before.' Suddenly he looked back at her with a grin. 'Saying that, they were always interested whenever I got into trouble.'

'Were you a very naughty boy?' she asked, matching his light tone, although she had caught a definite shadow in his eyes.

A gleam now shone in those same eyes. '*Sì*. I was a *very* naughty boy.' He leaned down to whisper into her ear. 'When we get home I'll show you what a naughty boy I can still be.'

Heat filled her from the tips of her toes to the long strands of hair on her head. 'I look forward to it.'

Suddenly filled with the urge to jump onto him and kiss his face off, which, given they were in full view of dozens of people, wouldn't do at *all*, she brought their conversation back to a less suggestive level. 'How come you joined the family business when your heart is clearly elsewhere?'

He shrugged. 'My father died. Luca had been groomed from birth to take over the business but none of us expected my dad to die so young. Luca held the fort on his own while I completed university but I knew he needed me. It wasn't fair for him to shoulder all the burden and pressure on his own. I'd spent my childhood playing the joker and it was time to grow up. Plus it was a good distraction from losing my father and from what Luisa had done to me.'

Her stomach contorted again, although whether this was because he'd mentioned Luisa's name or because of something physical, she didn't know, but it quickly passed.

'I think your father would be very proud if he could see you now, Pepe Mastrangelo.'

His eyes widened a fraction and glistened with something she couldn't discern.

'*I'm* very proud of you. And I know our child will be too.'

Before Pepe could respond, Georges Ramirez joined them, his pretty wife, Belinda, in tow.

Another, sharper pain cut through Cara's stomach.

Blocking out everything around her, she concentrated on breathing through the pain. This was definitely physical.

Cold fear gripped her.

'Not drinking?' Georges asked, looking pointedly at the orange juice in Pepe's hand.

'I'm driving.' Pepe could have used his driver tonight but he enjoyed driving Cara around, especially now she seemed over the worst of her travel sickness. He always made sure to drive her in the car with the sturdiest stabilisers and keep his speed at a steady level—too much heavy braking and up she would chuck. As good as his driver was, Pepe preferred to trust in his own driving ability to keep Cara free from nausea. In any case, it hardly seemed fair for him to be quaffing champagne when she had to stick to soft drinks. If she could make the minor sacrifice of forsaking alcohol for nine months, then he could do his bit too.

'Good—you can drive me and Belinda home. Stay for drinks...'

But Pepe had tuned Georges out.

Cara was *proud* of him?

Such a simple word but one that filled his chest with something so light and wonderful he couldn't begin to find the words to describe it.

Like a thunderbolt came the realisation that Cara had the capacity to bring him more joy than anyone else in the world.

Holding tight to her hand, he scanned the room, looking at some of the women who had once shared his bed and the women who, if Cara hadn't come into his life, he would have considered bedding.

There was no comparison, and it was nothing to do with the physical, although that certainly played its part.

Bedding all these women...

He'd been hiding. Tied up with his feelings of being second best to his brother and after everything Luisa had put him through, he'd sworn *never again*. Never again would he put himself in a position where he could be hurt. Those women had been nothing but a temporary affirmation that he was worth something, a good time, a boost to his ego.

Cara made him feel like a king, as if everything he did was worth something, if only to her.

At some point he'd stopped hiding the essence of himself from her—he didn't know where or when, it had been a gradual process born of their enforced intimacy over the past few months—and, even after seeing the real man behind the mask, she could still stand there and declare her pride in him.

And it came from her. The one woman in the world whose opinion actually mattered.

Because *she* mattered.

She mattered more than he had ever dreamt possible.

'Pepe?'

Even though he'd successfully tuned Georges out, Cara's whispered call of his name brought him back to sharp focus…and with it came the realisation that something was wrong.

Her hand, still clasped in his with a grip tight enough to cut off his circulation, had gone clammy. In the blink of an eye she had gone from being pale to totally devoid of colour.

He placed a hand to her forehead. It was cold. And damp.

'Cara?'

He'd hardly got her name out when she doubled over with an anguished cry and fell to the floor.

Rancid fear clung to Pepe like a cloak. For the first time in his life he felt helpless. Totally helpless.

The ambulance sped through the streets of Montmartre and he had to stop himself from demanding the driver go faster. The sirens blared but it rang like a dim distant noise, drowned out by the drumming in his head.

Cara's huge eyes, so full of pain and terror, didn't leave his. An oxygen mask had been strapped to her face. He wished he could take her hand but the paramedic had ordered him to keep his distance so she could do her work.

Dio.

Under his breath he said a prayer. A long prayer. He prayed for their child. But mostly he prayed for Cara. For the sweetest, most beautiful woman on the planet, who had brought such meaning and happiness to his life.

Caro Dio, please let him have the chance to tell her how much she meant to him.

When she'd collapsed he'd known immediately something bad was happening. And she had known it too. While they'd waited for the ambulance to arrive, she'd clung to him. He hadn't realised he'd been clinging to her too until the paramedic had prised him off her.

And now it was all out of his hands. Cara's fate and their baby's fate were in the hands of someone else. If anything should happen to her…

Caro Dio, but it didn't bear thinking about.

Cara didn't want to open her eyes. Didn't want to face the reality that opening them would bring.

Soft voices surrounded her then a door shut.

Silence.

She knew exactly where she was. In a hospital. The smell was too distinctive to be anywhere else.

She also knew why she was there.

'Cara?' A tender finger wiped away the single tear that had leaked out.

This time she did open her eyes and found Grace sitting beside her, her face drawn.

'Where's Pepe?'

'He's talking to the doctor. He'll be back soon.'

'I want Pepe.' It came out as a whimper.

Grace clasped Cara's hands. 'He won't be long, I promise.'

'I want Pepe.' This time it came out as an anguished howl.

Although it went against all regulations, Grace climbed onto the bed and wrapped her arms tightly around her, letting Cara sob as if there were no tears left to cry.

Pepe staggered along the corridor, the coffee his brother had given him hours ago still clutched in his hand, cold.

When he got to Cara's room, Grace and Luca came out before he could go in.

'Is she awake?'

'She was. She's sleeping again. Probably the best thing for her.'

He nodded mutely, Grace's words sounding distant and tinny to his ears.

Dimly he was aware of them exchanging glances.

Grace took his hand and clasped it in hers.

When he looked he could see she'd been crying.

'Luca and I have been talking and we think Cara should come home with us.'

'No.' He snatched his hand away.

They exchanged another significant glance.

Luca put his hand on his brother's shoulder and drew him away. 'Pepe, I know you're hurting but Cara needs to be with someone who loves her and that person is Grace. You told me yourself you were only together because of the baby.'

Pepe couldn't even find the strength to punch him.

You were only together because of the baby...

Was that really true? Had that *ever* been true?

He didn't know. His brain hurt too much to think.

Everything hurt.

It had all been so sudden.

One minute, everything had been fine. The next…

'Listen to me,' Luca said in a gentle tone he'd never heard him use before. 'It is at times like this a woman needs to be surrounded with love and compassion. Your relationship was only ever temporary. Cara and Grace are closer than sisters. Grace will take care of her. I guarantee it.'

'She's got to stay in hospital for a few more days,' Pepe said dully. 'She's had major surgery. She shouldn't travel.' The obstetricians had delivered their baby via a caesarean section. Cara had been knocked out for it.

He wished he had been knocked out for it too.

'We need to arrange the funeral. She won't want to travel anywhere until we've said goodbye.'

Luca winced at the mention of a funeral.

'What?' Pepe snarled, suddenly springing to life. 'You think I'm not going to give my baby girl a proper goodbye because she was *stillborn*? You think Cara will not want to say goodbye to Charlotte? You think we'll want to forget she ever existed, is that it?'

'No…'

Whatever Luca, who had gone white, was going to say was pushed aside when Grace stepped between them.

'Pepe, please, forgive us. All we want is what's best for Cara, and for you. Nothing more. And you're right— she won't want to go anywhere until after the funeral. When she's ready, she can come to Rome with me. Luca will go back to Sicily to be with Lily.'

'It's what's best for Cara,' Luca added quietly.

Pepe knew his brother was right. Although it ripped his insides to shreds, he knew it.

Cara would want to be with Grace. She wouldn't want to be with him.

He finally jerked a nod. 'Okay,' he said heavily. 'But only if that's what Cara wants. If she wants to stay with me then neither of you are to say anything to change her mind.'

Without waiting for a reply, he strolled into the private room and took the seat by Cara.

She was pale enough to merge into the white sheets.

He was glad she was asleep. At least if she slept she wouldn't have to remember, or, worse, feel.

He would gladly give up every organ in his body if it would take away her pain.

The next time Cara awoke, Pepe was sitting on the private room's windowsill, looking out.

'Hi,' she whispered.

His head snapped round and in a trice he was by her side.

He looked dreadful. Still in the same tuxedo he'd worn to the gallery; what had been an impeccably pressed suit was now rumpled. *He* looked rumpled.

He didn't say anything, just took her hands in his and pressed a kiss to them.

'I'm so sorry,' she croaked.

His brow furrowed, but he didn't speak.

'I keep thinking I should have known something was wrong...'

He placed a gentle finger to her lips and shook his head, his face contorted. 'No,' he croaked vehemently. 'Not your fault. It was a severe placental abruption. Nothing could have been done to prevent it. Nothing.'

She swallowed and turned her head away. Everything inside her felt dry, and so, so heavy, as if a weight were crushing her.

Time passed. It could have been minutes. It could have been hours. She had lost all sense of it.

'Has Grace spoken to you about going back to Rome with her?' Pepe asked quietly.

She looked back at him and mouthed a silent 'no'.

His lips compressed together. 'Grace wants to take care of you. She thinks you will want to be with her.'

More time passed as she looked into his bloodshot eyes. He really did look wretched, and no wonder. Pepe had lost his child too. He was suffering too.

'What about you?' she finally said, dragging the words out. 'What do you think?'

He shrugged, an almost desperate gesture. 'This isn't about me. It's about what's best for you.'

Oh.

Somewhere in the fog that was her brain was the remembrance that their relationship had only ever been temporary.

Nothing lasted for ever, she thought dully. Nothing.

She had no doubt Pepe would allow her to return home with him if she asked. He'd take care of her as best he could.

But he wasn't asking her to go home with him, was he? He was giving her—them—a way out.

And she knew why.

Every time he looked at her he would be reminded of the loss of yet another child.

And every time she looked at him her loss would double.

He'd loved their baby, not her.

She'd loved them both.

'I need to sleep,' she whispered, disentangling her hand and carefully turning onto her side, not quite turning her back to him.

She could hear his breaths. They sounded heavy. Raspy.

'So you're going to go with Grace?'

She nodded, utterly unable to speak.

It was only when she heard the door shut that the dryness inside her welled to a peak and the tears fell, saturating the pillow.

Incoherent with grief, she was unaware of the needle that was inserted into her arm to sedate her.

CHAPTER FOURTEEN

'ARE YOU SURE you want to do this?' Grace asked as the driver pulled up outside Pepe's Parisian home.

Cara nodded absently, gazing at the place she had called home. The place where she had spent the happiest months of her life. The place where the man she loved was holed up, alone.

'You don't have to do this.'

Cara attempted a smile. 'I know that. I *want* to.' How puny a word *want* sounded when describing the desperate yearning that lived inside her to be with him.

But Grace was right. She didn't have to do this. She could get on the jet that was waiting for them and fly off to Rome. The world would still turn. In time she would heal.

But her heart wouldn't. Without Pepe she doubted she would ever feel whole again.

'Are you sure you don't want me to come in with you?'

Cara shook her head. 'No. I need to do this alone. I want to say goodbye to him properly.' At the graveside Pepe had looked desolate. She'd had Grace on her arm, holding her up. He'd stood apart from them all, shunning even his brother.

She needed to satisfy herself that he was holding up. Who was taking care of *him*? she wondered. His mother was in Sicily taking care of Lily. His brother was already en route back to Sicily, having returned for the funeral. Pepe had rejected his attempts to stay with him, assuring both Luca and Grace that he was perfectly all right, and throwing himself into his work.

But he wasn't all right. He couldn't be. The few conversations they'd had to discuss the funeral arrangements had been almost too painful to recall. He'd sounded empty.

His friends, as lovely as she'd come to accept most of them were, were too wrapped up in their own lives to see beyond the tragedy of what had happened between them on anything but a superficial level. And now that the funeral was over, she suspected those that had been there for him thus far—if he'd even let them be there for him, which she doubted—would fall by the wayside.

She'd held off for a full twenty-four hours before caving in to her need to see him. Her mind was tormented with worries for his state of mind. She'd phoned the house and been assured by Monique that he was working from home. She'd called at the right time—Monique had been put on leave with full pay until further notice. She was only at the house at that time with the ostensible excuse of having to drop some dry-cleaning off. She too was worried for him.

'Make sure you take things easy,' Grace warned kindly.

Two weeks had passed since Cara's baby had been so cruelly taken from her. It would be another four weeks before she'd be allowed to lift anything heavier than a cup of tea. 'I promise. I'll call you when I'm done.'

'No rush. I'll wait at the house.' Since her discharge, Cara and Grace had been staying at the home of a friend of Pepe's who was away on business. 'The jet's ready to leave when we are.'

Swallowing her apprehension, Cara used her key to unlock the front door. The alarms were disabled, so she knew he had to be around somewhere, but only silence greeted her. Heavy, oppressive silence.

Slowly she walked through the ground floor. Everything was just as it had been when she'd last walked through this house, when the future had seemed full of hope, when they'd found a new level of intimacy and she'd believed that maybe miracles could occur.

But there were no miracles to be had.

Nothing had changed but the house felt like a shell of itself.

How could Pepe bear to live here all alone with only his own thoughts for company?

At least she had Grace. She would always have Grace and would for ever be grateful to her best friend for everything she had done for her and continued to do. But all Cara wanted was Pepe. It was his arms she wanted around her, holding her. Just holding her. Sharing their grief.

'Pepe?'

No answer.

'Pepe? It's me. Cara,' she added as an afterthought.

Where was he? Oh, please let him be okay.

There was another reason for her being here.

Taking a deep breath, she entered the garage.

All the stuff was there, exactly where she had left it, still in the boxes. The cot. The dresser. The pram. Even the baby bath. Everything.

The weighty nausea that had lined her stomach for the past two weeks began its familiar roll. She closed her eyes and leaned against the wall for support.

Her baby would never sleep in that cot or ride in that pram.

Her chest heaved as she fought back another fresh wave of tears. So many tears. So much grief. And the man she wanted so desperately to cling to could hardly bring himself to look at her.

Heavy steps came into the garage accompanied by even heavier breathing.

'Sorry, I was on a teleconference,' Pepe said tonelessly.

She opened her mouth to say not to worry. Instead, bile and hysteria rose in her throat. The boxes ripped at her.

'Are you healing well?'

She wanted to say yes, but all she could see were the boxes. 'I don't know what to do with this lot. I just don't know what to do.'

At first he didn't answer. 'I'll keep them here until you decide.'

She jerked a nod, and finally made herself look at him. 'Thank you.'

He raised a shoulder. 'No problem.'

Despite his casual air, she wasn't fooled. Not for a second. Pepe was hurting every bit as much as she.

He looked wretched too, even more so than she'd seen at the graveside, when she'd been too heartbroken and scared to do more than cast him fleeting glances. Scared she would take his hand and offer the support he so clearly didn't want. Scared his grief would make him reject her.

He couldn't have shaved at all since it had happened. The man who took such pride in his trim goatee now had a fully fledged black beard. His eyes were bloodshot and wild. Even his clothes were all wrong. He hadn't dressed. He'd thrown clothes on.

His feet were bare.

She longed to reach out but didn't know…

She didn't know anything. She didn't know how to cross the bridge to him.

What did she think she was doing? Pepe didn't want her there.

He didn't want anyone.

She straightened and inhaled deeply, closing her eyes as she said, 'I need to go.'

She took his lack of an answer as agreement.

Her hand on the door, she turned to face him one last time. 'Be kind to yourself, Pepe.'

Tears blinding her, she walked through the living room, fumbling in her bag for her phone to call Grace, who'd likely not even made it back to the house yet.

'Cara?'

Hastily brushing the tears away with the back of her hand and in the process clonking her nose with her phone, she stopped and slowly turned.

Pepe shuffled towards her, his hand outstretched. 'Don't go.'

Her brow furrowed in confusion.

Her legs too weak to carry her any further, her stomach feeling the strain of being upright for too long, she sank onto the chair right behind her.

When he reached her, he knelt down and placed his hand on her neck. 'I can't bear it,' he said hoarsely. 'I think I could cope if it was just the loss of our baby, but losing you too…'

A sound like a wail echoed in the room. It took the beat of a moment for Cara to realise the sound had come from *her*.

Pepe's face contorted and he looked down to her belly then back up to her face, his eyes searching for…something. 'I know what I'm asking is selfish but, please, *cucciola mia*, please don't go. I'll take care of you. I'll help you heal. Please, just give me the chance to show how much you mean to me and prove how much I love you.'

When Pepe saw the confusion and doubt ringing in Cara's eyes, he almost gave up. It was the tiny spark of hope he also saw that gave him the courage to forge on.

To put his heart on the line. Because if he didn't say it now it would be too late.

'When Luisa aborted our baby—and I believe with all my heart that child was mine—it was the loss of that child so soon after the loss of my father that ruined me. Her lies and deceit were supplementary. I never missed *her*. I'd been in love with a dream that didn't exist—in my own family I'd always felt like a spare part. Luca was the brother who mattered; I was just the spare, and, no matter how much my parents loved me, I always knew that. With Luisa, I dreamt of having my own family where *I* mattered.

'Cara, losing *our* baby has broken my heart. Our child was more than a dream. *You* were more than a dream, and you leaving…it's broken *me*. I don't know how to go on. I'm lost without you. I'm…' His voice went. All the desolation he'd been sitting on for the past two weeks burst through and choked him. He didn't even realise he was crying until Cara wrapped her arms around him and pulled his head to her chest.

She kissed his head, over and over, murmuring sweet words and cradling him with such love and compassion that for the first time in a fortnight a trickle of warmth cut through the ice in his chest.

'Oh, my poor love,' she whispered, her own tears falling into his hair. 'I've been so desperate to be with you.

I thought you wouldn't want me here any more. If I'd known how you felt I would never have gone with Grace.'

He raised his head and found his face being rained upon with her tears. 'I thought you *wanted* to be with her.'

She shook her head. 'I wanted to be with you. Just you. I love you, Pepe.'

'You do?'

What looked like a brave smile broke through her tears. 'How could I not fall in love with you? I always thought love between a man and a woman was about sex and power and humiliation. I had no idea it could be about sex and friendship and support. You're everything to me.'

'I'm so sorry for the way I treated you when you first came to me about the pregnancy. And I'm sorry for the way I treated you in Dublin.'

'I understand. You were helping your brother. While I don't agree with your methods, I can see it was something you felt you had to do for his sake. I would have done the same for Grace.'

'I was terrible,' he stated.

'It's done,' she said gently, 'and if it makes you feel better then know I forgive you. I forgave you a long time ago.'

Pepe hadn't realised how badly he'd needed her forgiveness until another trickle of warmth seeped into his bones. It would be a long time before the cold left him, but with Cara at his side he didn't have to freeze alone. And neither did she. Together they could bring the warmth back.

'A part of me always knew getting involved with you would bring me nothing but trouble,' he confessed.

'Really?'

'*Sì*. And I was right. It wasn't just that you were a virgin or that I felt guilt for what I'd done: I couldn't get you out of my head. The pregnancy came almost as a relief—it meant I had a legitimate reason to keep you in my life without having to acknowledge that my feelings for you ran far further than I could ever admit.'

Her bee-stung lip wobbled. He pressed a finger to it and then the tenderest of kisses. 'I used to tease you about being my concubine or my geisha. I can see now how wide off the mark I was—*I* should be *your* concubine because your needs are all that matter to me. The rest of the world can go to hell. *You* are all that matters to me, and whatever it takes to get us through this whole horrific ordeal I will do. I swear.'

'As long as you're by my side, I know I'll get through it,' she said gently. 'And part of that is you letting *me* help *you*. We can support each other.'

'Do you really mean that?'

'More than anything. I used to think wanting to be with a man meant weakness and that to fall in love would make me lose something of myself. But it hasn't. My mum's life is not mine—and you have shown me that. I know I can survive without you, Pepe. I know I can lead a fulfilling life on my own, but I don't want to. I want to be with you. I want to support you just as you've supported me. I love you. Seeing you alone at the graveside tore me in two.'

'Shall we go on our own tomorrow, to say goodbye together?'

Cara nodded through fresh tears then buried her face into his shoulder. Except these tears didn't feel quite as desolate as all the others had. Pepe's love had given her the hope and desire to see the silver lining on the dark cloud.

Together they would heal each other, and then who

knew where their love would take them? All she knew with bone-deep certainty was that wherever they went, they would always be together, united. As one.

As love.

EPILOGUE

'HAVE I TOLD you how beautiful you look today, Signora Mastrangelo?' Pepe whispered into his wife's ear.

She grinned up at him. 'You're looking pretty spiffing yourself. It's nice to see you've made the effort,' she added with a snigger, referring to the charcoal suit he wore with his salmon cravat.

The priest coughed and they forced their attention back to the proceedings before them. When instructed, Pepe carried baby Benjamin to the font, Cara right by his side.

Of course he'd made the effort today, at their youngest child's christening, just as he had for the christening of their twins. From the corner of his eye he saw a pair of miniature grenades launch themselves up the aisle, quickly followed by his elegant mother, who had been designated babysitter for the day.

A loud voice stage-whispered theatrically, 'Gracie and Rocco are being *very* trying today.'

Titters could be heard throughout the congregation. Luca and Grace were standing at the font with them, their heads bowed, their frames shaking at the precociousness of their eldest daughter, who sat in the front row looking self-important for all her five years of age. Their youngest daughter, two-year-old Georgina, was conspicuous by her absence, no doubt rifling through handbags in the hope of finding sweets. Pepe knew a couple of his artist friends had planned to bring sweets laden with sugar and additives in the hope of watching all the toddlers turn into Scud missiles.

Pepe still felt guilt whenever he recalled turning up at Lily's christening dressed more appropriately for a day out sailing than the baptism welcoming his niece into the world. Looking back, he couldn't believe he'd been so selfish. A child's baptism was one of the most wondrous days for all the family. Instead of appreciating that, he'd deliberately dismissed the event, determined to prove to himself that babies and marriage meant nothing when, in reality, family meant everything.

What a shallow life that had been.

Thank God for Cara.

He would never be able to express the pride he felt in her and the pride she gave in him. He would watch her chatting to clients at the gallery they owned in partnership with his brother and Grace, and which Cara ran, and be awed at her knowledge and the daily battle she fought to unlock her shy tongue and speak coherently. She'd even had another go in his helicopter, a trip that had been aborted after five minutes. Some battles just couldn't be won, and severe motion sickness brought on by helicopter travel was one of them.

Once the ceremony was over, all the guests trickled out and headed to the party being held at their Parisian home.

Pepe, Cara and their children lingered a little longer.

They walked to the altar at the side of the church, which held the memorial candles, Pepe holding a sleeping Benjamin in his arms. Cara gave the three-year-old twins, Gracie and Rocco, some change to put in the donation box, then helped both children light a candle.

'Is this for Charlotte, Mama?' Gracie asked.

Cara's eyes were bright with unshed tears but she nodded and smiled for their daughter.

Then it was their turn. Standing close together, they lit their candles and each whispered private words of love to the child who would for ever live in their hearts.

Once the five candles were lit—Pepe lit one for Benjamin too—he turned to his wife and kissed her, a chaste brush of the lips that sweetened the melancholy of the moment.

Only then did they leave the church, somehow managing to keep a hold of each other as well as their hyperactive toddlers and newborn baby.

In his heart he knew they would always keep hold of each other.

* * * * *

A sneaky peek at next month…

MODERN™

POWER, PASSION AND IRRESISTIBLE TEMPTATION

My wish list for next month's titles…

In stores from 18th April 2014:

❏ The Only Woman to Defy Him – Carol Marinelli

❏ Gambling with the Crown – Lynn Raye Harris

❏ One Night to Risk it All – Maisey Yates

❏ The Truth About De Campo – Jennifer Hayward

In stores from 2nd May 2014:

❏ Secrets of a Ruthless Tycoon – Cathy Williams

❏ The Forbidden Touch of Sanguardo – Julia James

❏ A Clash with Cannavaro – Elizabeth Power

❏ The Santana Heir – Elizabeth Lane

Available at WHSmith, Tesco, Asda, Eason, Amazon and Apple

Just can't wait?

Visit us Online

You can buy our books online a month before they hit the shops! **www.millsandboon.co.uk**

0414/(

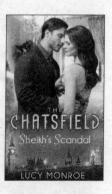

When five o'clock hits, what happens after hours...?

Feel the sizzle and anticipation of falling in love across the boardroom table with these seductive workplace romances!

**Now available at
www.millsandboon.co.uk**

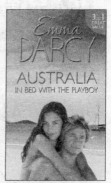

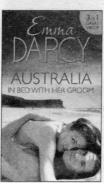

MILLS & BOON® Book Club

Join the Mills & Boon Book Club

Want to read more **Modern**™ books?
We're offering you **2 more** absolutely **FREE!**

We'll also treat you to these fabulous extras:

- Exclusive offers and much more!
- FREE home delivery
- FREE books and gifts with our special rewards scheme

Get your free books now!

visit **www.millsandboon.co.uk/bookclub**
or call Customer Relations on **020 8288 2888**

Discover more romance at

www.millsandboon.co.uk

- ❤ WIN great prizes in our exclusive competitions

- ❤ BUY new titles before they hit the shops

- ❤ BROWSE new books and REVIEW your favourites

- ❤ SAVE on new books with the Mills & Boon® Bookclub™

- ❤ DISCOVER new authors

PLUS, to chat about your favourite reads, get the latest news and find special offers:

- 🖪 Find us on facebook.com/millsandboon
- 🐦 Follow us on twitter.com/millsandboonuk
- ❤ Sign up to our newsletter at millsandboon.co.uk

The World of Mills & Boon®

There's a Mills & Boon® series that's perfect for you. We publish ten series and, with new titles every month, you never have to wait long for your favourite to come along.

By Request

Relive the romance with the best of the best
12 stories every month

Cherish™

Experience the ultimate rush of falling in love
12 new stories every month

Desire™

Passionate and dramatic love stories
6 new stories every month

nocturne™

An exhilarating underworld of dark desires
Up to 3 new stories every mo